RENATO'S LUCK

"Jeff Shapiro's tale of *Renato's Luck* embodies the power of rebirth for Renato the waterworks man, for his family, for his small Tuscan town of Sant'Angelo D'Asso, threatened with extinction, and, what's more, for the reader. Tender humor, pathos, touching despair, and resurgent hope abide in these simple, wise people whom you can't help but love, all of them fitting neatly into a lovely read, fresh and bubbling over with the spirit of caring—as if Shapiro had signed it 'Affectionately Yours.'"

—Susan Vreeland, author of *Girl in Hyacinth Blue*

"Bravo for Jeff Shapiro! Renato Tizzoni is a prince among men and Sant'Angelo D'Asso sounds like heaven on earth. *Renato's Luck* is a dream of a book—warm, wise, full of heart, and an absolute pleasure from beginning to end."

—Carrie Brown, author of *Rose's Garden* and *Lamb in Love*

"This is a delightful book. Jeff Shapiro has wonderfully captured the true essence of the Tuscan spirit."   —Jean Salvadore, author of *Villa D'Este*

"With his sharp attention to detail and his ability to quickly engage us with his characters' personal dialogues on meaty subjects such as love, death, and the quest for spiritual understanding, [Jeff] Shapiro has delivered a charming novel that unfolds with the vividness of a richly produced foreign film."

—*Milwaukee Journal Sentinel*

"*Renato's Luck* is a sweet and engaging tale."   —BookBrowser.com

"An engaging first novel. . . . The reader is drawn into the story and waits eagerly to discover how the fates of the townspeople will change."—*Publishers Weekly*

"*Renato's Luck* gathers homespun wisdom, offering some earthy insights into life's unsettling gyrations."   —*Los Angeles Times*

RENATO'S LUCK

RENATO'S LUCK

LUCK

Jeff Shapiro

Perennial
An Imprint of HarperCollins Publishers

A hardcover edition of this book was published in 2000 by HarperCollins Publishers.

HarperCollins books may be purchased for educational, business, or sales promotional use. For information please write: Special Markets Department, HarperCollins Publishers Inc., 10 East 53rd Street, New York, NY 10022.

First Perennial edition published 2001.

Designed by Christine Weathersbee

The Library of Congress has catalogued the hardcover edition as follows:
Shapiro, Jeff.
    Renato's luck / Jeff Shapiro.—1st ed.
      p. cm.
    ISBN 0-06-019418-9
    I. Title.
  PS3569.H34119R46   2000
  813' .54—dc21   99-34922

ISBN 0-06-093219-8 (pbk.)

01 02 03 04 05 ❖/RRD 10 9 8 7 6 5 4 3 2 1

To my father, Dan Shapiro. I wish he were still here.

And to Valeria, because she juggles snowballs.

Contents

Acknowledgments

Trena Keating and Larry Ashmead at HarperCollins have been vital to every part of the life of this novel: its conception, its birth, and its growth. I would like to express my deep gratitude for their kindness, their thoughtfulness, their patience, and their wisdom.

My friend Renato Bernini is dear to me as an inspiration in more ways than one. I would like to thank him and the many other people who live around me in Italy who told me their stories. Their contribution to this book is great.

Professor Alessandro Falassi, whose brain is a rich encyclopedia, was a wonderful font of research material. Art historian Claudio Bartalozzi provided invaluable information regarding the Late Roman period.

Fernando Franchi and Cynthia Foppiano at the Scuola 2F in Florence showed remarkable tolerance by keeping my teaching schedule flexible so that I would have time to write.

My brother Barry's encouragement was greatly appreciated. My parents, Ruth and Dan, and my sister, Suzan, proved themselves skillful readers. They tried their hardest to be objective about the work of their son and brother—naturally an impossible task. My father gave me a living example of what it means to never lose the taste of life.

Valeria Indice was invaluable as a sharp-sighted reader. She didn't mind when a book's worth of fictional characters inevitably came to live with us while I was writing. To the contrary: She opened the doors wide. Her name appears in the dedication, with love.

Author's Note

Born and raised near Boston, Massachusetts, I suddenly found myself living in Tuscany in 1991. Interesting experience, being an American amid a very different language and culture. Interesting, but also awkward and lonely at first. At times, almost overwhelming.

Yet stay somewhere long enough and you start to get a feel for the place. Talk to people and you start to get a feel for their lives.

I ended up making notes on all sorts of things people said. Without even planning a novel at first, I made notes because I wanted to remember. You know people better when you write them down.

My friend Renato told me about a strange dream he had that gave him a singular sense of mission, urging him to take a trip to St. Peter's Square in Rome. A dear friend, Signor Gorelli, died. After his death, his wife was left wondering how fifty years of life lived with someone could disappear in an instant, as if those years had never existed. A woman up near Monteriggioni, north of Siena, remembered being a child when the Allies came through at the end of World War II and detonated an unexploded bomb that had been dropped on a field where young men, already believing the war to be over, had been playing a friendly game of soccer. My beloved, Valeria, has an uncle named Zio Giacomino who at the slightest encouragement is quick to tell the story of how he returned to Italy on foot all the way from the Russian front. I watched and fell even more deeply in love as Valeria herself juggled snowballs on the banks of the River Po, near her grandmother's home. A barbershop became the forum for customers' tales of long-lost sexual prowess. A car mechanic named Cappelli had a way of turning blasphemy into an art form. (The Tuscan practice of inventing creative blasphemies dates back hundreds of years to the time when the Tuscans were sworn political enemies of the Papal States.) A sheep I met limped around pathetically even though veterinarians could find nothing wrong with her hoof.

The notes gathered together started to become a portrait of this part of Tuscany and of the people I had been getting to know. It was a kaleidoscopic and fragmented portrait. I spoke with several history experts to try to understand how the Tuscan present had grown up out of the Tuscan past. But those bits of information, too, were pieces of a puzzle that hadn't yet been put together.

Trena Keating and Larry Ashmead suggested I unify the individual sketches into a novel. All thanks are due to them. Thank you, Trena and Larry!

And this portrait of Tuscany, I believe, isn't as regional as it may seem. I suspect people find similar difficulties and joys in life wherever they live.

Renato's List

MARGHERITA—*In an instant,
a lifetime disappears like a dream.
But life renews itself.*

MILENA—*That things may change!*

PETULA—*You can only accept.*

DUNCAN—*The ephemeral is beautiful.*—ANGIE.

SCULATI—*The past is always present. It's just hidden
most of the time.*

MEG BARKER—*Choosing is good.*

TRIESTE—*Sooner or later the fabric of every life
gets torn. That's when life begins.*

PELLEGRINI—*I wish the impossible—to be
forever young.*

DON LUIGI—*Loneliness is the mother
of all other fears.
Have faith.*

CAPPELLI—*You are another I.*

RENATO'S LUCK

ONE

Daybreak and the Sheep

Dawn.

The coldness outdoors this morning woke up Renato's brain.

September. Yes, here was a good time of day, a good time of year. In fact, it was Renato Tizzoni's favorite time of year. Autumn was a season of brisk transition.

Renato's work boots clomped down the stone steps in front of his house. The sky was brightening from deep blue to the start of sunlight, pushing stars away. But the air was still dark and chilly inside the courtyard. Renato crossed the courtyard and stopped at the well.

The bucket he lowered into the well disappeared quickly in the blackness. He heard the splash, low and far away. When he hoisted the bucket back up, the metal of the pulley squeaked.

Inside their stall across the courtyard, the sheep heard Renato and responded with impatient movements. One of the sheep had a bell tied around her neck. The bell *clank-te-clanked*. One sheep went *be-e-eh*.

"A little patience, please!" Renato told the sheep, talking to the closed wooden door of their stall.

He set the dripping bucket on the ledge of the well and, leaning forward, washed his face with cold handfuls of water.

Renato was the waterworks man for the township of Sant'Angelo

D'Asso. It was up to him to make sure that every home always had water. All the same, each morning he splashed himself awake not with the town's water that came through his house's pipes but with the earth's own water, pulleyed up from the courtyard well. Every morning, every season. If you asked him why his first touch of water every day should come from the well, he wouldn't have known how to answer. Who needs to explain? Well water was part of his every dawn. One of the little things that gave life its taste.

An orange cat lived in the courtyard and in the sheep stalls and in the cellar under the house. The cat policed the mice around the place. He and Renato liked each other. The cat rubbed himself against Renato's ankles now while Renato rinsed his face with well water another time. Renato said, "Micio," for no one had ever thought to give the cat a name other than the word "kitten." He bent over and stroked the cat above the nose, just between the eyes. The cat closed his eyes and purred. "Micio," Renato said.

He walked across the courtyard to open the door for the sheep.

The four sheep pushed one another out of the stall like passengers getting off a hot bus in summer. Four were enough to give Renato the satisfaction of keeping sheep: He made pecorino cheese from their milk. The cheese was at its best, according to his tastebuds, when it was neither too mature nor too fresh. He liked it *semi-stagionato*, halfway aged, solid yet not hard, salty and tangy in the mouth. Four was the right number for sheep because once you had too many you became a shepherd whether you meant to or not. Renato's little flock was manageable.

Rushing out of their stall this morning, the four stirred up commotion. They bleated. They bumped into one another. Under them, udders bobbed. Hooves tapped on the stones of the courtyard.

Renato went into the stall, the air in there warm with sheep body smells, and made the milking corner ready. He righted the stool and put the metal milking pot on the ground. From a hook on the wall he took down the plastic feed pail. In the adjacent storeroom he filled the feed pail from a sack of grain. Beside the sack were some branches that he had cut from his olive trees. For the sheep, nibbling on olive leaves was a treat.

It was dark in the feed room, but Renato didn't need light to help him fill the feed pail. His hands knew what to do in the same way that his hands didn't need light to touch his wife's body in the dark. The hands knew what was where.

In the stall, Renato settled himself on the milking stool. The feed pail to his left, the milking pot in front of his work boots, Renato scratched his beard. "Ready!" he said.

The first sheep trotted back inside the stall, her bell clanking. She was a character, the first sheep. She was braver than the others, though bravery never amounted to very much in sheep. Renato didn't exactly have a name for the first sheep, or for any of them. He called them by their numbers—*la Prima, la Seconda, la Terza, la Quarta*—because that was the order they had chosen for themselves. Every morning and evening the spirited Prima was always the first to come into the stall to be milked. The four sheep knew their order as if they knew their own natures.

Prima was a character, all right. Wide-eyed curiosity set her apart from the others. If Renato ever had to be a sheep, he would probably be this one.

She put her mouth straight in the feed pail and started to chew, her flank leaning against Renato's knees. He took her udder with his right hand and squeezed with an undulating upward coax. Milk squirted into the pail. The sheep chewed.

When Renato finished, he slapped Prima on her rump. She ran out into the courtyard through the open door.

"Seconda!" Renato called, and, when he had finished with her, "Terza!" The second and the third were creatures of the flock. They gave birth, gave milk, gave wool, chewed grass, and stayed with the others. They never distinguished themselves in life. When they died someday, Renato wouldn't revisit either of them with a nostalgic thought.

The fourth set herself apart, but not with the courage of the first. To the contrary. She was delicate in build. And she could be neurotic at times.

Eight months ago a stone had gotten stuck in her rear hoof while she was being covered by the ram whom Renato had hired from a professional shepherd nearby. She limped around afterward with a frantic look in her eye, as if death were chasing her like a wolf. Renato had removed the stone but the limp had never gone away. She limped in June when she gave birth to her two lambs. She limped early in August, last month, when her lambs were killed for their meat. Renato had even called in the veterinarian to have a look, but the vet found nothing wrong. Quarta still limped, and she behaved as if she expected the others to understand the trauma she had endured. As if her experiences were any different from theirs.

This morning Renato had to call for her repeatedly before she stuck her muzzle inside the stall. "*Dai!*" said Renato: Come on! She put her head in, waiting to be convinced. "*Dai, Quarta.*" The sheep trembled, as if going to meet the slaughterer and not the man who milked her twice a day. "Oh! Don't play the pathetic one." Playing on pathos, Renato knew, was her game. He rose from his milking stool and ducked into the storage room. The fourth sheep watched him from the doorway. He emerged with an olive branch, which he broke in bits and put on top of the grain in the pail. Seeing the olive leaves, the fourth sheep quick-stepped in, almost forgetting to limp, and put her nose inside the pail.

When Renato had finished milking the sheep, he took the pot of warm milk down into the *cantina* under the house. He ran the milk through a strainer to purify it of woolly tufts. Later, he'd bring the milk up to the fridge inside the house. Tomorrow he'd make pecorino cheese.

Renato and the sheep climbed the hillside that rose up behind his house. Prima ran ahead of the others. Quarta limped behind.

The sky was bright enough now so that the stone farmhouses along the hilltops around him started to take on color. Renato saw his olive grove spreading up the hill beside his field. The olive leaves, wet with disappearing mist, shone silver in the sunlight that broke out.

Sunlight. No clouds.

And Renato did what he did every morning: He sat down on the ground. Sitting, like washing his face in well water, was a ritual he wouldn't have known how to explain. He happened to like the feel of grass and dirt and stones beneath him. These were elements of the hill he had known since childhood. Daily, he liked to renew bodily contact with the hill.

Sitting now, Renato looked down over the town of Sant'Angelo D'Asso in the first fresh light of dawn. He saw the stones of walls and church and houses glowing golden on the other side of the green valley. Renato felt an emotion wash over him, an emotion so strong it would overwhelm him if he wasn't careful. Seeing the town, and the old stone bridge over the river, he thought: *This is home.* The thought seemed tragic to Renato. It stuck in his throat like a sob. He looked away, trying not to think. He didn't want to think at all.

For a moment Renato lost himself, contemplating the town below him as he sat on the ground. A wind blew up from the valley. He shivered.

He recognized the shiver. Only recently the shiver had awakened him in the middle of the night. The frigid electric tingle had crept up along his back sometimes when he was at work under the sun, or even when he was cozy under blankets, busy making love to his wife. The shiver had come to him whenever he tried with all his might not to think. And there was so much not to think about now.

He pulled his collar to his throat. The ground was cold beneath his ass. He was sure for a moment that he could feel the coldness come up through the seat of his pants and penetrate his body, taking away all heat, even from his bones.

Renato shivered more. How could a whole town just disappear? he tried not to ask himself. Why were people disappearing around him? Why did everything have to change? None of it made any sense.

The first sheep nudged him, wanting to graze where Renato sat. Renato's thoughts returned to himself, to the four sheep around him, to the hillside field he was sitting in at dawn, to the next steps he would have to take to get on with today.

He would have to shower and change his clothes. He'd have breakfast with his daughter and with Milena, his wife, before Petula went to school and Milena went to open her parents' *bottega* in town, the way she did every morning. And yes, when he changed his clothes, he'd have to do something that he didn't like doing at all: He'd have to put on a tie. Aristodemo Vezzosi had died. The funeral was today. Renato would have to watch the old man, his friend, be put into the ground.

Mah. Che ci puoi fa'? What can you do? These things happen, he tried to tell himself. And he tried not to think about the death of the man he loved.

At least the weather will be mild for the funeral, he told himself. There were worse days than today for a send-off. The shiver had left him now.

Renato stood up. He turned and walked down the hill. Behind him the sheep tugged mouthfuls of grass. The bell on the first sheep's neck clanked.

TWO

Family

"There isn't any water." Petula was waiting for Renato when he got back to the house. She was halfway smirking. She leaned against the wall in the corridor and said to her father, *"L'acqua non c'è."*

Petula was seventeen years old. Her arms were wrapped around her waist. House slippers covered her bare feet. A towel was wrapped turban-style around her head.

Renato took his daughter in, wondering when she had changed into such a woman, asking himself further why she seemed weirdly triumphant in the news she was giving him. He said, "What?"

"There's no water," she repeated, her smirk very close to a grin. "Not even a drop."

"Why are you telling me this?"

"If I don't tell you, who am I supposed to tell? You're the water man, Babbo. No?" For a while now he had noticed this new tone of hers, a tone akin to condescension, as if it were she in charge of looking after him.

"Where's your mother?"

"Hasn't woken up yet."

"We should wake her. She has to go to work." Renato stared at his daughter. He said, "There has to be water today. I have to go to the funeral."

"I have to wash my hair. How can I wash my hair if there's no water? I'm full of shampoo! I was washing my hair when the water ran out."

"Let me see."

"You don't believe me?"

"Let me see," Renato insisted.

She took off the towel. Sure enough, her wet hair was all suds.

Renato said, "So?"

"What do you mean 'So?' I can't go out like this, with all the shampoo. I have to wash my hair."

"What's to wash? What's left since you cut it this crazy way to look like your friends?" Hair had become a sore issue between them since Petula had gotten her new haircut about six months before. The top and sides were normal enough, shoulder-length chestnut strands. But she had asked the beautician to shave the nape of her neck. The back of her head was now nothing more than silky stubble. It was the new fashion on the heads of her friends, boys and girls alike. And it was the look sported by one boy in particular, that Daniele, whose influence over Petula affected almost everything about her, not just the length of her hair. Renato thought she looked like a mutant soldier from a deranged planet. Why a pretty girl should go out of her way to make herself ugly was something Renato couldn't grasp. "Why not just leave the suds? Might be a new look, no?"

Petula looked horrified. "If I leave the shampoo in, it'll ruin the roots and my hair will fall out and I'll be bald."

Renato laughed. "Then maybe that boy of yours will imitate you for a change, and he'll go bald to look like you."

"Babb-o!" She half-whined the word for Dad.

Renato saw his daughter momentarily become a little girl again. *"Facciamo una cosa."* His voice was gentle. "Let's do a little thing. Get me the pasta pot."

"What for?"

"Get me the pasta pot, the big one we use when there's company. You'll see."

She turbaned up her hair and went to the kitchen. She got the pot from the cupboard. Renato filled it with water from the well and set it over a high flame on the kitchen stove. He said, "This way we'll wash your hair."

When the water began to steam, Renato said, "Wake your mother up. She can help. It's time for her to get up anyway." He carried the pot into the bathroom.

Milena entered, groggy, from the bedroom, wrapping her robe around her. She didn't snap at having been woken up. Snapping wasn't her way. She padded into the bathroom, bringing with her the perfumed smells of woman-sleep and warm bedding. Her voice was lovely when she said, "*Che c'è?*" She had a voice that could make the words "What's happening?" sound like a lullaby. Renato smiled.

Petula started explaining how the water had run out just when she had been washing her hair and how the shampoo would ruin her roots and make her bald.

Renato leaned against the bathroom door frame, scratched his beard, and watched. Petula took the turban off her head and leaned over the sink. Milena filled a pitcher from the pasta pot and then cascaded the water over Petula's head into the sink. The scene made Renato glad to be the father of a family. One bathrobed woman was pouring water over another bathrobed woman's head. Renato liked women. These were both his.

Seeing his seventeen-year-old daughter with her soapy, wet head inclined in the sink, Renato remembered Milena twenty years before when he and she had ridden around town together on his motorbike, when they had taken walks past the fields at night.

Milena had seemed so fresh! The fragrance of her skin had made him hungry. He used to kiss her neck as if she were made of something good to eat. And her pudgy hands had been soft and babylike. He had wanted to eat her hands, and her soft feet, too, and her thighs and her belly and her breasts. Her laughter this morning was still young.

Not that she was old now. Not that he was old either. They were both on the brink of forty. They had gotten married before they'd turned twenty. They had been kids.

Renato still could only think of himself as young. If anything, he was now enjoying the fullness of his powers. His body had never been stronger. He had lost the puppyish insecurities of boyhood. He had grown into what he believed it felt like to be a man.

Milena, too, was by all accounts holding up well. Her eyes were the same as ever. There were no bulges on her thighs. It was only that—

She used to be less tired.

Milena worked hard at the *bottega* that her parents ran. It was everything for the town of Sant'Angelo D'Asso: a bar, a cold meats and sandwich counter, a restaurant serving hot lunches and dinners, as well as a grocery store that stocked jars and bottles and tins on its shelves for customers who wanted a couple of things but didn't feel like going all the way up the hill to the supermarket. The only other place in town to get so much as a cup of coffee was the bar up by the train station, the bar run by Daniele's parents. Daniele, the boy who was turning Renato's daughter into a mutant soldier freak. The work that Milena had to do at her parents' *bottega* was infinite. Early in the morning until late at night. A few hours of sleep, only to wake up and do it again.

So of course she seemed tired sometimes now, Renato thought. And he, too, felt a fatigue that had been unknown to him twenty years before. Time was doing its work on both of them. Time was certainly at work on his body. There was the little layer of fat that sat permanently on his hips, and there was the reptilian hardness of his elbow skin. The hairs of his beard now bristled with gray. Why couldn't time simply leave the two of them alone, leave them as they had been when they were first in love?

He watched his wife and his daughter in their soapy, steamy bathroom. For a strange instant he believed himself to be a ghost, watching but invisible to the people he watched, as if foreseeing how they might live without him. At the same time he felt a happiness so intense it almost hurt. He loved this moment—his wife still youngish, their daughter still theirs to love—and he wished this warm, humid, shampoo-smelling image could last forever.

He was about to try to say something to his wife when the telephone rang.

"Telephone," Milena said to him, her hands soapy past the wrists. "Will you get it? It's for you, anyway."

"Maybe it's your mother. How do you know it's for me?"

"It's not my mother. It's for you. Sixth sense. It's Cappelli for you."

"How do you know it's Cappelli?"

"It's Cappelli. The phone's ringing again."

Renato left the two females in the bathroom. The corridor felt empty and cold. He reached the phone.

"Did you see?" said the man's voice on the other end. It was Cappelli.

"There's no water." Renato knew he was saying what surely was clear to them both.

"*Madonna maiala!*" Cappelli said, referring to the Virgin Mary as a promiscuous sow. Renato didn't get excited by his assistant's shouting. Cappelli was well-known for shouting that which could simply be said. He had some local fame, too, as a grand master in the age-old Tuscan art of blasphemy. Tuscans had taken to blasphemy centuries before as a rebellious gesture after a political dispute with the Papal States over a question of taxes. Swearing against sacred beings became a habitual manner of speaking, not a religious statement, and Cappelli had slipped into the local habit when he'd first learned to talk. So making a simple sentence sound like the apocalypse was nothing new. Today, however, Renato heard Cappelli's voice sing out with special vehemence. "What do you mean there's no water?" Cappelli screamed.

"What do you mean what do I mean there's no water?" Renato said. "There's no water."

"*Madonna lupa!*" cried Cappelli, now likening the Virgin to a she-wolf. "There's water everywhere."

"There's no water here."

"Oh, Tizzoni! Wake yourself! There's no water there because there's too much water here!"

Renato began to understand. A queasiness tightened his stomach. He could go to no funeral today, no matter how attached he had been to the man who had died. That much was clear. Instead, there would be work, but not just regular work. There would be the kind of work which, once you began, you would wonder whether you'd ever finish. Heavy work. Work that made your arms tired, and your shoulders, and your neck, and your knees, and your back. "Where's the water?" said Renato, humbled by the enormity of the task that awaited him.

"Everywhere!" Cappelli screamed. "*Maiala quell' Eva!* It's everywhere!" Now Eve, too, was lumped in among the sowlike and the lascivious. "Think, Tizzoni! You live in the bottom of the valley, so there's no water down by you because up here by us in town it's everywhere, *madonna bona!*"

Renato had already understood. "Tell me where it's coming from." He looked along the corridor to the open door of the bathroom. Milena was towel-drying Petula's hair.

"Didn't you hear me? It's everywhere!"

"More precisely?"

"More precisely—more precisely it's in the square. I can see it from my window here. In the square in front of the church. Coming up right from the ground. It would look like a miracle if it wasn't such a mess! Water coming right up from between the paving stones in front of the church. There's already people in the piazza, just watching, like some kind of miracle. They're waiting for us to do something about the water."

"*Dio boia!*" Renato usually wasn't big on blasphemy. But he let himself speak of God as the Executioner because, really, the crisis seemed too extreme. "*DIO BOIA!*" he shouted. In the bathroom, Milena turned her head to see, hearing her husband use those words. "It's the main pipe burst," he said to her. "The main pipe for the whole town, there under the piazza."

Cappelli went on. "What can I do here by myself? I'm hiding myself here behind my window. I don't know what to do."

"Wait for me, Cappelli. I'm coming."

"Don't make me wait! There's people in the piazza and the water's running down the street!"

"I won't make you wait. Just a little instant and I'll be right there." He hung up. He scratched his beard.

Milena put down the towel and came to him. In front of the bathroom mirror, Petula started going at her hair with the electric blow-dryer.

"So?" said Milena.

"So," said Renato.

"Breakfast?"

"What breakfast? I have to go."

"And the funeral?"

"The others can go to the funeral. Not me. Old Vezzosi would have understood. There's water in the piazza. Sounds like a flood. I have to fix the pipes."

Milena touched his cheek. He closed his eyes, wishing he could curl up and fall asleep inside her hand. "I'll get ready and go to the funeral," Milena said. "My parents can take care of the *bottega* without me for a couple of hours. Business will be slow anyway, if there's no water for coffee and cooking. Okay? And I'll come and say hello to you while you work."

"*Grazie,*" Renato said.

He walked to the bathroom. Petula put aside the blow-dryer for a moment. Renato kissed her on top of her head. Her freshly washed hair was soft against his lips, hot from the blow-dryer. "*Mi dispiace,*" said Petula: I'm sorry.

"Sorry about what?"

"Sorry that Signor Vezzosi died."

Renato smiled. His daughter was still his daughter, however much life threatened to change. He said, "I'm sorry, too."

In the corridor he kissed Milena on her mouth. He bent down and kissed her neck, pressing his mouth into her warm skin.

❧

Outside, the early morning air was full of sunshine, the sun now well over the hills. The light on the olive trees and on the green hillsides was still the warm light of summer, but Renato sensed the beginning of autumn in the breeze. At least he would work today, he told himself, in cool air.

THREE

Water

Walking toward town—the valley bright in sunshine now—Renato tried not to think about anything. But how can you make yourself not think? Think about not thinking and you'll find yourself thinking more troublesome thoughts than you would have thought if maybe you had let yourself think things through in the first place.

Renato was going crazy trying not to think.

He walked across the bridge over the River Asso, stopped halfway, and looked down. The swift water was so clear, he could see all the way to the bottom. What were the long shapes waving in the water? Fronds of grass? Trying not to think, he thought of eels. Soon, when the river was dammed up and the valley filled to become a lake, his own house, like every house in town, would be too wet even for human ghosts. Water creatures would live there instead. Fish chewing on algae. Slippery, slithering, stinking eels.

To divert his thoughts, he lifted his eyes to Sant'Angelo D'Asso on the road in front of him. The walled town climbed up from the bridge where Renato stood. The bell in the church chimed the time. The church was older than much of the town. The better part of the town was only six or seven hundred years old, but the church was Romanesque, built around eight or nine or ten centuries ago.

What Renato's eyes saw now inside the bowl of this valley was the only world he had ever known. He had been born into the world here, been a baby, then a boy, now a man. Everything and everyone he loved was here. Home. And all of it was about to disappear.

The proposal to build a dam farther up the river had seemed too absurd to consider at first. No one had taken it seriously. But the politicians had pushed and pushed. The lake that the valley would become once the dam was built would provide irrigation water for vast tracts of land in this part of Tuscany. Or at least that was what the politicians promised. Agriculture would boom. More grapes and olives, more grain and cereal could be produced than had ever been grown before. Legislators were persuaded in regional and national assemblies. Townspeople, backed by environmentalists, did their best to protest. But when is the voice of a small town ever heard in the big city rooms where laws are made? Appeals were attempted. They failed.

And only last week had come the ultimate announcement. There would be no more appeals. No decision would be reversed. Construction of the dam was due to begin in a few months. By next spring, the people of Sant'Angelo D'Asso would have to leave. Water from the dammed-up river would fill the valley. The old town would be submerged. Everyone, Renato included, would be somewhere else. Not here. Not home.

Where? Renato didn't know. The final decision had caught everyone off guard. No one had time yet to make any plans. Besides, how can you think the unthinkable? Renato tried to imagine where he and his family might go, but no mental effort could make the idea of leaving seem real. It was impossible to envision what he might eventually find. The only feeling now was that he was about to lose, about to lose his world.

Renato didn't want to think about the valley becoming a lake. He didn't want to think about water smothering the town. He rubbed his eyes to make himself not look at the town with its buildings glowing golden in the green valley. The town looked too fragile despite its stones. The fragility hurt Renato's heart.

Absurd! he said to himself. Absurd having to dread what water—
water—would do to the town. He was the waterworks man. He had
toiled his whole working life to see that the town never ran out of
precious water. But water, like everything else, was good only when
the dose was right. And soon there was going to be too much.
Ridiculous!

He stopped staring into the river from the bridge and quickened
his steps. He had work to do. He had to stanch the water that gushed
from a broken pipe.

He entered the old stone gate at the bottom of Sant'Angelo
D'Asso. Even before he reached the piazza, water came down the
stone street to greet him.

The church bell rang half-past seven just as Renato entered the piazza,
his shoes already wet from the torrents that covered the streets. Seven
chimes, then a pause, then two more chimes for the half hour.

Cappelli had been right when he had said there were people in
the square. Half the crowd stood around watching the water fiasco;
the other half got on with normal business, for another Friday morning had begun in the life of Sant'Angelo D'Asso. Water or no water,
there were still shops to open and errands to run. The midget who
operated the newspaper shop had the bulgy-eyed, flat-nosed, jut-
jawed, open-mawed, mouth-breathing mug of a pug dog. He was
busy setting up the outdoor magazine racks and the poster boards
that announced the day's headlines. The headlines spoke of yet
another high-ranking politician accused of corruption. The young
couple who kept the vegetable store on the piazza, right next to the
newspaper shop, were making pyramids of blood oranges on wooden
display trays. The tobacconist's wife was washing the cigarette store's
front step, as if there weren't already enough water about. Her lips
clenched a lighted cigarette.

Milena's parents had already opened the *bottega*. Renato was less
than delighted to see a group of customers standing out in front of the

bottega's open door. When they spotted Renato, they sent up a little cheer. *"Eccolo!"*: Here he is! "Decided to come, did he? Eh, Tizzoni, nice little job that's waiting for you here, no?" Old men having a ham sandwich and a drop of wine for breakfast gestured with their glasses in hand. He saw crumbs on the lips of one old man who was laughing with exasperating glee.

"Oh, Renato!" said Tonino, Renato's father-in-law, in the doorway wiping his hands on a dish towel. "Poor old bastard! You've got your work cut out for you today."

"Ah sì," Renato said. "Oh yes."

Then he saw his mother-in-law's unsmiling face from the back of the group. Maria Severina was a tough tree trunk of a woman. "How are we supposed to cope?" she accused him. "No water to make coffee with. No Milena this morning to give us a hand. When will you fix the water? We need water, you understand? We need the water."

Thank God Milena showed no signs of turning out to be like her mother, Renato thought. He said, "I'll take care of it. I'll take care of it," and kept walking.

Yes, many people were doing what they always did. But the others, those with no particular work to do, had congregated around the edges of the piazza to marvel at the sight in the middle. Dead center, before the stone steps leading up to the church, bright water hemorrhaged from the street. The earth's blood poured from the wound in the stone skin that had covered these streets since the Middle Ages.

"Ah, Tizzoni!" the tobacconist saluted Renato. The tobacconist was a fat man in a cardigan. His face always showed a smiling sneer, an expression that seemed to say he was the only person who ever knew what was really going on. "Decided to turn up at last, did you?"

"What 'at last'? It's not even seven-thirty."

"But if you'd waited any longer, we'd all be swimming. And they haven't started to build the dam yet!"

"I needed this?" said Renato, more to himself.

He looked up at Cappelli's house. Cappelli was at the window, peering out anxiously. Cappelli gave Renato a nod and lifted an I'll-be-down-in-a-minute finger.

The police *comandante* strode over. "Tizzoni. How long will it take to fix this mess?"

A few hours, if the repair went smoothly, Renato said. He didn't like the *carabiniere*'s accusatory tone. The tone insinuated that somehow this whole thing was Renato's fault. "With any luck," he told the man in uniform, "people will have their water in time to cook lunch. Of course," he added, "we'll have to dig up the street in front of the church."

"Don't make too much of a disturbance," the *comandante* ordered, for he was used to giving orders. "And there's the funeral to think about. Ten o'clock. Remember? All the people in the piazza, all the cars, the hearse. You won't hold up traffic, will you?"

"What can I say? We have to dig up the road."

"This had to happen today?"

"It was, what, fifty years ago? Fifty or sixty years? Let's say sixty years ago that the Fascists took up the street stones to put the water system in underneath." He was losing his patience. His voice held no apology now, but almost an accusation of its own. "Then they put the old stones back on top, and from that time until today that's how things have stayed. What do you expect, a pipe to last forever? *Che bel colpo di culo,* What a great stroke of luck, the pipe should choose today to burst! You think I'm happy? Do I look happy? I was supposed to go to the funeral myself. You want to blame somebody? Blame the Fascist imbeciles that their pipe had to break today!"

The *comandante* adjusted the cuffs of his uniform. "You see to it yourself that the people have water in time for lunch. And when you"—he made circular motions with his hand—"when you make a mess here, try not to make too much confusion. Take the traffic into account. This had to happen today!"

"Oh," Renato said with a shrug. "What can you do?"

Cappelli appeared by Renato's side. "So you see for yourself, Tizzoni?" he started. "*Madonna maia*—" Then he saw the police *comandante*. "Oh. *Buongiorno.*"

"Good morning." The *comandante* inclined his behatted head with a quick jerk. He took a step backward and went off to join his officers, who were making people keep their distance from the water coming out of the ground as if water were a dangerous thing.

"Good morning, my prick!" said Cappelli. He turned to Renato. "So?" Cappelli bristled with the agitation of a porcupine caught in a trap. His eyes were inflamed; Renato couldn't decide if the eyes were red because Cappelli had been drinking at breakfast or because he had gotten himself worked up over the burst pipe. Probably both.

Renato said, "Why didn't you go up the hill and turn the water off with the valve?"

"I was waiting for you."

"But you could have—"

"No, if you think about it," Cappelli defended himself, stiff gray hair quilling out from his head, "to close the valve we need the key to the waterworks building. And you're the one with the key."

Renato scratched his beard. Logic was logic. "Right," he said. "Let's go."

Up on the hill at the top of the town, at the far end of the Coop supermarket parking lot across the railroad tracks, there was the windowless single-room building that was the waterworks headquarters. Nothing fancy. It held the pumps and the main valves for Sant'Angelo D'Asso. The waterworks truck stood outside, waiting to serve.

There were no trees to shade the parking lot or the waterworks building. Hot, Renato unzipped his work jacket. The armpits of his shirt were sweaty from the walk up the hill. He looked at the sun, its light becoming heat in the blue September sky. The sun was laughing at Renato, the wicked laughter of a troublemaker about to pull a prank.

As the men approached the water building, they could hear the heavy hum of the pump. Renato took the keys from his jacket pocket and opened the door. Inside, over against the wall, there were extra lengths of pipe, pickaxes and shovels, and an array of WORK IN

PROGRESS road signs for when traffic had to be diverted. In the middle of the room was the pump.

Now the big pump roared like a raging god who refused to give up an impossible fight. Renato could smell the overheated metal. "*Dio boia!*" he said, touching the pump's trembling flank. He checked the temperature gauge. Any hotter and it would trip its own automatic switch. But who knew what damage the pump might do to itself in its fury? Mechanical creatures, he had learned in past crises, could never be relied on to act in their own best interests. Any more than sheep. Any more than people.

At the switch box Renato shut off the pump. It chuntled to silence.

Now the valve on the main pipe had to be closed. Otherwise gravity would continue sucking the water downhill from the underground reservoir beneath the waterworks building.

The valve handle was rusty. Renato had repainted and greased the thing many times, but years are years, and years corrode. The valve handle did not want to turn.

Renato leaned on the handle with all his weight. It crackled, coming away in his hand.

"*Madonna vacca!*" Cappelli erupted, classifying the Madonna as a cow. "*Puttana la miseria!* Misery is a whore!"

Renato let the rusty handle drop to the floor. "Get the big wrench from the truck," he said, his voice a disheartened whisper.

Cappelli went off. Renato waited. For a minute he couldn't breathe. The room was damp, as tight as a tomb. And this room was the headquarters for his life's work. He closed his eyes and rubbed them hard with his palms, thinking his head would explode. Suddenly he felt that not a single thing in his life was going right.

He opened his eyes and wanted to break something. He wanted to kick the walls. He wanted to punch the pump. He wanted to stomp on the pipes with his work boots until the pipes became soft, like human veins. But if he broke anything in here, he'd only be breaking himself. So he scratched his beard, let a lungful of air pass through his lips, and waited for Cappelli to find the wrench in the truck.

Renato thought about the hopelessness of fixing the water in town now, when soon everything would be water anyhow. His eyes stared at the floor.

"What the hell are you staring at?" said Cappelli from the doorway, the wrench hanging from his hand. "I'll close the valve myself if you're going to stand there like a deficient person."

Renato turned his head and stared at his assistant. Renato sensed that fortune was getting ready to kick him in the balls.

"Oh, Cappelli," he said, blinking. "Give me the wrench. I'll close the valve."

Cappelli handed him the wrench, yet he watched Renato the way you keep a careful eye on someone you think might be less than half a step away from slipping over the edge.

The valve good and closed, both men loaded up the truck with everything they would need to stop traffic in the town center and fix the pipe.

Across from the supermarket parking lot the gate was down at the train tracks, barring the road. Renato tried to be patient. He switched the engine off. He rolled the truck window down all the way and wished the hot air might turn into a little breeze.

On the platform at the train station, not far up the tracks, Petula was waiting for her train to take her to Siena, to high school. She was standing with a teenage boy. Renato watched them from the truck. The railroad crossing bells were ringing. Renato thought the bells were inside his head. He watched Petula and the boy, but they weren't looking at him. They were too busy looking at each other. The boy was smoking a cigarette. Petula was laughing as if the boy had just uttered the funniest words ever spoken.

Look at this guy Daniele, thought Renato. He's probably sleeping with my daughter. No wonder she's changed.

The boy's hair was cut just like Petula's: long in front, shaved silky short at the neck. His clothes were just like hers, the same mutant soldier look.

That Daniele. Of course Renato knew the boy. He knew everyone in town. Daniele's family, the Mangiavacchis, were known to be *grezzi,* coarse people. Renato didn't like the boy's father. He didn't like the mother. He didn't like the uncles or the aunts. Maybe Daniele wasn't old enough yet to have proved himself coarse, but give him enough time, Renato thought, and he will. And with Daniele as the center of Petula's universe, Renato did not feel disposed to like the boy.

From the open window of the truck, he heard Petula's lovely clear laughter, the laughter of a young woman in love. Cappelli was busy talking away in the passenger seat, blaspheming against the train and the town and its waterworks and the Madonna and the saints. Renato wasn't listening. His hands tightened on the wheel.

The train came. It took away his daughter and the kid who tossed his cigarette with a flick before climbing aboard. The train left, the gate opened, and Renato drove across the sunlit tracks.

FOUR

Digging Down

By the time Renato and Cappelli had put up the signs to block traffic, gotten out their heavy tools, and begun digging up the piazza in front of the church, both men's bodies smelled of sweat.

A crowd of people—mostly men—watched. Men love to watch other men work. Men can pass hours, eyes squinting, open mouths breathing, hands diddling with loose change in their pockets, minds concentrating on the spectacle of another man's labors. If, in a place with good public access, a man gets down to work repairing an engine, or felling a tree, or building a wall, or digging a deep hole to fix a big pipe, in no time he'll have a group of other men observing him, commenting on his every move. Old, retired men make for especially attentive onlookers. Past having to waste effort themselves, they leave activity to other folks now. So they watch for hours, not caring that their attention can be downright maddening to the guy doing all the work.

"Why are they using a shovel to pry up that paving stone?" asked an old man wearing a gray hat.

"How would I know why?" snapped an old man in a brown jacket. "If you were to ask me, I would agree with you. The pickax, of course, is what they should use. If they insist with the shovel, they'll break it. I tell you that myself. And then how will they dig a hole without a shovel?"

In fact, Renato had been about to ask Cappelli to hand him the pickax. But he heard the comments of the old men and he didn't want to let them have the satisfaction of being proved right. It was no good, though. He couldn't get enough leverage with the shovel. The paving stone wouldn't budge.

"Oh, here's the pickax," said Cappelli. "We should use this, no?"

"I suppose we could," said Renato, taking the pickax. He inserted the tip under the paving stone and moved it away with ease.

"Like I said," said the old man in the brown jacket. "It needed the pickax."

Renato played deaf. Taking up the shovel once again, he dug down in the earth under where the paving stone had been.

Not many minutes passed before the old men were arguing about the dam project. All conversations in town these days found their way to the dam.

"No, I tell you they did the same thing up in Vagli before the war," said the old man in the brown jacket who liked to have his say about everything.

"What before the war? It was after the war. After. Not before. I remember it well." The old man in the gray hat held firm. "Vagli, up there in the Garfagnana, past Lucca. Dammed up the river they did, and made a lake. After the war."

"You're both wrong," said a third old man who stood near them in the crowd. What conversation was ever private in Sant'Angelo D'Asso? "It was *during* the war."

"Ha!" the old man in the brown jacket said with a splendid show of sarcasm. "As if people didn't have better things to do during the war! No, it was during the twenty years of Fascism *before* the war. And who could argue with the government back then? Il Duce himself had the idea. So the people of the town of Vagli had to take their things and leave, just the same as us now. Don't you kid yourself. It's no easier to say no to the governmnent today."

"Il Duce?" The man with the gray hat would not be swayed. "Mussolini was already shot and hanged when the idea came up to make the dam at Vagli. I know it for a fact because my cousin used to live there, in the very town where now the only thing that pokes up above the surface of the lake is the steeple of the old church. My own cousin, you hear! Took the compensation money the government paid him. Left. *After* the war. I remember it myself."

"You're old," said the old man in the brown jacket. "You're old and your arteries have hardened. You remember wrong."

The third man was pursuing a thought of his own. "I think I'll try to sell my house. I mean, what's the use in waiting anymore? Only logical thing to do is sell and get out fast."

"Sell your house!" The old man in the brown jacket laughed. "And to what person are you going to sell? You think anyone wants to buy in a town that's already as good as dead?"

"He's dreaming," said the man in the gray hat. "No one will buy his house, or your house, or mine. Taking the compensation money from the government is the only way out. Simple people like us have no choice. Never have had. Never will. Government will send us out of here with a little bit of money and a big kick up the backside, and we'll have to make new lives for ourselves with no more help than that."

"I still say I can try to sell my house," said the third man.

"Then try, old imbecile," the man in the brown jacket said, laughing again, hiking up his trousers with his hands in his pockets. "Try."

Renato, digging, didn't want to listen. What they were saying was true, but it was too horrible to think about. He concentrated instead on his digging, heard the tip of his shovel crunch through gravelly earth.

He raised his eyes and saw the closed doors of the church, doors that would open in a couple of hours for the funeral of his friend. The coffin must be in there already. His mind was with the coffin while he dug. He imagined he was digging his friend's grave.

The more he thought about Aristodemo Vezzosi inside the coffin inside the church, the more everything around him seemed like a dream. He lost himself in memories and thoughts, but at least he didn't have to listen to the conversation of the old men who watched him work.

❧

A long time ago—long ago it now seemed, though his memories were clear—Renato had been a boy, and Signor and Signora Vezzosi hadn't become special to him yet. They were an older couple in the town, and there were lots of older couples in the town. Renato still had his parents back then. He was busy being his parents' son.

He was a dreamy boy with a tendency to lose himself inside his own imagination. Every now and then, though, his dreams had an unsettling way of making themselves real, so Renato grew up thinking that dreams were never to be ignored.

And of course there was the worst of all dreams that came to him when he had almost outgrown childhood. He dreamed his parents died.

It was a hot June when Renato had the dream. He had turned seventeen in February and had left school a year before. He didn't need a high school diploma because he had already started working as an apprentice to Aristodemo Vezzosi, the man in charge of the waterworks for the entire town of Sant'Angelo D'Asso. Vezzosi was starting to make himself special to the boy. Vezzosi was a small man, but his calloused hands were strong. When he and Renato mended pipes together, Renato would watch the eloquent intelligence of the hands. The edges of some people's mouths always seemed to hide a frown, but Vezzosi's lips were calm while his hands worked. His eyes were sharp, like the eyes of a beautiful bird. Renato wondered if his own hands would ever be so able, his own eyes ever so wise. Would he ever become a man?

One of these hot June nights Renato had trouble getting to sleep. When he finally did fall asleep, he wished he hadn't, because he dreamed that his parents died.

A terrible dream. Who could have imagined that such a vision would become true so soon after he had the dream?

The sun was cruel that long ago summer when Renato still had half a year to go before he turned eighteen.

Renato's father, forever a robust, zestful man, was diagnosed with cancer. *"Fulminante"* was how the doctors described the disease. Fulminating. As fast as lightning. In the course of a few weeks, the flesh seemed to evaporate from inside the man's skin. He became unendurably fragile. Then he was gone. The whole town came to his funeral.

Renato's mother had always had a weak heart. Not a month had gone by after her husband's death when she, too, died. In those short weeks of widowhood, Renato heard his mother say, "My heart is breaking into pieces." He tried to comfort her. He wanted to believe that it was only an expression, to say that a heart could break to pieces, but it was no mere expression for his mother. Her heart broke.

For the second time that summer, the funeral was attended by everyone in town.

The two caskets lay in side-by-side graves. As soon as the funeral was over, it started to rain. The metal-gray summer sky poured.

If Renato remembered correctly, it had been raining in the dream about his parents' death. Leaving the cemetery, he knew that everything had been shown to him ahead of time in a dream.

There were no grandparents to take Renato into their care, no uncles or aunts to contest his ownership of the house that sat across the bridge, just outside town. Important people of Sant'Angelo D'Asso, men with the power to make such decisions, decided that the boy was only six months away from legal adulthood. Midwinter he would become a man. Might as well let him live in the house on his own. He already had a job as apprentice to Vezzosi. Renato, they reasoned, could look after himself.

Renato spent a lonesome autumn in the house. When he thought he heard people moving about in the darkness, he knew it was only his parents' ghosts. More often, though, it was the wind.

At work, Vezzosi was especially gentle with Renato. Patiently he taught him all there was to know about the town's spring and pipes and pumps. When Vezzosi's eventual retirement came around, he wanted Renato to be his successor.

A childless couple, the Vezzosis never thought of adopting Renato; they wouldn't have been so presumptuous as to try to take his parents' place. But they invited him often to dinner in their home after work. They understood why he was silent while he ate. Silence was fine with them. They weren't particularly garrulous people themselves.

Renato was used to calling them Signor and Signora Vezzosi. This habit would never change. His feelings for them, however, did change in time. He never had reason to search for a word to define what he felt. All the same, the feeling that grew up quietly inside him was something very close to love.

He ate dinner with them in February on the night of his eighteenth birthday. He lifted his glass to theirs when the Vezzosis toasted him with their own wine. He felt himself smile.

Then in March he met a girl who would lift the loneliness from his heart.

Not that he *met* her in March. You can never meet someone new in a town so small. What's new is the way you suddenly see a person, as if for the first time. Magic happened to Renato when he first noticed Milena—noticed her differently—though she, too, had been living in Sant'Angelo D'Asso since the day she was born. And naturally, when he felt the need to talk to someone about the fact that he thought he was falling in love, it was to the Vezzosis that he turned.

Aristodemo and Tita Vezzosi had become family to the boy.

Now the boy had become a man and he was digging in the gravelly earth in front of the church, digging down to fix the broken pipe that was keeping him from going up the stone steps of the church to be near the body inside the coffin. He had to fix the pipe and he'd miss the funeral of the man who had been close to his heart.

And his daughter was becoming a mutant soldier and not his little girl anymore, and his whole town was about to disappear. And here he was sweating like a beast of burden beneath the same sun that had looked cool earlier in the morning but was now maliciously hot. So everything certainly seemed to point to the fact that, yes, *la fortuna*, fortune, was getting ready to give Renato a kick in the balls.

"But it is a shame if you think about it," said the man in the gray hat, still intent on watching Renato and Cappelli work.

"What are you talking about?" Renato said, gripping his shovel. If he wasn't careful—if he let his thoughts run away with him any-more—then he might find tears mixing in his eyes along with grit from the hole he was digging. "What are you saying?" he said almost angrily to the man in the gray hat. "What's a shame?"

"It's a shame that you have to fix this pipe instead of going inside for the funeral this morning. You and Vezzosi"—he held out the index fingers of both hands and put the fingers together, indicating closeness—"you were like this."

"True," Renato said. His shoulders relaxed. The man in the gray hat, like most of the old men in town, had been witness to the death of Renato's parents, witness also to everything else that had happened in Renato's life. And Renato had been feeling irked now because these irritating old men had been breathing down his neck while he was try-ing to get some work done, filling the air with their never-ending talk, when suddenly this old man in the gray hat should comment casually on what a damned shame it was that Renato couldn't go to Vezzosi's funeral, letting Renato know that not only was his work with the shovel being watched but the thoughts inside his head were being read as well. "True," Renato repeated, the muscles of his neck easing. "I wanted to go to Signor Vezzosi's funeral, but what can you do?"

The old man with the gray hat chuckled. A chuckle can take the place of half an hour full of words in a town where people have known each other for years. Renato realized he liked the man.

"But poor Vezzosi!" said the other man, the one in the brown jacket. "At least he didn't stay around to see himself made homeless by some accursed dam. That would have killed him."

"That's for certain," said another man in the crowd.

Renato went back to his work. He was still sad that he couldn't go to the funeral, but at least the man in the gray hat had noticed his sad-ness. The man's noticing had almost made things right again.

The man in the gray hat continued watching Renato work with particular affection. Many people in town thought of Renato with particular affection, because to them he had been, and always would be, the seventeen-year-old boy whose parents had left him suddenly alone. All parents have to die sooner or later, but the fact that Renato's parents had died one so shortly after the other made everyone in town take Renato's loneliness to heart. Ever since then they had put up with his dreaminess. He was the town's dreamy son.

Renato, naturally, was blind to the particular affection the town felt for him. What man ever knows how he is seen by other people?

Renato dug. The man in the gray hat watched.

"*Porca maiala,* the day's getting hot," Cappelli muttered. He ran a hand over his bristly hair and the hand came away wet with sweat.

FIVE

Dust to Dust

The church bells sounded the death knell, a fractured, descending scale devoid of rhythm. The bells played musicless music, oppressive notes that saddened the air throughout the town, turning morning into mourning, clanging the grim announcement that Vezzosi's funeral was about to start.

It was by now a high stinker of a September day. The breeze had vanished, leaving behind hot, stagnant air. Working, Renato had taken off his jacket. His sweater had also come off. He was down to his work shirt and his undershirt, and was now thinking about shedding the work shirt. On the skin beneath his beard, sweat was gritty with dirt. And he had expected today to be cool.

Cappelli helped with the work, but Renato couldn't decide if the help was really helpful or was merely useless activity cleverly disguised to resemble work. Cappelli took frequent pauses to go into the *bottega* on the piazza, "to refresh," as he said, and "to fuel the machine." Every time Cappelli returned from the *bottega,* Renato was sure the red porcupine eyes were slightly more inflamed.

Renato himself avoided the *bottega* this morning. He didn't feel up to dealing with Milena's parents. His father-in-law would have been good company, but his mother-in-law he could do without.

When Cappelli returned from another refueling trip to the *bot-*

tega, he came out wiping his lips and shaking his head. "How do you manage to have that woman as a mother-in-law?" he asked Renato. "She has all the feminine charm of a wild boar in a bad mood, *Madonna bona!*"

The funeral guests arrived at the church, mostly old people who had been Vezzosi's friends. The old man in the gray hat, and the old man in the brown jacket, and the other old men, too, filed into the cool shadows inside the door.

Renato worked on, right there in front of the church steps. His hair was wet with sweat beneath the work cap on his head. The earth he shoveled up was heavy with the water that had bled from the pipe.

And there was something about old people going to the funeral of a dead old man that made him think the old people were next in line to board the same departing train.

"*Ciao.*" He was cooled by the voice he heard. Soothed. It was Milena.

"*Ciao,*" Renato said, looking up at his wife from where he stood in the hole he was digging. "You look pretty, in your nice clothes like this."

"Has Tita Vezzosi arrived yet?"

"Not that I've seen."

"I'll go and wait for her inside the church. You need anything? From the *bottega* maybe? Something to eat or drink?"

"Thanks. No. Your mother is in a rage because you're not at work this morning."

"She can be in a rage. They can get by without me for one morning every now and then. It won't kill them. I want to be here instead. I'll go to work after the funeral."

"Thanks," Renato said again, loving her. "You go and wait for the *signora* inside. *Ciao.*"

Renato got on with his work.

Then along came Signora Vezzosi, accompanied by three or four of her friends. Old women and widows, all of them. Signora Vezzosi, the newest widow, hid her face behind a black veil. She stepped carefully around the hole in the ground that Renato was digging. Just before she climbed the stairs she stopped and turned. "Oh, Renato. Can't you come in?"

He took off his cap and wiped his brow with his forearm. "Look at me!" he said, spreading out his arms so that she could take in how dirty he was and how much work he still had to do. He smiled. "You know I want to be with you." He saw tears in the eyes behind her veil.

"Yes, I know." She blew her nose on a paper handkerchief that was already reduced to shreds. "Don't worry yourself. Do your work. And come and find me in the next few days."

"I'll come." He put his cap back on. "Count on it. In the next few days. But there's the water to sort out first. I'll be here all morning fixing this damned thing, and maybe all afternoon, too. But let's see if we can't get water to the people in time for lunch. You go in for . . . for the funeral. Know that I'm thinking of you."

"Fine," she said. "Good-bye, then."

"Good-bye, *signora*. We'll see each other later."

"*Ciao*."

Signora Vezzosi's old-woman friends held her by the elbows to help her up the steps. Of course she was old, too, thought Renato, but she was strong. She could heave baskets of grapes during grape-picking time as well as any man. She didn't need the help of the other old women. Or maybe she did. Renato didn't know. He hated seeing her that stricken. And he hated the way the other old women seemed to be welcoming her into the sisterly ranks of widowhood, even though their presence was probably a comfort to her. Renato was confused.

He got back to his work, trying not to think his own thoughts. Nothing could change the naked truth that Vezzosi was dead.

The police *comandante* and his officers sauntered by. "Try not to make too much confusion," he said with his tone of authority. Then he led his men into the *bottega*, where they would wait out the funeral until they would be needed afterward to control the movements of the mourning crowd.

Cappelli mopped his neck with his handkerchief. "We thought the summer was over, but it feels like it's only getting started."

Renato didn't answer. He didn't want to talk. He took the shovel and dug through the rocky mud, probing for the first metallic clink of the broken main pipe.

The church bells stopped once the funeral inside got under way. Digging down, Renato reached the pipe. It was certainly very broken; a good chunk of it had caved in from the top. No wonder so much water had bubbled up through the ground. The pipe on either side of the breach was so corroded that the metal crumbled away in Renato's hand. "*Dio boia!*" Renato said. This would be no easy repair. They would have to dig up lots more earth, at least another three or four feet in either direction before they would get to metal sound enough to withstand a new joint.

Renato kicked the pipe with his boot. More rust crumbled off. Above him, at street level, Cappelli snorted up mucus from the back of his throat and spit.

The shops around the piazza were quiet during the funeral: not many customers to buy things. Renato and Cappelli worked in silence, punctuating their efforts with an occasional grunt or curse. The voices of the funeralgoers inside sang out prayers and chants.

The hearse arrived. The driver was none too young, and turning the long hearse around was a great challenge for him. What should have been a three-point turn became an excruciating eleven-point operation. The policemen watched from the *bottega* window. Finding a way to make themselves important, they came out, directed by their *comandante,* and all of them gave the befuddled driver instructions: "Stop!" "Go left!" "Backward!" "Forward!" "There's nothing behind you! Go! Go! Go!"

Renato and Cappelli watched, buried up to their hips in the earth.

At the end of the funeral, men came out of the church bearing wreaths of flowers. These they carried down the steps to the hearse. They hung the wreaths off railings on the hearse's roof, the white flowers transforming the vehicle into something magnificent. Carnations perfumed the air.

Out came the mourners, some dabbing tears from their eyes. Others looked as if they were starting to think about lunch.

The mourners coming down the church steps divided into two ranks, leaving an empty walkway up the middle. They fell silent when Don Luigi the priest came out into the hot sunshine, the sun reflecting off his white robes. Behind the priest the pallbearers emerged from the door with the coffin on their shoulders.

Renato put down his shovel and stood, waist deep in the earth, by Cappelli's side. He looked at the wooden box, looking for something recognizable, some sign that it wasn't empty, that there was a person inside, that the person inside was the man he had loved the way a son loves his father. The box simply looked like a wooden box, showing no clue of the person it contained. And thinking about that man not being here anymore hurt Renato, and he knew he didn't want to think about how much it hurt.

Renato breathed in. He smelled the white carnations from the funeral wreaths.

The priest came down the steps and stood beside the hearse. The pallbearers descended. Signora Vezzosi walked after them, her black veil hiding her face. Milena was not far behind. The mourners were silent as the coffin came down the steps and was placed inside the hearse. The hearse started its engine, and the gears grated when the driver, not very good with the clutch, put it into first. Then it rolled downhill. The priest and Signora Vezzosi and her closest widow friends formed the front row of mourners.

"Come by the *bottega* and get something to eat if you want," Milena said, leaning toward the hole. "See you later on."

Renato said, "Later." He smiled.

The procession began its walking pace down toward the cemetery.

In the hole in the ground in front of the church, Renato was left with his shovel in his hand and a head far too full of thoughts. He wanted to leave. He wanted to go home and sleep. He wanted to cry. He wanted to go away. He was certain everything that had happened today meant something, but he had no idea what. He was hungry so he wanted to eat, but queasiness made him want to be sick. He wanted life to be something that it did not seem to be. He didn't know what he wanted, or what he wanted to do.

Before he could do anything else, though, he had a length of old pipe to replace. People would be walking home from the cemetery soon. People would need water to make the pasta for lunch.

A fly buzzed close to his ear. It was a high stinker of a day.

"Oh!" Cappelli called. "Oh, Tizzoni! Come and see!"

Renato let his shovel fall. He crossed the pit to where Cappelli was digging. "What is it?"

"Come and see! I was digging, and this old pipe is so damned corroded I thought I'd never hit solid metal. Then I came to this joint to the next piece of pipe. The next piece is sound. So is the joint. And look here! Look what I found."

With a dirty hand Renato wiped dirt away from the joint. The tough metal looked almost new.

There was an inscription on the joint. The lettering was much too regular to have been etched by hand. Evidently this piece had been tooled in the machine shop before it had been laid to mark its historical importance, a gesture typical of the Fascist era of the 1920s and 1930s, intended to give workers a sense of satisfaction for their participation in the building of a modern Italian state. The inscription read:

FIRST CENTRAL WATER SYSTEM EVER BUILT

IN THE TOWN OF SANT'ANGELO D'ASSO.

BUILT BY SONS OF THE TOWN.

LAID THIS DAY OF 4 OCTOBER 1935.

And beneath the inscription were the names of the men who had taken part in giving water to the town. Renato had a hard time reading the names because these had been etched in freehand, probably with a nail by the workers themselves. Straining to make out the lettering, Renato could sense the pride the men must have felt. The names scratched onto the joint were the signatures of artists who wanted to be remembered for their masterpiece.

Project Manager—M. Giannelli

was the first name,

Engineer—R. Lucatti

the second. The third name, that of the chief plumber, was harder to read. Time had nearly erased it. The first initial was indecipherable. To Renato, the family name seemed to be

Bernini

Beneath the other names was the final signature. Reading over Cappelli's shoulder, Renato saw:

Apprentice—Aristodemo Vezzosi

He recognized the handwriting. When Renato had worked as Vezzosi's apprentice, he had seen the signature many times on order forms and other official documents. Here was the same signature written with a nail when Vezzosi himself had been an apprentice, just learning the job. Why hadn't Vezzosi told Renato about his role in putting in the first pipes? Maybe because he had never been one to talk too much about himself.

Renato did a quick calculation. When he signed the joint, Vezzosi couldn't have been more than a teenage boy. What excitement he must have felt in putting his name on a pipe, buried for posterity, along with the names of the strong workingmen of the town. And the date: 4 October 1935. A national holiday was October 4. The feast of St. Francis, Italy's first patron saint. What a grand *festa* there must have been in town that day, the day they celebrated the new waterworks pipes!

And today of all days, thought Renato, this pipe had to burst. The day of Vezzosi's funeral. Powerful emotion rose in his throat. Too powerful. This was the kind of emotion that could dominate you if you didn't suppress it at once.

He blinked. He looked up at the sun. Salty sweat burned his eyes. "We'll put in the new pipe," he said suddenly to Cappelli. "But this joint is still good. We can use it again." He wanted to explain how important it was for water to run through the same pipes, for Vezzosi's joint in particular to go on forever, giving water to the town. But he would have needed too many words to retell the thoughts in his head, so he said nothing.

He and Cappelli worked for the next hours. Renato's hands welded the new pipe to the old joint. He looked one last time at the piece of metal Vezzosi had helped put into place more than sixty years before. Then, taking up his shovel, he buried it in the privacy of the earth.

The air still smelled of carnations.

SIX

In Bed

In bed, Renato hugged Milena from behind, aware of the perfume of her hair. He breathed in and the perfume filled him.

For a moment, breathing in his wife's warm neck, he nearly felt close to God, or to his version of God. To Renato, God was probably not very different from himself. God was a being who did things, created things, savored things for the pleasure of their color and smell and taste. The creation of man, maybe, was no big deal after all because most men were tedious, pragmatic creatures, like bulls or hogs, who thought of little more than the next meal and the next comfortable place to shit. But God had created woman as well, and it was for the creation of woman that Renato felt nearly close to God. In that act of creation, God had proved his artistic ingenuity. Woman was a poem to be smelled and tasted and touched.

He pressed his lips to Milena's neck.

Renato said, "I'm glad you came to the funeral."

"Shame you had to work outside and couldn't come in."

"Hmm."

His arm was around her. Renato loved this position. He always had. Her body wrapped inside his.

Petula was asleep in her own bedroom, up the corridor. The door to Milena's and Renato's room was closed. Their window was open slightly because it was a warm night. The breeze that came in smelled of trees in which nightbirds sang. The darkness in the bedroom was private for Renato and Milena, yet open to the night outside.

Renato's penis started to rise in the pleasing proximity of their bodies. He rolled to change his position. Milena turned her mouth to his.

Warm wet kiss in the darkness.

Then Milena did exactly what Renato hoped she would do. No word spoken, she sat up and slipped off her nightdress. His hand ran over the smooth skin of her naked back.

She lay down on the sheets.

He grasped her wrist and held her arm up over her head, nuzzling his mouth into the delicate hair in her underarm. The first sweat of excitation moistened her skin, sharpening her smell. She smelled delicious. A hint of spring onions. Salty to the tongue. He licked her with his tongue tip and felt her shiver.

She pushed him off, taking control. Her turn to taste him. She kissed her way down his chest, to the tingling skin of his belly. Then she took him into the warmth of her mouth.

Impatient to be inside her, all of him inside her, he pushed her to the mattress, lowered his mouth between her legs. "*Mi gusto questo gusto,*" he said. "I want to taste this taste." When she responded, he put his body up beside her and let the sensation of slipping inside his wife sink in, spread all over him.

They moved together and for a moment he imagined he had forgotten everything else in his world. But his forgetfulness was short-lived, for as soon as he had let himself enjoy the relief of not thinking about a thing, all the thoughts he had been hiding from caught up with him at once. Where would his life go now that he and everyone else would have to leave town? Who could guide him? Certainly not old Aristodemo Vezzosi, put to rest today. Suddenly Renato's life felt as crumbly and full of holes as the pipe he had been called on to fix in the town's main square.

All blood leaving his poor prick, Renato sagged limp inside his wife.

"What's wrong?" she said.

"If only I knew."

"Don't worry. Just relax yourself a bit. I'll do the moving."

Renato knew already that it was hopeless. With tender steadiness Milena pressed her hips into his, but, slippery and deflated, he fell out of her. He was soft beyond all dreams of ever being hard again. He sighed.

"Tell me, Renato," Milena said, lying back. "Tell me what's on your mind. Talk to me."

Panic held him by the balls. He had never had this problem before, but that wasn't what had him worried. Physical things take care of themselves if you give them time; it wasn't the physical part that upset him so. Instead, he was terrified by the question of what it implied. What did it mean, to be inside your wife—your favorite place in the world—surrounded by tastes and tingles and smells more exquisite than anything else on earth, and then to all of a sudden have that, too, disappear from your senses? What was happening to you when even sex—the exaltation of body and heart together—came to taste of nothing?

"Doesn't mean anything," Milena said to him, though he hadn't said a word. She always had possessed the uncanny knack of reading his thoughts. "Means maybe it wasn't the best night to make love, with your head too full of the day, too full of other things. But go ahead. Pour it out! Tell me and you'll feel better."

Renato wasn't listening. He was alone inside his fear. Life had lost its taste. *That* was his problem. That was the chill that kept coming over him lately. *Non sa di niente,* he said to himself. Doesn't taste at all. How can you live when life changes from lovely wine to tepid, weak broth?

"The closeness is nice anyway," Milena said, trying. "We can always make love another time. I'm happy to be here with you. *Ti voglio bene.*" She lay her naked body against his, snuggling under his arm. She kissed his chest, close to his heart. "It'd be better though," she said, "if at least you tried to talk."

"*Ti voglio bene,*" was all he managed to say. "I love you. Excuse me. Good night."

Renato stared into the darkness of the bedroom. He could hear his wife listening to his wakefulness.

Fine, he told himself. So life has lost its taste for me.

At least his sickness had a name.

Renato was bereft. Nothing could help him.

The bed underneath the small of his back was suddenly cold, and the chill spread inside him. It was the dead chill that had visited ever more frequently in recent weeks, the vertiginous queasiness that hollowed out his guts like the emptiness of loss. He had lost, he was losing, he would lose.

The empty chill chased away his closeness to God, made his wife's perfume disappear from beneath his nose, left him lonely and sad.

But God, as they say, prepares the remedy even before there is the wound.

SEVEN

Renato's Dream

Out of the darkness, a hand touched Renato on the shoulder. Renato mumbled into his pillow. The hand rested on his shoulder. He turned. The hand hovered in the darkness above his bed. He sat up. The hand floated.

The palm of the hand was wide, the fingers strong. On a finger glinted a heavy ring with a big red stone. The hand appeared to quiver momentarily, or maybe the trembling was caused by Renato's blinking, sleepy eyes.

Then the hand became clear and strangely luminous. It motioned for him to follow. Sensing the hand to be benevolent, Renato had no fear, so the fast fluttering of his heart was not terror but expectancy. His pulse raced, his breathing was loud, yet he rose from the bed with the light grace of a child. The darkness in the room was smooth and soft. Standing up, putting one bare foot in front of the other, he saw that the hand lighted his steps.

Milena's breathing disappeared behind him as he left the bedroom. He heard Petula breathing, too, when he walked past her open door. He followed the hand along the corridor. At the end of the hallway, the hand turned the knob of the front door and beckoned him outside.

Renato knew that the stone steps leading down into the courtyard were cold beneath his feet. He *knew* they were cold, but he didn't feel the coldness. There was warmth throughout his body despite the predawn chill. He looked into the darkness past where the hills would be. The sun had not begun to rise. Nightbirds called, voices like ripples of water. Stars were little lights overhead. He smelled the vanilla perfume of night-scented blossoms. Then the smells swirled, changed flavor, intensified. He smelled carnations. He smelled the warm animal musk of Milena's hair.

The hand preceded him. He floated to catch up.

The hand stopped above the well. He heard the tapping of the sheep's hooves in the stall. He heard the tinkle of the bell around the first sheep's neck.

Waiting for him at the well, the hand indicated that he was meant to look inside.

He went to the well and, as he stood there, the courtyard cat curled itself around his ankles and purred, caressing Renato's feet with vibrating fur. Radiance from the hand, as soft as candlelight, illuminated the vertical darkness inside the well. Renato could almost see a reflection of light far below, where the water was deep in the earth. He looked to where the hand led his eyes and saw a stone an arm's length beneath the well's lip.

He leaned into the well, blissfully secure of his balance. His fingertips were endowed with easy, heroic strength. Effortlessly he pulled away the stone.

He set the stone on the brink of the well and reached inside the hole where the stone had been. His hands touched wood. He pulled out the wooden box and placed it on the ground by his bare feet. The cat shut its eyes luxuriantly and rubbed its neck against the box.

Inside there were the treasures that you usually discover only in a dream. Gemstones were as plentiful as grapes in a bowl. Gold lay underneath.

Lifting his eyes Renato saw the dawn turn the sky to gold. His heart quickened again, but now with joy. He knew his luck had changed. His *fortuna* had been changed by a fortune, yet he was not filled with greed. It was beneficence that enlarged his spirit to the dimensions of the sky. There was more wealth here than he could ever want to spend. At last he would be able to give. He could give to Milena and to Petula. Give to everyone in town. The treasure was not for him; it was for everyone. Everything around him—the breeze on his skin, the cold stones beneath his feet, the sounds of the sheep in their stall, the purring of the cat against his ankles, the perfume of tree blossoms, the sleepy breathing of his wife and daughter inside the house—everything scintillated with life. He was rich; everything was rich with color, texture, music, smell, taste.

Renato, alone with his fortune, knew he was in a dream. He knew he would be awake soon. The fear of loss passed like a quick cloud. Then he was warm and relaxed because a promise took form in his head. The promise told him he would remember the dream forever because it had been sent to him.

Renato woke.

He mumbled into his pillow. He smelled Milena's warm sleep beside him. He felt the cotton of the pillowcase against his cheek. He blinked, then, remembering, turned his head quickly to look above the bed. There was no hand.

The empty darkness surprised him, for the dream had been so real. But that was a dream, of course, he told himself. You can't really expect a hand with a ring on the finger to float above your bed. He felt himself called to rise up all the same, and he found again the expectancy that had energized him in the dream.

The tiles of his bedroom floor were decidedly cold beneath his bare feet. Better bundle up a bit this time, he reasoned. This time it won't be so warm outside.

He went to the chair on which he had placed his clothes after undressing the night before. In darkness he put his work clothes on over his pajamas. He tiptoed out of the room so as not to wake his wife.

In the corridor, he almost wanted to run. The dream had been sent to him, and he knew a miracle was about to occur. He couldn't wait to see the treasure that waited for him inside the well. Now, however, he had to take every step weighed down by the gravity of flesh, disappointed that he could no longer float.

Outside in the courtyard the sheep were silent in their stall. But nightbird songs rippled like cool water, and Renato was reassured that the dream had been true. He went to the well; the courtyard cat rubbed around his ankles and purred. *"C'eri anche te, Micio,"* Renato whispered. His joy made him laugh aloud. "You were in the dream, too."

There was no dawn yet in the sky, only starlight. In the black mouth of the well, Renato's fingers felt for the edges of the stone. He found it. Its shape was identical to the shape his fingers had touched in the dream. He explored the outline of the stone and found no cementing mortar around the edge. There was room to insert his fingertips on either side. He held his breath. A certainty inside him told him not to doubt. He shifted all his body's strength to his hands. Amazingly, the stone moved.

Why had he never noticed the stone before? Why, when every morning he washed his face with water from the well, had he never seen this magical, appointed place? Because he had to wait for the dream, he explained to himself. He had to wait to be told.

The stone was more reluctant than it had been in the dream. His knuckles prickled as the skin was chafed. He heaved again. Gradually he dislodged the stone, as heavy and unyielding as it was.

His belly braced squarely on the lip of the well, he gave a final tug and the stone came away. *"Dio boia!"* he invoked God the Executioner, surprised by the weight. He was off-kilter. His back twinged. He huffed, hoisting the stone up to the edge. "God, it's heavy!"

He was free now to reach inside the hole. The cat pressed its nose and forehead into Renato's calf, prodding him to go on. "Patience, Micio," he told the cat.

Preparing himself for the discovery that would change his life, Renato reached inside.

Nothing. No wood. No wooden box. Only the grit of old eroded mortar. Renato was perplexed.

"So?" he said to the cat, waiting for an answer.

The cat rubbed his leg. It meowed. It purred.

He waited for a while, sure that something would happen, but nothing happened.

"Wake up!" he said to the darkness inside the sheep's stall, opening the door. He wanted someone to talk to.

He moved through the darkness to the small milking room. The sheep were not pleased to be disturbed. They clambered up to a four-legged stance, moving their mouths with a circular chewing motion as if grass left over from yesterday were still between their teeth. Tongues flickered about their lips. They bleated their complaint.

"Prima!" Renato called for the first sheep, settling himself on the stool. Always ready for adventure, even at this unusual hour, the first sheep trotted up to the milking stool. She was nervous, though, and her teat required a lot of handling before it would release its milk. He slapped the teat gently, imitating the movement that a lamb would make with its head.

"What do you make of it then?" Renato asked her when the milk started to come. "Was it just a dream or was it a message of what's destined to be?"

The sheep found olive leaves on the floor. She chewed.

Knowing she would understand him, Renato gave her his thoughts out loud. Of course it was no ordinary dream, he explained, because it hadn't *felt* like a dream. And surely he was experienced enough with dreams to know when a dream was just a dream and when it was a dream that was sent to change your life. This was a dream to change his life. And in this, his dream of dreams, he had felt what it must feel like to have his fortune transformed. No ordinary dream. Absolutely not!

But what did the dream mean? He didn't know, and the first sheep was no help on the subject. Neither was the second, or the third, or the timid, fearful fourth as he milked each of them in turn.

"What good are you all if you only listen to me but don't tell me your ideas?" he said to the sheep as he led them out of their stall. "How am I supposed to understand what the dream meant?"

The sheep were not accustomed to having their morning walk on the hillside in such darkness, but Renato wanted to be on the very top of the hill to sit down and wait for the dawn to appear.

He knew something wondrous was happening. Otherwise, why would he have been sent such an important dream? But how should he interpret its message? What would he have to do to make his fortune change?

"Fine then," he said to the sheep, sitting down atop the hill. "It's clear that I need to think about this some more. So that's what I'll do. I'll think about the dream. And the four of you can think about it, too. I mean, I know what my problem is lately: Nothing tastes of anything anymore, not even making love with my wife. Can you believe it? And I know this dream will give me the answer to everything. It promised to change my luck, right? And not only mine. But what is the treasure supposed to be? And what am I supposed to do to find it? I don't know what it means. Do you?"

The shy sheep, Quarta, opened her mouth and burbled an unconvincing bleat.

"You don't have to answer now," Renato said. "We'll all give it some thought. Then we'll talk more on the subject later. Another time. All right?"

The sheep started to chew grass. He watched them, his eyes getting used to the starlight. Maybe the fourth sheep was limping a little less this morning. Renato hoped so, though he wasn't sure. A dog barked outside a farmhouse across the valley. The first sheep, always alert, raised her head and stared. The dog barked again. The first sheep's ears twitched, catching the sound.

Renato sat on the hilltop and waited for light to come.

EIGHT

The Invitation

Later, midmorning, Renato sat on a wooden chair at a table against the shelves in his in-laws' *bottega*. There was work he should have been doing, naturally. Had he wanted to be busy, he could have replaced the handle on the main valve up at the waterworks building, the handle that had broken off yesterday. Or he could have done any number of small jobs. But today was Saturday and he didn't especially want to be busy. He could always work this afternoon, if necessary. Why not take a little time this morning and just sit?

It was a beautiful morning outside. Yesterday, all that digging and repairing while the funeral was going on had seemed a torture under the hot sun. Today he could enjoy the last of the summer's heat. Why not sit?

Petula was away for the morning, up in Siena. Milena was here in the *bottega* working with her parents. And maybe Renato needed a little human company, maybe he wanted to feel some family around. His head was far too full of unthought thoughts that were wearing him out.

And early this morning he had dreamed the dream that was sure to change his life, though he didn't know how to interpret it. He needed time to reflect. So why not sit? And it was a good time of day to be sitting here at the table inside the *bottega*. The early morning crowd had dissipated and the lunchtime business was still a couple of hours away. The customers at this hour were a manageable number. Men took coffee or wine at the bar, women bought cheese and cold meats from the counter or selected groceries from the shelves. Tonino was behind the bar, chatting with the men. They talked about the dam project. What else was there to talk about? Then conversation moved to yesterday's funeral, and poor Vezzosi. And the burst water pipe and how much water there had been, flowing from between the stones of the square. Renato listened, didn't say a word.

Maria Severina was at the cash register, ringing up the women. Milena was mostly in the kitchen, stirring sauces and preparing the meat for lunch. From his chair, Renato watched.

A sensation started to touch the back of his neck, like a slight breeze from an open window. Not a sensation, a thought. No. Not even a thought. A memory, or the memory of a memory. The ghost of a memory began to awaken some hidden awareness deep inside his mind. He searched for the phantom image, but it turned shy and fled.

And then there was his dream. He had been eager to tell Milena when she woke up this morning, but he hadn't said anything because he hadn't yet worked out what the dream meant and he would have looked foolish if he'd tried to explain that this, the most important of all dreams ever, would somehow change their lives though he didn't know how. So he would wait, he decided, until he understood it better before including his wife in the miracle that was sure to occur.

Not telling her called for unaccustomed discretion. He usually told her everything. And now all of a sudden there was this little secret.

Yes, Renato had to admit as he sat in the *bottega* now, yes, his dream had already become a secret between him and his wife, only because he hadn't told her when he first could have, or maybe should have. And now the dream was something that lived in him but not in her. Keeping a secret from Milena was something new. He wasn't sure where secrecy might lead.

"Anything else?" said Maria Severina from behind the cash register.

"Nothing else," replied an old woman customer. "No, wait. A little pasta. I almost forgot. I forget everything these days! Give me a little packet of pasta."

"Fine. Pasta," Maria Severina said. "What kind?"

"Any kind is fine," the woman said.

"Then take it yourself. It's on the shelf there behind the head of my son-in-law who is sitting in that chair doing nothing while we're all working."

The woman approached Renato, her string shopping bag clutched in her hands, already loaded with the rest of her groceries. She stood before him and squinted past him, focusing her old eyes on the shelf. "Have you got any spaghetti?"

"Of course," Maria Severina called out.

"But there's none here. I don't see any." She squinted harder. "None."

"The shelf is full of spaghetti!" Maria Severina was losing her patience, which was scant anyway.

Renato, trying to chase the memory of a memory that wanted to visit him, had been making himself distant. But the old woman right in front of him needed help and his mother-in-law's voice was closing in on nastiness. He turned in his chair, picked out a packet of spaghetti, and handed it to the old woman with a gracious, "*Prego, signora.*"

"Thank you," the woman said, appearing satisfied. Then she squinted at the packet in her hand and said, "No. Not these. These spaghetti are too big."

"How big do you want them?" Maria Severina said.

"*Che ne so io?* How would I know?" Now the woman was flustered.

"If you don't know," Maria Severina scolded, "who do you expect to know for you?"

"But how would I know?" the woman repeated, having found the sentence that best expressed what was in her head. "I don't know. Not these. These are too big."

"Maybe the spaghettini then?" Renato offered.

"Let me see the spaghettini." She squinted at the packet of spaghettini. "No, these are too small."

Maria Severina came around from behind the cash register, taking charge. "What? The others are too big, and these are too small? What kind of sauce are you putting on them anyway? Tell me, and I'll tell you what size pasta you need."

"What kind of sauce? How would I know?"

Renato smiled. He liked the woman's reply. Often in life, he thought, it would be good to answer challenging questions with a resounding *But how would I know?* His whole life now, in fact, could be expressed in the phrase.

"Go on!" Maria Severina's voice was harsh. "Meat sauce? Tomato sauce? Pesto? Mushrooms? What kind of sauce, and I'll tell you the pasta you need."

"I haven't decided about the sauce," the woman said, defending herself. "It's hard enough deciding about the pasta! You got linguine? Maybe linguine—"

"We've got linguine. Renato, move yourself and get out of the way!"

Renato had both women not more than a foot from his face. He remembered that yesterday Cappelli had likened Maria Severina to an angry wild boar and today he thought the description perfect. Her short legs were stiff at the knees. There was no neck to be seen between the shoulders and the jaw. The eyes held only rage. She gave him a shove with her hooflike hands. He leaned to one side, letting her reach to the shelves.

"Here are the linguine," Maria Severina grunted, sticking the packet in the old woman's hands.

The woman squinted very hard and said, "But the writing here says 'trenette'."

"Trenette, linguine, they are the same thing."

"Then why doesn't the packet say 'linguine'?"

"It does," Maria Severina said, animal menace audible in her tone. "It says the same thing."

"But why do they write 'trenette' if they mean to say 'linguine'?"

"*Madonnina benedetta e santa!* It takes the patience of the saints to deal with you!"

The fight of aging woman flesh occurring in front of him, Renato looked toward the door and saw the tobacconist come in, the man with the cynical, all-knowing grin.

"So?" said the tobacconist.

"So," replied Renato's father-in-law, Tonino, from behind the bar. He had done a fine job so far of ignoring the women altogether. "So."

"A corrected coffee," the tobacconist ordered.

"Corrected with Strega or with a drop of Sambuca or grappa or with some of this cognac here?"

"With the cognac."

The two women hadn't yet resolved the pasta issue in front of Renato's face when a middle-aged woman came in wanting to buy grated parmigiano cheese.

"Milena!" Maria Severina screamed toward the kitchen. "Come out here and grate some cheese! We have our hands full!"

Milena emerged from the kitchen, asked the middle-aged woman how much cheese she wanted, and got to work cutting the right-size piece from the big parmigiano wheel to feed into the grating machine.

"Or maybe the penne would be nice," the undecided old woman standing in front of Renato considered out loud.

"Certainly." Maria Severina glowered at Renato. "Certainly it might help things if this *coglione,* this testicle of a man, shifted himself out of the way."

"What have I got to do with it?" Renato said with grand indifference. He wanted tranquility. He wanted to reflect on the dream about the glowing hand with the red-stoned ring on the finger leading him to treasure, the dream that promised to change his luck.

Another woman entered the *bottega.* As soon as people noticed, they stopped talking. They knew who she was. They stared.

She walked to the bar. "An Irish whiskey, please," she said in English.

"*Un whiskey irlandese per la signora,*" said Tonino, pouring.

Everyone watched her first sip, then people got back to their conversations.

This was the new Englishwoman, the actress, who had bought an old, disused farmhouse not too far from town and had paid mountains of money to have the place redone. Renato had gone there once or twice to check out the water hookup, but she hadn't been there because she'd still been in London waiting for her house to be finished.

She had moved in only a week or so ago.

Here, in person now, she communicated an alluring paradox, a powerful mixture of strength and vulnerability. She could express herself with a movement of her hand, a glance of her eye. Maybe she could convey her feelings so well because she was an actress. Or maybe because she was a woman.

"You met her yet?" Tonino said to Renato in Italian, knowing the actress wouldn't understood his words.

"Her house, yes," said Renato. "Her person, no."

"She comes in every morning about this time," Milena said to him without looking up from the cheese she was grating. "Always has the same drink. This time of morning, can you imagine? A woman having a drink like that. Often comes in the afternoon, too. But they must have different ways, her people. Her drinks never seem to change her. She always walks straight."

She was dressed the way no townswoman would dress out in public. She wore jeans and a white T-shirt and light sandals on her bare feet. My God, she's long! thought Renato, looking at all of her from her light chestnut hair to the ends of her toes with their deep-red wine-colored polish.

He looked away, realizing that Milena had looked up from her cheese grating and had seen him watching the English actress. Staring at other women had never been his custom. Then again, neither had he ever been in the habit of keeping secrets from his wife, and he still hadn't told her about his dream.

The old woman and Maria Severina settled on some pasta—the standard spaghetti that she had said no to in the first place—and the old woman paid and left.

The English actress sipped her whiskey and looked at people in the *bottega*. She appeared not to notice that they were staring at her.

"She's the future of this place, you know," the tobacconist commented.

The actress's face was unchanged. Did she not know, or not care, that she was the topic of conversation?

"Clever, or just lucky, she is, like all those foreigners," continued the tobacconist. "Her house is far enough away and high enough on a hill so that when the whole town is sunk under the new lake when the dam's been built, she'll still be there. Might even have a lakeside view. She'll still be here when the rest of us are gone. *Che colpo di culo!* What luck! Those foreigners have all the luck."

What was her name? Renato asked himself. Something English and therefore incomprehensible. She hadn't been around long enough yet for him to have gotten a grip on her name. She had already become, though, the object of speculation and gossip. Everyone swapped stories about what "the English actress" was up to. The midget who sold newspapers on the piazza said he was sure he had seen her face in celebrity magazines, so certainly she must be a big fish.

The men in town looked at her a special way: Her beauty was out of reach for them. She was something none of them would ever have. They wanted her, all the same.

Foreigners were not uncommon in this part of Tuscany. Even Renato had made friends with an American named Duncan who lived up in Montalcino. Come to think of it, thought Renato now, a visit to Duncan wouldn't be such a bad idea. Duncan was Duncan, American or not. He came from a different world, yet he had a simple human heart and seemed to understand the simple human heart that lived inside Renato. In the next few days, Renato made a mental note, he would drive up to Montalcino to see Duncan.

And, yes, he owed a visit to Signora Vezzosi, though he was almost afraid to stare her grief in the face, never mind his own.

But here was this English actress. *Now.*

Surely there were other foreigners in the area. An American

writer or two. A handful of artists. A German sculptor. An Austrian musician. An Irish weaver. Some wealthy Swiss ex-hippies. And the tobacconist had a point. They always seemed to get the best houses.

Each, in his or her own way, had bought into the Tuscan dream. Each had spent a lot of money for a farmhouse up on some hill or other. Each had been gossiped about by the townspeople of Sant'Angelo D'Asso as a fresh curiosity and possible source of scandal. Each lived out his or her version of what all foreigners think Italian life in Tuscany really ought to be: long admiring walks in the countryside, afternoons drunk away at the bar with too much wine or beer, evenings of too much food and drink and loud talk in the *bottega* with visiting friends. Only rarely did these foreign lives ever touch the lives of the people who had been born in the town. *Stranieri,* they were called in Italian. Strangers. Inevitably the English actress would prove herself no different. *Che m'importa a me?* Renato asked himself. What's it matter to me?

She had come here six months ago, the English actress, along with an English film crew. They had come out to shoot scenes for a movie on location. For three weeks, actors, actresses, cameramen, directors, assistant directors, makeup artists, hairdressers, lighting people, and sound technicians took over a medieval castle just north of Sant'Angelo D'Asso, up in the middle of the chalk downs along the road to Siena.

A month later, after the film crew had driven off in their vans, the actress sent somebody from London to buy her a house. She wanted a piece of Tuscany for herself, a place she could come to when she wasn't making films. The farmhouse was halfway between the castle and the town. Orders were given to local builders as to how the house should be restored.

Moved in a week ago, and now here she was at the bar of the *bottega*. Renato shifted in his wooden chair, his back up against the shelves.

The English actress finished her whiskey, put the glass on the bar, and said to Tonino, "Um. I need a plumber. I'm having problems with a pipe."

Tonino smiled and nodded, not having understood a word.

"A pipe?" she persisted, keeping a brave smile on her own face. "Do you understand? A pipe?" From the back pocket of her jeans she pulled a paperback English-Italian dictionary. When she found the word, she announced, "*Pipa. Pipa?*"

"You hear that?" the tobacconist said, licking cognac-flavored coffee from his lips. "*'na pipata*. She wants to give somebody a quickie. *Pipare* seems to give her pleasure. Any volunteers?"

Other men in the *bottega* laughed.

The English actress straightened her back, knowing she was being laughed at but not knowing why. "*Pipa*," she repeated, looking around her to see if anyone might understand. She mimed her meaning with her hands, describing in the air something long and pipelike. "I have a *problema avec* I mean *con* a *pipa* at my house. *Casa mia.*"

"*Il tubo*," Renato said, understanding. "You mean a *tubo*. A *pipa* is something you smoke. Or it means other things as well. *Tubo*." He imitated her hand gestures, showing he had caught her drift. "*Un problema con i tubi a casa Sua.*"

"Exactly!" She smiled, delighted. She looked Renato in the eyes. Her eyes held light. Her beauty was an uncommon quality of light. Exquisite light seemed to be on all of her, as if the light on her cheekbones and the shadows of her throat had been designed by an artist. Her face itself was almost too handsome to be called beautiful, yet the face made the light surrounding it more beautiful than ordinary light. That was the beauty this woman possessed. "Can anyone help me with the *tubo* at my house?"

"Tizzoni here is your man," the tobacconist said. "That's his work, fixing ladies' tubes in their house."

"Behave yourself," Milena said to the tobacconist, laughing. "I know my Renato. He's not like that." Taking the situation in hand, Milena addressed the English actress. "*Mio marito può risolvere il problema con i tubi—*" She indicated Renato and spoke slowly. "Do you understand? My husband can fix the problem with the pipes."

"Him? This man?" the English actress looked at Renato. "Lovely." She smiled again. "*Tubo?*"

"*Sì, sì. I tubi,*" he confirmed. "But, Milena, maybe it's something a plumber could sort out. We don't even know what the problem is. If it's inside the house, I'm not supposed to touch it. Everybody knows that."

"Go, Renato," Milena said. "Who else is she supposed to ask for help? You go."

"Why?"

"Because it's your work."

"*Quando?*" The English actress surprised everyone by using exactly the right Italian word.

"*Dopo pranzo,*" Renato said. That was as precise an appointment as he ever made.

"*Dopo pranzo?*" the actress looked confused for a moment. Then she understood. "Right, then. After lunch."

The actress paid for her whiskey. She said, "Bye-bye, then. My house, after lunch."

"Bye-bye," Renato said, trying English.

"Bye-bye," the tobacconist echoed, laughing. He was laughing not at the woman but at Renato. When the woman was gone, the tobacconist paid for his coffee. He shook his head knowingly and said, "After lunch, then, eh, Tizzoni? Have fun."

"But what fun?" Renato laughed, disconcerted by the fact that his heartbeat had not yet slowed to normal, not since he'd understood he was invited to the house of the English actress who moved in that painfully beautiful light.

"Keep an eye on him, Milena," the tobacconist winked. "You know how men get after a certain age."

"I'll look out for myself," Milena said, "without your good advice. I know my own chickens. I'll tell you again: Renato's not like that." But the tobacconist had already left.

Renato's mother-in-law, Maria Severina, looked at Renato with cold eyes. She raised her chin and said, "*Mah.*" A single syllable that signified all: We'll see.

NINE

Temptation

Renato felt the tingle of weird, expectant, unknowing nervousness after lunch. He drove toward the English actress's house in his Fiat Ritmo. The windshield was dull with road dirt. He used the spritzer and the windshield wipers to clear two arcs of cleanish glass. He wasn't a man to worry about the appearance of his car.

He stayed in third gear on the curves. On the straightaway he shifted into fourth. He had to jerk the stick a good deal before he found the gear he wanted. A bad sign. One of these days the clutch would go on him. But why repair it now, while it still worked? Another problem for another time.

Suddenly there was that almost memory again, the memory he had nearly remembered this morning when sitting in the *bottega* on the wooden chair. The memory came close to letting itself be seen, a timid ghost. He thought he could begin to see the form. A young woman's face.

Then the memory retreated, delicately slipped back into the past.

Doesn't matter, he told himself, shifting gears gracelessly in his car. The present was nerve-racking enough. He was on his way to the English actress's house. Everything in him vibrated. The steering wheel trembled in his hands. He didn't know if the car needed a front-end alignment or if it was he who made the car shake.

Why should he be so agitated? He already had too many thoughts cluttering his head without having to worry about this tingling feeling, too. He should be busy sorting out his dream. What was the treasure waiting for him? It couldn't have anything to do with his appointment at the actress's house, now could it? He imagined finding treasure in a deep well.

The tingling expectancy was torture to him, especially because in bed with his own wife he had proved himself incapable of feeling the excitement he should have felt; torture, especially now, because he was already imagining— What was he imagining? He did not recognize his own thoughts. He was in crisis, he knew that. Crisis meant change. Everything was changing inside him and around him and all this changing scared him. And he didn't want to be thinking what he was thinking now. It wasn't like him to think this way. He was torturing himself hard.

But isn't it the way of every man, at least for a moment, to imagine that the answer to his crisis might be found below his belt?

Renato felt hot in his car as he drove toward the English actress's house. He opened the window all the way. Sweat from his armpit trickled down his arm, tickling him, making him shiver.

He didn't even know the English actress's name, had never touched her. But she, when she looked into his eyes at the *bottega,* had touched him enough to plant within him a green, sprouting seed of electric unrest.

He stepped on the brakes quickly, his tires stirring up a swirl of dust. He switched off the engine and stepped out onto the dirt driveway. For a moment he half-wished she wouldn't be at home; then he saw the Land Rover with the British license plates parked around the corner, beside the house.

As he approached the door he heard music coming from an open window. Something classical. He wasn't sure, maybe Vivaldi. Or maybe somebody else. Music wasn't something he knew about.

He looked at the door for a moment. He scratched his beard. His stomach jittered. He sighed. He heard a trumpet fanfare blast out of the stereo inside as if to announce the entrance of a king. He knocked.

No footsteps, only trumpets. Then the door opened. His eyes did a quick up and down. She had changed clothes since this morning. My God, she is long! Her feet were bare. So were her legs, or what he could see of the legs beneath her light skirt. Above the skirt she wore a white shirt with the tails untucked. Three buttons were open, revealing the muscles of her neck and the shadows between her breasts.

"*Buonasera,*" said Renato.

The English actress held out her hand and said, "Hello."

"Tizzoni," he said. Her grip on his hand was a pleasant pressure. "Renato Tizzoni. I guess we didn't really introduce ourselves before. *Piacere.*"

"Meg Barker. Pleasure." She brushed light chestnut hair out of her eyes with the fingers of her free hand. "Come in."

Their handshake was lasting too long. Renato was about to release her when the hand that held his pulled him inside.

From the CD player, throaty trumpets called.

"I was just having some wine." She shut the door behind Renato. "Want a glass?" Her smile was wide, teeth very white.

"*Scusi?*" Her perfume confounded his senses. The perfume was unknown to him, but he liked the smell. She smelled like wet wood, like wood in a forest after rain. "What did you say?"

"I don't suppose you speak English." She saw him listening to her voice the way a dog listens to the wind. "En-glish?" she syllabicated.

"*Inglese, no.*" He shrugged. "*Italiano, sì.*"

She laughed, which made Renato laugh, too.

"Shame. It would have been nice to talk with you." She knew her words were not understood. "I wonder if he knows how lovely he is," she said aloud, talking to herself.

"Here I can't understand a thing of what's going on," Renato responded, returning her smile, figuring, What the hell? If she planned on throwing unintelligble sounds into the air, he might as well play along.

She began again. She put a question mark in her eyes, and said, "*Vino?*"

"*Per me, no. Grazie.*" He shook his head to underline his meaning, and he pointed at his watch as if to say, At this hour? What, are you crazy?

"What did you say your name was?"

"*Scusi?*"

"YOUR NAME. My name's Meg." With her hand she patted herself between her breasts. "MEG. And you?"

"Tizzoni." He patted himself.

"Tisso—" She had trouble with the sound.

Helpfully, he said, "Renato."

"Renato," she repeated to their mutual satisfaction. "Renato." She patted her breasts again. "Meg."

But the vowel in her name was a problem for him. "Meh-eh-eh-eh-ek?" he heard himself bleat.

"Let's talk about it over a drink. Sure you won't have some *vino?*"

"*No, no. Grazie. No.*"

"Coffee? *Caffè?*"

"Oh, *un caffè?*" Coffee might clear his head. "But the work to do?"

"Coffee, yes?"

Why not? "*Sì. Un caffè, per favore. Sì.*"

He sat at the long refectory table in her terra-cotta-tiled kitchen. The music had changed from the trumpet fanfare to Gregorian chant. He wondered why anyone would listen to church music at home.

He watched her, all of her, surrounded as she was by that light of hers. She busied herself with the coffee machine. It was a very elaborate machine, some British designer's version of an authentic old-fashioned Italian espresso maker. Renato had never seen anything like it. A beautiful round brass body, lots of brass knobs. Meg Barker was unsure as to how it worked. She talked to herself under her breath; Renato didn't catch a word. Steam came out of nozzles and she swore. Renato watched her fidget. He wanted to laugh, so he coughed instead.

He was lonely for an instant. He wished his wife, Milena, were sitting next to him at the kitchen table. She would have laughed and he would have laughed with her, and they both would have enjoyed the laugh.

He made himself not think about Milena, realizing suddenly the disloyalty he was committing. Or was he? Had he done anything wrong yet? Was he about to? Did he want to?

And why would he? What could this woman give to him that his own wife couldn't? A new taste maybe, to make him taste again.

Renato looked around the kitchen. He glanced at the other rooms he could see through the kitchen door. Here was a whole different world. There were boxes everywhere. The actress woman hadn't yet finished moving in. So far she had unpacked only the things she considered essential. On the kitchen walls, a bright constellation of copper pots hung from nails. They were so shiny that Renato wondered if they had ever been used. He wondered if she knew how to cook. Or maybe it was all for show. How could you tell with someone from another world?

At the far end of the wood refectory table he saw the CD player. He didn't have one at home, not being a musical expert himself. But he had noticed CD players in shop windows in town. Certainly nice and clear, the organ music that came out now. You could hear the echoes and everything. Just like in a church.

On the table were a couple of empty wine bottles, an ashtray, a box of matches, an open pack of Rothman cigarettes. He wondered if her mouth tasted of smoke.

He looked at the floor. Probably hadn't been swept at all since the builders finished redoing the kitchen. He looked at her bare feet beneath her light cotton skirt.

He raised his eyes. Her attention was fixed on the fancy espresso machine, which sent up clouds of steam. Renato studied the back of her long neck, the interplay of muscle, tendon, and bone. Her hair was pulled up and tied in a knot atop her head. She was neither young nor old. Probably fortyish. But her body looked young, more muscle than fat. The topmost vertebra of her spine protruded when she inclined her head. He wanted to touch it with his fingers, to see how it felt beneath the smooth suntanned skin.

He turned away, focusing on the ashtray and the empty bottles of wine.

The music changed again, this time from pipe organ runs to Gregorian chant once more, for the CD was an anthology. "Vivaldi?" Making conversation seemed the right thing to do.

"What?"

"*La musica.*"

"The music? What about it?"

"Vivaldi?" Or maybe he should have guessed Verdi.

"Vivaldi?" she laughed. "Almost. Only off by a century. It is Venetian, though. Gabrieli. But I can never remember which one. There were two Gabrielis, isn't that right?"

He said nothing.

"Gabrieli," she repeated.

"Ah. Gabrieli." Renato didn't recognize the name.

"Music for a coronation in Venice. *Venezia.*"

"Ah. *Venezia.*" Renato was silent again, listening to monks chanting. There was no figuring some people's tastes, he thought.

Finally the espresso machine stopped squitzing. She carried two cups of coffee to the table and sat down at the head, close to him. He smelled her rain-washed forest smell. She was close enough so that when she crossed one leg over the other the toes of her bare foot touched the leg of his work trousers. He didn't pull his leg away. She didn't move her foot. Maybe she hadn't noticed. She said, "Sugar?"

"*Due.*" He watched her serve him two spoonfuls. He stirred his coffee and she stirred hers. Simultaneously they took their first sip. His was terrible. Dirty piss.

"I love Italian coffee," she said.

She took another sip, stared him in the eyes, smiled, and placed her coffee cup on its saucer. "Renato, you said your name was?"

"Renato. *Sì*."

"I think names are fascinating, don't you? I love finding out what they mean," she explained. "And Renato means?"

He sipped his coffee, not realizing a question had been asked.

She got up, walked to the far end of the table. He watched her move. From behind the bottles she picked up a paperback Italian-English dictionary.

She sat back down at her place, crossing one leg over the other again, touching his leg with her foot. "Renato?" She handed him the dictionary.

"*Scusi?*"

"RE-NA-TO." She pressed the dictionary into his hand.

"Ah! The significance! Fine, let's have a look." He flipped through the book, then scanned the correct page with his fingertip. "Here we are." He indicated the verb *rinascere*.

"'To be reborn,'" she read. "What a beautiful name to have. And your surname?"

Blank, canine stare.

"Renato what? Renato—" She made a drawing-out motion with her hand.

"Oh. TIZZONI." He seized the dictionary and flicked the pages fast. "I don't think they'll have it in this book of yours, but if you like the significance of my first name, what till you hear what my last name means."

She heard only a happy flurry of words.

"Tizzoni," he went on. "Tizzoni. How can I explain? It's like, you know when you've made a fire in the fireplace, and the fire burns itself down until you think it's gone out, I mean to say, you think the fire's dead? But it's not dead. There, under the ashes, there are still the hot pieces of wood, all glowing and alive. Those are *tizzoni!* But why do I imagine you can understand a damned word of what I'm saying to those ears? Tizzoni... Tizzoni... Ah, here we are. *Tizzone.* Which is the singular, naturally. But the idea is still the same."

She read above his finger in the book. "'Ember,'" she read. "Reborn Ember. Beautiful name."

He reveled in the moment, seeing approval in her eyes. He poured the rest of the coffee down his throat and didn't even notice the taste. "And you?"

"Me? Barker. I thought I told you. Meg Barker."

"Bah-keh." He imitated her accent.

"No, there are *r*'s in there. Barrr-kerrr."

"Ah. Bar-ke*r*."

Hearing his tongue roll the *r*'s of her name seemed to touch her like a caress. "Barrr-kerrr," she said smilingly, to make him say it again.

"Ba*rrr*-ke*rrr*." He handed her the dictionary.

"What's it mean? God, I never gave it any thought." She looked through the book and pointed to something that seemed to come close.

"*Abbaiare?*" He looked surprised. "Strange names you people have." He made a barking noise and started to laugh.

"No, I see your point. Can't mean that, can it? Why would they give anybody a name like that? Must come from something else."

Renato pointed to the second definition. "Ah, it could be this." He tapped the page decisively. The skin of a tree, he thought. That's why she smells like a forest after the rain.

"You think?" she said, looking at him sideways, wondering why he seemed so convinced that tree bark should have any relation to her.

"Meh-eh-eh," he bleated.

"MEG."

"*E significa?*"

"The meaning? God knows. Short for Margaret. Mar-gar-et."

"Ah, Margaret! It's the same as Margherita."

"Margherita in Italian," she said. "Yes, that's right."

"Margherita. Like the flower," he said. He looked through the dictionary until he found the word. "Here. '*Margherita.*'"

"Daisy?" she read. "Is that all it means? I'd hoped for something a bit more exotic."

She licked the last coffee drops from her lips and looked into Renato's eyes.

Now what? Something was supposed to happen. They both waited. Silence was stress.

Renato asked himself why he was here. And what did he think he was doing, sitting at a kitchen table over an empty cup of dirty-piss coffee, staring into those two luminous, intense, indecipherable eyes?

"Okay," he said, breaking the silence. "That little job? The water?"

"What?"

"The water." He pointed to the kitchen sink.

"Oh. Right. No, not here. Problem's in the bathroom."

"Because I heard that you wanted me to come and work," Renato explained, "though I still don't know what work. And really I should tell you that my responsibility ends as soon as the pipe enters the house, or not my responsibility personally so much as the responsibility of the Public Waterworks Department, which, of course is my responsibility, so really I shouldn't even be in the house because that with which we occupy ourselves at the Public Waterworks Department is everything between the town well and the place where the pipe enters your house. Inside the house, the problem is yours. I don't know if I'm making the idea clear. So let's hope your water problem is outside the house, where it is my right to work. Am I explaining myself well?"

Meg Barker looked startled. "What are you going on about? Didn't expect such nervousness from you. You didn't look the jittery type, not with that T-shirt and work jacket and cap of yours. I'd counted on a bit more rustic calm, to tell you the truth. Anyway, bathroom's this way." She stood up. He followed.

The bathroom smelled of her. Renato inhaled the thick air as if his nose had been beside her neck, under her hair. He looked around quickly, taking in the impression of the bottles and jars on the edge of the tub and on a glass shelf above the sink. Seeing everything, he felt himself standing in the world of her body. These things, he said to himself, are the things that touch her skin.

He saw the sink and remembered his work. It was half full of dirty, standing water. "That's the problem?"

"The problem? Yes. Stupid sink keeps filling up. Now it won't drain at all."

He blew air out between his lips. "I told you already. This isn't my responsibility. It's not that I don't want to help you, it's that I can't. I'm in charge of the Public Waterworks Department, and you call me here for a clogged sink, which is the work of a plumber? I can't go doing the plumbers' work for them, and they can't go doing mine. If I start doing the plumbers' jobs, the plumbers will hang me by the balls. *Mi dispiace*. I'm sorry. But you need the plumber. Yes, you need the *idraulico*."

"Hydraulics? What are you saying? Hydraulic?"

"*Sì. L'idraulico*."

"Hydraulic what? What are you talking about? I'd fix the thing myself if I were back in London. But this sink's different. Look, I tried to do it myself." She bent down under the sink and picked up a wrench she had left there on the floor. "I'm very handy, actually. Usually am, at any rate. I just couldn't find the right place to untighten it. You make your sinks different here. I'm not a helpless person. I just can't recognize a damn thing."

He saw her standing with the wrench in her hand, frustration in her widening eyes. There it was again: the mixture of vulnerability and strength he had first noticed at the *bottega*. For some reason, it pulled him in close.

"To begin with," he said, "you don't need that. A wrench doesn't serve. Get me *una bacinella*." Her turn now to have an empty stare. "*Una bacinella*. You know." He mimed a circular movement. "*Una bacinella*."

"A basin. Right. I think there's one under the kitchen sink. Hang on." She left him.

Alone, he swiftly opened a bottle of her French perfume and held it to his nostrils. It was like her smell, but sweeter. But it wasn't all of her smell. Another part of her smell maybe was her soap. Or maybe the rest of her smell was simply *her*.

Hearing her footsteps, he closed the bottle and fanned the air with his hands to chase away any lingering wafts.

Meg Barker returned carrying a red plastic basin, an ashtray, and a lit cigarette. She gave him the basin, put down the cover on the toilet, and sat down to watch, holding the ashtray on her thigh.

The music coming from the CD player in the kitchen changed once again, turned into a solemn sea tide of brass instruments, the phrases rolling over each other like waves. Above the instruments human voices sang out, "*Kyrie eleison.*"

Renato squatted in front of the sink, placing the basin beneath the drainpipe. "The wrench wouldn't serve," he said, "because this you open with your hand." He gripped the metal cup at the curve of the pipe, his fingers fitting around it easily. He had the feeling that she was watching his hand. He saw his hand as if through her eyes, noticing the sun-darkened skin, the muscular fingers, the close-cut nails, the strong knuckles. "I shouldn't be doing this," he said. "But it's such a nothing, this little job, it's not even worth your trouble to call a plumber."

"That's all there is to it?" she said, breathing out smoke. "Could've done it myself. Thought you needed a wrench."

"Little clog," he continued, talking aloud to himself. "Probably nothing more. Ah. Here." He removed the metal cup and held up the basin to catch the water that cascaded out. "You see? Dirty. That's all." The water was red with brick dust. "Those builders, if you ask me. I tell you that myself. Those builders weren't careful when they worked, and they probably washed their hands and their tools in the sink and left all this sediment behind."

Aware of her eyes on his hands, he put a calloused finger inside the metal cup to scoop out the muddy mixture.

"We should check in here, too." He inserted his finger into the pipe that entered the wall. He coaxed out a snarl of long blonde hair mixed with brick-dust mud.

She disappeared into a different room while he screwed the metal cup back in and rinsed the basin and his hands. He heard grit crunch under his work boots when he shifted his weight. He thought, She really ought to sweep the floor.

Meg Barker had an open wallet in her hand when she reappeared in the doorway. Renato saw lots of hundred-thousand-lira notes. Must be a million and a half in there, he thought. Does she always walk around with that kind of cash?

"How much do you usually charge?" She took out a hundred-thousand-lira bill. "Is this too little or too much?" She held the money out.

Renato's hands were wet under the tap. "No. I can't take anything for such a little foolishness as this. *Grazie. Ma no.*"

"No, really," she said. "Take something. I insist."

"No. Thank you. I insist."

She paused, then surrendered with a smile. "*Grazie,* Renato."

"You're welcome, Meg."

She was turning to take her wallet back to the other room when she let out a cry of pain. "Damn it!" she said, tossing her wallet to the floor, raising her foot to look at the sole. A heavy-duty carpenter's tack was stuck in the meat of her foot. Only the tack's head was visible.

"*Imbecilli!*" Thinking how much a tack like that must hurt, Renato winced to see her pain. "The imbecile workers could have swept up after themselves. Though, of course, a little pass with a broom wouldn't have been a bad idea on your part, too."

"Fuck," she said. "It hurts." She hobbled to the sink, putting her weight only on the heel of the injured foot. She lifted her leg to the sink. "Give me a hand pulling it out, would you mind?"

He pulled her foot into the center of the sink. To balance herself, she put an arm around his shoulder. She lifted her skirt up past the knee.

"This will hurt now, more." He grasped the head of the tack between his fingernails and pulled it out. Blood appeared in the neat round hole. "It entered deep," he said. "You should go to the doctor and get an injection *antitetanica*."

"Had a tetanus jab last year. I'm always cutting myself. Go barefoot most of the time. Ow! It stings! Was out in the garden, last year, you know, and cut myself on a bit of broken glass."

"We should wash this," Renato said. He took the round bar of wheat-germ soap and sudsed his own hands. The smell of the soap was edible, like soft grain. When he was sure his hands were clean, he put the soap to the sole of Meg Barker's foot. She held still, despite the sting, letting him wash her foot.

Voices from the CD player in the kitchen floating above the ever increasing tidal movements of the trumpets and trombones, the voices again took up their earlier song. "*Kyrie eleison,*" sang the voices in a melody that was melancholy yet sweet. "Lord have mercy."

Renato washed Meg Barker's foot, noticing every detail—the curve of the arch, the fine strength of the toes, the little wrinkles of the sole. He sudsed and sudsed. While he was there, he might as well clean the toes, too.

He caught himself stealing a peek up her skirt, for she had lifted the skirt high up on her thigh. She was naked beneath her skirt. He saw the hair between her legs, a shade darker than the hair on her head. He realized what he was doing: He was caressing her well-curved foot beneath running water, breathing in her fragrance of the forest after rain, staring at her bare thighs and at the hair between her legs. Her hair, in the shadows of her skirt, looked like wet mink.

He realized what he was doing and he thought: This is a step that probably leads to a next step. His heart beat fast.

Her eyes watched his hands on her foot. If she knew he could see between her legs, she gave no sign.

From the CD player the human voices sang their "*kyrie.*"

Meg Barker shifted her position, readjusting her balance. She pulled herself closer with her arm around his shoulder. She put her face closer to Renato's neck. He felt her breath against his skin where his beard ended. An electric erection started inside his underwear. When was the last time a woman who wasn't Milena had given him an erection? And last night, when he had tried to make love to Milena, his erection had gone away. Now it was back. Was this what he had come here to find?

"Hmm," she said. "You smell like honey." She emphasized a sniffing motion to make him understand. "Like honey and spice. *Miele,*" she said, remembering the Italian word. She breathed in again.

For a moment Renato was not Renato. He was tasting a foreign world, a different life. He could be any man, one of her men in London. This was what it was like to be with this London woman, to come to her house in the evening at some appointed hour after a day of different work. This was the flavor of being one of the men who had known her, men whom she had known. Renato almost wanted to be the kind of man he figured she was used to. For an instant he was an unrecognizable version of himself.

Or maybe he was nothing but the waterworks man from Sant'Angelo D'Asso and this London actress was a lonely woman who, after his leaving, would light a cigarette and pour another glass of wine.

Or maybe the only truth was that he had an electric erection in his underpants and that he and this woman with wet mink between her legs simply wanted to do what men and women always want to do. Nothing more than that.

He was there with her wet, naked foot in his hands and her breath on his neck. All he needed to do would be to turn his mouth toward hers and they would be kissing. And then ... But suddenly the shy memory that had been trying since dawn to visit him found the right entrance to his brain and his head was filled with the vision from years ago. Twenty years ago. The vision was clear. It was overwhelmingly bright. It was so beautiful and happy and sad that Renato wanted to cry.

His electric erection switched off and drooped. He rinsed the soap off her foot.

"It's clean now," Renato said. "Go to the doctor if it hurts. I have to go." He wanted to be alone in his car. He wanted to have time to sit in the company of his remembered thought.

Meg Barker didn't know what to say to the bearded man in the work clothes who suddenly seemed eager to flee her house.

They said *ciao* to each other at the front door. Meg Barker wondered about Renato as he raced his car out of her drive. Wondered if she might see him again. Smell, she had always believed, was so important between two people. And he smelled so *right*.

She felt a little empty going back inside her house with her beloved Gabrieli music still playing on her stereo.

❧

Once clear of her driveway, Renato gave himself over to the vision in his head. It was Milena, even before she had become his wife. Milena, the first time he'd noticed her as a person who was not merely another face in the town, the first time she had made herself precious to him.

Renato was eighteen years old and his parents had died the summer before. It was March now, a couple of weeks after his birthday, and a late snowstorm had hit most of Tuscany, making roads impassible, closing schools, creating an impromptu holiday for anyone who still had enough delight in life to rejoice at the wonder of silent flakes that turned the world white. Walking up the town's main street toward the pump house, Renato was alone with his quiet thoughts and with the sound of his work boots pressing his footprints into the snow.

He walked by the *bottega* that Milena's parents ran. Growing up, Milena had probably spent more time in the *bottega* than at her home. A kitchen to her meant something that fed forty people at a time. Bread was bought from the baker in basketfuls. Bottled water came in crates. Fruit was bought in crate loads, too. Things of the kitchen had been her first toys. Milena had learned a trick when she was only a little girl: Using tangerines instead of balls, she had been taught by her father how to juggle.

And that was how Renato saw her now in the snow on the street in front of her parents' *bottega*. It was the late afternoon pause before the tables had to be set for dinner. The sky was darkening and the street lamps had just come on. The snow was still falling. The lights were bright inside the big window of the *bottega*. A few men were talking at the bar. Savory food smells found their way out to the street. Renato could smell garlic and rosemary and wood smoke. He saw Milena, who was laughing. She dropped a snowball and bent over to pick up another one with fingers that the cold had turned rosy. When she laughed Renato saw the condensation of the breath from her pink lips. She, too, was eighteen years old. She pushed hair out of her eyes with the back of her hand.

"Do you know how to do that?" Renato asked her.

"Slippery with snowballs," she said, her smile looking as appetizing as a little cake, "but I'm trying."

And she succeeded. Renato stood watching Milena juggle snowballs in the snow.

He had been invited to dinner at the Vezzosis' house that evening. When he arrived, Signora Vezzosi noticed that his face was more relaxed than it had been throughout the autumn and winter.

The evening had a special flavor for Renato. After dinner, he and the Vezzosis were eating a treat that had always been a favorite. A slice of tangy pecorino cheese, smeared with honey and sprinkled with black pepper. The mixture was salty and sweet and spicy, yet harmonious. It gave the mouth every taste it could ever hope for all at once.

The Vezzosis asked him questions about his special smile this evening. He confessed the truth. He told them about Milena and the snowballs.

Signor Vezzosi smiled, seeing the transformation in the boy's face, hearing the ardor of his words. "Sounds like trouble for you," he said, shaking his head. "This is how it starts. Trouble for you!" he laughed. "You've gone and fallen in love! *Tarabaralla!*"

Of course Renato knew the word. The word was meant to sound like the noise of a car that maybe would or maybe wouldn't start. The meaning was, Well, let's just wait and see how this turns out. Might start. Might not.

But Aristodemo Vezzosi wagged a finger and repeated the word like a prediction. "*Tarabaralla!*" he said smiling, but ominous. "Eh, Renato my son, because you're like a son to me. *Tarabaralla!*" His word was an incantation. It said the machinery had now started in earnest and was destined to run its course.

A year later, Milena and Renato went to the church and got married. They moved into his house just outside town on the far side of the little stone bridge. The memory of Milena and the snowballs melted into the extraordinary taste of honey and black pepper and pecorino cheese.

This was the memory he had been catching hints of all day. The sight of Milena juggling snowballs. The sharp, peppery, honeyed flavor of falling in love.

Renato drove homeward, away from Meg Barker's house, feeling lucky, if only for a moment, to taste the past again.

TEN

Culo

Renato parked the Fiat Ritmo in his driveway a few minutes later and took the sheep out for their graze.

He sat on the hillside for a long time, until the sky started to turn the colors of sunset.

He needed to think. There were still all his unthought thoughts struggling for attention in his head: His friend Vezzosi had died; his daughter was growing ever more attached to a young man he couldn't much stomach; he, for some reason, could no longer make love to his wife; life in every other respect, too, had suddenly lost its taste; and soon the dam would be built, putting an end to the world of his town and forcing him to go away to someplace new and begin again, which, of course, was an unacceptable truth, an impossible certainty, an unthinkable thing. There was no shortage of thoughts to be avoided.

Now there were new thoughts, too, that whirred in his head. He had been tempted today to taste the different taste of the English-woman and her world. In the end he had fled, which was a kind of victory, even though maybe he should be feeling guilty anyway. He wasn't sure. But he had passed through temptation instead of giving in, and that couldn't be bad. He had caught up to the memory he had been chasing all day. Or maybe it was the memory that had been chasing him. And remembering how it had felt to first fall in love with Milena, he yearned for her now, though it was a strange, lovely, tormented yearning that ached inside, because he didn't know what he hungered for: Milena, or the feelings of being young again and alive and in love?

Had he betrayed their love today?

And an answer to everything had been promised to him before the sun had come up today, for he had been given the dream, which he still hadn't discussed with his wife, so the dream had become a secret between them, and it was a kind of secret to him as well because he hadn't come to understand what the dream meant.

Yes, he was keeping secrets now.

The dream. When would he ever manage to tell her about the dream? The sheep would listen to him, all right, if he needed to talk to someone about the dream, but how would a fellow human being react? Would his own wife consider him mad for being so moved by a vision that had come to him in the night?

We'll see, he decided. When the right moment presents itself, then I'll tell her and the secret I've been carrying around all day will be a secret no more. But I won't tell her about washing the English actress's foot.

What a day. So many thoughts to be thought or unthought. No wonder he needed time to sit on the hillside in the evening and look out over the valley while the sky changed color and the sheep stayed close around him, tugging on grass.

When the sky started to darken, he felt almost rested, ready to give thought to his dream, most promising of all thoughts.

"*Andiamo, ragazze!*" he called to the sheep. "Let's go, girls! I'll take you back to milk you, and you and I will see if we're any closer to understanding this thing."

He walked the sheep back down to the courtyard of his house and led them to their stall. He sat down on the milking stool and prepared himself for some serious thought.

"Prima!"

The first sheep trotted in.

"So? You've been thinking? Come up with anything?"

The first sheep let herself be milked, but seemed unwilling to offer any hypothesis as to what Renato's dream might mean.

"Fine then," he said, his hand coaxing her teat. "We'll think it through together. Let's start with the dream itself. What were the elements of the dream? The bright hand above the bed, the ring with the big red stone on its finger. The hand. And it led me outside, led me to the treasure box hidden in the well, and inside the box there was a fortune. A fortune! And I knew that fortune would change my fortune and the fortune of everyone around me, because I was meant to share it with everyone, and the fortune would make everyone's fortune change."

What could it mean? He had woken up and checked inside the well but there was no box, no fortune. Nothing.

But I was an idiot, he told the woolly white ears of the second sheep. Truly an idiot to think the dream was literal. Fool! Why should I think a wooden box is really a wooden box? Dreams don't work that way. They never have. No, it's symbolic, is what it is. But symbolic of what?

The sheep burped.

The trick is to first concentrate on the hand. What does the hand signify? Whose hand is it? The second sheep, undistinguished creature of the flock that she was, did not have a clue. The hand, Renato expounded, is not unknown to me. I've seen it before, but where?

The third sheep was of no more use. But that was fine with Renato, for with the third sheep he could reason aloud without being interrupted.

"*Il papa!*" The pope! That's the hand. The hand of the pope! I've seen it in thousands of pictures and in the newspapers and on television. I'm sure I recognize the ring. At least I think so.

But why the hand of the pope? I'm no churchgoer. It's not that

I'm an unbeliever, but I'm no great believer either. Why should the hand of the pope appear to me in a dream?

And what am I supposed to do? Something to do with the hand of the pope, as strange as it may seem. But stranger things have happened to people, don't you think? And I could tell right away that the dream was an important dream, because it *felt* important, so why shouldn't an important dream be about an important hand, like the hand of the pope?

The pope's hand above the water of the well. Water.

I've always been connected to water. Not only because I'm the waterworks man. Even my birthday in February is a connection, I suppose. I'm born beneath the sign of Pisces, the fish. Water. Fish.

And isn't that what was said somewhere in the Bible? "You shall be a fisher of men" or something like that? Said to Saint Peter and all the popes. Which is where the pope lives, there in St. Peter's Square. So you see, that's why I have to go to St. Peter's and seek out the hand of the pope. That's what the dream is telling me. Makes sense, no? He is the fisher of men. His hand is reaching out over the water, fishing for me, who by birth sign is a fish. Don't you see? Now it's all coming clear.

So. I am to seek out the hand of the pope. But why? To accomplish what end? Well, the dream made that obvious, didn't it? To change *la fortuna,* to change luck, for me and for everyone else. Isn't that what the dream promised? New luck, new fortune, like the fortune in the treasure box.

He could tell that the mysteries of the dream were explaining themselves through clear thinking by the time he had the fourth sheep's udders in his fists. She was a good listener, Quarta. Even if she played at being pathetic, she was nobody's fool.

With the dam about to destroy our world, he explained to her, with everything in my life going crazy and falling apart, I could do with a change of luck. And not just me, but everyone I know. That's what we all need, isn't it? A stroke of fortune. *Un colpo di culo* is what we need, I'll tell you that myself. *Un bel colpo di culo.* A stroke of ass. A stroke of luck.

Uh-HA! Fortune, ass. Ass, *fortuna.* Don't you see? *Culo,* ass. *Culo,* luck. A change is what's needed here. A change of *culo,* a change of ass, because as everybody knows, your ass is your luck. What do people say when something good happens? *Che colpo di culo!* they say. What a stroke of ass, meaning what a stroke of luck. And when something good is wished for, you say *Ci vuole un culo come una casa!* You need an ass—you need luck—as big as a house!

Yes, your ass is your luck.

And my luck is meant to change. That's what the dream is saying. That's the fortune to be found. *Un colpo di culo,* so I can maybe find what I've lost, so things will start to taste once again and I can be alive. A definite stroke of ass.

"I want my *culo* to change, can't you see that?" he half-screamed at the fourth sheep.

Hearing the vehemence of his voice, she got scared and backed away.

"Where are you going? Come here and let's finish this. Don't be afraid. I'm not going crazy. Or maybe I am. Doesn't matter, because it's all making sense now, don't you think? Here. Chew these." He gave her olive leaves.

She chewed the leaves but kept her eye on Renato, not sure what transformations were going on inside the man who milked her every day.

But what, he continued, what has my ass, my *culo,* my luck, got to do with the hand of the pope? I don't think the pope would ever want to lay hands on my ass, do you?

His thoughts were following the bright path of logic, though, and the images from his dream glowed brightly in his head, so he knew he was on the right track. See, he told Quarta while she nuzzled her mouth into another branch of olive leaves, you see, it all makes sense in the way the language of dreams makes sense. I don't know why, but if the dream is to be believed, which evidently it is or else it wouldn't have been sent, then I am to go to Rome and find the hand of the pope. If I touch the pope's hand, shake the pope's hand, yes, shake the hand of the pope, then my luck, my *culo*, will change. If I want my ass, my *culo,* to change, then I have to—

Yes, of course! Luck is a force of nature, the same as water. And water flows through conduits, like the pipes I run around fixing every day. The dream means that the hand is a conduit of luck, that this luck will flow from the pope to me if I touch his hand, flow right through me and change my ass, my own luck. And certainly the pope is not meant to touch my ass, but I can do that part myself. I must touch my ass in that very same moment in which I shake the hand of the pope. And then somehow this new *fortuna,* this luck, will change not only my *culo* but everyone's *culo.* Which would make *me* the conduit between the pope's hand and everyone else. Just as in the dream. The fortune in the treasure box was not merely for me but for everybody.

Why me? he wondered. But the why, he knew, was nothing he could ever expect to understand. He had not chosen the dream, after all. The dream had chosen him.

Renato felt humbled for a moment by the weight of responsibility the dream had placed upon him.

The fourth sheep flicked her tongue outside her mouth to better chew a piece of olive leaf.

If you think about it, yes. These things are probably destined long before we become aware. Think about it, I mean. My birthday, for example. February twenty-third. Think of the numbers games they gamble on down in Naples, no? Everyone knows numbers have magical meanings. Seventeen means a woman's thigh, which is a good number to bet on because it brings good luck. But the luckiest number of all, as everybody knows, is twenty-three because that's the number of the *buco del culo,* the very hole of the ass itself. What could be luckier than that? You see, don't you? he asked the sheep. I was born on the twenty-third, which means my *culo* is destined to change.

This is mystical, is what it is. Predestined before I was even born. And this morning the dream was sent to me. Mystical, if you think about it. Mystical. *Fortuna, culo,* ha!

"This thing is beyond doubt," he said, arising from the milking stool, slapping the fourth sheep on her flank as if she were a sturdier, less self-pitying creature. "It is a mystical thing and it's clear. I must go to Rome, as prescribed in the dream, and I must touch my ass while shaking hands with the pope. Then you will see how luck will change for me and for us all. Who knows what new *culo* is waiting for us? Ha!"

The fourth sheep ran, frightened, from the stall.

Renato took the bucket and poured the warm milk through the strainer in preparation for making pecorino cheese. He was at once elated and overawed. The stall was dark with the shadows of evening, but Renato felt surrounded by light as bright as the hand in his dream. Hope was making him strong. He smiled while he strained the milk. He was more alive than he had been in years. His mission had been revealed.

He scratched his beard. Outside the door to the stall, an evening swallow swooped.

ELEVEN

Tita Talks

The rightness of his mission was beyond doubt. But first things first. Before he could obey his dream, Renato had more immediate duties to carry out. Visiting Signora Vezzosi was chief among them.

Sitting at her table now, Renato found it hard to hold on to the sense of elation his dream had given him. Instead, he was eye to eye with the sadness of a person he loved. Elation felt far away.

"Another glass of wine?" Signora Vezzosi lifted the pitcher.

"Well, why not? But not a full glass. A little drop." Renato held out his glass and watched the old woman pour. At the house of the English actress, wine in the afternoon seemed unpalatable. With Signora Vezzosi, it was the most natural thing in the world.

He'd been buying wine from the Vezzosis ever since he had started earning money of his own; buying wine was as good an excuse as any to come and visit. And whenever he came to refill his wine bottles, he had a glass or two with the Vezzosis. Now, for the first time, he sat at the table with Signora Vezzosi alone.

"*Basta,*" he said, when she was about to give him too much "Oh! Enough. I still have things to do this evening. And on an empty stomach like this, the wine makes my head spin."

"I'll have another little drop to keep you company," she said, pouring herself a glass.

Renato's eyes watched. Half a glass was usually her limit. But she was upset. The funeral was too fresh in her mind. So was the image of Sculati the *becchino,* the cemetery's caretaker, who had bricked up her husband's vault in the cemetery wall. When Sculati slapped mortar on the final brick and slid the brick into place, Signora Vezzosi pictured the darkness that enclosed her husband's coffin inside the vault. Watching, she thought she would suffocate.

Sitting across the table from Renato, Signora Vezzosi put a hand on her chest. She breathed in deeply, reassured that air could still fill her lungs. She breathed out and shook her head. She sipped her wine.

Renato wanted to say something, but what can you say? He scratched his beard. "*Allora, signora?*" he said: So?

"So," she said. She stared at the wine in her glass and lost herself for a moment. "What can I say?" She spoke without taking her eyes from the glass. The circles under her eyes were nearly as dark as the wine: She hadn't slept much since her husband died. "*Siamo qui.* We're here. We are here, and he isn't. Simple, no? Simple but impossible. Yet that's how things are. What can I say?"

Renato sipped his wine. He looked at the tablecloth in front of him. It was an uninteresting floral print. There were leftover bread crumbs on the tablecloth now and flecks of grated cheese. He said, "Oh, when you've tried the pecorino cheese I brought you, tell me what you think. It's very tasty, I think you'll find." The cheese was on the table in front of him. He fingered the plastic bag that the cheese was wrapped in. He felt guilty. He and Milena should have invited her over today so that she wouldn't have been alone for her first Sunday lunch without her husband.

"*Grazie,* Renato. I always enjoy your pecorino. You always think of me. You're just like a son."

"And did you see? I put some fresh ricotta in the little bag, too."

"*Grazie.* Yes, I saw. *Grazie.* You shouldn't have." She sighed.

Renato's fingertips played with a bread crumb on the tablecloth.

After a while he said, "Oh. Did I tell you? The day of the funeral, when Cappelli and I were fixing the pipe, I mean, when you were all inside the church and I wanted to come in, too, but I couldn't because we had to fix the pipe, anyway, while we were fixing the pipe, did I tell you what I found? No? Well, I'll tell you. There on the pipe, or no, better, on the joint where the piece of bad old pipe ended, the piece we had to replace, there on the good joint there was an inscription. Everyone who had laid the pipe signed his name on the joint. October 4, 1935, was the date. And Signor Vezzosi signed, too. I saw the inscription. 'Aristodemo Vezzosi, Apprentice,' it said."

"*Davvero?*"

"Yes, really. Very important piece, that joint, no? I mean, not just the joint, but the fact that it was the first complete public water system the town ever had, and Signor Vezzosi helped lay it. That's important, don't you think?"

"Nineteen thirty-five." She smiled.

"But what I don't understand is why he never told me. When I was apprentice to him years ago, before he retired, and we worked on the pipes everywhere together, he never told me he had helped put in the main pipe, never mentioned it. Strange, don't you think?"

"Strange? No, I wouldn't say that. Doesn't seem strange to me." She reflected for a moment. "No, not strange. He didn't say anything because of his disillusionment, if you ask me."

"His disillusionment?"

"With the kind of people he used to work for. Bad kind of people. Not that he could have worked for anyone else in those days, because in those days they were the people who controlled everything. So if you wanted to work, even as an apprentice to learn a trade, you had to work for them. What else could you do?"

"The Fascists, you mean?"

"Who else? *I fascisti.* Though certainly when we were young everyone was a Fascist. Well, not everyone. Aristo's father, for example, was no Fascist. Not him! He was too far to the left, almost for his own good. Twenty years of Fascists before the war and he always stuck to the left. Didn't make things easy for him, I'll tell you that."

"And Signor Vezzosi?"

"Aristo? He was a boy. But he suffered the disillusionment all the same."

Without especially meaning to, Signora Vezzosi began to talk. Words came up from her as easily as water comes from a well.

She told him what he already knew, and she told him what he had never heard before.

TWELVE

Fifty Years

Who could remember a time when Aristodemo and Tita Vezzosi hadn't been together? They were together as soon as he was old enough to begin to think what it might someday mean to be a man, and as soon as she was old enough to suspect what womanhood might be all about. Someone who didn't know any better might have taken them for brother and sister. Yet everyone knew everyone in town. And everyone knew they were a couple of kids who would be together, who would marry, who would stay together for life.

Once they finished elementary school, they had more time to devote to work. Aristodemo helped his parents in their grocery store on the piazza. Tita helped her parents on their farm. On summer evenings after work, when the sun still burned for an hour or two in the sky, they rode their bicycles a few miles out of town to a place where the River Asso passed through a little woods. They cooled off in the shade there. When it was very hot, they stripped down to their underwear and sat in the river, laughing, watching goose bumps rise on each other's skin. Then they'd pedal home from the river while the fat sun sank into the fields of summer grain. Their bicycles squeaked, as did the crickets in the fields, as did the bats that swirled fast overhead to catch bugs. The color of those evenings was pink and gold and gray. Grain made the air sweet.

Tita was strong from her work on the farm. As for Aristodemo, a few years of lifting crates in his parents' grocery store had to pass before he developed muscles in his arms. He was shorter than she when they were children. She watched him grow taller than herself, though not by much. He never had to do more than incline his head only slightly when he put his mouth to hers for a kiss. She used to tease him before his muscles grew. *Pulcino,* she used to call him, for to her he looked like a baby chick. His nose was, in fact, beakish, and the eyes had a peculiar way of becoming round and bright. His eyes made Tita smile. And when Aristo's head was wet from the River Asso, his round eyes looked out from under hair that stood up on end, just as feathers stick up on the head of a chick.

In the thirties, the Fascists announced the waterworks project. First they built the public washhouse. The architecture of the wash-house was splendid, with Roman arches supporting the roof and vaulted ceilings inside. Two rows of stone tubs stood waist-high so that all the people of Sant'Angelo D'Asso would have one common place in which to wash their clothes. Water was piped in from the natural spring on top of the hill above the town. The tubs were always full. They gave a sense of abundance to all who came. Why had no one ever thought to undertake such a project earlier? The stone had always been there to make the tubs, and evidently the water had always been there, too, the spring inexhaustible. Organization was the only thing that had been lacking before, people reasoned. And if there was one thing the Fascists had a talent for, it was organization.

The washhouse was such a success that the Fascists decided to make water available in every home. Gone would be the days in which only the lucky few had wells beneath their houses and hand pumps in their kitchen sinks for drawing up the water. Gone would be the daily trips that everyone else had to make to the pump in the town square.

Water in every home. Sinks in kitchens with running water to wash plates and cook food. Bathrooms with taps in the tub and sink, and toilets you could flush. A dream, it seemed at first. But the

Fascists promised dreams; the washhouse was proof that they could turn dreams into fact.

"Dreams paid for with blood," was what Aristodemo Vezzosi's father told anyone who got him started on the subject. Most people ignored him. Customers in his grocery store knew that political talk only made the shopkeeper work himself up, so they talked about other things. Who cares if the man's something of a leftist? people figured. The products he sold were good and his prices were low. But some other people considered him dangerous. They did their shopping at the other grocery store farther along the main road.

Tita's father, unlike Aristo's, had long ago learned that the best opinion to have was none at all. He was a farmer, not a politician, he would have told anyone who asked, but no one ever asked. As for his daughter being engaged to the leftist Vezzosi's boy, that was their own business. Useless, he would have told anyone, to stand in the way of young people in love.

When Aristodemo turned fifteen, he leaned against the counter in the grocery and announced to his father that he didn't want to work in the store for the rest of his life. He had muscles in his arms now and he wanted to decide for himself as a man. He wanted to work outdoors. The waterworks people were looking for an apprentice to help lay the pipes for the public water system. In his opinion, he was the right man for the job.

Who would take over the grocery in the future? the father wondered. He had only one child. But he knew Aristodemo. He tapped on the counter in his grocery store with his knuckles to indicate the stubbornness of his son's character. "You've always been as hard as a pine cone," the father told his son. "No chance I could change your mind?"

Aristodemo laughed gently. "I'll help you in the grocery when I have free time."

"But you want to work with *them*?"

"I don't care who I work for. But you tell me, how could I look out from the shop window and watch them put pipes to bring water into every home? How could I watch without taking part myself?

And once we've finished putting pipes down in the town, we'll bring water to the houses outside town, too. You'll see, we'll have water in our own house."

"We already have a well."

"We'll have water that runs."

"What color shirt will you have to wear to work every day? No, let me guess. Black?"

He began as an apprentice. After work, riding bicycles with Tita, he told her everything he was learning about how the pumps at the pump house worked, about how the valves could turn on or turn off the water anywhere in town, about how pipes were welded and joined. Tita watched his mouth while he talked. His smile, his quiet, eager voice, made him seem like a man. His shoulders started to become strong. He liked to hug her too tightly sometimes, then he'd laugh, as if he didn't know his own strength.

Aristodemo was proud to etch his name on the water-pipe joint in front of the church. He felt that maybe he was working with people who knew how to get things done after all.

Aristodemo and Tita passed their eighteenth birthdays. Aristodemo rose from apprenticeship, becoming assistant to the man in charge of the waterworks. People were delighted with the water in their homes, but the new system needed lots of maintenance. Still living with his parents, Aristo managed to put money aside. He and Tita started to think that soon they would be able to buy a house. Once a house was secure, there would be nothing to stop them from getting married.

Then the war began. Marriage had to wait.

Aristodemo had just turned twenty-one when he was called into the army. Politics had never interested him. He became a soldier because he was given no choice. Still, he tried to convince himself, there was something manly and glorious in fighting for your country. He stared at himself in the mirror the first time he put on his uniform. Strange to see himself wearing the clothes of the people who had power. He asked himself why the face in the mirror still looked so young. His eyes became round.

He tried on his uniform for Tita. He was surprised that she wasn't impressed.

He was sent away for years. He came home for visits whenever he could. Aristodemo and Tita returned to their special place in the woods by the river when he was home. They kissed. They wondered if the war would ever end.

He was sent to Russia. It was a faraway place and he had no idea why he was there, or why he was supposed to feel any particular allegiance to the Germans he was fighting with or any particular animosity toward the Russians he was fighting against. The Russians, as far as he could tell, were doing their best to defend their own land.

Tita never would understand fully what happened to Aristodemo in Russia. He tried to tell her after his return, but what came out were fragments, fractured pieces of a mosaic that seemed too terrible to be looked at whole.

He told her that there had been 155 men in his company. And his company was only a small part of the nine army divisions of infantry-men and Alpine troops that Mussolini placed at the disposal of the Germans. All these men—boys, to Tita's mind—were sent by train to Germany, where they joined the German army. By train again they rode the first leg of the advance into Russia. In December and January they had to walk the remaining 715 miles to the front. On foot, 715 miles in 42 days, temperatures less than minus 20. These were numbers that Aristodemo later repeated so often they became a chant. Tita would always wonder what kind of Christmas the sol-diers spent during their march through the snow.

German and Italian troops completed the advance together.

Aristodemo's company dug trenches on the front line, at the banks of a frozen river. The Italians lived in the trenches. The Germans waited two miles behind the lines.

Across the river were the Siberian troops, far more accustomed to the cold. The Siberians had American-supplied guns and American-supplied tanks. Rumbling over the river was easy for the tanks because the ice was two feet thick.

The Siberians fired on the trenches. The Italians discovered that, in the minus twenty-degree cold, their own firearms didn't work.

Perhaps the withdrawal was orderly at first, but it soon became a retreat, and the retreat then became an escape. Of the 155 men in his company, 17 returned to Italy alive. "That's about one in ten who lived," as he later told Tita. "Which means nine in ten died." His comrades starved to death, or they froze. War to Aristodemo now meant no backpack, no gun, no food.

He and the few other survivors crossed Russia on foot. A good day was one in which they spotted a farmhouse where they could beg for food. The Russian women took pity on them and gave them potatoes to eat and let them sleep in the barn. He found it hard at first to understand the generosity of people who were supposed to be his enemy. One woman one evening made herself understood to the young Italian men eating at her table. "You are nothing but meat that's been sold at the market," she said. "Mussolini, your *Duce,* sold your flesh to Hitler. This shouldn't even be your war."

It was May of 1942, six months after the advance, when Aristodemo made his way across the Austrian border and back into Italy. He was taken to the Italian military barracks near Vipiteno. He had weighed nearly 160 pounds when he'd gone off to Russia. Returning, he weighed 81.

The army gave him lots to eat until he regained his strength. The officers told him he was not at liberty to discuss the retreat from the Siberian front with anyone. It wouldn't make for good news, they said. Wouldn't be good for the glory of Italy, they said. Wouldn't be good for the country's morale.

That was when Aristodemo's great disillusionment overwhelmed him. That was when he decided to leave.

Getting back to Tuscany from the north of Italy was a problem. He reckoned that the people back in his own town would understand why he left the army, but Fascist guards along the way would be less lenient. Their orders were to shoot deserters on sight.

He was on a southbound train, near Bologna, when the guards boarded. He saw them from the window, guns in their hands. He exchanged glances with the woman sitting beside him. She said nothing, but pointed to the space under the bench. He crouched beneath the bench as the heavy boots of the guards came up the aisle. The woman shifted her skirt to cover his face.

He got off the train in Siena and walked the final twenty miles to Sant'Angelo D'Asso. In his parents' house, he slept in the bedroom of his childhood, but he had lost the habit of sleeping on a bed. At three o'clock in the morning he gave up in frustration. He stretched out on the floorboards instead and finally fell asleep.

The next day he turned himself in to the Fascist authorities in town. He had calculated correctly, in that they didn't order him to be shot. They put him under a kind of house arrest instead. They assigned him a work detail: He was ordered to report every day to the public waterworks.

So he had his old job back again, even though officially he was being punished for desertion. Aristodemo couldn't have been more pleased. At night he sometimes sneaked away from home. He went to the nearby town of San Quirico D'Orcia where the partisans had managed to keep alive a cell of resistance fighters. He sat in on their meetings and pledged that he would do what he could to help the cause.

On other nights he sneaked out to meet Tita, to walk through fields together, to lie down beneath the moon.

At the end of the war, when the Germans were retreating, Aristodemo had a gun in his hand once again, this time to help the effort to make the Germans leave.

It was a warm spring Sunday evening that followed a week of rain, and the Allied front had nearly reached Aristodemo's part of Tuscany. He was full of joy. He and Tita had found a place to buy. The house was no more than the ruined foundation of what had once been a farmhouse, but there was lots of land and a perfect hillside where grapevines could be planted to make wine. The land was next to the farm that Tita's parents ran. Aristodemo couldn't wait to start work to resurrect the farmhouse from its fallen state. When the house was finished, he and Tita could get married at last.

To celebrate buying the house, Tita and Aristodemo decided to invite their friends for an outdoor dinner on the land that would soon be theirs.

Women had prepared food all afternoon. Now, this evening, tables and chairs had been brought. Fires were lit and big cooking pots set over the fires to make pasta and to grill the meat from a pig that someone had offered for the occasion. The women were busy making the dinner; the men played soccer in the evening light on the flat, grassy field by the house. The men had taken off their ties and jackets and they kicked the ball along the field in their black trousers and white shirts. The field was muddy after the days of rain, and the men were soon dirty. The sky looked freshly washed.

Half the town had come to the party. Children played beside the field. Teenagers sat with each other, and talked and laughed. One pair of teenagers was Maria Severina and Tonino, who would grow up to become Milena's parents. No, Maria Severina had never been any different from what she was now. Yes, she looked like a wild boar even back then. She had a way of attacking Tonino's ankles with a stiff-legged kick. That was her idea of flirting.

And Renato's parents were there, too, still only teenagers, a few years younger than Tita and Aristodemo. Now *they* were a couple well-liked by all. Good thing they were so young. Renato's father had been too young to get called up for the war. Happy pair, those two seemed together. Happy pair.

Sculati was at the party as well. He was a big, clumsy boy who drank too much wine. No one could quite put their finger on the strange quality about him, but the strange quality was there all the same. Was it really a surprise when he later grew up to be the gravedigger at the cemetery? He had always seemed half a step out of pace with the world of the living. Maybe he fit in better among the dead.

And Don Luigi was there. A long-limbed, serious, lonely boy who watched the soccer game that spring evening through the thick lenses of his eyeglasses, no one was shocked when he went on to become a priest.

Everyone at the party that evening tried not to think of the other young men who should have been there but who had been killed. Instead, people tried to let themselves relax. This was how evenings had been before the war. And people were hopeful, because everyone thought: The war is ending. This is how life will be again.

Aristodemo was tending the goal for his team. Tita was placing a glass with some wildflowers in it on the center of the table. She lifted her eyes from the table and watched Aristodemo. He had put weight back on since his return from Russia. He was respected at his job with the waterworks, even if the work was meant to be a punishment. She looked at the hills beyond Aristodemo and she told herself that these sunlit views would be theirs together from now on. She wondered if any person on earth had ever been so much in love.

Aristodemo felt her eyes on his body. He turned to her and waved.

Then the sky was ripped by noise as an American plane passed low overhead. The men stopped playing soccer.

Planes were nothing new. In the last weeks, there had been lots of planes to bomb the Germans during their retreat. And in the past few days, planes had swept by to clean out the hiding places where the last armed Fascists were holed up. The planes were making the area safe for the movements of the Allied land troops who were bringing the great wave of liberation northward along the Italian peninsula.

The men shaded their eyes with their hands to watch the plane as it went off toward the setting sun. They saw the plane bank. It circled back, much closer to the ground than before. The men, exposed in the middle of their muddy playing field, asked themselves how they appeared to the pilot. They hoped they looked like friends.

But the booming vibrations of the plane passing close to their heads prompted a fear that was swifter and more basic than reason or hope. One of the men, panicking, ran from the center of the field, and so did everyone else. Only Aristodemo stayed where he was in front of the two buckets that had been set up as the goal.

Tita saw the glass of wildflowers on the tabletop shake from the sound of the plane. For an instant she felt that everything was about to be taken away.

The plane circled again, this time higher. Before it reached the edge of the field it opened its hatch and dropped a bomb.

Everybody waited for the explosion, but none came. The bomb had slid like a knife into the mud in the middle of the field. Incredulous, some people laughed. A few had the presence of mind to wave at the plane when it came back to check on the damage. Maybe the sight of waving people dissuaded the pilot from dropping a second bomb. Whatever his reasons, he zoomed off and did not come back.

A week later the Allies liberated Sant'Angelo D'Asso, bringing with them chewing gum and Lucky Strike cigarettes and big band music and different dance steps and different ways to dress and all the thousands of little things which, in the years to come, would make Italy change. The war was over.

One of the Allies' first jobs in the area was to disarm unexploded bombs. They determined that the bomb in Tita's and Aristodemo's field had to be detonated. It hadn't exploded only because the mud it had landed in had been too soft.

They evacuated the area. Tita and Aristodemo went with their parents to the town's piazza to wait, along with the other people who had homes nearby.

The explosion was bigger than anyone had expected. It burst farmhouse windows and shook the ground so much that a well caved in a quarter of a mile away. Tita and Aristodemo came to see what was left of the foundations of what would become their house. The wall near the one-time entryway had collapsed, had fallen into the earth, and a cavern had opened up underneath. Aristodemo looked into the hole with a flashlight. He discovered an arched stone ceiling underground.

That was how Aristodemo fortuitously discovered the ancient *cantina,* the wine cellar, beneath what he would transform into his new house.

He built the house himself over the next two years. The Fascist who had been his boss at the waterworks was thrown out. All the most ardent Fascists lost their jobs. Aristodemo's desertion from the army and his participation in the partisan resistance were seen as points in his favor by the new body governing the town. They appointed him head of the waterworks.

Three weeks after he completed the house, he and Tita married and moved in. They planted vines together on the hillside and waited some years for them to mature. Aristodemo made new vats and barrels for the *cantina*. They began making their own red wine.

The years after the war were hard for everyone. Aristodemo and Tita, though, never lost the freshness of being in love.

Children would have been nice, but they never had any. They could never understand why. Who could tell why? And what difference would knowing have made?

As it was, their childlessness pulled them closer together. They were each other's company. In each other's eyes, they were always the kids who had fallen in love.

They escorted one another through the years, watching time change both their bodies.

One day Aristodemo entered their bedroom and found Tita staring at a picture that had been taken of her before the war. In the picture, her hair was glossy, her face smooth, her waist thin. She looked in the mirror above the chest of drawers to study what her face had become. She saw Aristodemo standing behind her. He, too, was looking at the reflection of her face. He, too, saw the graying hair, the lines around the mouth, the wrinkles on the neck, the lips that were no longer plump.

He put his hands on her shoulders and smiled at her in the mirror. They had begun their journey together, and going backward was a game that only the mind could play when it drifted off in memories or dreams. He bent down and kissed her, his lips to hers.

At the waterworks, Aristodemo Vezzosi took on the teenage Renato Tizzoni as apprentice. Having no son of his own, he was pleased to have found a successor in his trade. When the boy's parents died, Aristodemo and Tita secretly, mystically, felt that God had sent them a child. Renato was seventeen years old, and he made clear his desire to stay alone in his parents' house. Still, the Vezzosis were glad to have him over for dinner anytime he wanted to come.

When Renato told them he had fallen in love with Milena, they saw how he was transformed. The sadness that had shadowed him all winter slipped away. And they were happy for themselves, too. They knew they were important in Renato's life. Now his life would be joined to Milena's life, and through the young couple new life would come about. Participating in this was enough for the Vezzosis. They didn't ask for more.

After his retirement, Aristodemo Vezzosi got sick. Sickness, like love, was not a thing that needed to be discussed with words. The sickness was never called by its name. Instead, Aristodemo on occasion mentioned "the thing that's growing inside me," but he said this only when the pain seemed too much to bear.

The Siberian army and the Russian winter and the Fascist guards hadn't managed to kill him, and he saw no reason now why a few malevolent cells inside his body should prove themselves stronger than his will to live. The sickness, though, was slower and more insidious than any battle he had fought with a gun in his hand.

In the operating room they took out parts of his intestines. A year later they took out some more. Two years later they removed sections of his stomach, too.

At home Tita took over all the work. Aristodemo often felt too weak to do much more than watch her in the evenings while she tied the grapevines to their posts. When it was time for the more back-breaking chores of winemaking, Renato came around to give a hand.

Tita administered the many doses of medicine every day. She had a tray full of tablets and liquids. She gave Aristodemo shots. She hoped all the medicines would do some good, but she had doubts.

Aristodemo sat in a chair outside their house one evening in late autumn when Renato had come to help make things ready for winter. It was a beautiful, clear evening, but a wintry chill was already in the air. Renato hefted the potted lemon trees that had stood all summer in front of the Vezzosis' house. He put the lemon trees in a room beside the wine *cantina,* where they would be protected from frost through-out the season ahead.

"I had a dream last night!" Aristodemo Vezzosi said suddenly. "I dreamed I was in school again."

Tita laughed.

"You laugh because I never had much of a head for schoolbooks, and I never continued past elementary school. But neither did you!"

"And this dream?" she said, bending over to pull up the socks inside her rubber work boots.

"Last night. There I was in my dream, back in the old school-room. And all around me were all the other boys of the class. There was Petrioli, and Stori, and Vullo, and Morelli. You remember Morelli? The one who used to play, what was it, the clarinet? But the strange thing was, we were all young. Exactly as we had been then. And then I woke up, which was the strangest thing of all. Because for a moment, for a tiny little instant, I woke up and believed I was a boy again, with all my life still to be lived."

He looked at her and she saw his eyes grow wide. "*Pulcino!*" she said to him, touching his hair with her fingers. "Listen to the dreams of an old man! Still a little boy."

"Still a boy, yes. I feel the same inside. Nothing's changed. Then I saw myself in the mirror in the bathroom before I went to piss and I was so very confused. Someone had played a joke on me. Someone had turned my body old."

Tita saw his round eyes grow moist. "Listen to how you talk!" she said, not wanting him to cry in front of Renato.

He smiled at Renato. "You see how your old Vezzosi has been reduced?" He turned his gaze toward the storeroom where Renato had placed the potted lemon trees. "Beautiful, those little trees became this year. *Grazie,* Renato, for putting them away. When you come to take them out into the open air again next spring, I won't be here."

"What are you saying, Signor Vezzosi?" Renato said "Of course you'll be here."

That was the only time Renato heard Aristodemo Vezzosi talk about death.

Aristodemo was indeed there to watch the potted lemon trees come out of the storeroom in the spring. A happy surprise for everyone.

He did not live, though, to see the potted lemon trees put away again.

It was just the other day. *Just the other day.* He no longer had the strength to get out of bed. Tita did everything. She washed him, fed him, kept him company. She tried not to cry when she was with him. She waited for that until she was out among the grapevines.

One morning he said he didn't want to eat. Or he wanted to but didn't think he could. Around lunchtime Tita persuaded him to try a little broth. She propped him up on his pillows, kissed his head, and went to the kitchen to heat up the broth. When she came back in carrying the tray, she saw that he had changed position in bed. He was curled up like a fetus, on his side. Yellowed skin draped loosely on his bones. His eyes were open, round above his beakish nose. His eyes watched her come in the door. *"Pulcino,"* she said, seeing him. To her, he looked like a little chick whose shell had been broken before it was time to be born. She saw his mouth open to say something; instead, he exhaled for the last time.

"*Pulcino*," she said, and she felt that life had fled from her body, too.

On the chest of drawers she put down the tray with the bowl of broth. For many hours Tita lay on the bed beside Aristodemo.

THIRTEEN

A Scrap of Paper

Renato fingered the plastic bag that contained the pecorino and ricotta cheeses he had brought. He touched the bread crumbs on the tablecloth. He reached for his glass of wine and finished it in one gulp. He put the empty glass on the table. He scratched his beard. He was afraid to look at Signora Vezzosi's face. He knew what a strong person she was, but seeing tears on the face of a strong person is hard.

He saw her calloused old hand resting on the table. He took the hand and held it between both of his. "Signora," he said.

She let her hand be held for a moment, then pulled it away. "I don't know," she said, pulling herself back into her kitchen, back into today. "You know what thought keeps me awake at night?"

He saw the tears drying on the wrinkles of her cheeks.

"There's nothing left," she went on. "Fifty years together—you remember? We celebrated our fiftieth anniversary only a few months ago. What do fifty years mean? Fifty years, and now there's nothing. Gone, like a dream. Gone. Oh, there's the house. There are the vines. There's wine in the casks. But it's nothing. And whatever is left will soon be underwater anyway."

She poured herself more wine from the bottle, then held the bottle above Renato's glass. He protested, but she said, "Have just another little taste." She gave him a drop. "Taste. Go ahead."

He drank.

"You see? You taste something? For me, nothing. This bottle, he and I put the wine in this bottle together eight, nine years ago, even before his illness came to him. Now I drink"—she sipped from her glass—"and I could be drinking water. Fifty years and now there's nothing. For me, not even the taste is left. Now what can I do?"

Renato thought about the taste of the wine. To him, it tasted good. But he thought about what he had been feeling lately. He said, "I understand you."

"Fifty years and it all might have happened in the arc of one day. Not even a day. A minute. The minute before you wake up from a dream. Fifty years seem like a dream, and now I've woken up. Fifty years make no difference at all. What keeps me awake at night is the ugly sensation that fifty years didn't even happen. I drink my coffee in the morning; it doesn't taste. I eat a plate of food; it's like eating paper. I drink wine; I—" She shook her head. She wiped her eyes. "Nothing is left. In an instant, a lifetime disappears like a dream."

"*Sì,*" Renato said. "True. But it renews itself, too, even after everything seems to die. Life renews itself." Renato stopped. Why wasn't he a person of words? Had he been, he would have known what to say. Instead, he felt he was babbling. "I understand you," he tried. "I, too, lately—" He gave up.

Then an idea for action instead of words flowered inside his head. New energy came to his face. "Oh! *Facciamo una cosa,*" he said. "Let's do a little something."

"What?"

"Give me a piece of paper. Even a scrap is enough. Have you got a scrap of paper?"

"Paper for what?"

His turn to talk now. He started to tell her about how he had been feeling in general lately, but words threatened to dry up because it was too difficult to describe what happens to you when life loses its taste. So he told her about his dream, about the hand touching his shoulder in the darkness and leading him out of his house to the well. Yes, words ran fluidly because it's easy to retell a dream. He told her about seeing the hand with the ring on the finger suspended above the water in the well, pointing out where he was meant to look. He told her about the treasure in the dream, the treasure he found behind the stone inside the well. He told her about how he then had woken up and gone to look in the well, only to find an empty hole. He told her about what a mentally deficient person he had been to interpret the dream literally, about how, reasoning later with the sheep, he had understood the dream's real message. He told her how certain he was that now he had to go to Rome to shake hands with the pope. And how he had to put his other hand on his ass while shaking hands with the pope, and that way his luck, his *culo,* his ass, would be sure to change. "And now, signora, *facciamo una cosa.* Let's do a little something. Give me a piece of paper, and we'll do this thing."

He was too excited to contain himself now, so he grabbed for the plastic bag with the cheese inside and said, "Here's paper!" He took out the wedge of pecorino cheese that he had made himself with the milk from his sheep. The cheese was wrapped in gray paper. "All I need is a piece . . ." He tore off a strip. "But I don't have a pen. Signora, a pen or a pencil, have you got one?"

His eagerness was contagious. Without understanding why, she felt herself curious, the way you feel curious when someone starts doing a card trick and, even if you don't like card tricks, you're curious to see how the trick will turn out. "There's the pen I use to make my shopping lists over there in the drawer."

"Which drawer?" He started to rise.

"No. Sit. I'll get it." She got up, went over to the sideboard, and came back to the table with the pen.

"Good," he said. "Now, you see, the thing we will do is this: I will write your name on this piece of paper, and I will keep it with me here"—he patted his ass—"in my back pocket when I go to Rome. This way, when I shake hands with the pope, and touch my ass with my other hand, I'll have your name in my back pocket, and when my fortune changes, yours will change, too."

Signora Vezzosi was silent for a moment. She stared at Renato's face. Then she laughed. "Have we both gone mad?" she blurted out.

"I'm not even sure I'm such an admirer of the pope. Good man personally, no doubt. But officially? And touching your ass while you—"

"Neither am I!" said Renato. "I've never even thought about the pope before. He minds his business, I mind mine. But the *dream,* don't you see? The dream was sent to me, and I would be mentally deficient for real if I were to ignore a dream like this one. Who am I to doubt the message of a dream that's been sent? And in the dream, when I found the treasure, if you think about it, like I said, the treasure wasn't only for me, but for other people, too. So it's not only my fortune that's destined to change, but other people's as well. Your *culo* is destined to change, signora, and this is the way we have to do it to make your luck change. Doesn't it seem so to you also? Who are we to doubt?"

"And what does Milena say about all this, about the dream and your trip to Rome?"

"Milena? She doesn't say anything. I haven't told her."

"You haven't told your wife?"

"I'm waiting for it to come up. I mean, if the subject of dreaming dreams and shaking the pope's hand, yes, if the subject should happen to come up in some natural way in conversation with Milena, then of course I'll tell her about the dream. But the moment has to be right to talk about such a thing, no?"

"You've told me, Renato, but you haven't told her? Why not?"

"Oh, signora, what can I say? What if she thinks I'm crazy?"

"Then she'd have a point."

Renato exhaled. "Oh. But I want to do something to help you. So what do you say? Can I put your name on this piece of paper and keep it with me when I shake hands with the pope?"

"To me, it seems peculiar," Signora Vezzosi began. Then she started to think about how she would feel if Renato went off to Rome without her name in his back pocket. "*Very* peculiar, I would say." She thought about what thoughts she would be thinking later tonight when lying beside the empty space in her bed, and she knew she'd be thinking about Renato's dream. He had a strange way of reasoning, Renato had, but it was a reasoning you couldn't argue with. And dreams were known to be messengers, she'd heard it said.

Renato was already scribbling little circles on the corner of the cheese paper to be sure the pen worked.

"*Vabbene,*" Signora Vezzosi said, surprising herself. She recognized the sensation that rose like a sob of hope in her chest. It was a sensation she hadn't felt in the days since her husband had died. "Fine. Write my name."

"Good," Renato say. "You'll see. It will be good. Here I'll write, 'Signora Vezzosi'—"

"For something as personal as this, you would write my last name?"

"But I always call you—"

"I know what you call me, but that doesn't enter into it here. Here we're talking about *la fortuna.*"

"I understand this, but that doesn't mean you should reprimand me in this way!" He played at being offended. He was enjoying raising his voice with the signora. He was happy to hear how she raised her voice to him. A sign of life, he thought and hid a smile.

She said, "If you intend to do this thing in this manner, writing down only my last name before you go to touch your ass and shake hands with the pope, how do you expect me to react?"

"Forget the last name, then! I will write down your first name. Probably you're right, that it's more personal this way. I will write 'Tita.' All right?"

"Tita. Yes."

"Tita then." Renato was about to put pen to paper.

"No, wait! Maybe Tita is too familiar."

"But I've always heard you called Tita. Signor Vezzosi always called you Tita."

"And I always called him Aristo, I know. But it's like the inscription you discovered on the pipe. For a thing that important, he used his full name. Aristodemo. Write down my first name in full. Margherita. Please."

'MARGHERITA,' Renato wrote on the piece of paper. "No last name?" he asked.

"I've always been a simple person. I don't give myself airs.

Margherita is fine. Now let's go to the *cantina* and get you your wine.
You have the bottles in your car?"

Renato put the cheese paper with Signora Vezzosi's name on it
into his back pocket.

They filled the bottles in the same wine cellar that the Allied forces
had inadvertently unearthed more than half a century before when
they'd detonated the bomb in the field.

Renato put the bottles back in the car, then reached for his wallet.
"The big bottle holds five liters, and the smaller bottles are two each,
so that's seventeen liters," he started to calculate.

"No," Signora Vezzosi objected. "You gave me the pecorino and
the ricotta. I give you the wine. We're even."

"Signora, we're not even. A little bit of cheese—"

"A little bit of cheese, and my name in your pocket when you
shake hands with the pope. We're even, I say. This discussion will
become unpleasant if you continue to insist."

He put his wallet away. He opened the door of his car, ready to
leave, then he turned and held Signora Vezzosi in a hug. Holding her,
he felt the bones of her shoulders, the bones of her back. "Eat some
cheese this evening," he told her. "You're disappearing. See that you
don't forget to eat."

She kissed his cheek.

Driving away, he was full of thoughts. What could he do for
Signora Vezzosi? Nothing, probably. But he was trying.

Then the sense of responsibility arose in his head and weighed on
his mind. He felt the seriousness of his mission. Another person's destiny was at stake as well as his own. Signora Vezzosi's name was in his
pocket, next to his ass.

FOURTEEN

Milena Asks

"Don't sit there like a lost soul. You've finished eating. Get up and carry plates into the kitchen. Give Milena a hand. See what there is to be done."

Renato poured the last of his wine into his mouth. With the napkin, he wiped the corners of his lips. Like a cat washing itself after a meal, he used his fingers to flick away from his beard any bread crumbs that might have stayed behind. He held the wine in his mouth, bathing his taste buds in the flavor. I wanted to savor this taste, he told himself, but *she* shoos me away from the table as if I were a lazy kid.

She was Maria Severina. Renato watched her move among the tables of the *bottega,* an apron tied around her thick waist.

Renato swallowed his wine without noticing the taste.

He looked across the room to where Milena's father, a white dish towel over his shoulder, leaned with both hands on a table to talk to a couple of old friends in the middle of their dinner. Tonino was chuckling at something someone had said. He was fat, too, but his fatness was different. His abundance reflected the generosity of his spirit. How did this man, Renato wondered, ever manage to mount a woman as unappetizing as Maria Severina? Was any part of her soft and secretly delicious, or was she as tough as old boar meat through and through? Thank God, Milena had gotten her disposition from her father. Please God, she'll never wake up one morning and be like that sour, unwomanly woman who—

"Move yourself!" said Maria Severina, suddenly reappearing at his side. "Can't you see how many people there are to serve? Do something useful for a change. I only have two hands. How much do you expect me to do?"

Renato picked up his plates, his knife and fork, and his empty glass and carried them into the kitchen, half-hoping to hide in there, away from his mother-in-law.

As soon as he set foot in the kitchen, he was surrounded by good food smells. Milena stood before the old marble cooking counter. She was stuffing cannelloni. Baked pasta of this sort was a Southern Italian specialty, not Tuscan, but the tourist season wasn't over yet and many foreign visitors were never happy unless they had lasagne or cannelloni sitting on their plates. Renato knew this because the night before Milena had told him that today she planned to prepare cannelloni. She always discussed with him her ideas about what should or shouldn't be on the *bottega*'s menu.

"I thought I'd give you a hand," Renato said, putting down his dirty plates.

"You mean mamma told you to give me a hand."

"*Sì*. I mean your mamma told me to give you a hand. You need a hand?"

She laughed. Her eyes were on her work. With one hand she held a cannellone. She was pushing the meat stuffing into the tube with a finger of the other hand. Both hands were covered with the mixture of meat, egg, grated cheese, and spices. For an instant the hands looked murderous, as if she had ripped the heart from a living creature's body, grasping it by an aorta, and her hands were smeared with flecks of flesh up to her wrists. Then Renato saw the softness of the hands he had known for a lifetime. He knew every line of the palms, every fold when the fingers curled. A sudden appetite filled him: He wanted to put her hands to his mouth and lick off the last of the eggy, meaty mush.

She blew air from her lips, trying to blow back into place a lock of hair that insisted on dangling in front of her eyes.

"Here," Renato said. He brushed the hair out of her face, tucking it back behind her ear, smoothing the ponytail behind her neck. He kissed her above the ear.

"Thanks," she said, not taking her eyes off the cannellone in her hands.

"Tell me. You want some help in here?"

"I'm almost finished. Why don't you go out and help clear tables? When you come back, there'll be food to serve."

He turned, strangely saddened by the way she wasn't looking at him. Making cannelloni, of course, needed concentration, but couldn't she at least give him a glance? He felt sad because he sensed sadness in her. He couldn't name her sadness, which made her silence more powerful. "Oh. What's wrong?"

She shrugged, getting on with her work. "Nothing."

He turned to go through the door to the restaurant.

"Renato?" It was nearly maddening, the way she talked to him but seemed to be talking more to the bowl of meat.

"Tell me."

"Have you been with another woman?"

A question like this, and she gave him only her voice, not her eyes. "Who? Which woman? Of course not! Why would I be with another woman?" He saw her hands stuffing meat into pasta tubes and in his mind he saw his own hands washing the actress's foot in her bathroom sink.

"I've never asked you before. Never had reason, as far as I know. But I'm asking you now."

"Why do you ask such a thing?"

She was silent again. She placed the cannellone on the baking tray and started stuffing another one.

"Tell me," he said. "Why do you ask?" His heart thumped with dangerous speed in his chest. He was dizzy, as if the floor had disappeared beneath his feet.

The kitchen door swung open. "Oh!" Maria Severina barreled in, her arms loaded with dirty plates. "Do you have any intention of doing something useful or do you mean to stand around playing loving pigeons with my daughter? There are people. I need help."

"*Arrivo,*" said Renato. "I'm coming."

He left the kitchen and started clearing away customers' first-course plates, making room for the meat course that would follow. While he worked, the emptiness inside him made him queasy, as though, by means of some stupid carelessness on his part, his wife had slipped away from him, coldly, irretrievably, forever out of his reach.

Tourist faces in the restaurant were unknown to him. Other customers were from the town and he knew them all. Some were in the mood to chat, but Renato was distracted, hardly hearing what they said.

There was a time, his own voice was saying deep inside his head, there was a time when she was sacred to me. He remembered when they were first together, when he was a lonely kid living by himself in his dead parents' house, and some evenings she would sneak off from her own parents to spend time with him. He remembered how they used to lie on his bed and he would kiss her, frantically at first, as if her sweetness were something that would be taken from him, so he hungrily had to kiss her mouth and her neck and her belly and her armpits and her breasts before she disappeared. Her hands, with their lovely softness—the pink hands he had first noticed juggling white balls of snow—touched his back beneath his shirt, curled around his hair, caressed his still beardless face. Touched him. The first time he kissed her between the legs, he believed he was lapping from the well at the epicenter of the universe. That's what their time together meant to him.

Milena always made sure to return to her parents' home at a respectable hour. After she would leave him, Renato would lie alone and hug the pillow that still smelled of her, and everything she had touched would be sacred to him. One evening she was cold and she put on a sweater of his. When she gave him back the sweater, it was as holy to him as if the Virgin Mary herself had used it to keep her baby warm.

Now she was in the kitchen stuffing cannelloni and he was on the other side of the door among talkative customers in the presence of his in-laws, and the distance between Renato and Milena was infinite. She was a universe away. And he had created the distance by the silly contortions of his own mind, and now, he sensed, everything was about to explode in a final, annihilating, cosmos-quaking bang.

"You decided to help out tonight?" said Renato's father-in-law, laughing. "Always appreciated, your help is." Tonino laughed some more, and nodded, and got back to small talk with his friends.

Renato shouldered his way through the kitchen door, dirty plates stacked in his arms. He put the dishes down by the sink. The plates made noise when he put them down, for he put them down more quickly than he should have. Fine, then. He was glad for the noise. If she wanted to ask him about other women, let her ask. Why should he feel guilty about doing what he hadn't even done? Let her ask! If pushed, he might even tell her the truth and liberate himself from the heaviness he was carrying around inside.

Milena's eyes remained fixed on the meat stuffing. She fingered meat into a pasta tube. The meat squidged.

Silence.

The lack of words between them was tragic and tense, as if they had already fought.

"*Allora?*" Renato shot out. "So? You wanted to talk? Let's talk!" He almost hated her for her silence, for the way she kept her back turned to him.

She blew with her lips again to get rid of the hair in front of her eyes. She used the back of her wrist to push the hair in place. Renato took it as a defiant gesture, meant to demonstrate that she could sort out her own hair problems without any help from him.

He hated her for having found him out, the way you hate a roadside policeman who flags you down when you've done something wrong. He hated her for being hurt, even though she didn't know yet what there was to be hurt about. He hated her for pulling away, withdrawing into her sad silence. Had she screamed like a witch at him, or thrown a raw cannellone his face, he would have known how to react. He would have screamed back until he was purified, washed clean. He would have felt less alone.

Instead there was only her hurt, and her innocence, and her fear.

"You can tell me, you know," she said at last.

"Tell you what?"

"If you've been with another."

"I could tell you, you say? Thank you very much. If it happens to me, I'll let you know."

"Then don't tell me." She returned to her silence.

Who had ratted on him? Milena herself had made the appointment for him to go and unclog Meg Barker's drain.

Maybe it was the actress. Maybe she was going around town telling everyone that she and he had a story together. Her Italian was terrible, of course, so she must have done a lot of miming to get her point across, but she was an actress, after all, and actresses knew how to communicate without words.

Renato stood uselessly by the sink, trying to work out how Milena had found out. For an instant he considered washing the dirty plates he had just carried in, but then thought better of it, deciding his mother-in-law could do the washing later.

Yes, that must be what had happened, he reasoned. Meg Barker was circulating through town, inventing tales about him and her. Or maybe she had come here to the *bottega*. Maybe the *bottega* was the stage where she gave her reenactments of the love affair they had never had. She swallowed Irish whiskey by the glassful at the *bottega* every day. With her mind inflamed by alcohol, there was no telling what exaggerations she might dream up. Why would she do such a thing? Maybe she was malicious. Maybe she was deranged. Maybe strange things happen in the head of a woman of a certain age who lives alone in a foreign country. She begins to read meaning into little nothings. And in her culture, who knew what the significance was of washing a strange woman's foot in her bathroom sink?

"What's her name?" A question from the face with its eyes downcast toward the bowl of stuffing.

"The name of who?"

"You know who. The English actress."

"The English actress? The one whose house I visited to fix her pipes?"

"No, the other English actress in Sant'Angelo D'Asso, the one with the working pipes! Don't take me by the ass, Renato. Of course the English actress with the broken pipes. What's her name?"

"Why must I know her name?"

"You went to her house. You fixed her pipes. You don't know her name?"

"I fixed her pipes. Not even. Her sink was clogged and that was all. We didn't talk about her name." Liar! he screamed at himself. Drinking coffee at her kitchen table, you talked about nothing else but her name. And yours. She said your name was— What did she say? Beautiful, did she say your name was? Beautiful or interesting? What was it she had said?

"Her name is Barker," Milena informed him.

He shrugged. "If you say so."

"Not just me who says so. Everybody says so. A film of hers was on television the other week. And now she lives here. Everybody knows her name. Barker."

"So?"

"And her first name?"

"You watch television more than me, here in the bar. You tell me. Ask your mother. Your mother knows all these actress types."

"Her first name is Meg."

"You know the answer and you ask me the question. Does this seem right? In my opinion, no."

"Did you hear me, Renato? I said her name is Meg."

"Meg. So her name is Meg. So?" He turned on the taps of the big sink and started to wash his hands.

"Does Meg sound like a full name to you?" Milena placed the final cannellone on the baking tray. She looked across to Renato.

He looked over his shoulder and saw her looking at him. She was getting close now to exposing him altogether, but at least she was looking at him and talking to him, and anything was better than silence. "How do I know if Meg is a full name or not? They're funny people, the English. They have funny names."

Milena scraped her meat mush—covered fingers against the edge of the stuffing bowl. She carried the bowl to the sink and stood by Renato's side. "Meg is short for something. Any idea what? Move over. Your hands are clean and you're washing them. Mine are filthy and you're taking up the whole sink."

He took her meat-egg-cheese gooey hands and washed them under the running water from the tap. Now that they were talking again, he was feeling affectionate, almost enjoying the game. "Let me guess," he played along. "Meg is short for . . . Martha? Marilena? Mega-sega? Megalopolis?"

"Meg is short for Margherita." She yanked her now clean hands away from him. "Or however they say it in English."

"Interesting. Thank you for the information. Meg is short for Margaret, uh, or Margherita. Why is that important to me?"

"Because I found her name in your pants."

"What?" Renato couldn't make sense out of what was going on.

Milena grabbed a dish towel from beside the sink. Drying her hands, she walked off to put the baking tray of cannelloni into the oven.

He was stumped for a moment. Then his brain shifted into gear and everything was clear. He laughed; his secret was under no threat. Now he could talk and make things fine with his wife. "Give me the towel." He chased her across the kitchen. "I need to dry my hands, too." He put his arms around her waist. *Bischerina!* Silly! Getting yourself jealous like that over Signora Vezzosi."

"Signora Vezzosi?"

"*La Vezzosi. Sì.*"

"Tita Vezzosi?"

"Tita. Margherita. *Sì.*"

Milena thought for a moment, then laughed. "I was washing your pants and I—"

"And you emptied out the pockets first and you found the piece of paper. Yes, I understand. The piece of paper with the name 'Margherita' written."

"And I thought—"

"Yes. And you thought."

Then Milena asked him why he was walking around with Tita Vezzosi's name written on a piece of paper in the pocket of his pants.

Explaining was in order, he realized. He would have to tell her about his dream.

They served the meat course to the customers, then they got their hands wet again while Renato recounted the dream, for they had returned to the sink to rinse the food off the dirty first-course plates before putting them in the dishwasher. Renato told her about everything except the details of his visit to Meg Barker's. He told her about the cold panic that had been serpenting up inside him for some time now. He told her about how everything seemed to be going against him on the day of Vezzosi's funeral, with the town's main pipe bursting, and his not being able to go inside the church for the Mass, and his losing life's taste. He told her that everything was disappearing, even their own town. He told her how all these things weighed on him. He told her about his dream, what he thought it meant. He told her he should have told her about the dream before, but it felt too holy, too private, to expose it to the possible laughter of someone who maybe would not understand. He told her how he wouldn't have said anything to Signora Vezzosi either, but then he saw her loneliness and her sadness, and putting her name on a piece of paper to keep in his pocket when he shook hands with the pope was the only thing he could think of that might help.

Milena listened. She said she understood—more or less—and no, she wouldn't laugh at something as intimate as a dream. And of course he had always been a dreamer. Which was why she loved him, and why she sometimes asked herself if he could ever let himself be content with what was good enough for everyone else. Never quite contented. But that was him, she supposed. So yes, she understood.

But what she couldn't understand was *why*. Why did he think it was so unusual to sometimes be upset?

He tried to explain what it was like to live when nothing tastes of anything anymore. "It's like someone stuffed my ears with cotton, and my nose, and my mouth. Sounds and aromas want to penetrate me, but all I can smell is *white*."

He tried to explain how everything, even their daughter, had changed, how she was now more interested in her boyfriend than in them.

"She's growing up," said Milena, preparing sautéed spinach with garlic as a side order for a customer.

"Yes, of course. She's growing up. And that's fine with me, but she's changing. Everything's changing."

His mother-in-law charged into the kitchen to take the spinach out to the dining room.

Renato waited, as if waiting for a truck to pass, so that he could get on with his conversation.

"Everything's changing. Even you. No. I don't know. Have you changed? Or have I? When I fell in love with you, you were juggling snowballs in the snow."

"I was juggling snowballs in the snow." She smiled. "I wonder if I still know how." Milena was silent for a moment. "And when I fell in love with you, you hardly had a hair on your body. Now look at you! Your beard, the pelt on your chest, your belly. Can I ever set foot in the bathroom without finding your little hairs everywhere?" She laughed. "We're not kids anymore."

"No, but does that mean we have to be old? I remember so much. And there's still so much, but I can't reach it. There's something blocking my nose and ears and throat. Everything's there, but it's been removed. Distanced. I don't know."

"And me, too? Am I distanced from you?"

They were both frightened by their words. They were not used to hearing themselves say the words that two people say when maybe they won't be together anymore.

You were sad when I met you, Milena thought. Your parents were dead. You lived alone in your house. You were so very sad. And back then, all I had to do was smile at you and you came to life, like a miracle, like a bird that's hurt and afraid to fly and all it needs is a lit-tle time in a nice warm place, a little love. I was the first woman you loved. For me, you're the only man. "I always wondered . . ." she began to say.

"What?"

"Nothing." She realized her thoughts had escaped her lips through a force of their own. She carried the meat pan over to the sink, careful not to let the hot drippings spill.

. . . I always wondered when you'd get curious and start asking yourself what other women might be like.

Or maybe it's not even that, I hope. You're upset about the dam. Everyone's upset about the dam! Another year or two, who knows where we'll be? And your friend Vezzosi died. Like your father dying again. Of course you're sad now. There's little to wonder at. Surprising only that you're surprised because you're sad. And you'll do what you have to do to make yourself alive again. Then you'll come back to me. I hope.

She wanted to say all these things to him, but she sensed he wouldn't have wanted to listen to her explain him to himself. He would have denied everything. He would have pulled farther away.

Renato watched Milena as she carefully carried the meat pan to the sink. He watched her from the other side of the incredible dis-tance that magically, dreadfully, had appeared between them. He saw a stranger. He asked himself what he would think of this stranger if he were to see her for the first time. Would she catch his eye? Would he be curious to go inside her house, to enter her world?

He saw a woman in jeans and a light-colored flower-print shirt, an apron tied around her waist. If he didn't know the body the clothes concealed, would he be drawn to find out the secret inside? The ass inside the jeans was firm. The hips made the fabric strain a bit. The flower-print shirt was untucked. The apron string at the back of the waist was tight, cutting into a small roll of flesh. She looked soft inside the shirt, something that would be nice to touch.

On her feet she wore white clogs, the way the salesgirls behind the supermarket cheese counter wear clogs, the way nurses in the hospital wear clogs. Her feet were bare inside her clogs. The skin of her heels looked soft and very pink. Were she to slip a foot out of its clog, would his mouth water to bend down and give that foot a kiss?

She started to scrub the meat pan in the sink. He watched her neck, her downward-cast face. Her hair. Strands of hair were still intent on freeing themselves from the ponytail. The face appeared kind. The hair reflected light from the lamp above. The light around her, there in the kitchen, looked beautiful. Or maybe it was *she* who added beauty to the light.

The ear, as if it knew it was being watched, blushed red. The nape of the neck between her hair and shirt collar was strange to him, but he decided it probably would be inviting to his lips, after all.

He was about to walk over and kiss her neck, but then for a terrible instant he believed the fantasy that had grown up in his head. He thought she really was a woman unknown. You can't just walk up to an unknown woman and kiss her neck. You have no right. Who knows how she might react?

"I'm only being stupid. Probably." He spoke to break the ice, to remind her of their intimacy. To remind himself.

So he did walk over and put his lips to her neck.

She was relieved, but her neck muscles tightened all the same.

What surprised them both was that the kiss was like a kiss between strangers. Somehow the distance had become real.

Renato spoke. "You want me to help you some more? Here, let me finish washing the meat pan. You go and check on the tables outside. I'll take care of things in here."

"No," Milena replied. "You always offer to help when you really want to leave. You're thinking of going out to get a mouthful of air. It shows. Go. Don't worry. Where were you going?"

The stranger knew him well. "I don't know. Yes, I was thinking of driving with the window open. Breathe in the night breeze. I don't know. Maybe I'll drive up to Montalcino. I promised myself I'd visit Duncan. Haven't seen him for a long time. It's been a while since he's come by."

"Say hello to Duncan for me."

"Okay." He kissed her on the cheek, the way he would have kissed the wife of a friend. "I won't be back too late. See you at home. *Ciao*."

He was nearly out the kitchen door when he heard Milena say, "Oh. Renato."

"Tell me."

"So. You'll go to Rome, like your dream told you to do. And who knows? Maybe your fortune will change."

"Let's hope."

"Let's hope. Yes. But will you do something for me?" She closed the hot and cold water taps. She turned to him, drying her hands on the dish towel. She went to the counter where a spare pad of paper was kept for taking down customers' orders. Beside the pad was a pen. She reached into the pocket of her apron and took out a slip of paper. "Here," she said. "don't forget this when you go to Rome."

She handed him the paper with the name "Margherita" written on it.

She also handed him the pen. "You'll do something for me? Write down my name under Signora Vezzosi's. Maybe a change in my *fortuna* wouldn't be a bad idea."

Renato wrote her name, almost startled by the realization that she, too, might want her luck to change.

He folded the paper and put it in his pocket. He felt lighter now. He looked in her eyes. Her eyes were worried, but he and she smiled at each other.

In the hot kitchen of a *bottega* on the main street of an old stone town in the middle of night-covered hills, the smile between a bearded man and a woman with a ponytail was tenuous, but more tender than a kiss.

FIFTEEN

The Edge of a Breast

Milena had read him right. Getting out into the night air was exactly what Renato wanted to do. His headlights cut through the darkness as he drove around turns, higher and higher into the night on the road up to Montalcino.

The night seduced Renato. He opened the car windows. The air touched his skin, making the fabric of his shirt tremble against his chest. The strong wind that had come up was strangely warm. It was spicy with the smell of grapes on the vine almost ready to be picked.

Renato's heart rushed. He felt like a spy racing through the night to meet a lover, when all he was doing, he reminded himself, was going to visit his friend.

He parked his Fiat Ritmo under a tree in the square at the foot of Montalcino's main stone street. Under the street lamps of the town, the shops and bars were closed tight, always a melancholy sight. The warm wind pushed him up the street. He saw a light on in Duncan's window at the top floor of an old building. The hour was late, and he hadn't telephone ahead. But he never telephoned before he went to see Duncan. He knew he'd be happily received. He was glad to see the light on. Something warm came up inside his chest. He rang Duncan's doorbell, by the building's front door.

A moment later Duncan was leaning out the window. "Renato! *Ciao!*"

"Oh!" Renato whispered. "*Ti disturbo?*"

"You're not disturbing me at all. Come on up." Duncan pressed the buzzer to unlock the automatic bolt on the front door.

Inside, Renato climbed the stairs.

Duncan stood at the open door to his apartment with his shirttails untucked. His smile was like the smile in the eyes of a beloved dog when it greets you at the door.

The two men kissed each other on both cheeks. Renato wondered how his own beard felt against the smooth-shaven cheek of the other.

"I'm a little drunk," Duncan laughed.

"You have company?" Renato peeked around Duncan's shoulder.

"If only! No, no, no. No company." Endearing, the way his "no" was forever undeniably American. "Just me and a bottle of wine. Here. Come in. Come and drink a little, you too." His Italian was better now than it had been when he and Renato had first met, but even Italian idioms sounded foreign with that accent of his. Renato stepped inside.

A simple place. One room, with a big double bed against the wall, a table in front of it, and a kitchen unit in the corner, a stereo system set up on the floor, a bathroom through a door off to the side. And everywhere there were books. Books in piles. Books on the table, books beside the bed, books and compact discs on a little bookcase next to the stereo. Brick floor, white walls, exposed beams on the slanted ceiling, for the roof was right above. Renato relaxed in the familiar look of everything. Classical music came out of the stereo. He didn't know exactly what the music was, but it sounded like Duncan, it was part of Duncan, so he accepted the music the way he accepted the voice of his friend.

But there was something new in the apartment. It took him a moment to recognize what was different. Photographs. That was the difference. They hadn't been there a few months before, the last time he'd come. Now there were black-and-white photos everywhere, on all the walls. Photos of a woman, or rather *parts* of a woman. He

wanted to study the photos, wanted to ask about them. But, not wanting to be intrusive, he'd wait until the moment was right. Some of the
photos, he could tell, were of the intimate places of a woman's body.
He had to be delicate in his approach.

"Get me a glass," Renato said, turning to look at Duncan. "I don't
know why, but I want to get a little drunk, too."

They sat at the table drinking. He tried not to stare at the photos that
surrounded him like a breathing presence, as if the woman herself
had wrapped her body around his. He averted his eyes from the wall.
He drank his wine.

Renato would have been hard-pressed if anyone had asked him
how he and Duncan had come to know each other. They were friends;
that was that. Does it matter how friends met? Of course, if he had to
think about it, he'd remember that a couple of years before, when
Duncan had first arrived in Italy, the American lived in a rented house
in Sant'Angelo D'Asso for a few months while looking for a job. He
wanted to support himself so that his time in Italy could last as long as
he wanted it to. He bought himself a cheap old car and drove around
all the towns in the area, asking everywhere, until finally he got a job
working in the office of a winery in Montalcino. The winery had ties
to the export market to America. Brunello wine from Montalcino,
smoother and richer than Chianti, was in demand everywhere, and
having a native English speaker in the office was a business plus from
the winery's point of view. Duncan didn't earn a lot, but he survived,
which was all he wanted.

Those were the facts of Duncan's being here, but friendship isn't
based on facts. If anything, there was a mystery inside Duncan that
was far more the source of Renato's affection. Why was Duncan here?
Renato had no idea. Why would an American give up America, only
to find himself living alone in a one-room apartment in a hilltop town?
Renato didn't know what it was that Duncan was searching for, but he
knew he was searching, and the search itself made Renato want to
draw close.

❦

Two glasses of wine later, Renato was loosening up. "I'm living a strange thing," he said. "I don't know what it means." He saw the big eyes that looked into his own. The face was long, lending itself to a smile even when at rest. A lock of black hair fell across the fore-head, and Duncan now, as was his unconscious habit, used long fin-gers to push the hair out of his eyes. He wasn't much younger than Renato. Six or seven years, which would have made him just past thirty. Yet there was something puppyish still in his manner. He moved that tall, thin body of his as if he weren't yet accustomed to how long his arms and legs had grown. And when conversation struck him as funny, he'd laugh almost to his own embarrassment, for he'd cover his lovely lipped mouth with his hand. When talk was sad, his whole face was open in listening, as if he had no wall at all that protected his heart.

"Yes, a very strange thing that I'm living now," Renato repeated. The eyes that watched him were alert, the irises as deep and dark as pupils. Renato didn't know why, but he wanted to talk about the English actress. He had told no one; now Meg Barker was the name that filled his mouth like a musky flavor.

He wanted to talk, but he decided not to. What could he say?

"I almost made love to a woman. I mean, not my wife," he said, surprising himself that he was saying what he had decided not to say. Maybe that was the effect that Duncan's face had on him: truth serum. For a strange moment, he figured he understood how women probably looked at Duncan.

"*Almost* made love to a woman?" Duncan's eyebrows went up.

"Yes. Almost. I was washing her foot in a sink, and she showed me between her legs, not that she *showed* me, but I saw because I couldn't help but see. And I didn't do anything about it, even though I *thought* about doing something about it, and I keep thinking now and rethinking and rethinking about that and other things, though that's not the thing I want to talk about because there are, of course, other things, much more important things, to talk about."

"You were washing her foot in a sink?"

"Yes, as I said. I was washing her foot. It would take a lot of

retelling to make you understand why I was washing her foot. Maybe
I'll tell you now. Maybe another time. We'll see."

"What was her foot like?"

"It was a very beautiful foot. Do you understand?"

"I think so," said Duncan. "You were washing her foot and it was
very beautiful." That was Duncan's way. He took you seriously, but
his smile held laughter. Gentle laughter, no malice. "And that was
almost like making love."

"Yes. But no. There was more, too. She smelled me and said I
smelled like honey."

"That *is* more," Duncan said and smiled.

"Which is why I say I almost made love, because to my mind, she
was disposed to making love. But we didn't. Though since then, in
my mind, we did. I mean, I've made love to her more than once, since
then, in my mind. Which is why I feel we almost really did make
love."

"Which is why you feel guilty."

"Guilty? No, I wouldn't say that. Or maybe yes. But it was
strange, now that you say it, because what stopped me was that I
thought of Milena. I thought of my wife." He poured more wine into
both glasses. "I thought of her when we first met. Milena. Years ago."
He sipped wine, then cleaned his lips with his thumb. "I don't know.
But that's only the smallest part of what I'm feeling in these last days,
last weeks. Maybe last months. With the funeral, and the dam, and
everything. I don't know. You understand?" He laughed at himself.
"I haven't said anything, and I ask you if you understand."

Duncan said, "I took pictures of Angie's foot. Her foot was beautiful, too. You remember Angie? *Everything* about Angie was beautiful. Her foot's over there on the wall, next to the stereo."

"Ah! The photos. They're new, no? I saw something changed
here. Yes, the photos. I wanted to ask."

"New? A couple of months, I guess."

"And they're photos of Angie, you say? I remember Angie. The
English girl you brought to my house, no? Was it dinner we had
together or lunch?"

"Angie. Yes." Duncan fell silent.

"I thought she might be here when I came."

"She went back to England." Duncan laughed softly. "Forever."

It was Renato's turn to be silent. Then he said, "And these pictures are all of her?" He stood up and went to the wall near the stereo. "Here, this is the sole of her foot? Yes, you're right. It's a very beautiful foot. And this? It's—Wait, it's the place behind her knee?"

"Close. The curve of her elbow." Duncan rose from his chair and gave Renato a tour. "Here's her armpit," he said, pointing to a black-and-white near the kitchen sink. "Over here above the bed is that soft place at the center of her throat, and over there is the palm of her hand. There's her ear, and a nostril, by the door, and the edge of her breast is beside the window."

"Yes, I noticed."

"And her other nipple—nice close-up, don't you think?—is next to my closet. Her eye is above the window, and it watches me across the room when I'm in bed, and if you want to come into the bathroom, I've got a shot with her belly button in the upper left and the very beginning of her pubic triangle in the lower right corner of the picture. Looks almost abstract, like a dark moon in a white sky rising over dark, mysterious woods."

"Later. If I have to piss later in the bathroom, I'll take a look, *grazie*." They sat back down at the table.

"Her face?" Renato realized what was missing from the room.

"Exactly," Duncan said. "She didn't want anyone to recognize her." Silence. Duncan drank some wine.

"Tell me," said Renato, drinking more wine.

"Tell you what?"

"Everything."

"You tell me first, Renato. About almost making love. About the strange thing you're living in the last weeks."

"Not so important, the things I wanted to tell you. I can always tell you another time. But I came to see *you*. Tell me what you have to tell."

"There's not much to tell," Duncan said, pushing the hair out of his eyes. "Or maybe there's too much. I mean, it was a stupid situation from the beginning, which I knew, and I was almost glad about the *impossibilità*, yes the *impossibilità* of things. But then I did what I promised myself I wouldn't do."

"What did you do?"

Duncan said, "I fell in love."

SIXTEEN

Images

Angie. What can I say about Angie? I don't know if I can do it, tell you everything in Italian like this. Difficult enough in English. Maybe impossible.

Angie—a smell, a taste, a touch. Subtle colors. Definitely a touch against the skin. Magic, much too magical. Tears me to pieces.

I no longer know what part of her is real and what isn't. She's already become a myth. And maybe even when she was here, sitting there in the same chair you're sitting in now, her hand reaching out across the table, her fingers playing with mine, maybe all I saw was a myth of her, my myth. Did I ever see *her*?

Stupid, thinking this way, because I know that she was a girl. A woman. I mean, she was a person like any other. But I say that and it feels like sacrilege. She wasn't any other person. She was Angie.

Sacrilege. You see how far gone I am? I've turned her into a religion! My brain tells me I shouldn't. But since when did I listen to my brain?

I had been with other women before. Before coming here. One woman in particular. A long relationship, but you know.

You know when you see a woman who really hits you as a woman? That sensation of magic? I love the way you say it in Italian:

It's a feeling *of the skin*. Like something electric. That's what I was missing. Before Angie.

So when I came to live in Italy, I was looking, I suppose.

I mean, I had work in America. Good work as a photographer. Photos for newspapers. Weddings sometimes. Shots for advertising for smaller companies. And portraits. All freelance stuff. It was a living.

Yes, I probably could make a living here doing the same. Probably will someday, when I get tired of the daily job at the winery. But I don't know. I needed a break. I'm not sure I want to live by selling images of Tuscany. Another sacrilege, if you understand me. I *live* here. Do I really want to take picturesque postcard shots of grapes on vines, and terra-cotta tiles on rooftops, and old men walking with canes, all just to satisfy someone else's dream? Probably will, though, someday. Inevitable, in the end.

Anyway, that was my life.

I left it behind. Left the woman, too. Her last comment to me was that I was impossible to make content. And she made this prophecy that, because I was leaving her, I'd find myself lonely and nostalgic for everything that once had been mine.

Better to risk loneliness, I told myself, and perhaps find wild, ecstatic joy. Better to breathe with the windows open. Better to be free. Was that selfish? Was that wrong?

Hard to ever know the truth. Whatever.

Which is why I can't be angry with Angie now. Crazy, but I understand that she's trying to live. How can I be angry with her for taking herself away from me?

An interesting little lesson in any case. Hang around the world for a while and you get to try every role and see things from every angle.

I've had too much to drink. I'm talking too much. But you understand, don't you? I can see you do. My life or yours, doesn't matter. All interchangeable stuff.

That's why you and I are friends.

※

Angie, I was saying. I guess that's what I was looking for when I came to Italy. Totality. No more half dreams. No more half happiness. I wanted total life and total sex, total joy, total beauty. Total beauty more than everything else. And it *is* here.

Total beauty, which in some moments I think I've found. Surprises me, because much of the time I'm totally alone.

Total beauty. Angie. My God.

You know what happened. I came to Sant'Angelo D'Asso. Asked around, found the job here at the winery, found this apartment to rent. Didn't speak Italian. Started going crazy cooking dinner for myself and eating it at the table by myself and wondering what I'd do to make the evening pass before I could fall asleep.

Life at the winery was just work. But there was this scintillating expectancy to everything! Even in total solitude sometimes, even in being totally sad! An amazing feeling of waiting on the brink.

I mean, my first year here I was glad to know you and Milena, and it was great to come to dinner at your house—still is. God knows how we understood each other without words in common at first. But, you know, those were dinners. Every now and then.

I was waiting for, for someone to come into, to come into my bed. Blunt, but true. Not just sex, but sex, too. Yes, sex, too. Plus all the rest. Coffee in the morning. Dinner cooked for two. Evening walks together to look at fireflies like angels of light in among the olive trees. And your hand in somebody else's.

But even in the waiting, there's that expectancy that vibrates inside your skin. I was waiting, almost as if I was making myself ready inside. And the sunsets I saw by myself! The smell of jasmine in the night! Total beauty, waiting for another pair of eyes.

So this woman I work with. Secretary at the winery. No, nothing ever with her. But she travels a lot. Has friends from the rest of the world. Lives here in Montalcino. Just this woman and her cat. House in the country, outside town. Comes to work one day and tells me she's going away for a couple of months. Doesn't matter where.

What matters is that she tells me an English friend of hers named

Angie is coming to keep an eye on her house and the cat while she's gone. Says she knows I love animals, so could she give Angie my number in case she needs any help with the cat?

Maybe this woman was playing Cupid all along. I don't know. The woman goes and Angie comes.

I told myself not to expect anything. Still, every time the phone rang after the woman left, I kept wondering.

One day the phone rings and it's Angie. Introduces herself. The cat had gotten into a fight with another cat and Angie's all upset because she can't find the tail, which meant it was no longer connected to the cat, and she didn't speak Italian, and did I know how to get in touch with a vet, and how would she explain it to the woman if anything happened to the cat, and things were already bad enough because the cat was now without a tail.

No problem, I said. It was a Sunday morning. No work. I'll be there in ten minutes.

In the car on the way, I told myself she was probably old and ugly and unpleasant, even though her British voice on the phone had sounded beautiful and young. Don't expect anything, I told myself. Help her with the cat. Nothing else.

I get there. But you know her. You've seen what she's like. Maybe my first impressions weren't even so memorable. I mean, to look at, she didn't appear a wildly passionate person, but there was something in the way she looked that let you know there was a lot underneath. She looked like . . . But you know Angie.

Didn't she remind you of a cat when you saw her? I know all women are supposed to be catlike, but with Angie, didn't you think it was true? She could seem tense, to make you keep your distance at first. Then she'd purr, and pull you in close. And with that body. How slim she was. She had studied ballet as a teenager. Dancer's body. And that mane of dark, dark, red hair. And those eyes.

See that eye in the photo up there above the window? See the eye?

We get in my car and I drive her out to the vet. End of winter this was. Wasn't much blood coming out of the cat, but Angie was holding it in her lap, and she had wrapped a paper towel around the little stump that was left of tail, just in case.

She was holding this stumpy thing in her hand while she was talking, just a spot of red blood on the white paper towel, and she was telling me about why she was happy to be here, to be out of England, to get away, to try something new. She told me she had to get away from her boyfriend, because after four years, things weren't going well enough. Or maybe they were going fine, but she wasn't sure, and she had to be sure she wasn't compromising. Did I understand? she asked.

Yes. I said I understood. Yes.

And I was trying my hardest to listen without hoping for too much.

So yes, she said. They had decided to take a break from each other, or maybe even to finish with each other forever. They weren't sure. But they did know they needed time apart. And the way she was feeling now, she said, she had already started to think that she'd probably never want to go back again.

Then she was quiet, and looked me in the eyes with those eyes of hers while I was driving, and she gripped the cat's stump in her hand. Cat didn't seem to be in too much pain, to tell you the truth. He rubbed his forehead into Angie's stomach. Started to purr.

At the vet's office we found out the vet didn't have an assistant. So we helped. I was holding the cat. The vet gets out a needle to put in stitches to close up the wound, and the cat decides to leave.

I was wearing my leather jacket at the time, and Angie saw the cat clawing the life out of my jacket and said she was sorry because it was a nice jacket, and she felt that this was all her fault and she felt so sorry.

Don't worry, I said. It's only a jacket. And secretly I was glad for the chance to be magnanimous.

But she felt really bad, she kept on saying while I was holding the cat and the vet was stitching up the stump of the tail. And Angie asked what she could do to help. If you really want to be helpful, I said, you could get me a mint out of my jacket pocket. And she did. She fished the packet out of my pocket, because my hands were busy with the cat, and then she put a mint in my mouth. I felt her finger touch my lips.

I still have the jacket over there in the closet. The front is all scratched. It's become a souvenir, a reminder. You understand?

For a week after that, we had to give the cat an injection of antibiotics every day. We did it together. Angie held the cat on the bed, I gave him the shot. So we had dinner together at her place a couple of times after we gave the cat his shot.

One evening after dinner, she said she really shouldn't say what she was about to say.

I asked what she was about to say.

She said she was about to say she wanted to make love. Did I mind?

I said I didn't mind. We hadn't even kissed, and now we agreed to make love. We both felt awkward for a second, but then we laughed, and then we kissed, and a little while later we were in bed.

That was the first time I made love after, I mean, the first time I made love after a long, long time of being alone.

It was winter still, as I said. The end of winter. There was a full moon that night and the light from the moon came straight into the window of her bedroom and onto the bed. The sheets were white, but in the moonlight they looked blue. And Angie's skin was very smooth over those slim curves of hers, and her skin was very fair, but in the moonlight it looked silvery blue. I was stroking hair away from her face with my hand while I was looking down into her eyes, and her mouth was deep in blue shadows, and the shadows along the side of her neck were an even deeper blue.

That smooth skin and that clean, clean body, the welcoming eyes, the blue moonlight on the crisp, clean sheets around the naked two of us. So beautiful I thought I might cry for a happiness that I didn't know how to name.

And just then the cat climbed up on the bed with us and started rubbing its head against us. I almost got embarrassed to let go of myself with the cat there, as if he were a child or another person in the room, but then I told myself he was only a cat so I could go ahead and even enjoy the sensation of all that soft, purring fur while Angie beneath me was moving like a cat herself. And the cat seemed so happy, as if he wanted to take credit for doing a good job as matchmaker.

Whenever I think back to that moment—and I think about it a *lot*—all I see is blue.

About a week after that, she came to my place and we took the black-and-white photos. It was almost the start of spring, and we took the photos with the window open here. If you look, you can see the goose bumps on Angie's skin when the breeze blew in from outside. And that's when she told me that it would be best if I didn't take any full photos of her face, just in case her ex-boyfriend ever came to Italy, just in case the photos ever got into his hands, just in case he started asking why she let her body be photographed without any clothes on it.

And I told her what I had been telling myself ever since she had first started talking about her ex, or possibly ex, which was that I was almost relieved she was still halfway tied to someone else, because that would be a sort of natural limit to stop me from doing what I always tended to do, which was to lose my head completely and to start too soon to think about lifelong love. This way, I promised us both, we could enjoy each other for the moment, and neither of us needed to think about the future, because there probably wouldn't be love, but at least we could make the present an amazing, ecstatic explosion of whatever it was that was exploding.

And I said lots and lots of sensitive-sounding shit that I really believed at the time, because I was determined to love every moment we had together for as long as it lasted without letting myself fall in love.

You're right to laugh. Have another glass of wine.

Did I tell you she was an artist? She knew how to paint, though most of the art she did was to collect little things. She went around gathering bits of wire, pieces of string, tomato can labels showing old-fashioned maidens holding out baskets of fresh tomatoes, the absurd yet beautiful pieces of waxy paper you use here in Italy to wrap up oranges on fruit stands—she collected things for their aesthetic secrets, and then she assembled the things into something new.

Anyway, she noticed my erection when I was taking the close-up black-and-white photo of the soft skin just under her arm. I got embarrassed and said that great artists and photographers probably didn't get erections when they were doing nudes. She said that of course they did. She said it was precisely that tension that gave great nudes their electrical charge, "that feeling of about-to-fuck."

So we did.

My God. Sounds crude, but it isn't, the words, the way to think about these things, but it was so *physical*. A celebration, a sanctification of the body in the most jubilant sense.

Maybe it was because she was an artist, I don't know. But she had an astuteness, a way of *noticing* and making conscious every small physical sensation and impression, everything you usually leave unobserved. So everything became sex—brushing your teeth while taking a shower, putting on a jacket, getting a mint out of a pocket, walking down the street, breathing the air.

I think I'm getting drunk.

And I remember a comment she made once. She needed to earn some money, so she started working as a landscape architect, or a gardener, or whatever you want to call it, in other people's gardens. When the weather warmed up she liked to work barefoot so she could feel soil and pebbles with her feet. Otherwise, she said, there wasn't contact with the earth. She noticed things like that.

A couple of months later, it was springtime in full. The hills were green outside, and the wheat in the fields was still very young but it vibrated with that bright technicolor green color it has when the sun comes out after lots of rain and the wind blows across the fields like waves. One afternoon, it was a Saturday or a Sunday, we had made lunch here at my place and then decided to stretch out after lunch. The sun coming in the window was already too hot, so we closed the green shutters outside the window and the light that came in through the slats in the shutters was green; my whole apartment was as green as the inside of a curled-up leaf and the two of us lay beside each other on the bed.

And for a little moment there we were almost at peace. She told me she loved me. I had been feeling like a dead tree before we met, but lying in bed beside her, snoozing in the afternoon, life inside me felt all green and possible again.

Oh. Then there was, yes, then her boyfriend, or ex-boyfriend, or whatever, came to see her. She said she was nervous about his visit, but glad for the chance to settle things once and for all.

He came. I didn't exactly hide, but I took up my life again, while he was here, as if Angie and I had never met. To give them time together to do whatever it was they had to do. I tried not to think about them, about Angie's mouth on his.

I remember his name, you know. Of course I remember his name. But I don't like saying his name. I don't even like thinking it. Nice enough guy, I'm sure. But why couldn't he simply have died?

You laugh. I'm laughing, too, to hear myself.

Anyway, Angie telephoned me a couple of times during the week he was here. In secret—she found an excuse to go into town by herself and get to a telephone. She told me things were very tense between the two of them. Tense and sad. She said the days were passing terribly and that they spent a lot of time fighting and crying.

"And making love, of course?" I asked like an idiot.

"Of course. I thought that went without saying," she said. But their lovemaking, she said, was very sad and tearful because it was their way of saying good-bye.

I said, "We'll see." Saying good-bye is never as easy as it seems, I said. And he still had a few more days to go before he left, so now it was natural for them to fight and cry and rationally make plans to leave each other and all the rest, but when it's his last day here, I said, you'll see that sometimes the final good-bye just doesn't let itself be said. And sometimes, I said, it's only when two people face what it means to say good-bye that they realize they never want to say good-bye.

"But the relationship is over," she said. "He's leaving next week, and that's that."

I said, "We'll see."

"No, you'll see. I love *you*."

And that made me close my eyes on my end of the phone, because for a moment I let myself hope that it was true.

She made an appointment. Said that after he left she wanted a day to herself, to put a little space between being with him and being with me. But on Wednesday evening, after I finished work, could she come by my place?

I told her that of course she could come.

You wouldn't believe the lectures I gave myself, in those last few days until Wednesday, the good advice, the pleas for clear thinking. I talked to myself till I grew tired of my own thoughts. They're not saying good-bye to each other, I told myself. They're only now learning how to say hello.

Still, she'd said she loved me. And she knew better than I did what was going on inside her heart.

By Wednesday morning I was out of my head with hope and doubt. Doubt was more intelligent, but hope had the louder voice in my brain.

I woke up at a quarter to five. Couldn't sleep. Dawn was starting. Couple of hours still before I had to go to work, so I decided to take a walk.

I walked down the main street, out through the big stone gates, out into the fields outside the town. There was dew. A summer morning, and the green fields of wheat seemed more red than green. You know what it's like when the poppies are out. The hillsides go red.

Everything around was amazingly beautiful, and Angie was coming to visit me that evening after work; in my mind I had already done the dangerous thing, which was to attribute all beauty in the world to her, as if she had created it. All beauty came from her and belonged to her and was to be shared with her. You see how she had become a religion to me, despite my more intelligent doubt? I guess I was in love.

I walked back to my apartment an hour later with hundreds of poppies in my arms. To keep them fresh until the evening, I filled the kitchen sink with cool water and let the poppies float around. All day at work I wondered if the poppies had shriveled up or if they were still bright and fresh and red in my sink.

I left work a little early. The poppies had survived the day. I patted them dry with a dish towel on this table here, then I decided to play with the red color, to make something artistic for her because she was an artist and I wanted to talk to her through color, a language she might understand.

My house stank of poppies by this time. Did you ever notice how much poppies smell? The air in my house stuck in your throat. So I opened the windows wide.

Then I got to work on the white bedspread there on the bed. I started to write a word with the red flowers on the bed. It was the word that was closest to my heart. I didn't want to waste any time with evasions. Why not simply say what I felt?

Maybe saying it in English embarrassed me. Maybe saying "Welcome Back" in English seemed too silly and ordinary. But I wanted her to feel welcome again in my bed, wanted to say I was happy if she wanted to come back. So I wrote in Italian. We were in Italy, after all, and playing with the Italian language had been a little game between us.

That's what I wrote in big red letters of poppy flowers across the big white bedspread. *BENTORNATA!*

I figured she'd be so moved she'd hug me and we'd fall on the bed together and become all red ourselves, with the flowers touching our skin. Funny how imagination works, don't you think?

The doorbell rang just when I had finished. I threw away the last remaining stems and went to the door.

When I opened the door, she didn't seem to want to hug.

"Hello, Duncan," she said with an official-sounding voice, as if the State Department had sent her to tell me my brother had been killed in the war.

Then she sniffed the air for a second, catching the stink of the poppies, and she looked past me and saw the white bed all decorated in red. She went over to the bed, looked down at the lettering. She exploded like a storm.

"How dare you assume I'd be coming back to your bed?"

I could see from the first words where the conversation was going. Why had I been foolish enough to listen to Hope? Should have trusted Doubt.

Her voice softened after her explosion. She said she was just confused. Said I had been right on the telephone. When the moment comes to say good-bye forever, people do tend to rethink.

He was saying now that he wanted to marry her. He was sorry for cheating on her some in the past, for having taken his time to make up his mind. But now he knew his mind and he wanted to marry. He was offering everything she had always dreamed about: a house of their own in the English countryside, a garden of her own. Not just somebody else's garden to plant and water and weed, but a garden of her own that she could care for year after year.

She talked on and on. I looked down at the bed and saw the *BENTORNATA!* written in red poppies. I felt like an idiot.

She followed my eyes, then she started to cry. "But the problem is," she said, "I care too much about you. The flowers are beautiful. And so is the thought. No one's ever done anything like that for me before. I want to remember it forever. I wish I could have a picture of this bed, to cheer me up when I feel down."

"You want a picture?"

She laughed, even though she was crying. She said, "You're the photographer. Couldn't you take a shot of this for me?"

So I went to my camera bag. I had opened a box of film and was about to load the camera when she said, "No. Wait."

Then she said something that has been driving me crazy ever

since. She said, "The flowers are beautiful because they're ephemeral. The ephemeral is beautiful. Don't take a picture. Don't try to make the flowers last."

The ephemeral is beautiful. That thought kills me, because it means the opposite is true, too: Beauty is ephemeral. It blooms and dies. It doesn't last. Kills me, that thought.

And being with her had been so beautiful that sometimes I used to wonder if beauty was enough, if there could have been something more to hope for. Or maybe all we were to each other was a quick aesthetic high, like a little drug trip or something, thrilling and ecstatic, but then the effect wears off.

Problem for me is, though, I still feel the drug. I still feel the beauty. The smell of her perfume is still around the throat of my black sweater that she borrowed a few times. Her presence is still here, but she's gone.

Fine that the ephemeral is beautiful, but what good does it do you? It disappears and you have your memories left, but your memories hurt because the person is gone.

Does everything beautiful have to disappear? I don't know the answer to that one. That's what kills me.

We cleaned the poppies off the bed. Threw them away. "It *was* a sweet thing to do," she said.

She cooked some dinner over there in the kitchen. We sat here at the table and drank some wine and stayed up late talking. She said she had to get up early in the morning to do a job in the garden of a house not far from town. Said she really ought to leave now. But the wine was making her sleepy, and she had always liked my house, so would I mind if she spent the night?

Of course there was the cat to feed back at her place, the tail-less cat whose wound was all healed. She said she could go and feed the cat early in the morning on her way to do the garden at this other house. If I didn't mind, that was, her staying for the night.

In bed—there were little black poppy seeds all over the place—

she told me that in a couple of weeks she'd be leaving. Going back to England. Garden of her own, she said again.

And yes, we made love. Our turn to be sad and tender and tearful together.

She was gone when I woke up. She must have slipped out early.

That wasn't the very last time we saw each other, but it was one of the last. What's stuck with me, though, is an image. Mental image. Nothing on film.

It happened by accident. I couldn't get back to sleep once I woke up and found myself alone. I was cold. It was one of those strange, gray, wintry mornings that can happen even in early summer. I got dressed and figured I might as well drive out to the winery and start some paperwork I had to do.

The sun was just coming up over the hills when I drove through the gates, out of town toward the winery. Everything was gray and soft. And cold. And the sun was a dark red ball that came over the hill.

I stopped the car on a curve along the road to watch the red sun in the dark gray sky. I opened the car window and felt a damp breeze. I realized I was crying. The tears were cold on my cheek.

Then I looked down in the valley. Farther away than I could have thrown a stone, there was Angie. That was the garden of the house where she had to work, down there toward the valley. She had on the same jeans she had worn the night before, and she had on the thin gray sweater that she always kept in her car. I figured she must have been cold, though, because the wind was stinging.

She had her back to me. When the wind blew, I saw her straighten up, as if she were exposing her body to the wind on purpose, right through the thin sweater. That's the picture that's stuck of her. Angie standing alone in a garden on a chilly dawn, the wind touching her skin despite the sweater, probably raising goose bumps, her hands bare, her feet in work boots, her red hair thrown about by the wind, Angie standing up to offer herself, as if she welcomed the touch of the wind, as if she were a thing grown up out of the earth, like a strand of nerve, ready to receive. Gardeners are sensual people, she had said once. I thought: So this is what she meant.

That's the last picture I have of her. Dark gray everywhere with a touch of red from the dark red sun. Beautiful image, too. The last portrait of ephemera. Angie in the valley, her body probably tingling in the wind, too far away for me to call to, or touch.

SEVENTEEN

Ephemeral

Silence. Renato didn't know what to say. Duncan, he could see, was somewhere else, standing at the edge of the road in the cold dawn.

"Have you got a pencil?"

"What?" Duncan said, blinking.

"Have you got a pencil?" Renato asked again.

Duncan came back into the room as if waking from a dream. "Yes. I suppose. Why?"

"Because I need a pencil, that's why. *Facciamo una cosa*. Let's do a little something. Give me a pencil."

While Duncan stood up to get a pencil from the bedside table, Renato reached into his back pocket and pulled out the scrap of paper. He looked at the two names in his own handwriting:

MARGHERITA

MILENA

The piece of paper had already become great and important to him, though he would not have known how to explain why. It was a reminder of what he wanted to be sure not to forget. It held the names of people who mattered to him. And these were the names he wanted to have with him, close to him, when he did as his dream had instructed him to do. It was right for these people to be with him when that mystical change should occur.

Duncan handed him the pencil. Immediately Renato added another name to the list. He wrote

PETULA

beneath his wife's name. He didn't know what thing in particular his daughter would wish for, but of course her name should be on the list, too.

Duncan saw the piece of paper with the pencil-written names. His curiosity was tickled by the evident seriousness with which Renato wrote the name Petula. Duncan sat down, sipped from his wineglass, and said, "This list means?"

"Hmm?" Renato appeared startled, for he was deep in thought. "Oh. The list. I want to write down your name, if you don't mind. And I want to write down the thing you said."

"What are you talking about?"

"What am I talking about?" In Duncan's eyes he saw the smile that endeared the man to him. "*Bella domanda!*": Good question. "What am I talking about? It's not to be explained easily. I'm talking about, as I told you, the fact that I'm living a strange thing. A very strange thing. To say it in a few words, life doesn't taste of anything anymore. Sounds absurd, but it's true. And I don't know why. And I don't know how to find the taste again."

Duncan was quiet for a moment. He scratched the side of his head. He said, "Maybe that's just life. Maybe the taste is missing for everyone. I read this wonderful line in a book the other day. You make me think of it. I can't stand quoting, but I have to tell you this quotation. It's too good. The Portuguese poet Fernando Pessoa. He said, 'Literature, like all art, is the confession that life isn't enough.' I read that sentence and I thought, 'Oh! That's why I read so much!' It was almost comical, reading in a book the answer to why I read books. Yes, I think he's right, I'm looking for something. And maybe that's why I take photographs, too, trying to make beautiful things even more beautiful. Maybe that's why Angie is an artist. Maybe simple life on its own isn't enough. Maybe you're looking for something else, Renato. But, I don't know, are you sure there's something to find?"

"Am I sure?" Renato reflected. "Yes, I'm sure. Because I know what I've lost. That's the strange thing I've been living lately, as I started to say." He scratched his beard. "You know, I was happy before. I think I knew it. But anyway, I'm not a person to torture myself too much over whether I'm happy or not. But now all of a sudden, wife, daughter, work, home, waking up, going to sleep, making love, drinking wine—nothing touches me anymore. Everything in my mouth turns to sand. Now I know I'm not happy, but *I* am the thing that's changed, no one else's fault but mine. And I don't know how to undo the change. Do you understand what I say? Everything in the past used to have more taste. Now I can't feel joy. Not even sadness, really. And definitely not joy. Only the feeling of having lost something dear. No taste left.

"But think of yourself!" he went on, suddenly coming alive. "Think of the tastes you found, yes, even with Angie. With Angie in particular! You said it yourself. You said Angie was a smell, a taste. Think of the passion you felt with her. And the beauty you found was real."

"But it's gone. She was right. It was ephemeral."

"Yes! That's what you said. That's what I want to write down." Renato seized the pencil and wrote out the words.

L'effimero è bello.

"'The ephemeral is beautiful.' And next to the words we'll put your name."

DUNCAN

he wrote.

"And what was it that Signora Vezzosi said? Yes, that's what she said. She said, 'In an instant, a lifetime disappears like a dream.' And I answered her, 'But life renews itself.' I tried to convince her, anyway." He wrote the sentences in small letters, as an annotation beside her name. "And Milena? I suppose she didn't say any one particular thing. But she, like me, wants things to change. So that's what we'll write here, her wish: '*That things may change!*'"

Renato was not aware that he was speaking aloud while he wrote. Duncan watched. He said, "Renato?"

"Ah, yes. Excuse me. But now, you see, I've written your name on this piece of paper, too. Your name and what you said."

"I don't know what you're talking about," Duncan said, laughing.

"Then maybe I should explain." And Renato told him about his dream, about his wish to help Signora Vezzosi by putting her name on a scrap of paper, about Milena's jealousy when she discovered the scrap of paper. "Because she thought Margherita was that English actress woman and not Tita Vezzosi."

Renato talked and talked, explaining what had been happening inside him lately. When he finished, his American friend said, "You put my name down, too? Thanks," he said, laughing, "I guess. But why did you write down what Angie said, about the beauty of things that don't last? You wrote it down as if it were the answer to something, but I don't—"

"An answer?" Renato said. "No, I don't think so. Almost a question. But no, I wrote it down because you said that's what is killing you. You see, I listened to every word you said, and that's what you said, you said, 'That's what's killing me,' not so much that the ephemeral is beautiful but that beauty is ephemeral. It's killing you, you say, and I care about you too much for that. I don't want anything to kill you. An answer? Maybe no, but there must be an answer to that idea somewhere. You're sad because that thought makes you sad."

"I'm sad because I wonder if I'll ever find something with someone, something that will last. Right now, I don't think I ever will."

Renato stared hard at his friend. Staring hard, he saw him as he was. He saw a passionate young man who, capable of putting red poppy flowers on a white bed to try to touch a woman's heart, was certainly capable of doing such a thing again. And the time would come again. How could it not? Here he was, this man looking for

love, sitting in his house surrounded by black-and-white images of
his beloved's eyes, of the edge of her breast, of the sole of her foot, of
the corner of her mouth.

Renato wanted to say so many things, but how many things can
you say to another person, especially another man, even when the
man is your friend? Renato said, "You'll see. Trust me. You'll see."

"That's your answer? 'You'll see. Trust me'?"

"*Sì*. You'll see. You only have to wait a bit. Things have seasons.
It's a season of loneliness you're living now. But you think there won't
be new poppies when spring comes again? Of course spring will
come! Of course the poppies will come, too, and so much other beauty
that you, for now, can't foresee. And you want to know why? Because
I see the beauty that isn't so ephemeral, the beauty inside you. And if I
can see it, then some springtime woman will come and see it. Angie
saw it, too, I promise you. Even if she did decide to go away. She was
no idiot, that Angie. She saw inside you."

Duncan reached for the wine bottle. He filled his own glass.
"Some more?" he asked, but Renato wagged a no with his hand, saying it was probably time for him to leave. "My friend the waterworks
man," said Duncan. "Funny," he said. "I'm very happy you came."
He laughed to himself. "Can I ask you for a favor? Put her name on
your list, too. I want her to be happy."

"Of course." Renato took up the pencil again. "We'll put it here
next to yours. Next to the sentence about ephemeral beauty."

ANGIE

he wrote.

"I'll have to start writing smaller, or maybe write on the other
side, if I add any more names. Tell me, Duncan," he said, smiling
mischievously, "should we be magnanimous and forgiving and put
down the name of Angie's English boyfriend, too? You said you
know his name."

"I know his name, yes. And magnanimous would be the gracious
way to be, but, magnanimously speaking, I still want him to die.
Leave him off your list."

The wind was uncomfortably warm as it swirled into the car windows in the downhill darkness on Renato's way home. Could be the scirocco, Renato thought. The scirocco was a wind that nobody liked, for it brought only sweaty grumpiness and impatient discontent. But if the wind wanted to come, there was less than nothing Renato could do to make it go away.

La vita si rinnova, Renato said to himself. Life renews itself. That's what I told Signora Vezzosi, and pretty much that's what I told Duncan, too. Life renews itself, as I'm sure it will become new again for them. But when will life be born again in me?

EIGHTEEN

Noticing

It was hot. Renato twisted. The sheet and the blanket were too much. Renato smelled his own sweat. Rolling over again, he threw off the blanket. "*Dio boia!*" he said.

It was better with only the sheet covering him, but not much better. The window was open, but the breeze that came in was as hot and wet as animal breath. Renato scratched his beard, then scratched his scalp quickly, as if he had fleas. "*Dio boia,*" he swore again. He twisted over to his other side.

"I can't sleep either." A voice in the moist darkness.

"What?"

"I can't sleep either."

"How long have you been awake?"

"Since you returned. How was Duncan?"

"Duncan? Fine. No, maybe a little down. He's lonely. He misses love."

"I understand."

"How do you mean you understand?"

"I mean I'm sorry he's lonely, Renato. That's what I mean. How else should I mean? Don't be so touchy!"

"Me, touchy? I'm not touchy. I'm just hot." He rolled in Milena's direction, found her face with his hand, kissed her forehead. It was clammy. He said, "Let's try to sleep."

A minute later he was looking into the darkness, listening to her breaths. He knew she was listening to his breaths, too. Her breaths did not sound to him like the breaths of a sleeping person. Neither, he figured, did his to her.

"Milena?"

"Hmm?"

"You asleep?"

"Yes, Renato. I'm asleep in this very moment. And I'm having a dream. I'm dreaming I'm lying next to a man who has gone halfway out of his head."

"Oh, that's wonderful," said Renato, "because I'm having exactly the same dream." He turned over again, pulling the blanket over his shoulders. It was too breezy in the open-window bedroom for the sheet alone, too humid for the sheet and blanket both. Scirocco. No ease to be found.

Once, several years before, he didn't remember when, he had seen a television program about old torture instruments. One French device was a box, a simple box. What made it a torture instrument was its size. The dimensions were such that a prisoner, closed inside, could neither stand up, nor sit down, nor stretch out. The condemned was forced to assume bent-over positions that invariably became uncomfortable. The punishment was the body itself. The image of the box had stuck in Renato's mind. And now, trapped in his bedroom beneath the sheets of his bed, Renato understood how the condemned must have felt.

Bad wind, the scirocco. Truly a bad wind.

"Milena?" he said.

"Tell me," said his wife's voice.

"Do you ever notice things? Little things, I mean. Things that give you pleasure."

"In this moment, no."

"I don't mean now. In general, I want to say. Tell me something. Tell me something physical, a little detail, something that, when you feel it, makes you feel alive."

"Why do you want to know?"

"I heard about an Englishwoman who noticed all sorts of physical sensations, and it was an exciting, sexy thing when she described them."

"For the love of God! You're still talking about Meg Barker, the English actress!"

"What Meg Barker?" He had hoped that the subject of their fight earlier in the evening had passed, had been left behind in the restaurant kitchen. "Who was talking about Meg Barker? No. Duncan was telling me about the English girl. Angie. They came to dinner together. You remember her. She was always telling him about the little things of the body she noticed. Her descriptions pulled him close to her. So now you tell me. Tell me something you notice. Something you like. Not now. But in general, I want to say."

"Renato, are you putting me to the test?"

"No, of course not. Not really, I don't think. Not a test. A favor. I'm asking for a favor. Please. Can't you tell me one little thing?"

Silence. Milena breathed out. "Give me time to think about it. I can't pull something out of the air, just like that. Give me time. I'll tell you when I notice a thing. Okay?"

"All right. You'll tell me then. Okay."

More silence. "And you, Renato?"

"And me what?"

"Can you tell me some little thing that you like, that makes you feel alive?"

"If I could tell you that, Milena, I wouldn't be going halfway out of my head. I wouldn't be going to Rome to see the pope. I wouldn't be carrying other people's names in my ass pocket. I added Petula's name, by the way. And Duncan's. Did I tell you that? That I wrote down Petula's name? I don't know what she might want, but something inside me told me to write her name, too." He laughed in the darkness, feeling almost relieved. "If I could tell you one little thing that tasted of something, I wouldn't have asked you to tell me something you notice for yourself."

He found her face with his hand again, and this time kissed her lightly on the mouth. He rolled away, turning his back. "Good night," he said. "Let's hope to sleep, with this wind. And remember your promise to me, that you'll tell me when you notice something. Then you can recount it to me, and maybe I'll understand life inside your head."

"*Buonanotte*. If only I could understand life inside yours."

NINETEEN

The Hand Writes

Renato received with gladness the hand that hovered above his bed. The hand was masculine and strong. The ring on its finger, the red stone on the ring, shone with the light of authority and truth.

The hand summoned, urging him to rise from his bed, just as it had before. Renato floated along the darkened corridor of his house, past Petula's bedroom, flying with the same weightless ease. Whether or not his bare feet skimmed the ground as he floated, he couldn't have said. He felt cool. Confident, cool, and light. Happy to follow.

Renato was aware of rough stone beneath his feet only when he found himself standing before the well in the courtyard. His cat rubbed its sides against his ankles again. Renato felt the softness of the fur, heard the purr.

The hand disappeared inside the well, then came out a moment later. It held a fine feather quill.

A scrap of paper lay on the lip of the well. Renato recognized the scrap of paper. It was his list.

The hand rested on the piece of paper. Then, with the quill, it started to write. Renato could see the list as he had written it:

MARGHERITA—*In an instant, a lifetime*
disappears like a dream.
But life renews itself.

MILENA—*That things may change!*

PETULA—

DUNCAN—*The ephemeral is beautiful*—ANGIE

The hand was writing quickly, adding other names, other pieces of puzzling truth. The list grew before Renato's eyes. The names were so numerous that Renato couldn't move his eyes fast enough to read them all. Not now, not in a lifetime.

The hand continued to write. What touched Renato then was an electrifying sensation of complicity. The hand could have been his own, or his whole body could have been held in the palm, his own fist holding the feather pen. He knew it was right to be scribbling names on his list, though he didn't know what good it might do.

Falling backward into blind sleep, Renato felt sure the hand knew what he himself was doing, secure that the hand approved.

TWENTY

Petula

The next morning was like any other. Renato's rituals were the same as always, yet to him everything seemed to have changed. Or maybe everything was about to change. Hard to say what was in the air, but there was certainly something.

He got out of bed in darkness. While he dressed, he lingered in a sense of promise and reassurance from the visit of the hand in his dreams. But when he walked along the corridor past Petula's bed-room, that feeling quickly gave way to antsiness, as if everything known were about to become unknown, as if he might open the front door only to find that the stone steps had disappeared and he would free-fall to the hard courtyard below, or tumble off forever into space.

He opened the front door: The steps were still there. The scirocco had filled the courtyard with damp, uneasy warmth. He hoisted up a bucket of water from the well to wash his face. The water cooled him, and the cat rubbed around his ankles. "*Ciao,* Micio," he said, opening his eyes. But the cat looked up, and switched mood, suddenly becom-ing paranoid. The cat stared at Renato as if scrutinizing a stranger, then darted away.

The stamping of the sheep's hooves in their stall, the tinkling of the bell around the first sheep's neck seemed restless. Renato opened the door to the stall and all four sheep bolted out. The hooves tapped a nervous dance in the courtyard while Renato went into the stall to set up the milking stool and fill the feed pail from the sack of grain. Usually he liked the warm animal smell inside the stall. This morning the smell seemed an acrid stench. "Prima!" he called, but the first sheep didn't come. He saw her out in the courtyard: She pretended not to have heard him.

In the end he had to go out and haul her in, grabbing a handful of fleece at the back of her neck. She protested with a high-pitched bleat.

The second and third sheep were reasonable enough, but Quarta, the fourth, always prone to fears of cosmic persecution, was inconsolable when Renato tugged her teats. Even the olive tree leaves he gave her did little to calm her. She turned her head to watch him with the corner of her eye while he milked. She interrupted her chewing to open her mouth in burbled, pathetic cries.

Man and sheep were all relieved when the milking was over and it was time to take a walk up on the hillside behind the house. The sun was climbing in the sky and the breeze was damnably warm.

"Bad wind, this scirocco," he told the sheep as he sat down on the ground. He meant to comfort his little flock, to remind them that, when this particular wind blew, no creature was comfortable with life.

The sheep chewed grass.

Petula looked strange to Renato when he sat at the breakfast table. Milena was at the stove, pouring coffee into three cups.

How Petula seemed, he wasn't sure. How did she seem?

She seemed to have something in her. He recognized the look he had seen ever since she was a little girl, every time she transparently tried to conceal a secret. It was not so much her way of looking at him as her way of not looking at him. She sat at the table in her bathrobe and slippers, the same as always, but her eyes were fixed with fascinated concentration on the sugar bowl. She seemed to prefer staring at any meaningless thing to looking directly at him.

Usually when she wore her secretive expression, she appeared very much a little girl. This morning, though, she seemed a woman, intent on barring a man from touching something she had inside.

Milena brought the coffee to the table. "*Grazie,*" said Petula to her mother, the way a houseguest thanks a host.

She put sugar in her coffee in silence. She stirred. She sipped. Finally she said, "Babbo," looking Renato in the face.

"Tell me all, little mouse," he said.

"I want to have a key to the house." She dunked her breakfast cookie into her coffee, then bit it when it had gone soft.

"Why do you need a key? We're all here in the morning when you go to school. I'm always here for lunch. In the evening, even when *la Mamma* is at the *bottega,* you know you only have to ask for the key and she gives it to you."

"I want a key to have all the time. My own key."

"But why? Milena, when did you ever have a key to your parents' house?"

"Never," said Milena, sitting down in front of her coffee cup. "I was at home with my parents or at the *bottega* with them. Then you and I got married, and to their house I no longer needed a key. But things are different today, Renato."

"Why are things different today? I never had a key either. Not until my parents died and the house was mine. Fine for me. And it was fine for you, Milena. For Petula, why should it be different?"

Petula put her cup down too loudly in its saucer. "My God! What world do you live in? I'm seventeen years old and I'm only asking to have a key. Maybe sometimes I want to open the door by myself in the afternoon when no one is here without having to ask. It's logical, no?"

"According to me," said Milena, "according to me, she's right. Why can't she come into the house by herself?"

"Why not? I'll tell you myself why not. Because she doesn't want to come into the house by herself, that's why not! She wouldn't ask such a thing if it were only for herself. No! She wants to come into the house with that boyfriend of hers when we're not here, Milena, you and I. I'll tell you that. She wants to be by herself with him."

"He has a name, you know." Petula asked herself why, out of all the fathers in the world, hers had to be the stupidest and most stubborn. She snorted air out of her lips.

"Don't puff at me like that. Of course I know he has a name. Your boyfriend, like every other person in the world, has a name." A thought of Duncan flashed in his mind. Duncan, too, held secret animosity for an unutterable name. He, too, wished that the bearer of that name might go ahead and die.

"His name's Daniele," Petula said in the tone of voice people use when talking to an imbecile.

"This kid's staying with my daughter for what, a year, two years? and he cuts his hair in the same strange way she cuts hers, and together they look like a pair of mutant soldiers on patrol, and you think I'm not supposed to know his name? His name's Daniele. There! I said his name. Happy?"

"I don't care if you like my hair or not. It doesn't matter a pig's fart to me. Daniele likes my hair, and that's the only important thing to me."

"A pig's fart!" Milena laughed. "I like that."

"Fine," said Renato. "I'm happy for you that your boyfriend likes your hair, but he can like it outside my house. He can like your hair in the back of a car or under a tree or wherever it is you go so that he can like your hair, but coming in my house to like your hair when no one else is here, that's asking for too much. And you, Milena, instead of liking the pig's fart, you could do a little more to take my part in this one. Do you hear how your daughter talks to me?"

"*My* daughter? Now this daughter is only mine?"

"I'm seventeen years old," Petula said again, wrapping her bathrobe tighter around her torso. "And don't think that Daniele's never been here alone with me. He has. Lots of times. When Mamma's at the restaurant and you're out at work. You see, we come here together even without a key. So why not be open about this thing and do everything under the light of the sun? Why sneak behind your backs? Let's be adults here. I'm old enough to have a key."

"You've come here together, just the two of you, lots of times?"

Renato lost his rhythm. "Of course you've come here! Of course I knew that." He refound his stride. "Why do you think I didn't know that? And I'm not monster enough to try to forbid such a thing. It's natural that you and, that you and that boyfriend of yours should want to be alone. No, I won't forbid a thing of this kind. But to give you a key would mean to permit, to permit everything. To give you my permission and my benediction, and to say, 'Whatever you two do is wonderful for me.' But you can't expect that much from me. I care about you too much for that."

Petula was put off balance by words of affection. Then she said, "I care about you, too. But I also care about Daniele. And in my opinion, if I'm old enough to have a baby, I'm old enough to have a key."

"Then that's clear, no? You reasoned it out for yourself. You're not old enough to have a baby, therefore you're not old enough to have a key. Logical."

Renato looked at Petula. Petula lowered her eyes to the sugar bowl. Renato looked at Milena. Milena gave him an I-don't-know shrug. Renato took a mouthful of his coffee and noticed that it had turned cold. He put down his coffee cup and stared at the top of Petula's down-turned head. He said, "Petula?"

No reply.

"Petula?" he said again. "Come on, little mouse. What is it?"

Petula closed her eyes tight to stop herself, but a tear ran down her cheek. She sniffed and wiped her nose with the sleeve of her bathrobe.

"Petula?" Milena said, wrapping her arm around her daughter's shoulder.

Petula cried. Renato said, "Oy-yoy."

"But, Petula," said Milena, "but I thought you were—I mean, I didn't know."

"These things can happen," Petula said. "I've heard people say. And it happened to us. Happened to me."

Renato stared at Petula's mouth, which was wet with tears, wet from her running nose. He imagined that mouth with Daniele's mouth, that mouth on him, his mouth on her, their hands and fingers on each other and in each other. Natural, of course, he knew, but this was his Petula. And certain images he shouldn't be forced to contemplate. And she was, after all, still only a girl. He said, "Are you sure?"

She nodded. "The menstruation hasn't come to me for two months. I went to the pharmacy in Siena yesterday before school and bought a home pregnancy test. I did the test this morning. Just now. Yes, I'm sure. Will you give me a handkerchief?" she asked. Milena reached to the countertop near the kitchen table. She took a paper handkerchief from the packet and handed it to Petula. Petula blew her nose, then laughed. "So I decided it was time to ask for the key to the house."

Renato felt his intestines become as cold as his coffee. He blinked. "And the next step?"

"The next step?"

"The next step."

"Daniele doesn't know yet. I mean, I told him I thought I was pregnant, but he doesn't know the result of the test. I'll tell him later today. His parents have to go to Siena to buy things for the bar. He's working by himself today. I'll go and tell him. About the test."

"Does he want to marry you? Do you want to marry him?"

"You're joking! Marriage?" Petula seemed amazed. "We talked about the possibilities of what to do, but marriage wasn't one of them. We don't believe in marriage."

"I understand," said Renato. He nodded his head slowly, as if he understood, but he didn't understand at all. "You don't believe in marriage. *Dio boia,*" he said, nodding his head.

He thought for a while. Petula, holding the paper handkerchief in one hand, started eating her breakfast cookies with the other. Milena looked lightning-struck. She asked her daughter a lot of questions in as calm a voice as she could manage, and Petula replied. Renato was no longer listening. He was too busy with his thoughts.

He reached a decision. "Well," he said, "seeing how things stand, I want you to know that I'm disposed to help."

Petula said, "Help how?"

"Help in doing whatever's necessary."

"For example?"

"For example, I don't know. For example, if they need my signature, I'll sign."

Milena said, "Renato, what are you talking about? Who said anything about your signature? Your signature for what?"

"For the procedure. I mean, I never really thought about abortion. Is it right? Is it wrong? I don't know. Never thought. There never was reason to think before. But maybe it isn't so important, what I think. What's important is that you know I'm disposed to help. You're underage, but you can have my signature. And if money is needed, too, then I'll help pay for things also. Does the National Health pay for these procedures? Well, even if they don't, you can count on me to help."

Milena and Petula both looked at him as if he represented not only a different gender but also a different species, maybe a species from another planet, as if the words he said had been spoken in an alien and unintelligible tongue.

It was Petula who ended the silence. "No one is asking you to sign permission for any operation. Who's considering an operation?"

"I thought that's what you were asking me for."

Petula said, "The only thing you can do is accept things as they are."

"Accept things?"

"Only accept. You need to accept. You can only accept."

"Accept?" He shook his head.

Renato beheld the two women in their solidarity as if they were now the creatures from a different planet. Conversation at this point was useless. Conversation to say what? He had to think first. He needed time. They needed time, too. Petula needed time. Milena needed time. Time would clarify thoughts. Time would do *something* to put the world back on its course.

He swallowed the final mouthful of cold coffee, put down his cup, stood up, and announced, "I have to go to work. We'll talk more about this later." He leaned over and kissed Petula on the top of her head, the part of her that still seemed little girl-like. "*Ti voglio bene.*"

He kissed Milena on her cheek. "And you, too. I love you both. We'll talk more later. Now get ready for school and I'll give you a lift to the train station. I have to go to work."

"I'll walk to the train station if I decide to go to school."

"If you decide to go to school?"

"Yes. If I decide. But today, I don't know. Maybe I'll go to the bar and talk with Daniele instead."

"A wonderful way to start," said Renato. "Does this mean you plan not to finish school?"

"Of course I'll finish school. It's my last year. I should be able to finish before the baby. I'll finish somehow. I just don't feel up to going today."

"Come on, Renato," said Milena. "A day off from school won't do any harm."

"Wonderful. No school today. I have to work, all the same. We'll talk again later. *Ciao.*"

Petula said, "And the key to the house?"

"*Facciamo una cosa,*" Renato said, leaving. "Let's do a little something. Let's think for a time. All right?"

"I'm only asking you to accept," she said again.

"Then maybe you're asking for too much. *Ciao.*"

He grabbed his jacket and headed out the front door. Yes, the stone steps were there; all the same, leaving his house, Renato felt himself free-falling into the unknown.

Without thinking he patted the back pocket of his work trousers. The action had become a reflex. A quick double check. The list was exactly where it belonged.

He stopped by the well. He reached inside his jacket pocket and pulled out a ballpoint pen. He placed the list on the lip of the well. Beside Petula's name he wrote what she had said to him. He wrote:

You can only accept.

Accept? he said to himself and again he shook his head. Easy in theory, acceptance. But maybe Petula was asking for too much.

TWENTY-ONE

Petula's Boyfriend

Gunning his Fiat, Renato pulled out of his driveway and onto the main road. He had to go up to the waterworks building to check the pressure in the pumps.

Pregnant, he thought, shifting gears, feeling the clutch slip. My daughter's been making love. His body with hers.

He remembered how hungry his mouth had been for Milena during their first years together. He thought about Petula's boyfriend going at her with the same carnivorous zeal.

Daniele. Of course Renato knew his name! He knew his last name, too. Mangiavacchi. Daniele Mangiavacchi. What a terrible significance the name implied: Eater of Cows. Well, Petula was certainly no cow.

The whole Mangiavacchi family was a clan of *grezzi,* of crude people. The word around town was that Aldo Mangiavacchi, Daniele's father, ran the bar beside the train station up the hill only so that he would never have to reach far for a bottle. Most bar owners were decent enough people. But Aldo Mangiavacchi was always red-eyed and loud-mouthed from helping himself to his own stock in the same way that the man who ran the pastry shop was fat from sampling his own creations. Mara Mangiavacchi, Aldo's wife, was a shapeless, sullen woman. Her short-fingered hands were always quick to take customers' money.

Her mouth never thanked anyone. With people who frequented the bar she was not known to swap jokes, only complaints. "Look how they throw paper napkins and garbage on the floor!" she would grumble to anybody willing to listen while a group of customers laughed with one another and talked before catching their train to Siena or before going to work. "And who do they think will take the broom and sweep up their dirt? Fifty times a day I take the broom and sweep, if not a hundred times." Her heavy, bovine eyes watched Aldo with recrimination. When he talked to a customer, she muttered that he was wasting time. Every time he took out the glass that he kept for himself behind the bar, every time he refilled it, her eyes took note.

Everyone in town could recall the not very rare occasions when one of Mara's eyes was bruised. "She says she fell down the stairs again," folks would say in confidential tones, as if discussing a matter of secrecy. "What kind of stairs do they have in that house that she's always falling down them? Falling down against her husband's fist is more like it. But with people like that, what do you expect?"

When Daniele was a young boy in the town, Renato used to feel pain, almost, to think of a child growing up with parents like the Mangiavacchis.

Driving over the bridge and up the hill on his way to the waterworks building, he saw two cars coming down the road in the opposite direction. The first car, an old Fiat 126, was driven by an old man. The second car was tailgating the first car so closely that it seemed to want to mount the little Fiat 126 from behind. "Imbeciles!" Renato said aloud. "It's not necessary to give it up the ass to everyone else when you drive!"

The two cars passed him and he saw that the aggressive tailgater was none other than Aldo Mangiavacchi. His wife, Mara, was in the passenger seat beside him. In the brief passing, Renato had time to notice that Aldo was talking volubly, gesticulating with both hands, apparently unaware of the Fiat 126 he was busy buggering with his car. Mara's face was a switched-off lamp. If she was listening, she gave no sign that she cared.

Renato watched their car disappear in his rearview mirror. Strange that he should be thinking so intensely about the Mangiavacchis and their son, and then see them driving along the road. For a moment he imagined his thinking was so loud that the Mangiavacchis had heard his thoughts even from their car.

But of course not, he told himself. And his thoughts returned to Daniele, to the man-boy who had knocked up his daughter.

He remembered the first time he had really taken note of Daniele, really studied him. It was maybe two years before, when Daniele was seventeen, and Petula was fifteen, and the two of them began to be seen in each other's company. Petula talked her parents into going to see the concert of the Sant'Angelo D'Asso Musical Society Band. The concert was in the church.

So Renato found himself sitting in a church pew one evening, Petula on one side of him, Milena on the other, the three of them surrounded by an expectant throng of eager parents and sons and daughters and boyfriends and girlfriends, all come to hear their musically inclined loved ones play. When the conductor took the stand to great applause, when he prompted the band to start and the sounds of trumpets and trombones and tubas and flugelhorns and saxophones and clarinets and flutes and fifes and drums and cymbals and snares reverberated with monumental echoes off the church's vaulted arches and walls, Renato asked himself why he had come.

"That's Daniele," Petula said, pointing to a saxophone player in the third row.

"You don't have to tell me," Renato said. "I know who he is."

Petula was all eyes during the concert, watching her Daniele with the same evident adoration seen on the faces of the frescoes on the walls, the faces of saints and angels beholding the radiant splendor of their Lord.

She's fifteen, Renato told himself while the band played. She's too young.

He scrutinized the face that his daughter was busy worshiping. He saw a good-looking young man with the mouthpiece of a saxophone held tightly between his lips. The body was long. Long fingers played notes on the sax. The shoulders were becoming broad. The face was losing its childlike softness. Renato was looking at someone who was no boy. Not yet a man, but definitely no longer a boy.

Daniele's jaw was shaded by the beginnings of a beard. The hair was held in place by loads of gel, one single lock of hair falling across the forehead. *Tirabaci* was what the kids called a lock of hair positioned on the forehead that way. *Tirabaci,* a kiss attracter. During his pauses for breath, Daniele moistened his lips with his tongue. His lips grew swollen from effort as the concert went on.

Daniele's eyebrows knit together when he played, furrowing the forehead. His dark eyes were intense with concentration. He looked like an artist, his lean face consumed by the worries of the world. When the band finished its pieces and the audience applauded, his face became a smile. His eyes found Petula's, and between the puffy red lips white teeth flashed.

Renato was torn apart by recognizing all that was attractive in Daniele. Why couldn't he be ugly, or insensitive, or dim? He would have been easier to keep as an adversary.

During the intermission Petula ran up to be with Daniele. Renato could see how thrilled she was to have an intimate connection with one of the musicians, to be able to sit with him in the wing of the church where the band members had placed their instrument cases, to be included in the privileged world of musicians offstage.

"She's fifteen," Renato said to Milena during the pause.

"It's natural," said Milena.

"But he's seventeen. He'll eat her alive."

Petula came back to her seat for the second half of the program. Laughingly she whispered to her parents why Daniele had looked so fraught during the first half. "His reed was broken. He tried his hardest, but he couldn't play any notes at all."

Renato felt he had the upper hand for a moment, seeing that Daniele's situation was ridiculous. But the difficulty with the reed had only made him seem more tender in Petula's eyes. And now in the second half Daniele was relaxed, blowing into his sax. Renato couldn't single out the sound of the instrument, but he suspected Daniele probably played it well.

A year or so after that, Daniele started growing his hair long. Petula started cutting hers short. In the end they arrived at their common middle ground: shaggy and long in front, shaved close to the skin behind. As a couple they had their look. In his own head, Renato started calling them the two mutant soldiers. Bad enough for them to be together, but did they have to look like each other as well?

Renato pulled his car into the parking lot in front of the waterworks building. His driving had been jerky and too fast all the way there. He skidded slightly when he yanked up on the hand brake. The car stalled, cutting out before he'd switched off the key.

Now my child is with child, he said to himself. And she wants that other Daniele child to be her man.

And all of this, she asks me to accept. Does she truly think I'm crazy enough to accept such a thing?

The hot wind blew dust across the parking lot. Bad wind, this scirocco. Bad wind.

He opened the door to the waterworks building and heard the comforting, bestial roar of the pumps. He wanted to work hard today, to exhaust his body and leave no energy for his mind.

TWENTY-TWO

The Note

When Renato came home for lunch, the house was empty. Nothing unusual. Milena was always at her parents' restaurant for lunch, except for the one day a week when the restaurant was closed. Petula often caught the lunchtime train back from Siena, but not always. Sometimes she liked to stay with her friends in Siena, having lunch at a bar instead.

Today Renato had counted on finding her at home. He was hoping to have a talk. In which direction he wanted their talk to go, he had no idea. At work all morning, his thoughts had resolved nothing. He felt dizzy headed and befuddled, as if he had been punched.

Petula wasn't home, though.

He opened the windows in the living room and in the bathroom and in the kitchen. He wanted to change the air in the house, wanted to clear out the warm scirocco breeze.

He opened the refrigerator and stared in, looking without seeing, losing himself in thought, as if some answer lay waiting to be read between the jar of capers and the half a lemon.

In the end he took out a wedge of the pecorino sheep's cheese he had made himself the week before. The wedge was wrapped in gray paper. He shut the refrigerator door.

He could go to the *bottega* and eat anything he wanted, he knew.

Some pasta to start with, then a grilled piece of red meat or maybe chicken. A salad to follow, and then some fruit. But going to the *bottega* would mean dealing with Milena's father, who really was no problem, and Milena's mother—a person more problematic than Milena's mother would be difficult to find. Would Milena have told her parents about Petula's pregnancy? If she had, then Maria Severina's comments would be insufferable. If she hadn't, then keeping up the pretense of life not having taken a wild left-hand turn this morning would be unbearable, too.

Better to have lunch at home by himself. Better to eat cheese and bread.

He placed the wedge of cheese on the table. He opened the brown bag of bread from yesterday. He put the bread on the table next to the cheese.

A glass of wine, he decided, was perhaps more important than the bread, more important than the cheese.

He opened the cupboard where he kept a bottle of the wine he had bought from Signora Vezzosi. Then, before he had time to pour himself some, he noticed a piece of paper on the countertop, a note from Petula.

He read the note. Its contents made him sick.

In an instant he lost his appetite, lost all desire for a glass of wine. Not taking the time even to close the windows in the kitchen or in the bathroom or in the living room, he ran out of the house, got in his car, drove over the bridge and on up the hill toward town.

The note on the kitchen counter said:

Babbo,
I'm going to the bar to be with Daniele. Please come there as soon as you can. He telephoned me and told me his parents are dead. I beg you to come.
                                        Petula

TWENTY-THREE

In the Tunnel with No Light

By dinnertime, all that could be done for today had been done. The terrible events of the morning had been talked about, cried over, analyzed, and talked about again.

Now everyone sat around a table at the *bottega* of Milena's parents, the inevitable venue for the aftermath of important occurrences in town. The *bottega* was the natural place to go: There was Milena at the *bottega* and there was food.

Daniele did not talk much. He ran his fingertips over the prongs of his fork again and again while staring at the tablecloth. His fingertips were red from the scraping and almost started to hurt because of how many times he kept running them over the fork prongs. But that tingling fingertip pain was welcome, it was good. It was a relief from the disbelieving numbness he felt inside.

He smoked a cigarette.

His parents were dead. He was nineteen years old. This morning he had woken up with two parents. A few hours later he had none. He didn't know if his life was over, too. Or maybe it was just beginning. He didn't know what to think. His parents were dead. And when Petula came to the bar after he called her, she was all helpful and consoling. Then she cried with his crying, and in the middle of her crying it came out of her that she was definitely going to have his child. His parents were dead, and in six or seven months his girl-friend would make him a father. Those were the only two facts in his head, but those facts were big enough to eclipse everything else in the world.

Daniele stared at the tablecloth. He played with his fork. He stubbed out his cigarette and lit another.

Looking at Daniele in his seat at the table was like looking at a turtle without a shell. That's how Renato saw Daniele: vulnerable, unclothed. Never before had Renato felt so strong a temptation to give the boy a hug.

Daniele played with his fork. Renato, sitting across the table, drank from a glass of wine, his eyes on Daniele's downward-looking face. He saw a young version of himself.

Daniele did not say much, so Petula did the talking. She had been doing most of the talking all day. When Renato, after reading the note, had rushed up to the bar beside the train station, it was Petula who explained what had happened.

She told the story Daniele had heard from the police.

Aldo and Mara Mangiavacchi had been on their way to Siena to buy some things for their bar from a discount warehouse. The Siena-Bettolle *superstrada* had always been notorious as a dangerous road. Heavily trafficked, this highway through the countryside had only one lane in each direction. Slow-moving trucks were often followed by lineups twenty cars long. Cars tailed each other impatiently, nose to ass, nose to ass. And when the opportunity presented itself to over-take the truck clogging the road in front, the cars jumped lanes, com-peting to be the first to pass. This racing to get past trucks was con-stant on the Siena-Bettolle *superstrada,* and it occurred in both directions. Head-on collisions, the consequences of impatience, were common. Many people died on the Siena-Bettolle road. Volunteer ambulance drivers in small towns along the road were kept busy.

Daniele's parents in their Alfa Romeo 33 had been tailgating a gigantic trailer truck, waiting for the first chance to zoom ahead. Aldo Mangiavacchi flashed his lights at the truck and beeped his horn. But the truck driver had no place to pull over and let the Mangiavacchis pass. At least that's what the driver of the truck later told the police.

When the highway almost reached Siena, there was an open stretch of road leading to a tunnel. Aldo Mangiavacchi shot into the tunnel, only a few feet behind the truck, unable to see anything of what the truck might have had ahead.

When the truck's driver suddenly stepped on the brakes, Mangiavacchi was going too fast to stop himself, and the left-hand lane was occupied by a van. Having no place to go but straight ahead, Mangiavacchi slammed into the back of the truck.

The hood of the Alfa 33 crunched underneath the back of the truck. The steering-wheel shaft impaled Aldo's sternum. Mara's face broke the windshield.

Then a Mercedes, which had been shadowing all of their motions from one or two seconds' distance behind, hurled itself into the tail of their car, pushing the Alfa 33 the rest of the way under the truck. The roof of the Alfa was crushed.

Daniele's parents were dead.

The wounds to the Mercedes driver's face and head were minor, for his heavy car had protected him. He was able to tell the police what had happened, though in his recounting he added some extra distance between his Mercedes and the Mangiavacchis' Alfa. He was always a good driver, he assured the police.

The truck driver was unhurt. He explained to the police that he had been forced to slow down abruptly because in the dark tunnel he had come upon a small Apino three-wheeler that some farmer was driving, hardly creeping along at all. The farmer, whose little vehicle was loaded with crates of vegetables, had forgotten to turn on his lights.

There was no sign of the farmer or of his motorized vegetable cart. He had most likely continued on his way, unaware that he had caused death.

Numerous police cars appeared to redirect traffic, to take information from witnesses, to wait for the ambulances. It was an ugly thing, an accident inside a tunnel. Police work, clean-up work, was conducted in the close, echoing darkness that stank of fumes. Nasty place to work. Nasty place to die.

A police car was dispatched to give Daniele the news.

Daniele had been washing glasses in the sink behind the bar. He had been talking to customers waiting for their train to Siena. He had been smiling a lot.

The table at the *bottega* was cluttered with what was left of everyone's dinner. Plates held bits of green salad, chicken bones, yellow oil from the *bruschetta,* white pieces of fat trimmed off prosciutto. Some glasses had the remains of red wine; other glasses were half-filled with water, effervescence gone.

Daniele had eaten something; not much, but something.

Milena's parents took turns eating, getting up to serve other customers, fetching things from the kitchen. Milena was on her feet almost constantly, not letting herself sit down.

Renato caught on quickly that Milena had told her parents about Petula's condition, too. At one point, Milena's father sat down in the chair beside Renato. When he was sure no one else was listening, he said confidentially, "I'm sorry for the boy. Terrible thing to happen. Terrible thing indeed. But as for this other thing with my granddaughter, Petula, you listen to me, Renato. You do the right thing. Wait until discussions pass, and then you come in with the voice of reason. You see that a surgical intervention is done. They're too young, you know. And they have no intention of marriage. I'm sorry, but it's up to you to insist they do the proper thing." The man spoke into Renato's face. His breath smelled of meat.

"Petula doesn't want a surgical intervention," Renato whispered. "Maybe we have to let her decide for herself."

"She's too young to decide. You're her father. The decision must be yours."

As for Milena's mother, Maria Severina, ostensibly she passed no judgment in particular. But she moved through the evening wearing her pained expression. From time to time she let out a sigh, along with the words, "Poor Petula," or "Poor us," or "Poor Milena," even "Poor Daniele," though the Mangiavacchis had been a couple to whom she had not addressed so much as a *buongiorno* in more than ten years. Secretly she was pleased that her *bottega* this evening was the meeting place for the most interesting event in town. Everyone in town would be talking about the deaths on the highway, and the people closest to the dead couple were sitting here at the table with her. She made a great show of her grief. She was visibly grieved for everyone present, in her stout, boarlike way of showing grief, yet never once did she say "Poor Renato." She made clear, with sharp-eyed glances, that everyone was poor except for him. He alone was not the victim of circumstances; somehow these lamentable happenings were all his fault.

Renato couldn't think why his mother-in-law would want to blame him for the life-and-death happenings of the day, but he was not about to ask. What she thinks of me is of no importance, he said to himself.

He remembered Petula's words from this morning. He said to himself, I don't give a pig's fart what my mother-in-law thinks. He almost laughed.

He got up from his chair to help clear the plates. He left the plates in the kitchen, then went behind the bar to where Milena was making coffee for everyone. Renato could see that she was distracting herself with work. "And what do you think about all this?" he asked quietly, into her ear. "In the middle of everything, you still haven't told me what you think. This morning you seemed to take Petula's news with great calm."

Milena pressed the espresso coffee into the filter. "What does it matter what I think?" she said, not interrupting the rhythm of her work. "My thoughts I can think to myself later. She's my baby, that's all I know. If my baby has a baby, nothing changes."

"Hmm." Renato wanted to respond, but he was too full of feeling. So he said nothing.

Milena pointed to a place on the countertop. "Give me that tray. You can take the coffee out to the people."

"Can I pour you a grappa, or something?"

"Maybe in a minute. Maybe a little drop of grappa is a good idea. No, Sambuca instead. Take the coffee over and I'll come in a minute."

Back at the table, Renato handed out coffee. Petula, he noticed, was on her feet, going to get something from the kitchen. Renato gave Daniele a cup of coffee. "*Grazie,*" said Daniele, taking the cup.

Renato didn't know what to say.

Then Petula returned. She stood behind Daniele's chair and ran her fingers through the longer strands of his hair, the hair cut the same way as hers. Responding, Daniele closed his eyes, turned his head, and pressed the side of his face against her stomach.

Renato watched, transfixed by the sight of his daughter soothing the head of the young man. In that living image he saw everything there was between them. He saw how Daniele took comfort from Petula, just as Renato had found comfort in Milena ever since being orphaned before having fully become a man. He saw how much Daniele needed Petula, and how much she needed him, too, now that the life they had created together was growing inside the belly against which Daniele laid his head. The couple looked like a new family in Renato's eyes. He saw their friendliness together. He saw the natural touch that occurs between two people when they belong together. He was witnessing their love. She's still a little girl to me, Renato thought, but my little girl is living through a lot of woman things. She'll have a baby soon. And she's the only person in the world for the boy who lost his parents today.

Renato could *see* everything between his daughter and her young man. Seeing and accepting, though, are not the same thing. Keep your eyes open and you will see; to accept you have to open other parts of yourself. Renato was trying to keep a portion of himself closed. Things around him were changing too fast. If he opened himself too thoroughly, he might risk being torn apart.

"You want some coffee?" Renato said to Petula, interrupting their scene.

"Thanks," Petula said. She kissed the top of Daniele's head, pulled away, and took the cup of coffee from her father.

People's coffee cups were empty when the telephone rang. Milena's father answered it. "Renato," he called to the table. "Come. It's for you."

"Tizzoni?" said the voice on the other end of the line.

Renato stopped up his other ear with his free hand, to hear over the noise of the restaurant. "*Pronto,*" he said. "Who's speaking?"

Renato hung up the phone, came back to the table, and sat down. Milena was in the chair next to his.

"Who was that?" she asked.

"Will you give me a drop of your Sambuca?"

"Take it."

He sipped the clear liquid from her little glass. The taste of aniseed sweetened his mouth. "It's good," he said. He sipped again, leaving the rest for his wife. "On the telephone? Sculati. It was Sculati. Sculati the *becchino*."

"The *becchino*? The gravedigger? What did he want? Drink the Sambuca if you like."

"No. The rest is for you. I don't know what he wanted. He didn't say. Said only that it was important that I come to his house right away. Says we have to talk. Very urgent, he says. Very important."

"His house? But he lives in the cemetery." She sipped from the little glass, too. "Fine, Renato. If it's so important, you'll go first thing tomorrow morning."

"Even more important than that. Says I have to go there now."

"Now? But it's night."

"Now." He stood up from the table. Noticing him rise, people turned their eyes to him. "*Ciao* to everyone. Maybe we'll see each other later. If not, then tomorrow."

"Where are you running to?" Why did an innocent question from Milena's mother sound like an accusation?

"I have a little thing to do. *Ciao*. Petula, we'll see you at home later. Daniele, good night. *Ciao*." He bent over to kiss Milena.

She turned her face up to him to meet his kiss. Her lips tasted of aniseed.

TWENTY-FOUR

The Palace of the Dead

Renato drove over the bridge. Then, in the middle of the road, his headlights flashed against the swift beating of broad white wings.

He stepped on the brakes to give the owl time to fly away. Everyone said that owls were bad luck because they symbolized a visit from death. Renato wasn't afraid. He liked the oversize white-bellied birds.

Anyway, death had already come. Death had been all around him for a while. He was swimming in death. What more could death do to him now?

The gravel parking lot to the cemetery was unlit. Renato parked.

The only points of light to be seen were the rows of flame-shaped lightbulbs that marked the vaults inside the cemetery walls, creating the unsettling illusion of lit-up windows in the palace of the dead.

The cemetery wasn't far from Renato's house. Like his house, it sat on the out-of-town side of the bridge. The cemetery was wombed off from the surrounding country by its high walls and ranks of cypress trees. The black trees stood tall, like gigantic, deep-rooted ghosts.

Renato walked, invisible to himself. His boots crunched on the gravel, and he smelled the evergreen smell of cypress sap. He came to

the gate and pushed. It was open. Renato was surprised. Oh, the
becchino left it open for me, he told himself.

Renato didn't know that Sculati never locked the cemetery gates,
not even at night. There was no need. Vandalism, desecration of
graves, didn't happen in a town like Sant'Angelo D'Asso. Besides,
there were some people who preferred to come at night to visit the
graves of the dead people they still loved. Renato was not one such
person. He had never been to the cemetery at night. He hadn't been
there that often during the daytime, either. He'd come a few times
when the plumbing needed attention, but his own personal visits were
rare. He came once a year with Milena on the second of November, the
annual Day of the Dead. The whole town went to the cemetery on the
Day of the Dead. If Milena didn't see to taking flowers to his parents'
graves, Renato would have been content to leave well enough alone.
What was the point of flowers? His parents couldn't see the flowers.
That was a fact. And the flowers did nothing to him one way or the
other. They didn't add to his loss; they didn't gladden his soul.

But probably he was glad anyway that Milena did take the flowers to his parents. Other families transformed the cemetery into an
open-air exhibition of brightly colored flora every year. Maybe it
would be a shame, after all, if his parents were left out.

He walked along the pathway down the middle of the cemetery
toward the chapel, and on the second floor the gravedigger's apartment. That was where Renato had to go.

In-the-ground graves flanked him on both sides. He walked by
his parents' grave, aware that he was passing them, but he didn't turn
his eyes to look because he wasn't sure he could deal with seeing their
grave at night.

The unwelcome notion came to Renato that if anyone ever got
around to asking him how he would want to be buried, he'd decide to
be placed naked in the earth. No clothes. No coffin even. No box to
imprison him in an airless cubicle of darkness. Only his nakedness
and the earth. Then rain would come down through the ground and
he would melt. He would become water and dissolve downward. He
would trickle into an underground water table. Then he would rise

again, *rinato,* like his name, reborn, reemerging upward to open air through a spring. He would evaporate and transform. He could become rain. He could become a cloud, then fog, or dew, or snow, or the sea. As water he would live forever.

He tried not to look around him until he reached the door beside the entrance to the chapel.

He rang the bell. He realized that he had been holding his breath. He exhaled.

He heard footsteps inside. "Who is it?" a voice said from the intercom beside the doorbell.

"*Buonasera,* Sculati. It's me. Renato Tizzoni."

"Come," said the voice. An electrical buzz unlatched the door and Renato went in. The stairwell in the stone building was dark and cold. He started to climb, then a moment later the door at the top of the stairs opened and he saw the silhouette of the gravedigger fill the lit-up doorway. The gravedigger was a big man.

"Sorry about the dark stairs," said the silhouette. "I need to change the lightbulb, but I keep forgetting."

"Don't worry," said Renato, reaching the top and letting himself be shown inside.

"Thank you for coming, Tizzoni. Now I'll tell you what I have to say and you'll understand why you had to come tonight. Come, take a seat here by the table. Make yourself at home."

Renato sat down and looked around him. The one-room apartment showed that a man lived alone here, that there was no woman to soften the bare functionality of table, chairs, bed, dresser, sink. Sculati, like Renato, was employed by the town: Renato to take care of the water, Sculati to take care of the dead. The town provided Sculati with the apartment at his workplace. Gravediggers in more modern towns no longer lived in cemeteries, but Sant'Angelo D'Asso was not one of the more modern towns. And the town administration, knowing that most men are useless at cleaning up after themselves, sent in another employee, a cleaning woman, once a week.

The apartment was clean enough. The whitewash on the walls was fairly fresh, the floor tiles recently swept. The bed was unmade, and the dirty dishes in the sink awaited the cleaning woman's next visit; still, there were no unpleasant smells.

All the same, Renato said to himself, this is no place where I'd want to sleep.

Sculati. Poor Sculati! Not that there was anything especially poor about the man, but people in town, on the rare occasions when they referred to the *becchino,* inevitably said, "Poor Sculati." Maybe because of his name. What a name! Sculati. Who could ever have given a family such a name? The Sculati Family. The Family of Unfortunates.

The gravedigger Sculati had lived alone in the cemetery all his adult life. No wife, no family, no anyone. Only the dead to keep him company. Maybe his name wasn't the only reason people called him "poor."

Yet there was something likable about the man. Looking at him, you wouldn't have been surprised if a deep laugh suddenly exploded out of his lungs. He had a large face that *should* have been given to joy. Instead, he was not known to do much laughing. He had a natural, heavy-footed dignity, which made him seem at home in his job. Still, behind the bulk of the body, behind the shovel-holding hands, behind the big, watery eyes, behind the fat-lipped mouth, there seemed to hide the laughter of life.

"Here," said Sculati, his hands putting down a bottle and two glasses on the table. "Keep me company while we talk. I have something to tell you. I'm thirsty." Sculati sat down. He had a way of making everything around him look small—the table, the bottle before him, the wooden chair on which he sat. His dusty trousers failed to contain his belly.

"None for me," Renato said. "What are you drinking anyway?"

"What am I drinking? I'm drinking what I always drink. Water. See? Water in the bottle. Nothing else. Everybody always says I drink. But you ever seen me drunk?"

"I can't say yes."

"*Bravo.* You can't say yes because you've never seen me drunk." He poured into both glasses. "Have some water with me, and I'll tell you what I have to tell."

Renato drank. The liquid seared his throat. "*Dio boia!*" he said. "If I drank this water every day, I'd have a liver this big!" He held out his hands to demonstrate the proportions of something swollen and about to burst. "You always drink grappa in such generous doses?"

"Not grappa," Sculati said delicately, "water. Remember, only water in this house." He poured all the liquid in his glass down his throat as if indeed drinking water. He closed his eyes for a moment, waiting for warmth to arrive. When it arrived, he opened his eyes and mouth and said, "The stories I could tell you if you wanted to listen, Tizzoni! Things I've seen for myself. Things I've seen people do. And you're a person who knows how to listen. It shows. I can see. Which makes me want to talk. I would tell you about the young woman whose daughter died, so now the woman—very pretty, to my tastes anyway, you know her, the daughter of that old witch who has the dress shop up the main street? Very pretty young woman she is, you know the one I mean, and her little daughter died only last year, but this young woman comes every day. Every day, would you believe it? And she brings dolls and toys to the tomb, and sets them up as if the little girl could come out and play.

"The things I would tell you, Tizzoni. The things I would say."

"This is why you called me?" Renato didn't want to be rude, but he could see that the grappa was taking hold of the man, and he didn't know where a conversation like this might end.

"They're like a club, you see," Sculati continued, refilling his own glass. "This young woman who brings the dolls, and the other mothers of the dead children. They're like a club. They visit their children every day, polishing the gravestones, cleaning up as if they were tidying their children's rooms, and they talk together like mothers waiting in the afternoon at the gates of the schoolyard." He drank his glass in one swallow. "There's some meaning in there, if you're willing to look for it, Tizzoni. The Dead Mothers' Club, I call them to myself. But of course the mothers aren't dead, but their children, yes. You see, there's a meaning in there somewhere. And you seem the kind of person who has the head to read meanings for what they are." He raised his eyebrows and smiled, waiting.

Waiting for what? Renato asked himself. What does he expect me to do? What meaning am I supposed to see in the way this drunken man talks?

Renato said, "Is this why you called me and told me to come?"

Sculati's smile dropped. He blinked. He poured himself another glass. "No, you're right, of course not, that wasn't why. No, I called you about something else, which we have to talk about right now. More water, Tizzoni? No? Then I'll drink some more myself. What I wanted to tell you is this, Tizzoni. The discussion is this. The choices you have are three."

"Choices?"

"Choices. Three possible. It's up to you to decide."

"Decide what? Here. Let me have another drop." Renato poured for himself.

"It's good for you, the water. Drink as if you were at your home. Decide? I will tell you. You will have heard about the Mangiavacchis? The barkeeper and his wife up at the bar by the station? You will have heard what end they came to today?"

"*Sì*. I've heard. Their son is with my daughter. I was finishing dinner with him and my family at the *bottega* when you telephoned. How could I not have heard?"

"Yes, then. Well, you have heard. But now there is another discussion. Now there is a question of their graves. Where to put them, if you understand me. We are a small town here, and the cemetery is smaller still. People die every year, and all must be accommodated in some place or other. Difficult, you know, when the cemetery never grows any bigger than its walls, but the dead people keep coming, more and more of them every year. Think how many old people there are in town! And they will need some place soon. You understand what I'm saying?"

"So far, yes."

"Good. Therefore, as you know, as I know, as we know every one of us, it is necessary sometimes to reposition some of the older dead to make room for the new. Some families, to avoid the repositioning of their dead, make provision, you know. They buy permanent vaults in the wall, or they buy permanent plots of ground, or the families that maybe once were noble have their family tombs. But these provisions mean lots of cash." He rubbed his thumb against his first two fingers, making the gesture of money. "Lots and lots of cash. It isn't cheap to make permanent provision. Cheaper to buy a car. Cheaper, almost, to buy a house. But this you already know. Which is why most people never buy at all, but pay the rent on relatives' graves, paying year by year."

"Is the payment due on my parents' graves? Is that why you called me here? Though I'm sure my payment isn't late. Tell me if I'm wrong. Of course I'll pay."

"Your payment's not late, Tizzoni. That's not what this discussion is about. Instead, the time has expired, Tizzoni," said Sculati the gravedigger. "That's the discussion here. The expiration of time."

"Now I don't understand."

"Then I will explain. It was twenty years and a couple of months ago that your poor parents died. Twenty years and a couple of months. I know because the records tell me the date. I know also because I remember it myself. It was I who dug their graves twenty years ago this summer. Twenty years ago, and I still remember you, young as you were, when you came to their burials. How young you looked! Looking like a young beast, a little lamb or calf or something, with the legs not yet steady enough to hold the body up straight! But you had to stand on your own in any case, didn't you? Of course you did! You had no choice."

Renato felt something move inside him, something that made him want to cry, something as powerful as a young man's fear, or sadness, or love. With his fingertip he played with the lip of the glass in front of him. He pushed the feeling aside. He said, "So?"

"I saw you, you know, and I remember," Sculati went on. "You see? I see everything. People think I drink, but I don't. People think I don't see everything, but I do."

"Where are you going with this discussion, Sculati? Twenty years, you were saying. Twenty years and a couple of months. So?"

"So the time has expired. Rented grave space in the ground lasts for only twenty years. As it is, you've had a couple of extra months. But that's not a problem. The problem is that the twenty years have expired—twenty years, as the regulations say, because that's usually enough time for decomposition to be complete, for only the bones to be left—and now the moment has come to decide quickly about the repositioning. Quickly I say, because the Mangiavacchis died today and the funeral is tomorrow and we have no place to put them. We must make room by repositioning the other dead whose time has now expired."

"My parents, for example?"

"Your parents, for example, in particular, yes."

"But you need my consent. And what if I say no?"

"Your choices, Tizzoni, are three. One, you can buy the plots of land where your parents are now sleeping. Do you have the money for that? You tell me yourself. Two, you give consent and we reposition them to a vault in the wall. Decomposition has probably finished, as I say, so they wouldn't even take up two big vaults in the wall. We can do what we usually do, which is to collect the bones from their graves and put them into the small caskets, for bones. Much smaller, as you will know. Take up much less room. That way we can put both little caskets of bones in the wall together, and even with the two of them they will need only one vault, shared. The headstones aren't a problem. Those we will mount on the wall to show which tomb is theirs."

"Or the third choice?"

"The third choice is the *ossario,* the common bone room under this very building where you and I are sitting now. It's under the chapel, just below our feet. Here is where we put bones from old graves when it becomes necessary to reposition the dead who no longer have families to pay the rent. It's not a bad choice, if you choose it. Simply a place of bones, promiscuously mixed." He paused. "I'm sorry to ask you to choose, Tizzoni. I have no alternative. All of the other ground space in the cemetery is either old graves purchased by families or rented plots that still have not expired their twenty years. There are no other candidates, as fortune would have it. The common bone room could be an answer, if you don't want to buy the in-ground plots, or if you don't want to buy even the less expensive solution of the vault in the wall. Or of course . . ."

"Or of course?"

"Or of course, if you don't decide at all, I mean if you don't give your consent, then the common bone room is where your parents would end up in any case. But the choice, as I say, is yours. And I hear your thought, you're thinking so loud! You're thinking, Why all this fuss now? Why worry about where to put old bones and new dead, when everything'll be underwater anyway as soon as the dam gets built? That's what you were thinking, no? Of course you were! And you're right to think such a thing. But think it through some more. The cemetery here is far enough out of town, and high enough out-side the valley, so as not to find itself underwater when they build the dam. Funny, if you think about it. I'll be one of the few people in town to stay in the same place, even when the new lake comes. I'll still be here to keep an eye on the dead! In any case, the decision you must make must be made now. Am I making the discussion clear?"

Renato's fingertips slowly circled the lip of the glass. "Why not just put the Mangiavacchis in their own wall vault and leave my par-ents alone?"

"They would need two, not one. And who will pay all that money for their wall vaults? Their son, Daniele? Now that he has the bar to run all by himself? I don't think he has that kind of cash. Do you think he does? He will have inherited work to be done, but not much cash. Was it any different for you when your parents left you in your house by yourself?"

Renato started to think. He was quiet while his brain turned over the possibilities. He felt the gravedigger's big wet eyes watching him, but he didn't care. He needed time to think, though there wasn't time. Yes, he calculated, he probably could get the money together to buy his parents' plots outright. Maybe he didn't have all the cash in the bank, but he could go to the bank first thing tomorrow morning and ask for a loan.

But Daniele? Where would Daniele's parents go?

But Daniele wasn't his problem. Renato's duty was to think about his own parents. What had Daniele ever done for him, except knock up his daughter? No, he must do the right thing for his own poor parents. The common bone room was out of the question. He couldn't have their bones dumped in with centuries' worth of nameless body parts. His parents deserved better. And they deserved better than having their graves opened after all these years only to have their bones shifted about. They should stay where they are, and nobody should disturb them.

But Daniele?

Renato sighed.

But Daniele.

"Fine," he said at last, returning the look of the watchful wet eyes. "We'll move their bones to the little caskets and put them together in the wall vault. *Va bene*? Is that what you wanted me to say?"

"Why should I want you to say something? The choice is yours."

"Then I've chosen. Daniele Mangiavacchi can have my parents' grave for his parents. Fine. Here, give me one more drop of the grappa."

"Water."

"Water. Whatever you say."

Sculati poured a glass for Renato and a glass for himself.

"And when is it that we need to, you know, to do the thing, move the bones?"

"Early, early tomorrow morning, to be in time for the Mangiavacchi funeral. We'll move your parents' bones and this way the graves for the Mangiavacchis will already be dug. Two pigeons with one bean."

"Early early? Like half-past seven?"

"Even seven o'clock would be fine."

"A quarter past seven, then. I'll milk my sheep early and I'll be here at a quarter past seven. I mean to say, I should be here for this thing, shouldn't I?"

"As you want."

"Then I don't know. But yes. If you're going to move my parents, I should be here to watch. To help. Whatever." He lifted his glass as if toasting Sculati. "I'll need this to sleep tonight. Sleeping would be good, but I don't think it will come easily."

"Water is always good." Sculati finished his own glass. "Tomorrow morning at a quarter past seven, then. If I can get up earlier, I might even have the holes already dug. That way I will wait for you only before opening the caskets. And I'm sure everything will be fine. With the decomposition, I mean. Otherwise, you know."

"What do you mean 'otherwise'?"

"Nothing. I mean, you know sometimes the decomposition isn't finished, in which case I don't know what we would do, because it's not like we have a lot of space to play with here in these cemetery walls."

"And if it's not finished?"

"Nothing. As I was saying, you know, when we open a casket and the bones inside aren't ready—still lots of flesh attached, I mean—then naturally we have to put them back in the ground, usually for two more years, to finish up. We might even leave the lid off the coffin, to help the contact with the earth. Faster that way, you know."

"You're telling me we will open my parents' caskets tomorrow and find them still intact? *Dio bono,* Sculati! Now I'm beginning to have some doubt!"

"No, stay tranquil. Everything will go fine tomorrow. You'll see. I swear everything will be fine. I remember how we used to bury twenty years ago. I remember your parents grave inside. We didn't put the casket in a sealed zinc container as we do nowadays. Much faster when there's no zinc. No, they'll be good and decomposed. Stay tranquil. I know my profession. You'll see. Oh! You want Don Luigi to be here?"

"The priest? What's the priest got to do with it?"

"The priest is usually here for these things."

"I'm not a church man, Sculati."

"Neither am I. But take my advice. Let me ask the priest to come. Priests are good for things like this."

"Fine, then. But you ask him. You see to it. The priest, too." Renato laughed and shook his head. "Why not? We'll have the priest, too. And I'll ask Milena if she wants to come."

Sculati lifted the bottle. "Another little drop?"

Renato declined. He stood up, saying his good nights, feeling the gravedigger's apartment swirl around him when he moved. He had drunk too much. "Tomorrow at a quarter past seven," he said, leaving. "Let's hope we sleep well."

"*Buonanotte,* Tizzoni. See you tomorrow. And by the way," said the big man. "Your three choices? Of course what I think doesn't matter. But according to me you made the right choice."

Renato was at the door when Sculati said, "Oh! If anyone asks you, what will you say? Do you see me drunk?"

Renato stared. In all honesty, he couldn't say that Sculati had changed since before he'd poured his first glass. "No," he said. "I can't say yes."

Out shot the big laugh that had been hiding inside Sculati all along. "*Bravo,* Tizzoni! Well said. You, I must say, look a little unsteady, but you can't say yes that I look drunk. *Bravo!* Anyone asks, you tell them exactly that!"

When Renato stepped outside he noticed what he hadn't noticed before: The warm scirocco had passed. The wind no longer blew up from the south, with its sticky African heat. Now it blew down from the north. It was fresh. It smelled of cypress sap.

Walking past his parents' graves, Renato didn't look. He'd be seeing them anyway in a few hours' time. He'd be back here soon enough.

TWENTY-FIVE

Old Bones

Renato woke up early, when the morning breeze pushed inside his open bedroom window and touched his cheek.

In the valley where he lived, air itself was an erogenous thing. It was soft, and scented like a woman's skin. It touched you and you felt naked even if you were clothed. It whispered against your neck and you tingled with the tickling shiver you felt when touched by illicit love. Half fear, half lust. Yearning.

Air in the country could be that way, filled with the light of sunrise, with the smell of grass, with the singing of birds.

This morning a breath of that air pushed inside the window to stir Renato. He woke with his penis erect.

He put his lips to Milena's sleeping cheek. She smiled in her sleep, nearly opening her eyes. Renato felt alive. He thought: This is how I ought to feel always.

Then he stopped kissing Milena and let her fall back to sleep. How could he make love to her? How could he let himself be alive? There was death to deal with today. He had an appointment to open his parents' graves, then the funeral later to put Daniele's mother and father into the ground.

He wanted to be alive, but death had been circling him lately like a predatory wolf. First Signor Vezzosi had gotten sick and died. Now

Daniele's parents were dead, and today he had to look inside his parents' coffins to see how much of them was left. Life was more seductive to Renato because it seemed to be slipping away, a lover with her foot out the door. Seductive yet hopeless, suddenly out of reach.

Renato got out of bed. Each thing he had loved was strange to him. Maybe he was dying. Could he ever let himself be reborn?

That's why I have to go to Rome as the dream instructed, he thought while getting dressed. Could he dare to hope that his fortune might really change after all? Or maybe, said a fear somewhere in his rib cage, a fear like a foul-breathed beast, maybe I'm being called to Rome only to die. Who knows what dreams might mean?

He walked up the corridor, past Petula's room. *Dio boia!* he said to himself. God the Executioner! My baby's pregnant.

He went outside to milk the sheep and take them to graze up on the hill.

Milena stood, her arm interlocked with Renato's, at the cemetery. Don Luigi the priest was near them. Thick-lensed glasses, white hair, black trousers, and a white robe. Sculati the gravedigger was down in the hole. He had gotten up earlier than everyone else to do his digging. Renato looked into the ground. One hole, as big as a matrimonial bed, held his parents' coffins side by side.

Sculati was slipping a rope under one of the boxes. He slipped another rope under the coffin's other end. "See?" Sculati said. "The past is still here. The past is always present. It's just hidden most of the time. Buried. That's all. But it's exactly where we left it. Here, give me a hand up," he said to Renato when the ropes were in place. "Will you give me a hand?"

Renato reached for Sculati's hand, and helped the man clumsily get the bulk of his weight back up on the living side of the mouth of the grave.

"We're one man short," Sculati said. The idea of counting the people present had occurred to him only now. "Easier when there are four men, one on each end of the two ropes under the coffin. Four men can haul it up like lifting nothing at all. But, don't you worry. Renato, and the father, yes, that's right, Don Luigi, you go over there and take that other end, you two pull up on that rope and I'll take both ends of this rope myself. Three's just as good as four. You'll see."

"And I don't count for anything?" said Milena to the gravedigger. She turned her eyes to Renato. "*Andiamo.* I can help, too."

Renato shrugged. "If you want to, I suppose. What do I know? Sculati, what do you say?"

Sculati had already closed his eyes and raised his hands to make chivalrous protests against the thought of a woman helping in the heavy work. Then he felt a muscle twinge in his lower back. Digging holes wasn't as easy on the body as it had been a few years before. "Unusual for a woman to offer such a thing," he said, deciding against chivalry. "But if the signora insists, what can one say?"

The quartet pulled on the ropes, Sculati and the priest on one side of the grave, Renato and Milena on the other. The width of the hole made it difficult for the lifters to get any leverage. Everyone felt the strain in their backs. They congratulated themselves when the coffin sat securely on the ground beside the hole.

Sculati was winded. "Leave it to me," Renato offered, climbing inside the grave. "I'll take care of putting the ropes under this other one."

With the ropes in place, the three men and one woman took their positions again and hoisted the other heavy box.

Renato and Milena brushed dirt off their hands and off their clothes. "How clever we were to put on fancy clothes!" said Renato. Why hadn't he dressed in his work clothes, as if today had been just another day of digging up waterpipes, not coffins? He wished he hadn't put on a jacket and a tie, but somehow it had seemed the necessary thing to do.

Milena straightened her dress. "It's clean dirt," she said. "It'll come out in the wash."

She looked at her husband and saw the tension in his eyes, eyes which, had they been asked, would have chosen not to peer inside coffins.

Don Luigi the priest was muttering inside his robes. "For this kind of work"—he slapped dust from his sleeve—"I'm getting too old."

"*Dai!*" Sculati encouraged. "Come on! We'll do this thing, then afterward, whoever wants to can come up to my house for a drop of water."

Renato heard himself laugh. "Take that crowbar of yours, Sculati, and go ahead and take off the lids," for Renato had seen the crowbar laid out on the ground beside the hole. "Go ahead! Courage! *Vai!*"

Sculati said, "Yes, give me the crowbar, would you? We could use a screwdriver to get the screws out, but they're probably too rusty. The crowbar is faster anyway."

Renato handed him the crowbar, then stood back and watched. He remembered.

What did he remember? His father's funeral and then, only a few months later, his mother's. Looking now, he realized he hardly remembered the coffins. Or at least he did not recognize them. In his memory they were very big, very shiny, very dark. Ceremonious. Grim. Ominous. Grand.

The two boxes on the ground beside the hole this morning were the same color as the walnut kitchen table at home, only the two boxes had lost their shine. This wood was dirty. The corners showed signs of rot.

Twenty years, thought Renato. Twenty years can change a lot. Twenty years, wood starts to rot. Twenty years, people change. His life had changed, but Renato still felt the same. The same and not the same. Standing near the boxes, knowing his parents were inside, he felt the same now, the same as the seventeen-year-old who had stood in exactly the same spot twenty years before when the coffins, lowered into the ground, had looked polished and sturdy enough to resist eternity.

Milena soothed his arm with her hand, and he realized he had been clenching the muscles just above his elbows. It was something unconscious he did whenever he was agitated or afraid, one of the innumerable little signs that spoke as clearly as words to the woman who knew how to read his body. She touched him with her hand and his muscles relaxed. He patted her fingers with his.

The priest sneezed.

"Bless you," said Sculati.

"Thank you," the priest said, sneezing again. "Aya! Must be allergies." He pulled out a handkerchief from a pocket somewhere inside his robe. "Though allergies in this season, to what I wouldn't know." He wiped his nose, then gave it a blow. "Or maybe it's the dust." He indicated the coffins with his handkerchief hand. "I don't know." He sneezed again.

"Bless you," Renato said.

Milena said, "Bless you."

Renato heard her giggle for a second. He wanted to giggle, too.

A woman let herself in through the cemetery gate. Sculati looked up. Recognizing her, he gave a nod. She responded with a small wave, then walked to the far side of the cemetery. There she set about arranging things in front of a vault in the wall.

"That's the one I told you about," Sculati said under his breath to Renato. "Last night I told you. Remember? The Dead Mothers' Club? She's the head, I suppose you could say. She's the one who comes every day, and brings toys and things to her daughter's grave. But you recognize her from town, no?"

Renato looked. He did recognize her.

"The others will be coming soon," said Sculati. "They always do. Every day. Heat or rain. Other mothers to visit their *bambini*."

Watching the mother for a moment, Renato thought that there was no telling just how deep the wellsprings of grief must flow beneath the surface of some people's lives.

Renato turned his attention back to what Sculati was doing to the bigger of the two coffins lying on the ground. He watched as the monstrous man attacked a corner of the coffin with the crowbar. Years of lying underground had softened the wood around the metal of the screws that held the lid in place. The wood yielded to the crowbar without much of a fight. Sculati went to work on the other corners until the lid was no longer fastened down.

Renato caught his breath, expecting that the moment had come.

Sculati, however, went to the other, smaller box and started prying up the corners. Was he trying to build a theatrical effect, Renato wondered, getting both coffins ready so that they could be opened at the same time? Or maybe in his own way he was following his personal sense of due ceremony. Whatever.

The crowbar creaked when it jerked the last screw out of the wood and the operation was finished.

"Good," said Renato. "That's done. Now we can lift off the covers. Courage!" He couldn't wait any longer. It was intolerable not knowing for sure what was inside, waiting in dreamlike anxiety to reveal a different dimension inside the boxes, an alien world of unforeseeable phantasms and crawling monsters and ancient emotions. What if there were insects everywhere?

"Come on!" Renato encouraged Sculati, who went around to the far end of the larger coffin. "Let's get this done with!"

Together they took off the lid, putting it on the ground beside the coffin. Renato looked in. He saw a white sheet, which had turned brown in splotches. Water stains. Earth-colored spots.

They removed the lid from the other coffin, too. Another white sheet. Similiar stains.

The priest surprised everyone: He made himself useful. He rolled up his sleeve, reached into the bigger coffin, and pulled away the sheet. Then he did the same for the smaller coffin. "You see?" Don Luigi said, as if some reassuring words he had spoken were now proved true. "Here they are uncovered. And everything seems to be exactly as it should be."

He was right. Looking in, Renato saw nothing gruesome. There was no monstrous other dimension. What he saw in the open wooden boxes were pieces of this earth, decayed clothing. No glistening streams of insects, though there were spiderwebs in both coffins. And he would have thought that spiders preferred to stay where there was light. There was lots of dust, too. A layer of dust covered the bottom of the coffins. The dust mixed with traces of soil near the walls where the wood was weakest.

"They're not joking when they say 'dust to dust,'" Renato said aloud, talking more to himself.

"Yes," Milena said. "Who would have thought?"

"It's no poetry," Renato said, shaking his head. "It's fact." Human flesh, after twenty years, had become simple dust.

In the middle of the dust and limp clothing there were the bones. The hungry earth had digested everything soft about Renato's parents, leaving only hard bones. The skeletons that reclined in their boxes were smaller than the walking, breathing, speaking people of Renato's memory. Maybe his mind had made the people bigger than their real size. Or maybe bones, deprived of muscle and skin, always looked small. He had no way of knowing.

The bones were not white, as bones always appeared on television or in films. They were an earthier, dingy yellow, almost light brown. The color of *tufo* stone, Renato thought. The color of cliff faces in many of the ravines between the hills in this part of the countryside.

For the past twenty years his parents had been so intimate a part of his dream world that he could scarcely be sure such people had existed for real. Strange to see the tangible evidence now. Memory might make the past appear an invented dream; in truth, though, Sculati was right. The past was still here. Concrete.

"Nice," said Sculati. "Fine. As I had thought, decomposition has happened perfectly. And now we see that things couldn't be better, so I would say let's continue, wouldn't you? Tizzoni, if you'd give me another hand, there in the little work room beside the chapel I've prepared the small caskets. Come with me and we can each carry one. All right? I could carry them both myself, of course. But it's better if you participate. This way you have less time to think. Believe me. I know my profession. So, Tizzoni, if you'll come this way with me? *Prego.*" He extended an arm like a restaurant maître d'.

"Fine. I'll go with you," said Renato.

"Go," said Milena.

"Go," said the priest. "It's better not to think too much. Sculati is right."

"I'm going!" Renato said. "Who's thinking too much? I'm going."

He followed Sculati to the little work room, then returned with him to the graveside, each man carrying a more modern-looking miniature casket in his arms.

"The account for the caskets we can settle later," Sculati said. "You'll see I chose the simple models. Dignified, but nothing too deluxe. For now, in any case, let's concentrate on getting the bones put away in the proper way."

"The proper way?"

"Well," Sculati said with a modest shake of his head, "I call it the proper way, but maybe there is no proper way. Years ago I observed how saints' bones were placed in the glass caskets in *reliquiari,* on display in churches and such, you know. There, of course, the asthetic side is more important, for people to see the lovely disposition of the ribs and femora. You will all understand, naturally, that these things are less important when we put the bones in the little wooden caskets. No"—he spoke with the tone of an expert lecturing on a favorite subject—"with the wooden caskets the concern is more practical, making everything fit in neatly to the limited given space. Put the smallest bones in the casket first—starting with the fingers of the hands and feet, obviously—and then the less small, and less small still, until you arrive at the bigger bones, the ribs and similar, then the long femora as the second to last, and finally the skull. Trust me. You will see."

The gravedigger finished speaking. Renato and Milena and Don Luigi were staring at him as if none of them had ever before thought that so much planning was required to stash away some bones.

"Fine," Renato said. "Then let's begin."

"Which one first?" Sculati asked. "Your poor mother or your poor father?"

"*Dio mio!*" Milena said, tempted almost to laugh. "This really is too much."

"Too much indeed," Renato said, laughing for her. "Sculati, let's do it this way. Since you are standing there closer to my father, you do him. And while you do him, I'll do my mother here."

"You want to participate this much? Fine with me, if you insist."

"Do I want to? Let's not exaggerate. What I want is to get this thing done." He squatted down and reached a hand into his mother's coffin. "Little bones first?"

"Fingers of the hands and feet first. *Sì*. Here. Do like this. Take a bone"—he lifted a bone from the father's foot—"and tap it against the side of the coffin like this. You see how the dust comes off? Why not take advantage of the opportunity to put the bones in their new home all nice and clean?"

Following Sculati's lead, Renato reached into the coffin.

"Let me help." Milena squatted by his side and helped him arrange the small bones. "I think the vertebrae should be next, after the fingers. Is that right?"

"Yes, yes, signora," Sculati said. "Vertebrae next."

They worked without much conversation. Renato tried not to think.

In no time they had transferred the ribs and the collarbones, and the sterna and the sacra, and the long bones from the arms, and the pelvises, and the bones from the legs, with the femora coming last.

"Sculati, wait!" Renato called out when he saw that only the skulls remained. Sculati was already tapping the skull against the wood, getting out the last of the dust from inside the cranial cavity. "Sculati, please wait. I'll take care of the heads. Please. Let me." He stood up.

He went to his father's coffin and Sculati handed him the skull.

Returning to his mother's coffin, he picked up her skull as well. He held them both with his arm, cradling them against his chest, using his free hand to brush the last of the dust from the crowns of their heads.

With a skull in each hand, he turned them to look at their faces. There were no eyes to look back at him.

Suddenly his breath stuck in his chest. "This is difficult," were the only words to come from his mouth. These were his parents. They had lived inside these heads, the two souls who had given him love. Now what was left for him?

When he had been a child, he had thought he would live forever and that his parents would never die. Part of him knew they weren't immortal, but their death was unthinkable; even more unthinkable was his own, for they surely would die first. Parents do that service for a child: They place themselves between the child and death. Then Renato's parents died, leaving him alone in the world of life.

Not even ten days ago, Aristodemo had died, leaving Renato once again on his own. On his own against what?

I'm next, Renato said to himself. His life seemed to him precarious and small, a butterfly's wing in the face of the wind, now that no one older who loved him remained. Yes, Tita Vezzosi still lived, and she was strong. Yet for all her strength, she was vulnerable in her pain.

This was Renato's chill. He was a chick only now beating his wings outside the warmth of his shell. Not far from forty, and only now a chick. Every passing breeze made him cold.

Tenderness filled him for the two people whose heads he held in his hands. If only for a minute, half a minute, even less—for the single beating of his heart—if only he could feel his mother's and father's love.

Closing his eyes to stop tears, Renato put his lips to the foreheads of his parents' skulls.

"Well," he said, clearing his throat. He put each head in its separate box with its separate bones. "That's done."

He became aware that Milena was next to him, and that Sculati and Don Luigi were there, too. He had forgotten them.

Sculati was about to put the lids on the small coffins when the priest told him to wait. "The benediction first," Don Luigi said. He reached into a pocket inside his robe and pulled out a silver water shaker, covered in its silver case. Unsheathing the water shaker, he sprinkled holy water over the bones in each box, then made the sign of the cross.

The wall vault in which Sculati placed both little caskets was very close to the wall vault with Aristodemo Vezzosi's name and black-and-white photograph on it. "I'm glad they'll be together," he said to Milena, holding her hand while they watched Sculati brick up the opening. "My parents, I mean," he said, realizing that Signor Vezzosi was still physically *here*. "My parents close to each other, together, I wanted to say. But yes, I'm happy, too, that they'll be close to him."

"And we'll leave the hole they were in open for the Mangiavacchi funeral this afternoon," Sculati said. "That way, this evening I'll only have to fill it in, which is easier than digging." He was talking to himself.

The priest said his good-byes and went on his way.

Renato and Milena thanked Sculati for everything. Sculati said that he would wait for Renato to come another time to settle the account. He'd be seeing him later on, anyhow, for the Mangiavacchi affair.

"Oh," Sculati said. "Before you go, Tizzoni, I have something to ask you. A favor."

"Ask."

"Before you go to Rome, will you put my name on your list?"

Renato looked at Sculati. Then he looked at Milena. Milena raised her eyebrows in an expression that said *I didn't tell him, so don't blame me.*

"No one knows I'm going to Rome, Sculati. How do you know I'm going to Rome?"

Sculati laughed. "Everyone knows you're going to Rome, so I know you're going to Rome. And everyone knows about the list."

"What do you mean everyone knows? This is a private thing, something I'm doing for, uh, I don't know why. But it isn't something for everyone to know, or everyone will think I'm a fool."

"They've always thought you were a fool, so why should you start to worry now?"

"Who told you, Sculati? I want to know. Was it Tita Vezzosi? Because I wouldn't have thought Signora Vezzosi to be a gossip."

"No, relax yourself. It wasn't Tita Vezzosi. I didn't even know she was involved. It was a woman standing next to me in the pharmacy yesterday when I went to buy some liniment for my back. Been giving me trouble lately, you know, my back. And I use this liniment that works well, if you are ever looking for a liniment that works. Anyway, it was the woman standing next to me, you know her, the baker's wife, and she had heard it from the butcher's wife. And the butcher's wife had heard it from—" He stopped talking and scratched his head. He rolled his big eyes apologetically toward Milena. "You will excuse me for saying, signora, but he asked me, so I must tell him the truth. The butcher's wife," he said, turning back to Renato, "heard it from your mother-in-law, from the signora here's mother herself."

"Your mother, Milena? And how would she know such a thing?"

"Don't be dim, Renato," Milena said. "My mother saw us fighting the other night in the *bottega* kitchen so she asked me what was wrong."

"You told your mother about my dreams and about the list!"

"I can't speak to my own mother? You may not like her, but what other mother have I got?"

Renato sighed. "So your mother told the butcher's wife, and the butcher's wife told the baker's wife, and the baker's wife told Sculati the *becchino* and who knows who else!"

"So you'll put me on your list?"

"What for? What reason? What do you expect to change in your life?"

"Doesn't matter," said Sculati, putting an affectionate bear paw on Renato's shoulder. "I'll leave the reason to you. You think of something. The important thing is that I want to be on your list. Tell me, Tizzoni. Can I count on it?"

What could Renato say? He said, "All right, Sculati. I'll put you on the list."

"And I can count on it?"

"Count on it."

A handshake with Sculati sealed the pact.

As he turned to go, Renato felt all shell-less and shaky, leaving the palace of death to confront life and mortality alone. He also felt an absurd delight in the ridiculousness of his situation. Everyone in town knew about his list. They thought he was crazy, but Sculati, for one, was entrusting him to carry out some sacred charge. His mission had found confirmation.

I know what I'll write, too, Renato thought. I know what I'll write next to Sculati's name. I'll write what he said about the past: The past is always present. It's just hidden most of the time. That's what I'll write.

Walking out with Milena, he put his fingers up and touched Signor Vezzosi's picture. "*Ciao,*" he said. "*Ciao.*"

TWENTY-SIX

Skatablang!

"*E poi?*" Cappelli's eyes watched Renato's face, waiting for the next words. The eyes, red around the edges, were small. Porcupine eyes.

"How '*E poi?*' How do you mean 'And then?'"

"I mean *e poi*." Cappelli licked the corner of his mouth, his tongue tasting the drop of coffee corrected with Sambuca. "What happened next?"

"There was no next, Cappelli." Renato finished his own espresso. The final sip was the best because the sugar had accumulated in the bottom of the little cup. "No, there was no next. Like I said, Milena and I left the cemetery, and then we had to go back there a few hours later for the funeral of Daniele's parents. And the funeral was, you know, it was a funeral. How do you expect a funeral to be?"

"I understand." Cappelli didn't look at all satisfied. "*Va bene.*" He eyed the row of bottles on the glass shelf behind the bar to see what he could drink next. "You took your parents' bones out of their old coffins and you put them in the new little coffins. And that was every-thing?" Somehow Renato's storytelling should have arrived at a more momentous punchline.

"What do you want me to say?" Renato scolded, thinking a glass of mineral water would do nicely now to wash his coffee down. What was he supposed to recount? What did Cappelli expect of him? No, he hadn't recounted all his feelings, all the longing and fear that had come up inside him when he saw his parents' bones unearthed. And he hadn't said anything about how he had kissed his parents on the foreheads of their skulls. But there were limits to what you could say to another man. With a woman you could say anything. Everything. Maybe. Depended on what there was to say. And with Duncan, too, words just came out, wanting the whole truth to be expressed. Strange, talking to Duncan was more like talking to a woman than to a man. Who knew why? Maybe sex disappeared in friendship. Or maybe Duncan, being American, came from a different world, and that difference gave Renato permission to open himself, to reveal what he had inside. But Cappelli? Cappelli was his assistant, someone he had to see every day at work. He was a man in Renato's town. How much of yourself do you want to show to people who already know you too well?

"Will you give me a glass of mineral water?" Renato said, catching the eye of Tonino, who was tending bar.

"Natural or with gas?"

"Natural, without gas."

"And to me," Cappelli said, licking his lips, "and to me you can give another little drop of that Sambuca, but this time without the coffee. Here. Pour it here in this coffee cup. Don't trouble yourself giving me a clean glass. Sambuca in the coffee cup is even better, with what's left of the coffee still in the bottom." Tonino poured and Cappelli said, "Thanks."

It was a quiet moment in the *bottega*. Milena was in back in the kitchen preparing things for dinner, to be served later. Maria Severina, at a table behind Renato's back, sat with another woman. She was busy complaining. Didn't matter what about. Her complaints could be about the weather, about her no-good son-in-law, about how swollen her ankles were because she spent too much time on her feet. Renato paid her no mind. He was careful only to lower his voice when he spoke to Cappelli so that Maria Severina couldn't spy on his every word.

"Let's go, Cappelli," said Renato. "Come on. We still have work to do this afternoon before we go home. This was supposed to be only a little pause for coffee before we go to change the water meter up by the gas station. If you get yourself too ballsed up with the Sambuca now, you'll be worse than useless, and we have a lot to do."

"Worse than useless you say? Listen, my dear one. I'll worry about my own drinking, thank you very much, *Dio bono!* You know that this is my fuel, and without it my engine doesn't work!" He scratched the gray bristles on his head. "It takes a little fuel to make the engine work, don't you think?"

"Do as you wish," Renato said, realizing that there was no hope of changing the porcupine-man by his side.

"I wish to drink this little drop of Sambuca," he said, drinking it. He gave a gratified "Ah!" when he had finished, wiped his mouth with the palm of his hand, and said, "And tell me again why you went to the funeral of the Mangiavacchis. It's not that there was much friendship between you and them. Not that anyone should die like that, poor bastards. But I mean, you and they . . ." He shrugged.

"*Sì,* as I was telling you, I told you that. Nothing. You're right, I didn't get along very much with the Mangiavacchis. But their son for some time now has been with my daughter, as you know."

"As everybody knows," said Cappelli, his eyes returning longingly to the bottle of Sambuca on the shelf.

"Yes, as everybody knows," Renato went on. "So. There you are. Their son is with my daughter, for some time now, as I say. So it seemed only right to go to their funeral, don't you think? And after all, you will remember in the story that I just told you, it was to make room for them that I had to go and meet with Sculati the *becchino,* and move the bones of my poor parents. Really, I suppose I had an interest in going to the Mangiavacchis' funeral, wouldn't you say?"

"What do I know?" Cappelli signaled for Tonino to pour him another little drop of Sambuca.

Renato wanted to talk. He wanted to tell Cappelli how Daniele Mangiavacchi had gotten Petula pregnant, and that *that* was why he suddenly found himself having closer involvement with Daniele than he would have wished. And he wasn't sure what to make of any of it, of the pregnancy, of the Mangiavacchis' death, of Daniele's new look of disarming vulnerability. He wasn't sure what to think. Talking would have helped. But here? In this *bottega* with both his in-laws around him and his wife in the kitchen? And could he really say such things to Cappelli? Maybe it was better to respect the natural distance that existed between two men. Better to keep his mouth shut.

He looked out the window toward the piazza. His eyes followed the bright afternoon sunlight up toward the church. A backlit figure crossed the line of his vision. The form entered the bar. He recognized it by its shape, by the length of the legs, the leanness of the body, the carriage of the head, the flow of the hair. His heartbeats redoubled. An animal instinct made his nostrils open wide. As the figure walked toward him, he recognized Meg Barker's musky smell.

"*Buonasera,*" he said, wondering who in the bar was listening. He heard sudden silence behind his back, and knew his mother-in-law had heard him greet the English actress and was now listening with open ears.

"Oh! *Ciao,* Renato," she said. "*Ciao.*" She told Tonino that she'd have her usual. She spoke in English, but Tonino, having caught her meaning, poured out her glass of Irish whiskey.

Cappelli's own animal instincts were turned on to full because of the female presence. "She calls you by your first name, I see," he said sotto voce, recognizing that some things had to be said carefully when in-laws were around.

"You know" Renato began, "probably she would find my last name too hard to pronounce, so it's easier for her to use only the first."

"Could be as you say," Cappelli considered, not in the least convinced. "Could be. Or it could also be that you didn't tell me what really happened when you went to her house the other day to see to— What was it, anyway? A broken pipe?"

"Clogged sink, in the end. Of course I shouldn't have done the job, should have left it to a plumber. But it was only a clogged sink. Only took two minutes."

"Unclogged her sink, did you? And?"

"And nothing." Renato glanced over his shoulder. Maria Severina's eyes were watching him. On the other side of the bar, Tonino was pretending to busy himself with dirty coffee cups in the sink, but his attention, too, was on Renato.

"Nothing, you say?" Cappelli said between tight lips. "And now she comes here and calls you by your first name. I begin to have my doubts. But I must say"—he appraised her through red porcupine eyes—"*Madonna rana!* A true piece of woman indeed! If I had been in your clothes, Tizzoni, I would have unclogged more than just her sink!"

Renato felt himself blush. Absurd. When was the last time he had blushed? He was glad that the better part of his face was hidden by a beard. If Meg Barker were to look at him, perhaps she wouldn't notice how pink his cheeks surely had become. And yes, he knew she couldn't speak Italian, but what if she understood a word or two? How would she feel to hear Cappelli's appreciation of her beauty? How would she react to hearing Cappelli liken the Virgin Mary to a frog?

"Babbo?" Milena emerged from the kitchen behind the bar, calling Tonino. "Babbo, have you seen the knife sharpener? This big old knife is no good unless I can find the sharpener." She saw Meg Barker at the bar, standing close to Renato. "Ah. *Buonasera,*" she said, nodding toward the English actress.

"*Buonasera,*" Meg replied.

"It's here," Tonino said. "The knife sharpener. I was using it on the little knife, the one for cutting lemons."

"*Grazie,*" Milena said, though she was looking at Renato and Meg. "Oh! Look at these dirty cups!" She pushed her father away from the sink. "I'll take care of the cups, *Babbo.* You have other things to do, no?" And she started running water over the dirty coffee cups in the bar sink, just across the counter from Renato.

Renato stood at the bar with Cappelli on his left and Meg Barker on his right, his wife in front of his face, a kitchen carving knife on the counter beside her.

He was filled with a sense of precariousness. Since his encounter with Meg Barker's foot in her bathroom sink, a strange power had been given to him. He hadn't yet exercised the power; he hoped he never would. All the same, Meg Barker had given him the power to make his marriage go *skatablang*. Not only his marriage. His whole world might explode. *Skatablang!* A few words, that's all it would take. *Milena,* he could say—even now, if he should lose control of his tongue—*I was washing Meg Barker's naked foot in her bathroom sink because she cut it, you see, and it made me want to make love. Her face was close to my neck and my desire grew even more. I happened to see up there between her legs and I tell you, it looked like wet mink, like something good to touch, to slip myself inside. I didn't want to feel that way, but the feeling happened to me anyway. I almost wanted, no, what almost? I did want. I wanted to make love. And I want to make love to you, Milena, to you more than to anyone else, to you, my wife, but lately it hasn't worked.* Mere words. But those words, if spoken, would be as life-changing as a bad car accident or a death. They would make his world go *skatablang*.

His heart was certainly beating quickly as he sipped his water. Looking in the mirror behind the bar past Milena, he watched Meg Barker sip her Irish whiskey, and he asked himself with a sense of rising panic if he should say something to her, though God knew what words he might speak, or ignore her, or finish his water quickly and leave the bar, giving her only the minimal social courtesy of a head nod and a mumbled *buonasera*. Yes, he should get out of there fast, and to speed things up he could offer to pay for Cappelli's drinks and his own coffee and—why not?—he could be a sport and pay for Meg Barker's Irish whiskey, too, though on second thought that might look a bit forward on his part, such a gesture being seen through the eyes of his wife, and father-in-law, and mother-in-law, and the other people in the bar, so really thinking about it, things would be better if he let her pay for her own drink, because, after all, he certainly didn't expect her to pay for his, so why should he pay for hers, seeing as how they were not even friends, really, only two people who hardly knew each other despite the fact that he had washed her naked foot in her bathroom sink and had felt her warm breath on his neck and had seen the wet mink between her legs.

"Renato!" she said, breaking his thoughts.

"*Sì?*"

He was visibly so awkward, so unaccountably awkward in her eyes, she had to laugh. "Wanted to tell you. Sink works beautifully since you fixed it. No more clogs. Doesn't seem right, though, that you wouldn't let me pay you. You sure I can't offer you something for your troubles? Maybe cook you a dinner sometime?"

Renato smiled with the same uncomprehending smile that would have appeared on his face had someone asked him for directions in Urdu or Cantonese.

So Meg Barker did her best with hand gestures to make herself clear. "No way I can repay you? A favor for a favor?"

"What's she saying in her language?" Renato wondered aloud.

"'*Un favore per un favore,*' she's saying," Milena said, some special intuition becoming a bridge across the language gap. "She seems to think she owes you a favor."

"*Sì,*" Meg Barker said, pleased to hear her words transformed into Italian. "*Un favore per un favore,*" she echoed.

"Oh. That's what she means." Renato said. "For unclogging her sink, she means."

"Naturally," Milena said. Her voice held a tone Renato had not heard before. He heard the hard tone of a woman who does not want to lose.

"*Sì,*" Renato said to Meg. "I mean *no*. No favor for a favor. It's not necessary."

Meg Barker wanted to say something, but it's difficult to speak when you don't know the words. She wanted to tell Renato that she was truly grateful for his having fixed her sink, but more than just that. She recognized something in him, something that made her want to pull close. She wanted to let him know that she did not see him merely as a workman who was useful to her because he could unclog her pipes. He was not simply an Italian in the picturesque Tuscan town where she had bought her house. Not a charming part of the landscape in her eyes. She saw the person inside him. She wanted to know that person better.

She smiled at him, hoping her meaning was clear in her eyes. She sipped her drink, watching Renato's face over the lip of her glass.

Who knows, she asked herself, if this man feels the same about me?

She turned away from him and looked at herself in the big mirror behind the bar, looking straight past Milena. For the first time since buying her house in Italy, she felt absolutely lonely in the isolation of wordlessness.

Looking in the mirror, Renato watched the frustration on her face. He saw that she would have told him something if only she had had the words. And he, too, might have shown his own willingness to listen if he had known which words to say. If he hadn't been so surrounded.

But there were no words between Renato Tizzoni and Meg Barker. There were only Meg's thoughts. And the turbulence of Renato's thoughts, too.

TWENTY-SEVEN

Wife

Seeing Meg Barker smile in the mirror behind the bar, Renato felt his penis give a twitch in his underwear.

Perfect, he thought. This is all I need. Why must the body respond? Isn't the mind spinning enough already without the body's help?

He hated himself for having a penis in that moment, hated himself even more because the troublesome appendage inside his trousers seemed determined to react to this woman who, for now at least, was peripheral to his life.

Feeling this way was nothing he was accustomed to. His faithfulness to Milena in all the years of their marriage was unblemished because never had he been tempted in any other woman's direction. But now there was this woman living near his town. She, and the forest-after-the-rain smell of her, and the sculpted curves of her foot, and the wet mink he had seen between her legs. She would be there. She would not disappear. No getting around it: Sooner or later he would have to make some kind of choice. His penis, if nothing else, was giving him an irksome prod.

Or maybe his penis had nothing to do with it, he told himself. Let his penis respond. So what? That's what penises were there for. Nobody ever admired a penis for its intelligence. He was more than just a penis bearer, though. He was supposed to be the person in charge. He had never been a slave to his penis before. Why start now?

His penis wasn't all of it. This much he knew. What he was feeling had little to do with the hunger to chase after a few minutes of exhilaration between some other woman's legs. It was the new taste Meg offered that intrigued him. It was the possibility of taste itself. When was the last time he had tasted anything in his life? Looking at Meg in the mirror behind the bar, he saw what might be the chance to change everything and perhaps to start to taste again.

But what could hold greater taste for him than his lifelong love affair with his wife? How much would he ever want that to change?

Meg waved a finger at Tonino, saying, "I'd love another."

Tonino poured more whiskey.

Renato watched Meg's mouth touch the lip of the whiskey glass. That mouth has been close to my neck, he said to himself. If I ever went back to her house, which of course I would never do, still, if I did . . .

"Oh, another drop of water in the glass before we go," Renato said to Tonino. His mouth was dry with inexplicable thirst. He looked at Milena and wondered if she could read his thoughts.

Tonino poured.

Renato drank his water. Looking in the mirror behind Milena, he watched Meg Barker watching him watching her while she drank her whiskey.

Cappelli finished his Sambuca. Again, he wiped his moist mouth with the palm of his hand.

"So then," Renato said, talking aloud to himself. "So nothing." He put his hand into his ass pocket to get his wallet. "Oh, Tonino. I owe you for Cappelli's corrected coffee, and his Sambucas," for Renato always paid at the *bottega,* never taking advantage of the fact that the owners were his in-laws, "and for my regular coffee, and the water, too. How much?" His gestures were jerky and graceless. His list fell from his pocket when he pulled the wallet out.

Stooping to the floor to pick up the list, Renato found his eyes on a level with Meg Barker's knees. She wore blue jeans. Her feet were bare inside sandals with thin straps. He looked up and glimpsed the folds of her jeans at her groin.

Meg Barker reached into her large leather handbag and took out her purse. "I'll pay for the gentlemen's drinks," she said with a circling motion of her hand to indicate the empty coffee cups and water glass in front of Renato and Cappelli. "How much is that?"

Renato stood up quickly. "No, no!" he said to Meg Barker, to Tonino, to Milena across the bar, to Maria Severina at the table behind him, to anyone else in the *bottega* who might be listening. "Don't take the lady's money for what we drank! What, are we joking? Of course not."

"She wants to pay for you," Milena said without smiling.

"Oh. It would be for courtesy, no? I mean, she's only offering for courtesy, for the little job I did on her pipes. But I can't accept drinks from a woman. If anything, I should be gracious. We all should. I should offer. Polite thing to do, no? Listen, tell me what her drinks cost and I'll pay for those, too. Are we crazy here? The lady wants to pay for our drinks?"

"*You* want to pay for *hers*?" Milena said, something like fear in her eyes.

"Only out of courtesy," Renato said. "Only because she offered to pay for Cappelli's and mine."

Tonino stood, trying hard to decide whose money to accept. "But if the lady wants to pay for your drinks, Renato," he said, smiling mischievously, "then I say why not let your lady friend pay?"

"Now she's my lady friend?"

"She's offering to pay for your drinks," a voice said from behind Renato's back. It was Maria Severina. How could she not have taken note of everything going on?

"How much did that come to then?" Meg repeated while conversation flurried around her.

"*Sì*, she's offering to pay. But it's only out of courtesy. Why should it be anything else?" He slapped a ten-thousand-lira banknote on the bar. "Is this enough for the lady's drinks and for ours?"

"No, *caro*. That's not enough." Tonino wouldn't drop the smile, which was starting to get on Renato's nerves. "Eleven thousand and six."

Renato fished in his pockets for the change. "There you are. Thank you." He turned to leave.

"My turn to thank you again in that case," Meg said in English. "*Grazie,* Renato."

"For what?" he said with a quick laugh. He wanted to disappear.

Cappelli poked Renato's shoulder. "Eh, Tizzoni. Do I have to thank you, too?"

"You don't have to thank me," said Renato. "It's enough that the next time we're at the bar, you pay."

"She's waiting for you to say something, you know," Cappelli said.

"She can wait. What am I supposed to say?"

"If I were in you—" Cappelli began.

"But you're not in me."

Cappelli said, "They say she's very famous."

"That's what they say. So what? To me, what difference does that make?"

"True piece of woman," Cappelli whispered so softly that only Renato could hear.

Meg Barker pushed herself to speak what was on her mind. "Come by sometime." She hoped her smile looked relaxed. She did not feel relaxed. She felt the way she had felt the very first time she had spoken to the darkness of a theater from the brightly lit stage. Crazy to feel this way, she told herself. But the man leaving the bar awakened many long-slumbering emotions inside her. "If you want," she added. "Come by, if you want. For dinner, for a drink." Seeing he didn't understand, she said, "To my house." She pointed to herself. "*Casa mia.* Come by *casa mia* when you want. If you want. If you get a chance."

There it was. An invitation, clear in any language. In front of his in-laws. In front of Milena. No escaping it. Renato's moment of choice had come. His heart jerked in his rib cage. And he imagined he could hear Milena's frightened heart pounding from across the bar.

In the silence that followed Meg's invitation, Renato looked in her eyes for a moment, reading her, seeing also the embryonic possibility of a different life for himself, a life unlike anything he had ever known.

He took his eyes off her and looked at Milena's frightened face for a moment.

Then he turned to Meg Barker and spoke.

"*Signora* Barker," he said.

"*Signorina,*" she corrected.

"What?"

"*Signorina,*" she repeated, emphasizing her singleness.

"Doesn't change anything," he said with a hint of exasperation. "Fine then. *Signorina*."

She smiled. "But call me Meg."

"*Signorina* Barker, Meg. I don't believe you have ever been properly introduced to my wife." He placed his open hand on the bar. Milena wiped her hands on a dish towel and placed her hand in his. "Milena," Renato said. "*Mia moglie.*" I want no other woman, he thought, than the one I've got. I've got a wife. Holding Milena's hand in his, he felt triumph and joy flowing from her fingers.

Meg Barker looked puzzled, not understanding. "*Moglie?*"

"*Moglie,*" Renato said, thinking: What a beautiful word. Wife.

"The woman behind the bar?" Meg Barker said. Then she looked, understanding. She looked at Milena, then at Tonino, then at Maria Severina, understanding the family connections between the people who, since her arrival in town, had been pouring her daily whiskey. "I see. Your wife," she said in English. English was no good, so she tried French. "*Ta femme*."

"*Sì,*" Renato said, because everyone knows a little French. "*Ma femme. La mia donna.* My woman. Meg Barker," he introduced, "Milena Tizzoni. My wife. Milena, Meg Barker."

Milena let go of his hand and with a smile held out her hand to the English actress. "*Piacere,*" Milena said, shaking the other woman's hand. "Pleased to meet you."

"How do you do," Meg Barker said politely, knowing that her acting expertise could help her hide anything, even disappointment.

"My father, Tonino," Milena said, introducing him.

"But we know each other by sight already," Tonino said as he shook hands with the actress. "*Piacere*. Tonino."

"Pleasure," said Meg.

"My mother," Milena said, indicating her. "Maria Severina."

Maria Severina stood stiffly from the table and smoothed her skirt. She was queen of the *bottega,* but she blushed in anticipation of a handshake with a person so famous. "I am happy to make your acquaintance," Maria Severina said, mustering as much formality as she could manage.

"Well," said Meg, briefly touching Maria Severina's hard, hooflike hand. "Delighted to meet you, too, I'm sure."

"And me?" Cappelli prodded Renato. "Did I suddenly disappear?"

"My colleague Cappelli," said Renato.

But when he shook Meg's long, elegant hand, Cappelli could think of no words, so he inclined his head, hoping to appear gallant.

"We're going. *Buonasera,*" Renato said to Meg. "And you," he called to Milena, "I'll see you after work." He went toward the door.

"*Ciao,* husband," Milena said, her smile as proud as the sun.

"*Ciao,* wife," he laughed back. He left with Cappelli at his heel.

"*Ciao* to everyone," he heard Cappelli say.

Outside, Renato felt the smile on his own face. Every now and then, he thought, choosing is good.

TWENTY-EIGHT

Cappelli Knows

Renato and Cappelli crossed the square. They walked past the bakery. Renato smelled hot bread.

"Look at this sky, will you?" Cappelli said as the two men walked toward the waterworks truck. "I don't like the look of those clouds. Is it sunny or is it going to rain? Can't say. *Madonna, che tempaccio!* But it's to be expected, I suppose, because the summer is finished and now the season is changing. And people become strange when the season changes. Feel strange inside. You've become strange, Tizzoni, in the last weeks. You've become strange. Must be that you are changing season, too, no?" He whistled through his lips. "So. You changing season, Tizzoni?"

"What are you saying, Cappelli?" Renato said, unlocking the waterworks truck. "I'm changing season? Get in and let's go, or else we'll never get the water meter changed at the gas station. Come on. Get in. What are you saying, that I'm strange? I'm hardly strange."

"Oh yes, you've become strange. *Sì, sì, sì.* You tell me, Tizzoni. What am I to think? Out of the blue sky the famous Englishwoman calls you by your first name and wants to buy you drinks. Invites you to her house. And not only that. You act strange. You seem to be full of thoughts all the time. You walk around dreaming. And everyone says you've become strange with this list of yours."

"My list? You know about my list?"

"Everyone knows. I'm only surprised you haven't had every crazy old woman in town line up in front of your door to ask for a blessing. If it hasn't happened yet, it soon will. But tell me a thing, Tizzoni. Is it true what they say, that you intend to go to Rome to meet with the pope to present your list to him?"

Renato started the truck. The engine roared, then switched itself off. He started it again. "We'll let her warm up before putting her in gear." The engine revved. "True and not true, Cappelli," he answered at last. "Present the list to the pope? No." Then he told Capellini about his dream-sent mission to go and shake hands with the pope.

Cappelli looked out the dusty windshield of the truck. He whistled low. "*Madonna vipera,* Tizzoni," he said, using the big guns of blasphemy, for he called the Virgin Mother a viper. "You have become strange indeed. And you are sure this is what you have to do?"

"Very sure."

Cappelli scratched his head and made a grunting sound. "And you're sure you've understood this thing the right way?"

"Absolutely sure. Unless of course I understood the dreams all wrong. Which could always be the case."

"And you're going to do this thing anyway. Even if you're not sure you're maybe not understanding it all wrong?"

"I'm going to do this thing. Yes. Who is ever sure?"

Cappelli laughed. "Dear Tizzoni, the season is changing for you. That's for sure."

Renato laughed at himself. "I seem crazy, I know. I feel crazy, too. But this thing feels right. Oh. Listen, Cappelli. If you like, I can put you on the list, too."

"Me? *Madonna lupa benedetta!* What kind of benediction would you hope to receive for a blasphemer like me? I don't know, Tizzoni. I have to think. I will think about it and I will tell you. There's time, no? You're not leaving tomorrow, I mean."

"Tomorrow, no. But soon."

"Then I will let you know. And that famous English lady with the long legs and the nice tits whose pipes you happened to unclog. Are you going to put her on your list?"

"Now you're reading my thoughts, Cappelli. I was thinking about that just now. Hand me that pen from the glove compartment. I don't know what to think, or what to hope for her when I go to Rome. But she's become—"

"She's become important in your head."

"In a way, yes. Important and maybe not so important after all. But I should put her on the list in any case. As a favor, you know?"

Cappelli gave him the pen, adding, "I knew it. Funny change of seasons you're going through."

Renato took the list out of his back pocket. Cappelli tried to look, but Renato shielded it with his hand. Using his left thigh as a writing surface, he wrote:

MEG BARKER

He stopped and chewed the pen, thinking what to write next. He thought about the choice she had cornered him into by stirring up an erection inside his underwear and by inviting him to her house. He thought about her. He thought about his wife. He wrote:

Choosing is good.

He gave Cappelli the pen, and put the list away in his back pocket.

"So what did you write?" Cappelli's reddened eyes were alight with the expectation of being included in a great secret.

"You'd like me to tell you, wouldn't you?" He put the truck in gear. "*Andiamo,*" he said. "We've got the water meter to replace."

TWENTY-NINE

Torn

Renato didn't like admitting it, but there was no denying facts: Cappelli had been right.

"Everyone knows," Cappelli had said. "I'm only surprised you haven't had every crazy old woman in town line up in front of your door to ask for a blessing. If it hasn't happened yet, it soon will." Facts were facts: Cappelli had been right.

Not that crazy old women started knocking on Renato's door. Not exactly.

But people—all sorts of people, people whom Renato had known merely as faces around town—found ways of sidling up next to him and starting conversations. People who had never much bothered with him before were eager to get in good with him, to get a piece of something he had or was about to receive.

He was not sure he liked being the object of speculation. His list, so private and precious, had somehow become public property. Renato didn't know what to think.

He had the impression of being transformed into an ear. An attentive, listening ear. People talked to Renato. People disclosed themselves unexpectedly, revealing themselves like songs. Renato became interested in discovering what there was to be heard.

❧

Il Piccino, the midget who ran the newspaper store. *There* was a melody.

One evening Renato was walking along the main street on his way to have dinner with Milena at her parents' *bottega*. He passed the newspaper shop, which was about to close. From the corner of his eye he saw something through the window that halted his steps.

He entered, said a quick *buonasera* to Il Piccino, nodded to the two other customers, and turned to look at the magazine rack near the window. There on the cover of the guide for the new week's television programs was a photo of Meg Barker. Renato had never before seen a magazine cover bearing the image of a person he knew.

Embarrassed that somebody might see what he was doing, he went to the magazine rack and picked out the television guide. His hand trembled slightly as he opened the cover, ran his finger down the table of contents, and flipped to the page that held the story about Meg Barker's film. It was one of her old films, made twenty years ago, dubbed now in Italian to be shown on television.

Renato heard the door to the shop close. The other customers had left and he was alone with Il Piccino. Il Piccino was staring at him. Feeling caught, Renato closed the magazine and slipped it back into the rack, pretending he hadn't been reading anything of particular interest.

"I have something to tell," Il Piccino said.

"To me?"

"To you. People are talking about your trip. I want to tell you what I have to say."

Il Piccino was not a talkative person. Renato was disconcerted by the intensity with which the waist-high pug-faced man stared into his eyes. He said, "Tell me."

"Everyone calls me 'Il Piccino,' the little one, but my family name is Trieste."

"It's a nice name."

"It's a Jewish name."

"Oh," said Renato. "I didn't know."

"Many Jews took their names from the towns where they lived. That was hundreds of years ago. And then my people came to Tuscany. To Siena, more precisely. Siena is where I was born. I'm Jewish. Did you know?"

"No," Renato said. "That's fine. Even though I'm not sure I know what it means."

"It means I belong to the same religion that gave birth to the man who is your Lord."

"Yes. That everyone knows. But I never met a Jew before. I don't know what it means."

"Should mean something good, because my religion is mother to yours. We're brothers, one could say. But too many people haven't thought about it that way."

"I understand."

"You understand." Il Piccino laughed, then shook his head, for Renato hadn't understood anything. "There used to be a good number of Jewish families in Siena. There are only a few left now. The Germans came and took them away."

"I've heard this said. I'm sorry."

"It was before you were born," Il Piccino said. "I was a young boy. I'm older than you, you know." He stopped. "When the Germans came, my parents hid me in a trunk in the attic underneath old clothes. Smelled of camphor." He sniffed. "I'm a small person. Even smaller at that time I was, even smaller than now.

"Strange, you know," he said. "I remember—before the Germans —when my grandmother died, and I saw my grandfather the day of the funeral. The rabbi went to my grandfather, attached a black piece of cloth to the breast of his jacket, just over his heart. The rabbi took a little pair of scissors and made a cut in the cloth. I asked my grandfather about it later. He told me in the old days, in the days of the Bible, when someone you loved died, you had to tear all your clothes. But in modern times a little symbolic piece of cloth was enough. 'But why did the rabbi cut it?' I asked. And my grandfather said, 'Because my heart is torn,' and he started to cry as I'd never seen a man cry before.

"I thought about that a lot after the Germans came and took everyone away, almost everyone but me. I was easy to hide. Lucky, no? A few managed to come back after the war. Very, very few. I kept thinking about that little rip."

He looked Renato hard in the eyes. "I grew up anyway with the help of good people, Christian people, in Siena. Didn't want to stay there, though. When I was old enough, I came here and set up this shop.

"It was true, what my grandfather had said about a heart being torn. He was taken away. My parents, too. And the funny part is, when he told me about the little rip, at that time I thought my life was already imperfect, already had a tear in it because I was so short. Then the Germans gave life a much bigger rip. Much bigger indeed."

Renato didn't know what to say to the eyes that stared at him.

"I don't complain, though. Want to know why? Because I looked around after growing up some, and you know what I saw? The fabric of every life gets torn. If it hasn't happened yet to a person, it's enough to wait awhile. Sooner or later the rip comes. Somebody dies. Love is lost. Things change. A town becomes a lake. Sooner or later there's the rip. With the town about to go underwater, I'd say that's a pretty big tear for all of us, wouldn't you?" He smiled, and lowered his eyes, relieving Renato of the stare. "Which isn't necessarily a bad thing," Il Piccino said. "Because that's when life begins. The interesting part is what you do with life after it's been torn."

Renato was silent. Then he said, "You're right, I think. But why are you telling this to me?"

"Because from what people are saying about you, I knew you were beginning to open your eyes to things as they really are. There. You can write on your list what I've said, if you want. If it makes any difference to you. Or you don't have to write a thing. Doesn't matter to me. I told you what I had to say. That's enough for me."

"But if you don't care about the list, why was it so important to tell me?"

"I told you because, I don't know. I suppose I told you to feel less alone. A little bit less alone."

Renato was silent. Then he said, "Got a pen?"

Il Piccino handed him a pen from next to the cash register.

Renato wrote:

> TRIESTE—*Sooner or later the fabric of every life*
> *gets torn. That's when life begins.*

He didn't show the list to Il Piccino because the list was private for Renato, private for the other people whose names were written down. But Renato did say, "Good. I wrote down what you said."

"Thank you." After a pause Il Piccino added, "That's the only thing I miss, you know. I don't care about my height. But it's the only thing I miss."

"What?"

"Company," Il Piccino said.

The door opened just then and a woman came in asking to buy a magazine on embroidery. In the presence of a customer, Il Piccino's face closed, like the door to a vault. "Did you find the magazine you were looking for?" Il Piccino said to Renato, now with the voice of a courteous but distant shopkeeper.

"Can't remember what it was now that I came here to find." Renato laughed. "Funny trick my stupid head played on me. If I remember, I'll be back. *Buonasera,*" Renato said to the lady customer. "*Buonasera,*" he said to the short man behind the cash register.

He let himself out of the shop.

THIRTY

Barbershop

Yes, word of Renato's trip to Rome was rippling through town, growing like circles on the surface of water. People found a way to talk to him wherever he was. "Renato," said the wife of the man who ran the gas station while Renato was filling up the waterworks truck. "Listen to me, Renato. My niece was supposed to get married next month, but her fiancé left her two days ago. Can you imagine anything unluckier than that? Poor girl, she needs her luck to change. She needs good luck. Can you do something for her when you go to Rome?"

"Come here for a minute, Tizzoni," said the man in the hardware store when Renato went to buy caulking. "A word about my poor old mother. Her veins, as you know, have never been good. And now they tell her they have to operate to fix the veins in her legs. With the miserable luck she's had all her life, she's terrified something bad will happen when they get her in the operating room. Of course I'm not a superstitious person myself, but she's my mother, you understand, and why take chances? You couldn't put in a good word for her, could you?"

"Oh, Renato," said the woman in the fish shop. "Do something to give my son good luck on his high school exams and I'll see that you and your family get a nice discount on fish for the rest of your life. Or at least as long as we still have a town to live in. While you're at it, maybe you might do something to change the luck of the whole town, if that isn't asking too much."

What can you do when people ask? You might not be so sure yourself of your power to do anything, but you see the eager need in their eyes, and you wish you could help. What do you say? "I'll keep your daughter in mind while I'm in Rome," was what Renato said. "I, too, wish your mother the best of luck." "My hopes are with your son for his exams." "Change the luck of the town? There's nothing I'd like more."

One Saturday afternoon he went to get his hair cut. A lively conversation was under way when he walked in and sat down in one of the chairs, waiting for his barber to be free. The men in the barbershop were discussing the dam. Of course.

The town's banker was having his hair cut. His was the most outspoken voice on this subject, as it always was on any subject. "I tell you," he said to the other customers and to the barbers, "I tell you all. Your debates, your argumentation, all your carrying on, it's all wasted breath. Such great orators you all become! But I tell you you're wasting your breath. And as to that school of thought that says we would do well to refuse the government compensation for our homes and businesses, the supporters of the notion, I tell you, are nothing but *bischeri:* fools. And I will remind you of our own Tuscan history, in this case to explain how we got the word *bischeri,* and you will understand how foolish it is indeed to think we might strong-arm the government.

"Look a little to the north, as far as Florence. It was there, five centuries back, that Luca Pitti wanted to build a grand palace, one that would be even grander than that of his rival, Cosimo de' Medici. So he bought up land across the River Arno and commissioned the construction of the Pitti Palace. Before construction could be started, of course, there was the matter of compensaton to be settled. Property owners in the area were offered a fair price. One family, however, the Bischeri family, wanted to hold out for more. They refused the cash compensation, thinking themselves terribly clever. In the end their property was seized and they were paid nothing. Zero. Clever people, these Bischeri? No. Total fools. And their family name lives on today as another word for idiots. *Bischeri* we say of people who don't know how to act in their own interest. And that's what I tell you now. Anyone who thinks about fighting back against the government in the dam project for this town is nothing but a *bischero*. Useless it is to fight against the people in power at any given time. Power is powerful and must be treated as such. If it weren't, then why would it be called power? Logical, no?"

"It's easy for you," said the customer who was just leaving. "Your bank will transfer you to another office. You'll still have a job, even if it is somewhere else. Your shoulders will always be covered. You'll always be rich. Easy for you to speak. But the rest of us? What life have we got, if not in this town?" He took out his wallet and said to Domenico the barber, "How much do I owe?"

"Thirty-five. Same as always."

"Good-bye, everyone," the customer said and left.

"Good-bye," voices said.

It was Renato's turn to occupy Domenico's chair. He noticed a new and nervous silence when he sat himself down in the barber chair in full view of all the men present. Conversation was usually so fluent here, for the barbershop had always been a place of easy discussion, discussion that turned boisterous when politics were spoken about and philosophical when women were the subject. But today Renato found himself watched by the customers in the barber chairs on either side of his own. Silently they observed him in the mirror while Domenico spread the barber sheet over him and tucked white cotton around his neck so that no hairs would fall inside his shirt collar.

"So?" he said to the mirror when he could no longer stand being stared at by the several pairs of curious, reflected eyes.

"So nothing!" said the man in the chair next to him. Conversation started up again. A relief. The men, having tired themselves with talk about the real-life problems of the homelessness they'd be facing soon, talked instead about whether the Ferrari team was likely to win the next race on the formula one circuit. Here, too, the banker spoke as if with great expertise.

Renato looked in the mirror and studied the banker, in the next chair over. Renato had never much cared for him. The banker liked to give the impression that he owned everyone in town, though really, Renato reminded himself, the banker held nothing more than the titles to businesses and homes, not the titles to souls.

No, Renato told himself. Better not to think about the banker. Why not think of pleasant things?

He breathed in deeply and smelled shaving cream, shampoo, hair tonic, aftershave lotion, disinfectant liquid for scissors and combs. Clean barbershop smells. He felt his barber's fingers on his face. He heard the quick, snipping scissors as the barber trimmed his beard. The barber had always been one of Renato's favorite people in all the world.

The barber's name was Domenico, of course, but secretly, Renato thought of him as Figaro. Though not an opera fan, Renato knew that once, in some place, there had been a barber named Figaro who had acquired renown because of his talent for stirring up intrigue. Domenico seemed such a Figaro. He was a robust man with the gray hair of a biblical saint and the face of a smiling lion. A well-clipped beard and mustache decorated the area around his grinning mouth. Bright, mischievous eyes watched the world in amusement over the half glasses that perpetually perched on his nose.

"I think it's a grand thing you're doing," Figaro the barber said suddenly, with a smile in his voice, and Renato could tell conversation was about to take a strange turn. "And if anyone tells you you're crazy, you just tell them to go to the devil."

"Who's been saying I'm crazy?" Renato said.

"No one." He snipped the beard at Renato's throat. "But even if they were to say such things, you take my advice. Tell them to go to the devil."

"I, for one, think you're crazy," said the banker.

"*Ah sì?*" Renato said. "In that case, go to the devil."

"*Bravo!*" Figaro laughed.

Renato's house was his own. He was employed by the town, not by a business that depended on the bank. Employed for as long as the town would continue to exist, in any case. The banker and his bank played no part in keeping Renato alive, so the banker might just as well go to the devil.

"Go to the devil you," the banker rebutted ineffectually. Then he added, "You and that list of yours for the pope."

"Leave my list out of this," Renato said, pushing Figaro's scissors away from his face so that he could defend himself without interference. The banker retreated in silence, but with a self-righteous smirk. Renato, victorious, eased back into his own chair and let Figaro resume the beard trim.

"Don't send me to the devil for saying so," said the customer in the chair on Renato's other side, "but I think you're crazy, too."

"Leave Renato in peace, will you?" Figaro cut in. "He's come here for a trim. Not for a jury trial."

"No," Renato said to them all in the mirror. "I'm curious to know what people are saying. Curious but also indifferent, because at the end of the day I will do exactly what I want anyway, whatever people say."

"*Bravo* again," Figaro said, patting his shoulder like a trainer in his boxer's corner of the ring.

"If you let me finish what I had started to say," said the other customer, whose name was Pellegrini, "then you will hear. What I started to say was that I, too, *think* you're crazy, but this little thought of mine doesn't change the fact that I also want you to ask for a blessing for me."

"*Aya!*" screamed the banker, for the barber cutting his hair had taken tweezers to a single dark strand growing from inside the banker's ear. The banker's barber was bald himself. He was not known for the delicacy of his touch. Perhaps he harbored a silent grudge against the hairier members of his species. "Warn me next time before you yank!" scolded the banker.

"Would a warning have made a difference?" the barber asked.

"You want it shorter?" said Figaro.

Renato said, "What?"

"The beard."

"No, this length is good. Don't you think? Let's concentrate now on the hair."

"You want a shampoo before I cut?"

"How much is a shampoo?"

"Ten thousand lire more," Figaro said, "but you know it cuts better when it's wet."

"Then wet my head with the spray bottle and spare me the shampoo. I'll shampoo myself when I'm at home."

Figaro took his plastic spray bottle from beside the sink. He baptized Renato's head with a fine mist.

Renato closed his eyes.

But he heard the other customer say, "As I was saying, I would like your blessing all the same. You see, I have an idea."

"Let's hope it doesn't die of loneliness," said the banker.

"Let's hope what doesn't die of loneliness?" Pellegrini said.

"Your idea," the banker explained. "It's not as if you have one every day."

Renato opened his eyes through the mist to look at the other customer in the mirror. Pellegrini's face had turned red with the humiliation of a man who does not know how to reply. He was not a talkative sort. He had a shoe-repair shop at the far end of the main street. Most of his days he spent alone with other people's shoes. When he went to the bar in the evening to pass a few hours, he tended to disappear under the bravura of other men's conversational technique.

"I can't say that I know how to bless anyone, but tell me your idea," Renato said.

"My idea is the following," said the cobbler. "You remember eight years back when I had that growth inside my brain? You remember how they sent me to the hospital up in Torino, and there they operated on me, taking the bad growth out?"

"I could be unkind here," said the banker, "and say that the surgeons were clearly mistaken, for they took out the good parts and left behind only the parts that did not work. But I would not say such a thing, for I would not dare be so cruel."

"Then thank you for not saying it," said the cobbler.

"Let him finish speaking," Renato snapped at the banker while Figaro set to cutting his now dripping hair. "Yes, I remember," he replied to Pellegrini. "I remember your operation. So?"

"So ever since then," the man went on, "I have had to take tablets every day to keep the blood pressure down in my brain. Otherwise, say the doctors, if the blood pressure gets up too high in my head, then something might pop. A vein or artery or something. In any case, it would be my end."

"But the pills work, no?" Renato asked. "They keep your blood pressure under control?"

"Only too well."

"Then what's the problem?"

"The problem is, they keep my pressure down *everywhere*. Not only in my brain, but in my other little head as well. *Il povero uccellino!* My poor little bird! When I was a young man, I used to"— he made a pistonlike movement with his hand—"I used to do it all the time. Nothing out of the ordinary, of course. Nothing to boast about. But the normal dose, you will understand. And especially with my wife. Now, since the operation, since I'm taking the tablets that don't let my brain pop . . ." He shook his head.

"Hold still," said the barber behind Pellegrini. "If you keep moving while I cut, you'll have a missing ear to add to your problems."

"Now, as I say," said the cobbler, "it's been eight years. Now for my poor little bird, the clock always stands at half-past six."

"Half-past six?" said the banker, curious despite himself.

"Half-past six. Think of a clock's hands when it's half-past six. Everything hangs down."

The banker laughed. Then he said, "You have nothing to complain about if you ask me."

"I didn't hear him ask you," Renato said.

"Nothing to complain about," the banker continued, ignoring him. "What is the saying they say? Better one day as a lion than one hundred days as a sheep. You've had your day as a lion. You said so yourself. And now you must content yourself with your memories. Age is like that for everyone. You've attained the peace of your senses. They don't trouble you anymore. You should be content."

"But I'm *not* content!" said the cobbler with passion. "Why should I be content now if the rest of my life means living like a sheep?"

No one had an answer. Renato thought about what it might mean if his own senses ever reached a static state of peace in which he no longer hungered after anything. Terrible it would be. Terrible. At least now, in his own turmoil, he was hungering after hunger itself, yearning to find the taste of things once more.

He said, "I'm sorry, Pellegrini. I would help you if I could, but I'm no doctor. And I've never performed a miracle in all my life. There's nothing I can do."

"You're waiting for a miracle to happen, though. Isn't it true?"

Renato reflected. "In my own life, perhaps. Yet I have such fragile faith in what might happen for me, how can I promise anything to anyone else?"

"I want to be on your list all the same," the cobbler insisted, the color of conviction now rising to his cheeks. "Would you do this thing for me? Right now! Now, before you forget. Get out your list. Put my name down. Please."

"But you said yourself that you thought I was crazy!"

"Crazy, yes. But every blessing is a crazy thing. If it weren't, where would the miracle be?"

Renato looked in the mirror and exchanged glances with Figaro, who stood behind him, scissors in hand. "Now?" Renato said. "In this very moment now? My hair is wet. Domenico is cutting my hair. I'm wrapped up in this barber's sheet. Let's do a little thing. Let's wait until we're done, at least."

"Now, please," said the cobbler.

Again Renato and Figaro looked at each other in the mirror. "I'll wait for a moment," the barber said. "I'm happy to wait. Get out your list. Do what you have to do."

So, reaching under the barber's sheet into his back pocket, Renato pulled out the list. "Anyone got a pen?"

Figaro produced a pen from his breast pocket, where it was tucked in beside a spare comb.

Renato shifted in his chair and leaned forward, laying the list on a dry place beside the sink. He shielded the list with his free hand so that no one might read what else it contained. "Tell me then. What should I write?"

"Write my name," said the cobbler. "Pellegrini."

"Pellegrini," Renato said, carefully writing out the syllables he pronounced. All eyes in the barbershop watched him as if witnessing a mystical rite. Scissors had ceased their snipping. The aromas of aftershave lotion and hair tonic, like incense, spiced the air. "Good. Pellegrini. I've written your name. Then?"

"Then write the following: I wish I could be—" Something caught in the cobbler's throat as he heard himself utter his own words. He swallowed. "I wish the impossible—to be forever young."

And those were the precise words that Renato added to his list:

> PELLEGRINI—*I wish the impossible—to be*
> *forever young.*

"Good," Renato said when he had finished. He returned his list to his pocket and handed Figaro back his pen. "I promise you less than nothing," he said, getting settled in his chair under the barber's sheet, "but I respect your wish. I'll take it with me to Rome."

"Thank you," said the cobbler as his own barber resumed cutting his hair. "Of course it's impossible," he said. "I think I'm crazy to ask." He laughed, finding again his habitual sense of embarrassment.

"You're one more crazy than the other, the two of you," said the banker as the bald barber behind him got out the tweezers again and started eyeing another errant hair, this one growing from the lobe of the ear, "though I wouldn't know who to bet my money on as the crazier. *Aya!*" he screamed as the tweezer-armed barber went in for the kill.

Somehow the snideness of the banker made all the men in the room comfortable once again. Their world had returned to order.

As noisy as cicadas, Domenico's scissors snipped around the crown of Renato's head.

People, thought Renato. People are expecting *a lot*.

THIRTY-ONE

Cool Air After the Rain

Renato was just finishing up in the barbershop when the weather changed, from one minute to the next.

A sharp wind came from the west, from the Mediterranean Sea, blasting away at last the *anticiclone,* the heavy mass of high pressure that had parked itself over Tuscany for the past few days and had kept all storms away. Now the good wind came, making temperatures drop in no more time than it took for birds in their nests to notice that the tree branches were blowing once again, like boats suddenly moving in full sail after a long, dead calm.

Renato returned home and took his four sheep for their evening walk up on the hillside above the house. They raised their heads every time thunder rumbled from the clouds that were accumulating in the western part of the sky and were blocking the sunset behind the approaching rain. The sheep twitched their ears, their mouths chewing in unceasing circles, tongues flickering fast over lips. Prima was feeling frisky. She pranced for a moment, the mood coming over her. Quarta took the longest to trust the sky before lowering her head again for another mouthful of grass.

Renato milked the sheep in their stall and felt the building shake with thunder.

Later he lay in bed beside Milena and listened to the rain thrum on the roof. He heard it gush over everything in the blackness outside, washing away the last of the heat. Renato felt washed, listening to the rain.

He dreamed of the hand again. The masculine hand with the ring on the finger was outside his front door in the nighttime courtyard, hovering above the well while rain raced down inside the well and splashed in loud drops on the surface of the water. The hand was the only luminous thing in the black, wet courtyard, hovering like a dove, glad for the rain. The hand was vigilant outside his door, waiting still to lead.

The world looked fresh the next morning. The dawn gave light to a crisp blue sky that smelled like autumn. The wind was chilly, making Renato happy to be sitting there on his hillside with his sheep. White clouds were vague in the incredibly deep-blue sky; higher up a few clouds looked solid, well cut from some magical white stone, weightless and pure.

Quarta bumped against Renato. He looked at her, looked at the grass blowing on the hillside, looked at the valley, the far away cypresses, the sky, the clouds. Everywhere he looked, everything seemed so beautiful it almost hurt.

The cool wind followed Renato throughout the day, running its fingers over his skin inside his clothes. He drove to work, leaving the windows of his old Fiat open; the wind surrounded him in the car. He switched vehicles, taking the Sant'Angelo D'Asso waterworks truck, along with Cappelli, to check the levels in a water depository that served several farms near town; the wind came, too. "*Madonnina!*" Cappelli said. "What a wind!"

Back in Sant'Angelo D'Asso the wind walked with both men all the way to the *bottega,* on the main street, which was bright in the sunlight. Then, after Renato had finished his coffee and Cappelli his topping-up dose of Sambuca, the wind was waiting for them as they stepped outside to the open square, ready for more work.

❦

Evening was coming. It was half-past six and the sky was still bright, the colors of dusk about to start.

Renato had finished work. He was at home, where he exchanged a few words with Petula. She said she was going out. She would have a sandwich or something for dinner with Daniele up at his bar by the train station (*his* bar alone now that his parents weren't alive). And maybe she'd give him a hand with the bar. In any case, she was on her way up there and she'd be back late. She told her father not to wait up.

"Fine," Renato said, feeling he had lost the right to say anything else. "Fine. Come back late if you want." Talking to her had become strange since he'd found out she was pregnant. Polite, friendly, but distant. It would stay that way, he knew, until he could bring himself to say what she was waiting for him to say. But words didn't come to him, only confusion and an empty feeling in his stomach, as if she, his baby, had been yanked from some mysterious womb deep inside him, which of course was ridiculous because everybody knew that a man had no womb, but he felt as if he had had one anyway, once, or not a womb but her, Petula, inside him for years and now she had been pulled out of him and stood there watching him from the outside, judging him for his inability to do something that seemed impossible. Acceptance was as hard as that.

It was too difficult and confusing. So he said, "Fine."

The house was empty when she left. Renato didn't want to milk and walk the sheep just yet. He wanted human company instead. He realized he wanted to be with his wife.

Walking into town, he was accompanied by the wind through the crowd of people out taking their evening stroll. There were still another forty-five minutes until seven-thirty, when the *bottega* would serve its first dinner customers.

Milena's mother watched Renato walk in. She said, "Oh. You. If you're looking for your English actress lady friend, you'll be disappointed. She came, had her whiskey, and left hours ago."

"*Cara* Maria Severina," he laughed. "You know perfectly well I haven't got a lady friend." Indeed, Renato hadn't been thinking of Meg Barker. She no longer tormented him mentally. She, at least, was one question he considered resolved. Milena was good for him. She was his woman. In her there was every woman in the world. "Is Milena here?"

"If not here, where do you want her to be?" said Maria Severina. "She's in the kitchen, working harder than you."

Tonino stepped out from the kitchen just then, carrying a tray of glasses to be put on the tables. "Oh," he said. "*Ciao.* Looking for your wife? She's in the kitchen finishing the meat sauce."

Renato patted the man's arm as he walked past. "Milena," he said in the kitchen, "*vieni con me.* Come with me. Let's go out for a little while."

"Come with you? I have the meat sauce to finish. Where do you want to go? We're serving dinner soon. Why do we have to go out in a hurry? Is anything wrong?"

"Your mother can finish the meat sauce. Come with me. Nothing bad has happened. I want to walk with you, that's all. Let's go, all right?"

"What's come over you lately, Renato?" She stirred the sauce. "What do you mean, you want to walk? I have the meat sauce to finish and there are a thousand things to do."

"I want to walk. Is that a strange thing to want? When was the last time you and I took *la passeggiata* together? When was the last time we went for the evening stroll?"

"The last time? It can't have been long ago."

Renato watched her face while her thoughts went backward until she was a younger woman and Petula was a little girl and the three of them, together, a young family, walked with the rest of the people along the town's main street, when the future was something imponderable and not worth too much thought anyway.

"A little bit of time has passed," Milena said, "now that I think about it. But this evening we have to do it?" She indicated the sauce with her hands.

"Tomorrow evening will be no different. Or the evening after. You'll always have the sauce to think about. There will always be too much to do with your parents here. So let's take our stroll this evening. Why not? It's beautiful outside. I want you to see the light on the buildings. I want you to feel the wind with me. It smells like autumn already. Come with me. Shall we go?" He held out his hand, waiting for hers.

Milena untied her apron strings, and hung up the apron by the sink. She washed her hands, then tightened her ponytail.

"I'll be back before we serve dinner," Milena said to her mother on her way out. "Will you take care of the sauce?"

"But there are things to do," her mother said, looking with accusation at the couple, as if Renato had never been anything but a corrupting influence, as if Milena should have known better than to let herself be led astray.

"There will always be things to do," Milena said. "This evening Renato and I are taking a little walk."

"*Buona passeggiata,*" they heard Tonino say behind them as the door closed. "Have a nice stroll."

THIRTY-TWO

Figs

Milena linked her arm with Renato's.

They started out uphill, toward the church across the piazza. Any stroll worth being called a stroll had to include more than one simple *vasca,* one lap. Renato and Milena went uphill along the town's *corso,* the main street, so that then they'd have the luxury of retracing their steps downhill, continuing their next lap farther down, past the *bottega,* perhaps all the way to the end of the *corso* and to the end of the town itself.

It had indeed been years since they had taken *la passeggiata,* but with the first steps their feet immediately refound the proper pace for a stroll. Strolling was not like walking. Walking was transportation to get you where you wanted to go. Strolling was more a question of watching, of giving the eyes the time they might need to take in everything there was to see. Strolling was all process, no goal.

Milena's eyes looked up above the ground floor of buildings already in shade. She looked up to the topmost floors where, on both sides of the street, brick façades were touched by the changing colors of the sun. The bricks and the windows shone rose-colored and gold. Farther up was the glass-blue sky.

"Look, the swallows!" Milena said, pointing up with her free hand at the swift, dark swallows that swirled and swooped in the evening air. "I've always loved the hour when the swallows appear."

Renato, too, watched the acrobatic circlings of the birds whose elongated tails and wing tips gave added grace. With the autumn not too far away, who knew how much longer the summery swallows would be here before they set off in migration toward Africa, to the south? And when they returned next year, eager to renew their nests beneath the eaves of the buildings, the same nests to which they had been coming every year for each of the many hundreds of years since Sant'Angelo D'Asso had been built, would they even find a town? Or would they fly here again only to look down in their flight upon a lake where once there had been a valley and a town? Where would they go then to make their nests?

Renato and Milena strolled. Neither had any special intention to be silent, but easy silence came to them as they looked at everything around, a silence rich with complicity, for the eyes of both of them observed the same things. Each walked with the other, each head thinking its own thoughts. And the thoughts prompted by what they saw were probably so similar anyway that they could have been thoughts filling a single head.

Milena and Renato saw two young mothers walking side by side, pushing babies in baby strollers. One mother did most of the talking. She was retelling the very big story of some very insignificant slight someone had committed against her and of the consequent dressing-down she had given the wrongdoer. The other mother nodded ruminatively and said *No!* and *You're joking!* and *But of course!* at all the right moments. The two mothers stopped in front of the open door of the newspaper store. Nothing in the store prompted their stopping; the story being recounted had merely reached an important point that needed to be emphasized by a total halt in motion. And once they came to full agreement that the more talkative of the two women— *poverina!* the poor thing—was unquestionably justified in the acts of vengeance she was now planning against the person who had offended her, then the two mothers would shove on again, rolling their baby strollers up the hill.

Il Piccino, inside his newpaper store meanwhile, seemed vexed because the two talking mothers were blocking his doorway, preventing paid-up customers from going out, stopping would-be customers from coming in. The talking mothers were oblivious.

Children chased each other along the main street, boys more interested in playing with other boys, girls sticking mostly to themselves.

Teenagers along the *corso* were not nearly so careless as to run about without a thought as to how they might appear. No, the teenagers moved with the self-conscious artistry of fashion models on a runway. Some stood like classical groupings of statues, waiting to be admired for their beauty and for their seeming indifference to the world. But no pose, no look, no personal style of dress, however casual in appearance, had been left to chance. Clothes, even jeans and midriff-revealing T-shirts, had been ironed by mothers at home. Cuffs had been intentionally frayed, hair meticulously coiffed with mousse and gel to give it that natural look.

Young guys in groups straddled their parked motor scooters, young knights astride their mounts, eyeing the damsels who floated past. Many eyes were masked behind cool-looking sunglasses, though the street itself was in shadow by now.

Other young men preferred not to stand around with switched-off motorbikes but to walk, taking advantage of the opportunity the *passeggiata* afforded to let themselves be seen in motion. Some walked pigeon-toed to look tough. And what would happen to those feet later in life? Would the feet eventually turn outward to a more linear gait, or were these young men destined to seek coolness forever, until they became wrinkled old men who simply walked funny?

A beautiful girl walked past. Flanking her were two girls of lesser beauty, ladies-in-waiting attending the queen. The three walked with arms interlocked, their pace slow enough to let onlookers take in the central girl's long hair, long neck, and coy, regal, down-turned eyes.

Why was it that everyone seemed to resemble a famous person? The guys imitated the way rock stars dressed. The girls looked like some television starlet or other. Everyone had an image to maintain.

Everyone's appearance was a bargain-basement copy of an image that belonged to someone else.

A rich middle-aged couple strolled by. They lived in a villa in the next valley over, well past the town's old walls. They wanted to look like horsey English country gentry. They wore jodhpurs and tweed, and carried a rolled-up Burberry umbrella. Neither of them had been near a horse for years, if ever.

Passing Milena and Renato, the couple said, "*Buonasera*."

"*Buonasera,*" Milena and Renato replied.

The *comandante* of the police walked by, shoulders back, chest out, hands clasped behind his back in fine Mussolini fashion. His boots were shiny, the crest of his hat very high. He walked as if he expected people to pay him homage. Few people lived up to his hopes. "*Buonasera,* Tizzoni," he said to Renato, somehow managing to make an evening's greeting sound like a warning.

"*Buonasera a Lei,*" Renato said, walking past, giving Milena's arm a squeeze with his own.

Older people walked along the *corso*, too. Older women still wore nicely pressed blouses, still scented themselves with perfume, still put on lipstick and rouge, but inside them was a secret rage against futility, for no amount of hair teasing or personal grooming could ever stop the march of time. Some older men had given up the fight, letting themselves relax to drink and play cards at tables in front of the bar, legs splayed, belts unbuckled, without caring whether or not the stripes on their shirts clashed with their pants. Or maybe they hadn't given up entirely, for the shoes of many card players showed a recent shine, and wafts of masculine cologne came off newly shaven old necks. Maybe no one ever really stopped caring.

An ancient woman with a permanently bent-over back stepped out of a shop in front of Renato and Milena. She was a sweet woman. If you ever gave her time to say what was on her mind, she'd get her mouth going first, working the words around in there between her tongue and her false teeth. Half a minute later her words would find their way out and she'd say, "I was a real *garbereccia* as a girl. A real looker."

This evening she saw Renato and Milena. She smiled, and her mouth started to go to work.

"*Buonasera*," they both said, not quite having the patience to wait for the arrival of her words.

Her hand gave a small wave. "*Buonasera*."

A very old couple walked slowly along, their arms, too, interlocked like Renato's and Milena's. They looked disoriented amid the noise of the crowd. They grumbled their way through the youthful throngs as if a bad joke had been played on them, as if the young were no longer recognizable as members of the same species, as if it were the young who had changed.

Milena's and Renato's arms were crossed lightly at the wrist. The very old couple's arms were locked tight at the elbows, links in a chain trying hard not to break.

Milena and Renato were walking downhill now. They strolled by Sculati on his way up to the bar. "*Buonasera*," said Sculati. He looked in a hurry to get to the bar. Maybe it was a drink he was eager to reach, maybe a little company among people who were still alive.

"*Buonasera*," said Renato and his wife.

All along their walk they greeted and were greeted by people of the town, people they had known their whole life. They walked past the barbershop, exchanging a *buonasera* with Figaro, who was closing up shop, and Renato realized how many of these people had their names written on the list that he carried in his pocket next to the left cheek of his ass. He felt the weight of the duty that would go with him to Rome to shake the pope's hand, as if the *culo,* the luck of the whole town, was waiting to be changed by that handshake alone.

Only in a town like Sant'Angelo D'Asso could you walk and recognize almost everyone you saw.

"A beautiful stroll," Milena said, mirroring his thoughts. He took Milena's hand, turned it over in his own, and gave her palm a kiss.

Milena and Renato reached the end of the *corso*, down past the pharmacist's house with the ancient Roman mosaic floor hidden in its basement. They approached the big stone gate that marked the end of the town. "I should get back to the *bottega*," Milena said. "You can go on home. I'll see you after work. Thank you for the stroll."

Renato looked out past the arch of the gate, his eyes following the road into the countryside, toward their house. The evening appeared brighter out there than it did in among the buildings of town. "Wait," said Renato, not wanting to let Milena go. "Let's just do a little more of the road. Only over the bridge. Then we'll walk back. All right?"

"It's almost half-past seven. We open soon. What difference does it make to walk a little more?"

"No difference," Renato said, laughing. "Exactly. So let's walk."

She let herself be corrupted. She put her arm around his waist and kissed his shoulder, savoring the delicious irresponsibility of playing hookey, if only for a moment, a sensation she hadn't felt since she and Renato had sneaked away together, years in the past.

Smells of the countryside were in the air on the road outside town, the mixed perfumes of grain in the fields, grapes on the vines almost ripe enough to be picked, animal manure in farmhouse stalls, trees in green woods at the edges of hills.

Renato and Milena were almost at the bridge when they saw something that neither of them had ever noticed before. At first it appeared little more than a green clump beneath the curl of the road as it turned over the bridge, a bush, perhaps, just below the uppermost edge of the riverbank. Getting closer, they saw that it was no bush but a tree, a fig tree. When they were even closer, they observed that the tree was bigger than it appeared from a distance. The green leaves reached only a couple of feet above the ground along the incline of the riverbank, yet the trunk of the tree was hidden inside a hole. The leafy branches covered the better part of what looked like the mouth of a little grotto.

Renato gave Milena his hand so that she wouldn't slip down the riverbank as they went to have a better look. They saw the top of a stone arch, a quarter dome crowning the hole in the ground in which the fig tree grew.

"I'd love a fig!" Milena said. "Are there any ripe ones left, or have the birds eaten them all?"

They searched together among the fig leaves, which came up no higher than their waists. It being nearly the end of September, the fig season was almost finished. The figs that remained were either hopelessly shriveled or split open from over-ripeness, with tiny ants swarming over the skin to the moist meat inside. Renato said, "Look at these!" when he discovered a small branch holding two perfect figs. He reached over to pick the fruit, leaning against the stone arch for balance.

He handed the figs to Milena and said, "But what kind of place is this? Strange we never noticed it before. From a distance it looks like nothing. And maybe it's only this year that this fig tree grew tall enough to make itself seen over the edge of this hole in the ground. Looks more like a buried building than a hole."

"What beautiful figs. I hope they're sweet."

Renato took a penknife from the front pocket of his work trousers. "Take this," he said.

With the knife Milena cut one of the figs, opening it into a four-pointed star. She raised the fig to her mouth, scraped her teeth along the inside of the skin, and sucked in the glistening faintly red flesh. "It's delicious!" she said, delighted by its sweetness. "Here. Try." She held the open fig out to Renato.

"Oh. You'll feed it to me?" he laughed. "Well, why not?" He ate from her hand.

"Very good, indeed!" he said, wiping his mouth. He smiled at Milena, surprised to find himself feeling the way he felt when they made love together, when they made love well. This was almost more intimately titillating, eating figs in the pinkish light of the evening sun.

"Shall we eat the other one?" Milena smiled wonderfully, and she cut open the other fig, letting Renato eat half from her fingers first, then eating the other half herself.

"Strange, this place," Renato said, his teeth chewing through pulp to the little seeds. "Oh! I can't resist the curiosity. I have to take a look down inside."

"You won't hurt yourself?"

"I climb down inside wells almost every day. This hole doesn't even look too deep."

Renato pushed aside the branches of the fig tree and lowered himself inside the hole in front of the arch. Feeling with the toe of his boot, he found footholds. Carefully he went down, reaching the bottom in no time, for the hole wasn't much deeper than he was tall. His eyes needed a moment to adjust to the relative darkness. Then he saw that the arch was, in fact, the top of a doorway of some sort. There was so much dirt and so many rocks filling the doorway, it was difficult to say whether he stood before the entrance to a natural cave or to a man-made room that reached back into the earth of the riverbank. Rough stones were evenly spaced around the doorway and the arch above: Evidently this was the ancient and simple architecture of man. The fig tree was rooted strongly in the soft soil in front.

"It's dark in here," Renato called up. "Hard to know what it is. Could be an old tomb, or something. I'd need a flashlight, but it doesn't look like there's anything in here except the roots of the tree."

"Careful of little animals," Milena said. She never did have much affection for *animaletti,* as she called bugs.

Renato looked, but he saw no bugs. He didn't see much of anything. For a moment he remembered his first dream in which the hand had revealed a treasure for him hidden inside the well of his own courtyard. His heart beat fast thinking of his dream.

But he was quickly disappointed. There was no treasure to be found here. Most likely it was simply an old tomb. Everyone knew that there had once been Etruscans here, even before the Romans had built a small town where Sant'Angelo D'Asso now stood. The Etruscans had put their houses high on hillsides, but their tombs they would often construct on lower ground. The river, naturally, was the lowest point in the valley. Tombs had been discovered before, the artifacts and treasures they contained taken away to museums throughout the region. This little cavern in front of which Renato stood, this underground room, or tomb, or whatever it was, held no treasure. It was a hole in the ground.

At least there was a fig tree, he told himself, and the figs were very good. He'd come back another time to collect more figs, maybe next year if the town hadn't been put underwater yet. A fig tree was a nice little treasure, he tried to convince himself. These figs were especially sweet.

He looked around then to refind a foothold so that he could climb out. With his eyes now well used to the shadows, he saw a metal object on the ground beside the roots of the tree. It was not much bigger than an egg. He bent over, picked up the object, then climbed out of the hole. The light above had turned to the gold of sunset. Milena helped Renato brush the dust off his trousers and shirt, then Renato handed Milena the object.

"How lovely!" she said. "You found this down there? What is it?"

"I don't know. An old metal something. Corroded as hell. Here, look. Looks like a little boat, doesn't it? Could be a child's toy. Some kid must have lost his toy boat."

"I like it, though," Milena said. "You could polish it up, and who knows how pretty it might be."

Renato smiled so as not to spoil this moment with Milena in the evening light, but inside he was disappointed. Disappointed, yes. His dream had promised a treasure, and he couldn't help but hope to discover some physical treasure with magical powers.

Fine, he told himself so as not to lose his smile. This discovery of the toy boat was not the realization of any dream. *E allora?* So what?

There didn't have to be a so what. It was a pleasant evening, and he and his wife had taken a nice stroll together and had found some wonderful figs. That was enough. And now there was this old toy boat as a little reminder. Why should he expect more?

"Here," he said. "You keep this, just to remember the figs we ate."

"Renato, this crisis you've been living lately, how bad is it?"

"Bad," he said. "But nothing to worry about. Happens to everyone sooner or later, I think. Who knows why?"

"I don't satisfy you?"

"Milena," he said, "you're everything to me."

"Yes." She looked at him. "But is everything enough?"

He kissed her mouth and said, "Here. Take the little boat to remember the figs."

"You keep it," she said. "I'll remember the figs anyway. With what you're going through, maybe you need the reminder more than I do."

She knows me, Renato thought. It almost scares me to think how well this woman knows who I am. "*Grazie.*"

They started to walk back toward town. "In any case," she said, taking up the conversation she had maybe wanted to start a moment before, "I suppose we have other things to worry about now. Have you been thinking about Petula?"

"If I could not think about her it would be a miracle."

"There's nothing we can do but accept," she said. "And Daniele, you know, isn't a bad boy."

"His parents were bad."

"But he's making himself better. Petula will help him with that. And now she's carrying his child. We have to accept, don't you think?"

"In theory I know you're right. But I can't put it in to practice. I can't bring myself to—" He made a circular gesture with his hands. He shrugged. "Give me some time."

They walked in silence, entering the town through the stone gate. Bats now swooped above them to catch insects, taking over from the swallows, who were returning to their nests.

"I wish I didn't have to go back to the *bottega,*" Milena said as they walked up the main street. There were fewer people on the *corso* now; most were in their homes getting ready for dinner. "It would be nice once in a while to spend an evening at home just by ourselves."

At the door to the restaurant, she said, "Will you have dinner in here tonight?"

"No. I'll go back home and have a bite. I have to take care of the sheep. There's some cheese in the fridge and some slices of ham. I want something light. Petula's out with Daniele. I'll wait for you to get back after work."

They kissed each other on the cheek. Renato went off feeling happy and sad at the same time.

He was walking down the mostly empty street when he saw the priest coming uphill in the direction of the church. "Oh, Tizzoni!" the priest said, surprising him, for it was not the priest's habit to bother with him very much.

"*Buonasera,* Don Luigi. On your way to the parish house, I see? Then *buon appetito*. I'm going to have some dinner myself."

"Yes, Tizzoni. *Buon appetito* to you, too. But there was more I wanted to say to you."

THIRTY-THREE

Don Luigi the Priest

Don Luigi was about as tall as Renato, but larger in girth. The priest's hair was silvery white and thinning on top. The most remarkable features of the face were the mouth and the eyes, or rather, the eyeglasses. Between the priest's eyes and the outer world were two thick panes that made the eyes appear small and far away. Looking into those eyes through the depths of the glass, Renato wondered just how much of the world the eyes managed to see. It was a queer impression, because, reasoning a bit further, he knew that eyeglasses served to improve vision. With that much improvement, the priest's view of the world was probably very sharp indeed. Yet the strange impression persisted beyond reasoning, for the glasses suggested that Don Luigi saw the world through twin telescopes, as if the eyes were watching the earth from some galaxy light years away.

The mouth was almost always curved in a benign brotherly grin, as it was now. But with the eyes seemingly so distant, Renato asked himself what remote thought could possibly make the mouth smile this much. Maybe the priest was smiling about what was happening elsewhere, not here.

"Tell me, Don Luigi. You have something particular to say to *me?*"

"Yes, Tizzoni, to you. I've heard talk, you know. I've heard people talking about what you're doing. About your visit soon to Rome. Is it true what they say? That you're going to see the pope?"

"Public information I see it's become. I would have preferred to keep it quiet. But what can you do in a town like this? Really, it's no big thing. True, yes. But it's not a big thing. A private little trip. That's all. I can't be the first person from Sant'Angelo D'Asso to make a trip to Rome."

"Not the first. But you're wrong when you say it's no big thing. It has become a big thing, Tizzoni, become a big thing for many people in this town. So that's why it has become a big thing for me." The priest wore a long black cassock that reached all the way to his black shoes. He extended an arm in the direction of the church. "I'm on my way uphill to the parish house. May I take you out of your way? Will you walk with me for a while in this direction, even though it will make your way home longer?"

How can you say no to a white-haired priest? Renato told his stomach to be patient for dinner. "Of course," he said.

The two men turned to walk the main street in the deepening shadows. Street lamps switched on. Insects came to swirl around the light, and bats swooped in to eat the insects.

"My little trip to Rome has become important to you, you were saying?" Renato asked. "This surprises me."

"Don't be surprised. It's what everyone talks about these days. And I am, after all, I try to be, the shepherd of this flock. You keep some sheep on your land, I believe, don't you, Tizzoni? And if your sheep were agitated, all of them about one particular thing, wouldn't that thing become important to you?"

"Naturally," Renato nodded. "But if you were to know my sheep a bit better, the fourth one especially, you'd know as I do that sometimes it's better not to take too seriously the things they say to each other. Quarta is given to her little hysterics and she tries her hardest to convince the others that every fear of hers will come true. So I try to ignore most of what they say."

The priest was perplexed by Renato. Was it possible for a man to talk so earnestly about his sheep? "I think you are taking my analogy about the sheep too literally." The smile on his mouth became hesitant.

"Try telling that to my sheep!" Renato laughed. There was something about men in cassocks that brought out a schoolboy's naughtiness in Renato. "But no," he caught himself, not wanting to make the priest feel too teased, "I didn't miss what you meant to say. And I was trying to say something, too. I wanted to say that maybe the shepherd shouldn't worry too much every time the sheep start to bleat about this or that. Maybe they're just making noise."

The priest laughed as well. "Yes, a lovely observation. I like that. But tell me something. Are the sheep just making noise this time? I've heard talk about a dream of yours. About a list of people's names. About you becoming some kind of, I don't know, emissary, representing the people of this town to the pope. If this is the case, don't you think you should at least let me know what this is all about? Because, if you give the matter some thought, I myself am the pope's emissary to this town, through the channels of the cardinal and the archbishop, of course." He stopped in his steps and put a strong hand on Renato's forearm. Don Luigi smiled. "You see, Rome has sent me to you, to all of you. And now it sounds as if something is sending you to Rome. Worth, at the minimum, a little conversation between the two of us, don't you think? Or were you planning to wait until closer to your departure before you came to see me?"

Renato didn't know what to make of the hand that held his forearm. Was it a threat or a fraternal clasp? Was it meant to hold him back or to encourage him to go on? He looked at the hand. It was no hand he recognized, certainly not from his dream. He raised his eyes to look into the milky pools of the priest's eyeglasses. "If I have to tell you the truth, I would say that I'm not sure—that is, I mean, I can't say with certainty that I would have come to see you before my departure. I'm not certain, if you hadn't asked for a word this evening, that we would have spoken at all."

The priest's eyes stared through their glasses and his smile seemed to freeze. He exhaled loudly. He and Renato started their walk again up toward the church. They walked in silence.

They started climbing the stone steps in front of the church, the priest's house off to the left side. Just then the priest turned, looked at Renato for a moment, then sat down suddenly on the steps. "Sit yourself, Tizzoni," he said, tugging on Renato's trouser leg. "Sit and talk to me some more while we look at the evening together."

Renato sat down, waiting to hear what the priest would say next.

Don Luigi didn't say anything at first. Instead, his eyes, from behind their lenses, looked over the length of the main street that ran down from the bottom of the steps where the two men sat. Renato's eyes followed the priest's. The sight before them was very beautiful. Many of the shops along the *corso* were just closing their doors for the night, but the shop fronts were illuminated, casting golden light onto the street. Bright lights came out from the large window of the *bottega* where Milena was working with her mother and father. Street lamps all along the *corso* sent out conical areas of white light in the shadows of the buildings. High above everything else were the silhouetted outlines of the hills at the edge of the valley, set against the sky, which was still bright with the pink and gold of sunset.

"Beautiful," said the priest. "No? Beautiful, but somehow almost sad. Don't you think?"

Renato looked at the distant light of the sunset. Yes, a sadness came up inside him. Maybe the sadness came because there was always something a little sad about sunsets when the summer was coming to an end. The seasons were changing now, which tended to make everyone melancholy and uneasy, and, as Cappelli had said, some season was changing inside Renato, too.

But Renato had an inkling that he was also feeling some deflected sadness emanating from the priest. Looking at the windows with their lights on—kitchen windows bright with lamps suspended over tables where food was being prepared and where families would soon sit down to eat—Renato realized that cozy domestic scenes of this sort were unknown to the priest. Oh, he had probably participated in family dinners as a child, but as an adult? He was always a guest in some other family's house, or if he ate in his own home, he was alone. The names of other priests in nearby towns were often mentioned in rumors of illicit affairs with various women or girls of the congregation. But, thinking about it now, Renato could not recall any time he had heard such a story about Don Luigi. He wondered what it must be like to live an entire life without so much as the possibility of a wife.

Trying to read the priest's thoughts, Renato said, "Sad, you say? Hmm. There's a certain loneliness in looking at lit-up windows from the outside, I suppose."

"*Preciso*. You know, in all the many sufferings I see people living through I've come to believe that loneliness is the mother of all other fears. It's the biggest fear there is. Bigger than the fear of hunger, or poverty, or pain, or even death." Don Luigi laughed. "Loneliness."

The priest was quiet for a moment. Then he said, "It's been a lifetime since I've seen you in confessional, if I'm not mistaken, Tizzoni. No?"

"A lifetime, yes," Renato said.

Silence from the priest.

And what was Renato supposed to do? Apologize? Explain? He didn't feel inclined to offer apologies or explanations. But he had to say something, so he said, "Listen, Don Luigi, it should be no offense to you that I haven't been to confession for so long."

"Offense? Why should I be offended? Confession exists for the sake of the person who confesses, not for the sake of the priest."

"Yes, of course, but what I mean to say is that, I mean, I am simply not—how would one say it?—I'm not a church man, and by this I mean a man who goes to church often, a churchgoer, one might say."

The priest smiled. His eyes were fixed on the scene in front of him: the evening street of the town. "Not a man of the church. Then tell me this, Tizzoni. Why are you going to see the pope?"

"Good question, that one. It would be a long story to tell."

"My supper can wait for me. Can yours wait for you?"

A wind blew across them, a little taste of the weather that would arrive in the coming months. The priest drew his cassock around his body.

"Naturally my supper can wait. It's only that explaining everything is difficult, you see. But you've asked me, so I will tell you. I'm going to see the pope—and it wasn't my idea, you understand, but an idea that was sent to me—I'm going to see the pope because, uh, because life doesn't seem to taste of very much anymore."

Renato could almost hear the priest smiling. Don Luigi said, "*Capita*. It happens."

"It happens, in what sense?"

"In the sense that it happens. Life loses its taste sometimes. Happens to everyone, I think, for a time at least."

"For a time, you say. Meaning the taste comes back?"

"I would say yes. Yes, decidedly. I tell you yes. And there's nothing so tragic if it happens, that for a time—"

"Nothing so tragic?" Renato was shocked. "But it is very, very tragic. I've always been a person who has loved every little taste. Every little one. Food. Smells. The smell of my house, the fields, the sheep when I milk them. The smell that things make when you throw them on the fire—tangerine rinds and rosemary sprigs, and things like that. The smoke. And the smell, you will pardon me, of my wife. And touches. The sun on my skin. A sweater on the body when it's a chilly evening like tonight. Sounds. Sensations. Everything." Renato heard himself speaking. Strange, how close he felt to confessing everything. Turn a valve and what was inside him came out. Was he really as easy to open as that? And the temptation was strong to go all the way with confession, to tell the priest about other temptations he felt, about how he had almost been tempted by Meg Barker. Yes, maybe he could confess to Don Luigi. And then Don Luigi would maybe offer him absolution and the consequent state of grace.

But something in Renato made him hold back. Did he really want everything inside him to gush out now, here on the steps of the church?

"The taste of things," he picked up what he had been saying, choosing more general words instead. "But now, now it's as if I'm alive but not alive. Because nothing tastes at all. And I suppose I'm looking in all sorts of directions to get the taste back again. You know."

"I understand," said Don Luigi. "If you say it like that, then I understand that this is a great loss. But help me to understand. You want the taste of life to return to you. You want to be reborn to the world, in effect?"

"Reborn to the world! Exactly! *Rinato*. Like my name Renato. I want to be reborn."

"And going to Rome, to the pope, will in some way, you think, give you the—"

"But I told you already! It wasn't my idea that I had to go to Rome. It was sent to me as an idea, and who was I to argue with a strong idea that was sent?" Renato could tell the priest wasn't following him anymore. No way around it. He had to tell him about the dream.

So Renato told Don Luigi about his dream.

The priest was perturbed. "Let me understand this. Because of your dream, you tell me, you have to go to Rome and shake hands with the Holy Father while with your other hand you touch yourself on your ass?"

"Yes! That's the message."

"I wonder if it isn't verging on blasphemy." Don Luigi shook his head. He took off his glasses and rubbed his eyes. "And other people are involved in this?" He put his glasses back on. "This would be the list that everyone is talking about?"

"Well, yes. I was talking to Tita Vezzosi and she was telling me of her loneliness. Yes, the mother of all human fears, as you said yourself. She told me of her loneliness, and sadness, and desperation, and I became desperate myself, wanting to do something to help. So I put her name on the paper in which I had wrapped up the cheese, the cheese from my own sheep. I said to her, '*Facciamo una cosa*. Let's do a little something.' And I wrote her name down and put it in my pocket after telling her, too, about my dream. And I promised her that her fortune would be sure to change as well. A strange idea, I know. But what else was there for me to offer her? And I told her that she would see, in time. Life has a way of regenerating itself. And from there, it's clear. The thing simply grew." He didn't mention the phrases he wrote on the list along with the names. That wasn't the priest's business. The phrases were memoranda for himself. "A list of names along with Tita Vezzosi's. Because other people had things they needed to change in their lives, too. You understand?"

Don Luigi breathed. "All this from a dream—which maybe was the result of indigestion from something you had eaten that night—a dream that you're not sure you interpreted in the right way?"

"But sure I'm sure! Because that wasn't the only dream. The hand came back to me, keeps coming back in other dreams. And I saw the hand holding the list once as if it were reading it and adding other names with a feather pen."

"Tizzoni, this all sounds very irregular. How can I send you to Rome when I know you're going to touch your ass while you're shaking hands with the pope?"

"Send me? Excuse me, but you're not the one who's sending me."

"I mean"—the priest was getting flustered—"I mean, send you off, I mean, with my blessing, if that's possible. A benediction, if it would help, to let you and everyone else in town—for everyone seems to be participating in this thing—to let you all know that my best wishes, indeed, my benediction and prayers, go with you. As if we all didn't have enough problems right now! Becoming extinct as a town isn't enough? In any case, a meeting with the Holy Father should certainly be an important pilgrimage. But with a mission like yours, Tizzoni? To touch your ass? All because of a dream?"

"Am I mistaken," Renato said, "or doesn't the Bible talk a lot about some very strange dreams? There was that one with the fat cows and the dried-up cows. It was Joseph who dreamed that, wasn't it?"

"It was the pharoah. Joseph interpreted it."

"Fine. Whoever it was. But the point is, it was a dream about cows, everybody could have said. But did they think that? No! They knew the dream had been sent, and they knew it was of great importance. And there were other dreams, too, no? There was Jacob who had a dream, and I can't remember right now but I think there was another one in the Bible."

"Now he's giving me catechism lessons on the Bible." Don Luigi shook his head again.

"Don Luigi, the dream was sent to me, though I didn't ask for it. It was sent, and I'm doing my best to follow it. It's become important to me, the most important thing in the world somehow. The dream, and the list of people whom I'm carrying around even this very moment with me. Because it's become important to them, too. And yes, I'm terrified by the responsibility. How do I know what will happen in Rome? I hope something good happens. What else can I say? Maybe this doesn't seem important to you, although you say I have to understand that it's become a big thing to you—you said so yourself—because this being papal business, it falls under your domain. Fine, then. That's how it is. And the only thing I can say to you is—"

"Tell me, Tizzoni. What is the only thing you can say to me?"

"The only thing I can say to you is: Have faith."

"'Have faith'?" Don Luigi was stunned.

"Have faith in the goodness of this thing. I don't understand it completely myself, but the dreams keep coming back to tell me I'm doing the right thing. So have faith, Don Luigi. Have a little faith."

The priest thought for a moment. What's the worst that could happen? he asked himself. The worst thing that could happen would be for the man sitting next to him now to carry out his sworn intention. Reflecting a little more, the priest decided that the pope was wise enough to know how to handle a man who was touching his own ass. The pope was no fool. Surely he had been called upon to deal with worse. So the question was, did the priest have faith in the pope's ability to deal with Renato?

"All right then, Tizzoni." His usual smile returned to his mouth. "I will have faith." Then he remembered his duty as shepherd to his flock. "And, if you will permit me, Tizzoni, I'll give you a word of advice."

"Tell me."

The priest smiled while he waited for the right approach to come to him. When it came, he said, "Think of things that fly. Think of the swallows that were flying around right here before the sunset. Tell me, Tizzoni, what is it that lets them fly?"

"Easy," said Renato. "What lets them fly is their wings."

"Something other than their wings, I mean. Smaller, but stronger in a way."

"Ah. The feather, I suppose. The lightness and strength of the feather. Without that, birds couldn't fly. Take away a bird's feathers and—yes, you're right—he'd still have his wings, but without the feathers he'd crash to the ground and die."

"Then it's a kind of feather I'm talking about. Light and yet very strong, as you say." Don Luigi was in his element now. Metaphors, similes, and parables were, after all, essential tools of his trade. "But it's not the kind of feather you touch. It's something inside. It's the creature's faith. You tell me to have faith, Tizzoni? Very well. And my advice to you is: Have faith. Your own words back to you. I don't know what things in particular have brought about your crisis, but as for the answer, have faith."

"If only!" Renato said, keeping the priest company in laughter. "What can I tell you? It's not easy."

"No, it's not easy."

"Not easy at all to have faith," Renato said. "But I'm trying. I'll try."

Sensing an end to their conversation, the two men stood up.

Renato said, "Not a bad benediction you left me with, Don Luigi. Thank you."

"Glad you like it. And when you're ready to go off to Rome, maybe I'll give you another benediction a little more publicly. People like a good show, you know. Something to bring people together."

"See you when I'm ready to go, then." Renato shook the priest's hand and started to walk down the steps.

"*Buon appetito,* Tizzoni," Don Luigi called after him.

"*Buon appetito* to you, too."

Renato was hungry when he got home. He told his stomach to wait some more, though, because he had his sheep to see to first.

When his sheep had been milked and fed, he went inside. The

house felt very empty when he switched on the light in the hall, what with Milena at work and Petula away at Daniele's bar. This solitude, he thought, is how Don Luigi lives. He turned on the light in the kitchen. Before he went to the refrigerator to get something to eat, he placed the list on the kitchen table. He wrote:

> DON LUIGI—*Loneliness is the mother*
> *of all other fears.*

Then he added:

> *Have faith.*

THIRTY-FOUR

The Toy Boat

The hand came to Renato again that night. He was relieved to see the hand because he had been unsettled by doubts before he had fallen asleep. Perhaps he had said too much to Don Luigi and had revealed too much of what was going on inside his head. If you speak too much about a cherished dream, if you expose it to air and to light and to the uncertainty of other people's questioning, then the dream may even appear to fade. Renato had spoken a lot to the priest, and the priest had asked many questions. The questions did not make Renato lose conviction in his dream, but they did make him feel almost ridiculous and fragile in his continued belief. Could it be that his interpretation of the first dream had been mistaken, that he had mis-read the signs? What if a true dream had indeed been sent to him, but he had forced his own shape onto the dream instead of letting himself be shaped by it?

Then the hand returned to him that night, after his conversation with the priest, and by its very presence reassured him, telling him that he was following in the right direction, that he was doing well to let himself be led.

The dream was strange. He was aware of its strangeness even while he was dreaming it. And the dream moved him, letting loose an emotion so strong it threatened to overpower him.

In the dream, the hand was luminous in the darkness above his bed, as was its custom. This time when Renato followed the hand he was conscious of the strangeness of things. He floated behind the hand along the corridor of his home, and certainly everything was known, everything was loved—the smell of Milena on the sheets of their bed, the sound of Petula's breathing as he drifted past her bedroom door, the purr of the cat outside in the dark courtyard, the stones of the well—and everything was also distant in time. He floated behind the hand and he noticed the elements of his life with nostalgia, as if everything were already lost.

The hand guided him away from his home, out to the road, away from town, up to where the cemetery stood. He stopped outside the cemetery wall. Over the top of the wall he could see black cypress trees rising up against the night sky, vertical shadows, black on black. The atmosphere inside the cemetery, faintly perceived above the wall, glowed dimly with the orange lights that burned in front of the rows of tomb markers.

Outside the wall, Renato lowered his eyes to the ground. In front of his bare feet the earth bulged up in a mound like a freshly covered grave. Staring at the mound he knew that buried beneath was something or someone very dear to him, some persons or things that he loved, though he couldn't say who or what it was. Pushed by an emotion stronger than himself, he lay down on the mound, his cheek to the earth, his arms stretched wide to embrace whatever was buried underneath. Hugging the earth, he felt beneath him the presences of many things, of his mother and father, of the recently dead Aristodemo Vezzosi whose picture had been set in glass beside the name written on the marble stone of the wall vault, on the other side of the cemetery gates. And Renato, running his hands over the damp earth, sensed his own daughter Petula under him, or the little girl she once had been but was no more. He sensed himself as a young boy. He sensed the entire town. He sensed these many presences lying in the earth beneath him and he started to sob, surprised by the might of his own crying. Helpless, he sobbed and sobbed, wetting the dirt with tears, as if the hand had disappeared forever, as if no comfort could even be imagined.

Just then he felt another body next to his, a living body that rubbed against his ribs and pushed its head up under his arm until its cheek was beside his own. He breathed in deeply and recognized the perfume of Milena's skin. He moved his face and rubbed his beard into her hair. He felt her body snuggle close. She put her arm around his shoulders to quiet his sobs. He put his arm around her, grateful for her.

The hand reappeared, touching him on the shoulder to rouse him, to call his attention to something it held in its palm. He opened his eyes, his crying finished, and saw that the hand offered him an object. It was the toy boat he had found by the roots of the fig tree that grew in the hole in the riverbank. In the dream, the little boat had been polished to a beautiful shine. He examined the boat and discovered a figure etched into the side. He did not recognize the shape. It looked like this:

He memorized the design, then wrapped his fingers tightly around the toy boat. Shutting his eyes again, he hugged Milena to his side, happy to feel her lying close.

When Renato woke from the dream, Milena's body was pressed to his, her cheek against his beard. Had he woken up at all or was he still in his dream?

Milena felt him wake up. She said, "You were making noises in your sleep, as if you were in pain."

He hugged her and kissed her forehead. "Go back to sleep."

He was awake and refreshed by his sleep when the first traces of dawn came in through the window.

Before leaving the house, he stopped in the kitchen, took the toy boat from the table, and put a little bottle of metal polish and a soft rag into the pocket of his work trousers.

The courtyard cat rubbed himself around Renato's ankles while Renato washed his face with water from the well. Renato filled the feed bucket with grain and let the sheep munch away while he milked them, in their daily order, from Prima to Quarta. All four sheep trotted behind him as he led them up to the hillside. Together they watched the sun come up. It was a clear morning, the sky free of clouds.

While the sheep nibbled grass, Renato pulled the bottle of metal polish and the rag from his pocket and sat down on the ground. Then he pulled out the toy boat.

Polishing the little boat proved a slow process. At first the white polish, coming in contact with the metal, became ugly black-green slime. Renato rubbed away at the boat and still no bare bronze showed through. This thing's been lying on the ground getting rained on for years and years, Renato thought. Probably centuries, by the looks of it.

As the layers of corrosion came off, revealing the original metal beneath, Renato knew that the boat would never have a golden shine. The years had bitten into the metal, discoloring it forever. It was well made, though. It even had two little sailors standing up on the deck, one in front, one in back.

Renato poured another dab of polish onto a clean corner of the rag. He set to rubbing again. "*Dio boia!*" he said a moment later, holding the little boat up to the light. He could hardly believe what he saw. Engraved in the metal there remained the better part of an insignia of sorts. The form was not as perfect as it had been in the dream, but the shape was unmistakable:

He had no idea what it meant.

Whatever the meaning, he knew he had been destined to find the little boat, though materially it seemed no more important than a child's toy. And his dream had shown him the symbol etched on the boat's hull, even when corrosion had made the symbol impossible to see.

"Come on, girls!" he screamed at the sheep. "Let's go home!"

Prima, the bold first sheep with the bell around her neck, responded immediately to his instructions and headed downhill for the stalls. The second and third sheep didn't care much what they did. They followed the first sheep without enthusiasm. They would have been just as happy, he suspected, to stay out on the hill and eat more grass. The fourth sheep, Quarta, was suddenly beside herself with skittish energy. She bumped into Renato's legs and kicked her heels, spinning herself in a half circle, only to bump into him again.

She's gone crazy, Renato thought. Or maybe she's simply the most sensitive of the lot and is showing that she understands what's happening inside me. "Come on, Quarta," he said, not without gentleness. "Don't be so silly. Let's walk down the hill together and you just try to relax yourself." She looked up into his face, her eyes opened wide with agitation. "I don't know who's crazier," Renato said. "You or me." He patted the wool on top of her head. "Let's go."

THIRTY-FIVE

Cappelli the Mystic

Cappelli and Renato were working one day up around the back of the church. In the ground under a grassy hill just behind the church lay a water-holding tank, and a pipe leading from the tank had broken.

It was getting on to noon. Renato and Cappelli had been working to repair the pipe since not long after dawn. Renato straightened his back and let his shovel drop. The air was clear and cool. Looking out from where he stood, Renato could see all of the town of Sant'Angelo D'Asso below him. Much farther away he could see the slopes of Monte Amiata to the south and the towers of Montalcino, where Duncan lived, to the southwest. Turning, he saw the tower and cathedral of Siena breaking the horizon far to the north. "I'm so hungry I could kill someone," he said.

His mouth was gritty with dust. On the street below he saw an old man in a sleeveless undershirt use his hat to chase away a fly. "Crazy if you think about it, Cappelli. We're breaking our balls fixing pipes and things here in town, but before you know it we'll all be leaving and everything will be underwater anyway. Still, every day, we carry on breaking our balls. Crazy, don't you think?"

"I'll tell you what I'm thinking in this very minute." Cappelli put down his pickax. His cheeks had gone past red, to purple, after his long morning of labor. "I'm thinking we've done enough work for now. Let's get some lunch in the *bottega*. And then we'll have the whole afternoon to think about getting this pipe fixed. I can't take any more. We'll work better with a full stomach, and maybe, if we're lucky, maybe after a little nap as well. And you're so hungry you're getting nasty. I've worked with you enough years now to recognize the signs, *Dio bono*. You're a nice enough person when you're stomach is full, but once you're hungry, you start getting this way."

"I start getting what way? How do I get?"

"You get like the way you are now." Cappelli laughed. "Unbearable."

"Now you're becoming a wife to me? Is that what you mean to say?"

"I mean to say let's eat. Come on. I need a drink, too. This healthy exercise will be the end of me. I need some wine or else I can't carburete. And besides, there's something I have to tell you after we eat a mouthful. I'm too excited to contain myself. I've been trying to keep silent since we started this morning. But it's no use. What I have inside me insists on coming out!"

It wasn't Cappelli's way to be eager to communicate in long speeches with many words. Yet Cappelli was like an overexcited hedgehog today, the stiff hair on his head sticking out, alert. What could be going on under those gray quills? "All right," said Renato. "Let's go to the *bottega*. Then you tell me what's turning over in your head. First, though, we eat."

Renato and Cappelli stood in the *bottega* with the counter and the glass-windowed fresh food case in front of them and the tables and grocery shelves to their rear. They felt tall above the mob of short old ladies who had come to buy meat and cheese for their lunch tables. Tonino and Maria Severina and Milena all worked behind the counter, rushing to take care of everyone's orders.

"Give me a little slice of that salami," said a stout woman whose head came up no higher than Renato's armpit. "No," she said, poking at the glass of the fresh food display case, "that one with the bigger pieces of fat in it. My husband loves the fat."

"One should think about cholesterol," advised another woman

customer, as thin as a strand of dried fish. "It was the cholesterol that killed off that husband of mine."

The stout woman was not to be dissuaded. "He's always been this way, my man has. Always has loved the fat. He is made that way. What can I do? He wants fat, I buy his salami fat. And in my opinion he'll live another fifty years after I'm gone, in any case."

"A slice of the salami with the big pieces of fat it is then," said Tonino from behind the counter, picking the meat up in his meaty hands, using a knife to cut away its skin before loading it onto the electric slicer.

Yet the mention of cholesterol had the effect of a lit match set to a nest of brittle twigs. Among these women, it didn't take much of a spark to ignite a crackling fire of medical complaints. A stooped woman started in with her perennial litany about her neck pains. Another said her digestion had been working poorly. She had eaten onions for lunch three days ago and those onions had been sitting heavily on her stomach ever since.

"But of course! What do you expect?" clucked a little woman with a chicken's beak for a nose. "Onions are a blow to the liver." She made a chopping motion with her hand toward her own abdomen to demonstrate how violent an insult to digestion an onion could be. "Za! A blow to the liver like this. Za!"

"You can joke!" said a waist-high woman with no teeth. The thin wisps of white hair on her head did little to hide the pale blue veins that wormed beneath the skin at her temples. "But I remember my sister's husband's cousin's son-in-law who ate a piece of melon on a hot day once, then went in to bathe in the cold water of a river. He almost died of the congestion, he did. People die that way, you know. I'll tell you that myself. You can joke!"

Maria Severina raised her knife from the loaf of bread she was cutting, stopping herself midslice. "Ah, the congestion is a terrible way to die, to be sure. Touching water after you eat is a guaranteed way to kill yourself. Sometimes when I put my hands in water to wash the coffee cups here in the sink after I've had only a snack, I can feel my digestion blocking."

Renato couldn't stand it. He had come to eat, not to listen to a seminar on absurd anatomical perils. "What do you mean, he almost died of congestion? I don't believe a word of it."

"Who?" said the waist-high woman, focusing her eyes on Renato's face.

"Your sister's cousin's—whoever! What do you mean he almost died?"

"It was the son-in-law of my sister's husband's cousin. In any case, I tell you this, the boy almost died."

"But what does it mean to almost die?" Renato wouldn't let go of the thing. At least arguing made him forget his hunger.

"I mean, he almost went into a coma!" The waist-high woman stabbed her finger into the air.

"Oh, my!" said Maria Severina behind the bar, shaking her head, resuming her work with the bread knife.

Renato scratched his beard hard, as if a bee, trapped against his cheek, were trying to sting its way out. "Come on!" he growled. "Do you hear what you just said? 'He almost went into a coma.' What does that mean? Almost a coma? You're either in a coma or you're not in a coma, no? There is no halfway. So tell me, what is this supposed to mean, that this fellow almost died from almost being in a coma, all because he had some melon before sticking his ankles in a stream?"

"It's true, I repeat, it's true!" the waist-high woman insisted. Renato imagined that he saw a vein in her forehead start to bulge. "Why would they have told me such a thing if it wasn't the truth?"

"Hearsay." Renato folded his arms across his chest. "I don't believe a word."

Cappelli and Milena eyed each other. "He's hungry," Cappelli explained to Renato's wife.

"I figured. When he gets this way . . ."

"Hmm," Cappelli said, nodding. "Unbearable."

"Unbearable indeed," Milena said, weighing some tuna that she forked out of a big round tin.

Renato pretended not to hear the comments passing between his wife and his assistant. Instead, he was holding firm against the women around him. "Not a word, do you hear me? I don't believe a word."

The stout woman who had ordered the fatty salami stepped in to settle the question. "Then you'll believe me when I tell you that exactly the same thing happened to me, only last week. To me, I say it happened. Now is that what you'd call hearsay? And only last week."

"What happened, signora? You ate the same melon by the same stream?"

"No, but almost exactly the same thing. I was sleeping peacefully, as I always do, except for when I can't sleep. But that night I could sleep, so I was sleeping as deeply as a lamb when suddenly I couldn't breathe and that's what woke me up, because some saliva had gone down my throat the wrong way."

"Yes!" a chorus of women agreed.

"It's terrible when that happens!" said one.

"Ooh, I don't even like to think about it!" said the waist-high wispy-haired woman, glad to have found other voices to back her up.

"And I tell you all," said the saliva-suffocated stout woman whose husband liked his salami fat, "I know just what it feels like to almost go into a coma, because by some miracle I started to breathe once again, but if I hadn't started to breathe, then I wouldn't have been here now to tell you this story."

"It's true, poor dear," said several women. "It's true."

"Oh, and, Tonino," for the stout woman's attention had been captured again by the food behind the glass of the display case, "give me one of those little packets of tortellini. And a little bag of grated cheese. I think I'll make some broth for supper tonight."

"You're young," the waist-high woman said to Renato before turning away. "Of course you don't listen. The young never listen. Don't know what's good for them."

Renato knew the conversation had ended and he knew he had lost. He had convinced no one. Instead, everyone present took him for a deficient person who didn't understand what was obvious. "By the sound of what you all say," he tried as a last shot, "life is very, very dangerous indeed. What with saliva and melon and onions lying in wait to kill us when we're not on guard. What a miracle we've all managed somehow to stay alive until today!"

No one was listening. Renato began to think he hated them all.

"Oh, Maria Severina!" Cappelli called out to Renato's mother-in-law, intervening to make sure Renato did himself no further harm. "Give us some of that bread you're slicing, will you? Three or four slices for each of us. And some of that nice prosciutto to go with it. And a piece of that pecorino cheese. Have pity on us and give it to us fast, or else we'll never get the water fixed, and Renato here, if he doesn't put something in his stomach, will get nastier than he already is. Oh, and a bottle of wine, too. We'll eat outside."

"I've only got two hands," Maria Severina said. "But I'll get to you as soon as I can."

"I'll wait outside for you, Tizzoni," Cappelli said to Renato. "And it's your turn to pay."

"I thought it was your turn," said Renato.

"Next time is my turn," Cappelli said. "Next time, if it happens, it's on me."

They sat on the ground in the shade of a tree on the grassy hill behind the church. "You see," Cappelli began, wiping bread crumbs from his lips with the back of his hand, "what I had to tell you happened yesterday when I was feeling at least as nasty as you were feeling just now, before you had something to eat."

"I wasn't nasty." Renato could be magnanimous with the world now that his stomach was full. "I was simply hungry."

"You were nasty, *Madonna lupa!* But don't worry. It happens."

"Anyway, you were saying? You were saying the thing you had to say?"

"Ah. Precisely. I was saying." Cappelli drank some wine. "It was yesterday afternoon. You remember how in the afternoon you asked me to go and buy some extra nuts and bolts, just in case we needed them for the maintenance of the pumps or for whatever?"

"Yes, I remember. I haven't lost my memory yet like the old ladies at the bar. Nuts and bolts. So?"

"Nuts and bolts. So I decided to go to Siena to buy them. I could have bought them in town or anywhere else, but I thought: Why not take a nice little drive?"

"That's where you disappeared to! You went to Siena just to buy some nuts and bolts? Clever you are, to make an entire evening's mission of a few nuts and bolts so as not to return to work!"

"Clever? Could be. In any case, I wanted a nice little drive, *Dio bono,* so I took myself a drive." He poured himself more wine from the bottle, set the bottle on the ground against the trunk of the tree, and drained the glass in one gulp. "As I was saying, I was driving to Siena."

Cappelli had taken the Siena-Bettolle highway, he explained. Always a nasty road. The road on which Daniele's parents had been killed. And yesterday, as if the road didn't already have enough traffic problems, a crew was repainting the white lines separating the two lanes. A long stretch of the highway had become a work site, squeezing traffic into a single lane. Cars coming from the two directions had to take turns passing through the narrow stretch.

Impatience got the better of drivers, as it always did. Somebody had jumped his turn. In the end, a dump truck and a bus full of Japanese tourists were deadlocked nose to nose in the middle of the single lane, neither having room to get around the other or to let cars pass from behind. And half a mile of backed-up cars beeped their horns on the hot road.

"*Dio boia!*" Renato started to enjoy the story. "A beautiful mess! And you were stuck in the middle, you say?"

"Stuck, yes, while the bus driver and truck driver yelled, sending each other to do it up the ass. And people from behind them were all getting out of their cars to join in the screaming, and the Japanese got off the bus to watch everyone sending everyone else to go and do it up the ass. '*Vaffanculo!*' on the left; '*Vaffanculo!*' on the right. And it was hot there on the asphalt, horns honking, engines running, stinking up to the sky with fumes."

"And you were swearing too, I bet."

"Me?" Cappelli raised his eyebrows. "I was too hot and tired to have the strength. But I was angry inside. That's certain. Angry inside. And you know what happened then?"

"How would I know if you don't tell me?"

"I saw someone. By pure fortune I looked to my side, where there's the electric company storage shed next to the road. And do you know who I saw?"

I can imagine, thought Renato. That's where the prostitutes waited for customers to pull over. Everybody knew about them. They were roadside fixtures, like signposts and trees. And Renato started to wonder if this was about to become a story of Cappelli's sexual adventure with a prostitute. Could he bear to listen to the details of Cappelli's sex life, if indeed such a sex life existed? He said, "No, Cappelli, I don't know who you saw."

"I'll tell you. I saw a lovely young woman. She smiled at me," Cappelli continued. "So I smiled back. And you know what happened next?"

Renato tried to envision Cappelli engaged in intimate activity. It was not a pretty picture. "You're killing me with this story, Cappelli. But go ahead. Tell me. Tell me what happened next."

"I'll tell you, but first remember what kind of mood I was in. I was feeling as hot and pissed off as anyone else on the road. As nasty as you were feeling an hour ago in the *bottega* before we had lunch. I hated the world. Inside myself I swore against the traffic and against the dickhead truck driver and against everybody else. '*Madonna puttana!*' I swore to myself. That whore of a Madonna! 'Damn her and damn whoever goes into that wretched church of hers to pray to her!' That's what I was swearing to myself."

Renato had to laugh. "You were using the heavy guns, I can see."

"Precisely," Cappelli said, not without some pride. "And that's the mood I was in when I looked next to me, at the young lady standing there next to my car stuck in that traffic."

"I understand your mood."

"And you'll never guess what happened next."

"Oh, Cappelli. Am I supposed to act surprised? Who doesn't know about the girls along the Siena-Bettolle highway? All the girls in all the colors. Black girls from Senegal. White girls from Russia and Romania and Macedonia. You're telling me she was one of those girls, no?"

"You mean, a whore?" Cappelli seemed to lose the strand of his story.

"Of course I mean a whore. Isn't that where this is going? Or are you trying to tell me the girl wasn't a whore but was just out for a walk to get some fresh air for her health?"

"As you say it now, you're probably right," Cappelli said. "She probably was a whore. I hadn't thought. I was too hot and agitated in the traffic to think that way. It doesn't make a difference anyhow."

"I'm not following, Cappelli. What happened with this girl? Was she or wasn't she a whore?"

"It doesn't matter, I tell you. What matters was what happened next. I looked at her, smiled back at her after she smiled at me. And that's when she said the thing that she said." Cappelli shook his head, apparently drifting in the sweetness of his memory from yesterday afternoon.

"What did she say?"

"She said, 'Ciao. Come stai?' 'Hi. How are you?'" He stopped talking and seemed to be still under the spell of the words.

"That's it?"

"What else do you want her to say? But she continued and said even more. She said, 'I bet you'd rather be someplace else.' She had a strange accent, as if maybe she wasn't Italian. But she spoke well enough. And the way she spoke to me . . ." He made a gesture with his hands as if his heart had poured out from his chest.

"But what did she say?"

"I told you what she said. Didn't you hear? 'Come stai,' she said. Don't you see? She didn't know me, because we had never met before, but this fresh, pretty stranger called me 'you.' She gave me tu. She didn't call me Lei, the way most strangers do. She called me you, tu. Just in the moment when I hated the world and was ready to send everyone to go and do it up the ass, she spoke to me like a real person. She called me you. And that little way of speaking of hers, how can I say this? It made an explosion go off in my head. It made me think . . ."

His words ended.

"I'm listening," said Renato. "It made you think?"

"How can I say what it made me think? Are there words for such things? And I'm no good with words." He snorted through his nose. He scratched his head. He poured more wine and drank another glass. "What can I tell you?"

"Tell me what the girl who talked to you made you think. Tell me about the explosion in your head. Go on! Courage!"

Cappelli shoved the last piece of bread and prosciutto into his mouth. He chewed, then wiped a snowfall of crumbs from his chin. "*Porca vacca,* Tizzoni!" he erupted. "Even when we were kids in school they taught us to be polite and call people *Lei,* which is like calling another person IT, if you think about it. And I have my balls overly full of being called IT and having to call other people IT. And you know how it works. Your parents die and so do your uncles and aunts, and your pals move away, and suddenly even the people in your town—people you've known all your life—have to disappear because of a stupid dam. And the longer you live you're left every day with less people who see you as *you.* To most people, you're nothing more than an IT. That's what she made me think, the girl next to the traffic, when she called me YOU.

"Truth is, people get so used to calling you IT that in the end they forget there's a YOU inside. And you start to forget the same thing about them. But say YOU to another person and it's almost the same thing as saying I, because it means you believe, deep down, that there's no difference between I and YOU. Every person is in the same boat. YOU are another I. Am I drunk, Tizzoni, or am I making sense?"

"Both." Renato poured himself some wine. "You know, Cappelli, underneath it all, I always suspected you of living some secret life in your head. Now I know I was right. *Dio boia!*" he said, laughing. "Go on. Say more of what you were saying."

"So that's the calculation, the sum of it, I was saying. There's people I can count on the fingers of one hand who even call me You. And then there's millions and thousands of millions of other people in the world and for them I'm nothing but a turd. That's a sad thought, Tizzoni. A sad thought, I tell you that myself.

"But what if the opposite were the case? You see? That's what the girl beside the road exploded inside my head, like that!" He snapped his fingers. "Because she was a person who didn't even know me, yet she smiled and asked me how it was going for me, and she could see I was sitting in all that traffic, sitting there and hating the world, ready to kill everyone, like you wanted to kill everyone when you were hungry and waiting for your prosciutto and cheese in the *bottega* just now. She stopped her little life for a moment to look into the window of mine and she called me You, the way a sister would speak to me if I had one.

"If people for maybe five seconds stopped and thought that maybe they weren't surrounded by Its to be treated like turds but were surrounded by other Yous. For five seconds. What do you think would happen?" He looked into Renato's face.

Renato waited for an answer. None came. "What?" Renato prompted.

"No, no. You tell me. What do I know? If that happened for five seconds, what would happen next?"

"You're the one with the vision, Cappelli. You tell me."

Cappelli looked disappointed. "How the hell would I know? Maybe the world would end. Maybe it would go BANG in fireworks of joy. I was hoping you had an idea." He shook his head. "In any case, Tizzoni, that's what the girl beside the road got me to thinking yesterday. And now it's like there's this radio singing this loud, happy song inside my head with the volume up high."

He stopped. He looked at Renato, who was sitting on the ground beside him, looking back at him. They looked at each other for a moment.

Then Cappelli said, "You're looking at me funny. What do you want from me?"

"Excuse me," said Renato, embarrassed. He looked away.

Cappelli looked away as well.

So they sat not looking at each other, each man embarrassed inside himself, because the two men had revealed themseves to each other.

"No, really," Cappelli said, making things all right again, "before you get worried and start to think that soon they'll come to cart me off to the place where the funny people live, I promise you this: The feeling will pass. Feelings always do. Bad ones and good ones alike. Give them time and they pass. It was just a thought, is all it was. Just a thought. Couldn't keep it inside myself. Told you my thought. *Basta.* That's all."

Renato looked around for a moment. He looked at the tree they were sitting under and saw the light come through green leaves. He looked at a stone lying on the ground. He saw a small black beetle crawl in a straight line, then take a detour in its path to walk around the stone. He heard a bird chirp.

"And then?" Renato asked. "What happened after she said hello and asked you how you were, calling you *tu?*"

"And then nothing. We chatted. Talked about the weather. The traffic. Nothing. Then the dump truck and the bus unblocked themselves and the traffic started to move again, so I said good-bye and drove away."

"Well," said Renato, rising suddenly, brushing dust off his trousers. "Let's get back to work."

"No nap?" Cappelli asked.

"I don't need a nap now. You?"

Cappelli shrugged.

"I like your thought, Cappelli, though. I like your thought very much. Wait a minute. Let's do a little something. I'll show you how much I like your thought." He dug his list out of his ass pocket. Patting his shirt pocket, he found a piece of pencil. He knelt beside Cappelli and used his own thigh as a writing surface.

Cappelli—*You are another I.*

"Did I say I wanted to be on your list?" Cappelli asked.

"You didn't say so. I said so."

"And what else do you have on your list, Tizzoni? Show me who else you've got."

Renato folded the list and put it in his pocket. "Don't you worry about the others. You're on my list. What else do you care?"

Cappelli scratched his hedgehog head, yawned, and worked his way up to a standing position. "Fine," he said, tucking his shirttails inside his pants. "No nap. We'll get back to work."

While they worked to fix the pipe, Renato thought about the girl. If I had seen her, I would have dismissed her as a whore. But she was a sister in Cappelli's eyes. A lovely young sister who called him You. He's as crazy as a camel is Cappelli. But sometimes even crazy people can have a good idea. Even if five seconds is all it lasts.

THIRTY-SIX

Addio

In small towns little things grow into big things fast. Sant'Angelo D'Asso was a small town. The little thing that grew big fast was Renato's departure for Rome.

The first mention of his plans was barely a breath. "I think I'll leave next Saturday," he told the sheep one brisk morning while they grazed and he sat on the hill. At breakfast he told Milena and Petula. "Saturday," he said. "I was thinking that Saturday after work might be a good moment to go to Rome."

"Renato's thinking of leaving for Rome on Saturday after he finishes work," Milena told her mother later that morning in the kitchen of the *bottega*.

"Saturday, Sunday, or Monday, makes no difference," Maria Severina said, smacking rock salt on to chickens destined for the roasting oven. "He'll go to Rome, then he'll come back home looking like the same fool he is. Everyone's talking about this trip of his. Who knows what people think of this whole business?"

"Don't worry about people," Milena said, peeling the paperlike skin off garlic cloves in preparation for making tomato sauce. "People are talking, yes, but they're talking hopefully. What else have they got to look forward to these days?"

"People are talking, and that's embarrassing enough." Maria

Severina stuffed handfuls of sage leaves into the gutted caverns of the chicken carcasses. "And I suppose people will want a big send-off dinner for him."

"You think so? I don't know." Milena brushed hair from her eyes with the back of her hand. "Renato wouldn't like that. He's not one for public events. He's going to Rome for something that's private to him, even if other people have become involved. A big dinner? No, Renato will probably just finish work, the way he does every day, and have a quick something to eat at home, then get in the car and go."

"You mean you'd send your husband off to Rome without so much as eating dinner with him?"

"Oh Mamma, since when do you care if Renato and I eat dinner together or not? What, do you think I'd leave you here alone on a Saturday night? Don't worry. I won't take the evening off."

"You don't have to take the evening off." Maria Severina gave her version of a smile.

Always a worrying sign when Mamma smiles, Milena thought. It means she's out to get something. But what could she want?

"You tell Renato to come here for dinner," Maria Severina continued. "And of course, since everyone's been talking so much, I expect people would want to come here, too. Who knows? We might even have to get out some extra tables from the cellar."

"No, Mamma," said Milena, understanding. Clearly her mother couldn't resist the thought of Saturday night bringing a full house's worth of business. "Renato wouldn't come if he thought he'd be in the middle of everyone's attention."

"But what in the middle of everyone's attention? We'll have just a small dinner for the family. You'll be here and Renato will be here. And Petula, of course. And your father and me. The only other people in the restaurant will be the regular Saturday night crowd. What could be more private than that?" She put her hand in the hole where the back end of a chicken had once been.

"Mamma says you should come to the *bottega* on Saturday night. Says we should have a family dinner before you leave," Milena told Renato after turning out their bedroom light.

"You told your mother I'm leaving on Saturday?" Renato faced the darkness over the bed. "Is it any of her business?"

"Renato, she's my mother."

"Yes. Could I possibly forget? And it's her idea that we should eat dinner together? When has your mother ever wanted to eat dinner with me on purpose?"

"Maybe she cares. She says everyone in town cares about your trip to Rome. She was even thinking a lot of people would want to come."

"Ah! So she wants to get the restaurant full of people. Now I believe you, that she cares."

"*Sì*, but don't worry. I made her promise she wouldn't go telling everyone. It'll be just a dinner for the family. Then you can get in the car and go." She reached for his hand under the sheet. Finding it, she raised it to her lips and gave the hand a kiss. "What Mamma wants doesn't matter to me. But I want to have dinner with you and Petula. It will be nice. A nice little dinner together. You've never gone away from us before."

Did Renato want a big deal to be made of his leaving for Rome? No. Did he trust Maria Severina not to mention the dinner to every customer who came into the bottega between now and Saturday? No, again. But was there any way he could protest against his wife, especially now that he was feeling the softness of her lips against his hand?

He said, "We should invite Signora Vezzosi."

"That's a beautiful idea."

"She's lonely. She's sad. She's an old woman sitting there on her own, and Saturday night, while we're having dinner together, I don't know. I think we should . . ."

"Certainly we should invite her. She's not just an old woman, Renato. She's the closest thing you've got to a mother in this world."

Renato smiled into the darkness. "You know me well."

Milena rolled over toward Renato and hugged him. "*Buonanotte*," she said. "Call Signora Vezzosi in the morning. Tell her to come on Saturday night. *Sogni d'oro.* Golden dreams."

All day Saturday the weather switched schizophrenically from sunshine to cloud to sunshine again, as if it couldn't decide whether or not to storm.

At the end of the afternoon, Renato finished work and gave Cappelli the keys to the waterworks truck. "Just in case you need to take care of any emergencies during the next couple of days while I'm gone." As he drove home to milk the sheep before dinner, he saw that the sky had become a badly stitched patchwork of different climates all at once: sunshine and clear blue on the western horizon, nervous windswept wisps of white cloud directly overhead, black banks flashing sharp with lightning to the north.

At home Renato threw a few extra clothes into the overnight bag which he put on the seat beside him in his car. Fresh and showered now, he wore an open shirt, a jacket, and a pair of trousers. He wanted to look decent for the dinner and for the trip. In the hip pocket of his jacket he carried the brass toy boat he had found. He would take it to Rome as a reminder of Milena and of the figs they had eaten together. In the back pocket of his trousers he had the list.

He drove his Fiat Ritmo into town and parked along the street near his in-laws' *bottega*.

The restaurant was crowded when he walked in the door, but apart from the "Here he is" that one or two people said, most customers didn't seem to pay him any special attention. Maybe I can get away with a quiet dinner after all, he told himself.

Two tables had been put together on the far side of the room. Tita Vezzosi was seated beside an empty chair, evidently saved for him. "Come and sit," Tita said as Renato bent over to kiss her on both cheeks. Milena and her parents were on their feet taking care of other tables. Petula was seated. Beside her sat Daniele.

"*Ciao,*" Petula said, half-rising to kiss Renato's cheeks.

Renato noticed that Petula and Daniele were holding hands. "*Buonasera,* Daniele," Renato said, sitting down, wishing there were a way for him to tell the young man to keep his hands to himself. Why did Daniele have to be here at all? Wasn't this supposed to be a dinner only for immediate family? But Daniele, thought Renato, is about to become immediate family. Now *there's* a tricky thought to accept.

"*Ciao,*" Daniele said. In the past Daniele's eyes had always looked unwelcoming to Renato, for Daniele had seemed eager only to appear cool. Now, in their new vulnerability since the Mangiavacchis' death, the eyes in the young man's face had become open doors. Renato wasn't sure he wanted to let himself step inside.

Tita Vezzosi was sitting between Petula and Renato. Renato was almost glad for the distance, for Petula was busy with Daniele.

On Renato's other side was the chair where Milena would sit.

The door to the kitchen swung open, spilling out heat and steam rich with the smells of sauces cooking and meat roasting. Milena came out, carrying a tray loaded with the *antipasti*.

"You made it." Milena put the tray on the table so that everyone could help themselves. Sitting down, she smiled and said, "You look handsome. Eat."

Dinner was what it always is when eaten at the table of people who run a restaurant: a series of fast forkfuls swallowed during the constant stand-up and sit-down dance of running back and forth to the kitchen to get other courses and to wait on other tables. Tonino kept popping up to get customers drinks from behind the bar. Maria Severina spent more time in the kitchen than at the table. Renato didn't miss her when she was gone.

"I'll be back in a minute," Milena said after eating only a couple of bites.

"Let me help," Petula said. Maybe she wasn't growing up so badly, Renato thought.

But she's still growing up, he told himself. She needs more time. How can she become a mother now?

Renato talked mostly to Tita Vezzosi. He didn't know what to say to Daniele, who was sitting up there at the end of the table. It was a relief when Daniele got up to help Tonino serve drinks.

"Listen. I wanted to tell you. I don't know how long I'll be in Rome. Not more than a day or two, I wouldn't think." Renato said to Tita. "But you need anything while I'm gone, you just telephone Milena and Petula. You promise?"

"What would I need? I'll be fine."

"And then when I get back, I'll come and help you with the grape-picking. I've heard people say that next week will probably be the right moment to pick the grapes. How are your vines doing? Will they be ready next week? You can count on me being there to help."

"Help me do what, Renato? It's crazy to pick grapes this year. Why make wine? My husband isn't here any more to make the wine with me, or to drink it. And wouldn't the picking be a lot of work for nothing? Can you tell me that my *cantina* will even be here next year when it's time to drink the wine? Then what would we do with all the wine if I have to move away to some apartment building some-where? Where could we take it? Or would we just leave the wine there to sit in its vats at the bottom of the lake that the valley will become? You see? Oh, it makes my head spin just to think about all these changes! Makes my head spin and my digestion block. Why add to my troubles by worrying about the wine as well? Why pick the grapes? Why not let them rot on the vine?"

"I don't know, Signora. I can't give you a reason. Still, it's seem strange to me to think that Signor Vezzosi and you planted the vines together and worked for so many years—fifty years together, no?— only to stop caring now. Seems too strange for me to think about. Maybe it doesn't even matter if we can say that we'll still be here or not to drink the wine next year. Maybe we have to make it anyway. I don't know. Think about it some."

Thunder exploded in the sky outside the *bottega* then, rattling the glass of the big front window.

"Looks like you'll have rain while you drive to Rome," Tita said. "Don't you mind driving through rain?"

"I'll be dry inside the car. What difference does rain make?"

"Drive carefully anyway." Tita looked at Renato. "Tell me something," she said. "Tell me the truth. You still believe you can change things by going?"

Renato rubbed his beard with the palm of his hand. "Believe? When the dream came for the first time, I hoped there was a way to change *fortuna* for all of us. Maybe it's impossible. What can we do?"

"But you're going to Rome in any case, no?"

"In any case? *Sì.* I'm still going to Rome, even though things begin to seem more hopeless than ever. A dream is a dream after all. Who am I to argue?" He took a mouthful of red wine from his glass.

"Good." The smile Tita Vezzosi gave was even more warming inside him than the wine. "You haven't changed since when you were a kid."

It was toward the end of the pasta course that Renato realized what a big thing this little dinner had grown into. One by one, more people started to arrive. "Good evening to everybody," a voice said from the door. It was the priest.

"*Buonasera,* Don Luigi," diners in the restaurant said.

"Ah, Tizzoni. Good. You're still here. I wanted to give you my good wishes before you left. If you don't go soon, though, I think you'll catch some rain. The heavens look like their getting ready to open up."

"*Venga,*" Daniele said from his end of the table, rising to get the priest a chair. "Come and sit."

Since when, Renato wondered, is Daniele so nice to the priest?

"You'll want something to eat, I suppose." Maria Severina stood up from her place, already heading for the kitchen.

"Well, my usual bowl of broth I already had at home. But if there's any more of the pasta left, I wouldn't say no to just a little."

Tonino was on his feet, too, to get a glass from behind the bar. "Wine's on the table, Don Luigi. Help yourself."

"Sit, Tonino, sit," said the priest, accepting the glass. "Don't trouble yourself."

"I haven't sat for more than thirty seconds all evening," Tonino laughed. "Why start now?"

"Tell me something, Don Luigi," Renato leaned across the table to ask. "How did you know I was leaving tonight?"

"Who doesn't know? Your mother-in-law told me when I came by for a coffee yesterday morning. Told everyone else, too, I expect. She's better than the Evangelists themselves when it comes to spreading the word, Maria Severina is."

"But what are you saying?" said Maria Severina, arriving with a plate of food just in time to catch the end of Don Luigi's sentence. "Use that mouth for eating instead of talking. Your pasta will get cold."

A hand touched Renato's shoulder when people were finishing their meat course.

"Duncan!" Renato said, looking up.

"Duncan," said Milena. Duncan leaned over and gave her a kiss on both cheeks.

"No kisses for me?" said Petula.

"Of course. For you, too." He kissed her cheeks as well.

"Happy to see you," said Renato.

"Sorry I'm late. I had to finish work in Montalcino and it took me some time to get here."

"Late? Why? Did you have an appointment here at a certain time?"

"Petula told me to try to get here at eight o'clock."

"Petula?" Renato raised an eyebrow at his daughter.

"I knew you'd want Duncan to be here. I was right, wasn't I?"

"My daughter," Renato laughed. "I'm very happy you came, Duncan. Find a chair somewhere. Hurry up and take a seat if you want to get something to eat."

"Daniele," Tonino called out. "Let's go to the cellar and get an extra table. Come and give me a hand."

When Tonino and Daniele returned, the two tables joined together became three.

Duncan sat down at the far end and served himself from the tray. As Renato watched him, his thoughts had nothing to do with pasta or with trays of meat. He needs a woman, is what Renato thought. No way around it. He's unhappy alone. He'd be good to a woman. He needs to find a woman who'd be good to him.

Renato sat there, feeling waves of affection for the young man, knowing at the same time that his affection wasn't enough because no amount of friendly social company could ever be a substitute for a woman's love.

The big front window rattled once more after another rumble of thunder, this one closer than last. In through the door walked an unexpected couple: Cappelli, accompanied by Morelli, the mayor of the town.

"Cappelli!" Renato said. "When I said good-bye to you after work, didn't you tell me you had a game of *bocce* to play this evening?"

"I lied," Cappelli said, his eyes scanning the table for an empty glass.

"Wait," said Tonino, who, with a bartender's instinct, was quick to recognize the signs of another man's thirst. "I'll get you a glass from the bar. Wine's on the table."

"A glass, yes," Cappelli said, licking his lips in anticipation of what he really desired. "But not an empty one for wine. I'd prefer a drop of that nice grappa you have. A big drop."

"And for you, Mr. Mayor?" Tonino asked.

"Wine would be fine," Mayor Morelli said. "Grappa would be better."

"Two grappas," Tonino said on his way to the bar.

"Who would ever have expected so many people?" Maria Severina said, her smile genuine now because she had succeeded in getting what she wanted. The restaurant was packed, and people were eating and drinking with as much abandon as if someone else were paying the bill. "I think we'll need another table from the cellar soon. I hope there are enough chairs."

"What do you mean you lied about playing *bocce*?" Renato said to Cappelli.

"I mean I lied." Gratefully Cappelli received his glass of grappa from Tonino's hand. He poured some into his mouth. With his lips still wet, he said, "Mayor's orders. All part of the surprise."

"What surprise?"

"The surprise," Mayor Morelli answered, "is that I have decided you can take the waterworks truck to Rome with you. Cappelli had to come here to give you back the keys."

Cappelli shrugged. "I can always play *bocce* next Saturday." He drank more grappa.

"The truck?" Renato did not understand. He knew Mayor Morelli to be a serious man. His answer to any problem had always been work. Earnest, patient, diligent work. In every matter, the mayor with the dark mustache tried his pragmatic hardest to do what was best for his town, "doing only the possible," as he was fond of saying.

"The waterworks truck is the only sensible solution," Mayor Morelli said now. I'm concerned that your old Fiat isn't up to the job."

"What job?"

"The job of going to Rome."

"My trip to Rome has nothing to do with my job. Cappelli will cover for me if anything needs doing. That's the job part taken care of. Why should my trip concern the mayor's office?"

"But the Fiat, it isn't in good enough shape to make the trip. Your clutch slips," said Mayor Morelli. "Everyone knows it. Everybody hears it slip every time you drive anywhere. Your mechanic says he would fix the thing but you never bother to get it fixed."

"My slipping clutch is my own affair, I would think. Wouldn't you think so, Mr. Mayor?"

"I would think so, normally, yes. But not in this case. Your trip has become a public affair. And that's why I, after much reflection, have decided that you should take the waterworks truck instead. It's old, but its clutch doesn't slip and it had its inspection just last year so it ought to be more reliable, no?"

"More reliable, yes, I suppose. But tell me, Mr. Mayor, why are we swelling this thing out of proportion? With all respect, I'd imagine you would have more important things to reflect upon, like the fact that our town is about to disappear."

"Priority for the town, Tizzoni. That's what we're talking about here. You know I don't have to defend my political record as far as the dam project is concerned. I petitioned the Regional Government. I appealed to the Parliament in Rome. I sought help from the National Ministry of the Environment. And all this opposition served what end, Tizzoni? Nothing. So what can you chose to do when you have no choice? Set yourself new priorities is all. And the only priority right now can be the people's morale, even as we face our inevitable end. Am I explaining myself, Tizzoni? Is the discussion clear?"

"We've gone mad," Renato said. "That's what I think. We've all gone mad."

"Think what you want. You are taking the waterworks truck, in any case. That's an order. We're both public servants, you and I, but your job is to take orders from this public servant, as long as we have a town to serve. Besides, Cappelli has already moved your little suitcase into the truck."

"Thank you, Cappelli. How thoughtful of you." Renato said, tempted almost to laugh, but not wanting to offend the mayor.

"What could I do?" Cappelli said, finishing off his grappa. "I was under orders." His eyes caught Tonino's. "Any more of this in the bottle?"

"I'll take care of it," Daniele said, getting up so that Tonino could eat for a moment.

"Thanks," Cappelli said. "Any more of the food going? I had some ham at home. But there's always room for food." And Cappelli and Mayor Morelli helped themselves to empty chairs up by the priest, near Duncan, while Petula brought them clean plates.

"*Grazie,*" Renato heard from the bar behind him. The word was said with an accent that was clearly not Italian. "Oh hello, Renato!" He heard Meg Barker's voice saying his name. In her hand she held the whiskey that Daniele had poured for her at the bar.

Renato turned in his chair and started to stand up, then decided in favor of a gentlemanly nod of his head instead. "*Buonasera,* Meg," he said.

"I heard there was a party of some sort. Even I managed to understand that." She spoke in English. Her words flew past Renato, impossible to grasp.

"*Benvenuta,*" he said, not knowing what else to say. "Welcome."

"I think we can find a free seat up here," another voice said in English from the far end of the table. It was Duncan who had risen to reach for a chair from the corner. "I heard you speaking English. I think we're the only two in the whole place."

"Finally! Someone I can talk to without having to mime my every word."

Who knows? Renato thought, as he watched Meg sit down at Duncan's side. Who knows how many things in common they might have to talk about, two fellow foreigners like that. Who knows?

By the time cheese and fruit were served, other people had come, "just happened to drop in," as they explained. Il Piccino just happened to drop in for a little glass of after-dinner cognac. Pellegrini and his wife just happened to drop in for a cup of decaffeinated espresso. Sculati the gravedigger just happened to drop in and let himself be talked into a glass of grappa, though he insisted his usual custom was never to touch anything but water. Figaro, the barber, just happened to drop in, as did the banker. Tables were added to tables. Chairs were found for everyone.

Renato sat and watched. Cappelli, he observed, was trying his eager best to make conversation with the English actress. Her shoulders were turned to Cappelli, though, because her smiling face was offered only to Duncan.

He watched the priest talking to the mayor. He watched the banker teasing Pellegrini.

A big shame, he told himself. "A big shame," he told Milena beside him, giving voice to his thoughts. "A shame to think that all this will vanish. I'm glad we had this little family dinner, though."

"I'm glad, too. I think everyone's glad. Maybe everyone needed it."

"How do you mean?"

"I mean if people didn't get together to celebrate now, when's the next chance we'd have? When? The Day of the Dead? Hardly reason for a feast. Christmas? No. If you ask me, it'll be a sad Christmas this year because it will be the last. The New Year? Nobody will feeling like giving a party, because who knows when the government will hand us our compensation checks and tell us to pack our bags and be gone? No, Renato, I tell you this myself. If people don't have a little party now, they never will again."

"Everyone is saying *addio* to each other tonight. That's what you mean."

Milena looked at him. She wiped her lips with her napkin, then leaned forward and kissed him on the mouth.

Renato kissed back. "*Grazie,*" he said. "Why this kiss?"

"I hope your trip is good," Milena said. She picked up her knife and cut herself a piece of the peach she held in her hands.

Renato wouldn't have known how to describe the feeling that came over him as he sat beside his wife. There was something brave and frightening and thrilling in this moment, as if it were a wedding feast for Milena and him. Whatever the quivering inside him was, he and Milena sat with their chairs perched on the brink of some precipice. That much was for certain. And the chilliness that had been surrounding him and had been icing up the guts inside him for quite some time suddenly included Milena, too, in this moment. They were both of them exposed to the cold winds of uncertainty. Strangely, the sensation made them both seem sexy and young and alive. That was how Renato felt.

He put a hand under the table, high up on Milena's thigh. She turned to him. With his other hand he reached for a bottle and refilled her glass. "Here," he said. "Have some wine."

It was while people were eating their cakes, and Milena was up serving coffee, that Renato leaned across Tita to talk to his daughter. He had probably drunk too much wine, he realized. He wanted his words to come out right, but he had little faith that they would.

"Petula," he began, "I don't want you to think I'm hard. I'm not being hard. It's only that, don't you realize how risky things are? Do you really want to bring a baby into this world right now when you can't even say for sure where our home, your home, Daniele's bar, any of us, will be in not many months' time when the baby would be born? Can't you see how crazy it all is, everything up ahead?"

"It's my future to decide," she said.

"A baby coming," Tita said, nodding. "I see." Father on one side of her and daughter on the other, Tita found herself caught in the middle.

"I would have told you about it soon anyway," Renato said, realizing the wine had loosened his tongue.

"I could tell something was in the air," said Tita. "I just wasn't sure what it was."

"It's a baby," Petula said. "Mine."

"Yours and Daniele's, I would say," Tita said.

"That's right. It will be ours."

Tita thought for a moment, then said, "A good couple. You look happy together. You look good for each other."

"Then please tell that to my father. He keeps acting as if he wished he could wake up from the whole thing and find it was nothing but a bad dream."

"Tell him yourself, Petula," said Tita. "Tell him you're doing what you think is right for you. He's a stubborn person, too. He should understand."

"*Babbo,*" Petula said, leaning across Tita. "I'm doing what I think is right for me. There are some things in life you can't change. You can only accept."

"Again with the I-can-only-accept!" Renato said. "Then I tell you again, little Petula, you can't expect too much from me. Maybe you're expecting too much."

"I thought you were strong enough to be flexible, not rigid," his daughter told him, sounding womanly beyond her years.

Renato grabbed his glass and swallowed more wine so as not to say any more wrong words. *Idiot!* he screamed at himself. Why was he speaking harshly, when he had wanted to be comforting and soft? And maybe she was right. Maybe rigidity was a show of weakness. Maybe flexibility took more strength, more faith.

"Accepting is hard," Tita said. She was talking about herself. She shook her head, getting lost for a moment in her thoughts. The death of her husband wrapped itself around her like a heavy, unwanted coat. She couldn't accept that death. She wanted none of it. All she wanted was her husband back.

Renato was about to try to speak to Petula again when a loud popping sound came from behind the bar. "Spumante!" people called, and indeed Daniele was standing behind the bar with the freshly uncorked bottle of sparkling wine.

"We have to make a toast, don't we?" Daniele said, smiling.

Renato hated himself in that instant. Damn me, he thought. The kid is trying so hard to make me like him. Why can't I let myself give in?

Tonino stood up to hand around glasses. Daniele opened another two bottles, so many were the glasses to be filled. When spumante bubbled in every glass, it was time for the toast. Daniele spoke. "A toast to Renato Tizzoni," he said, raising his glass. "Let's hope his trip goes well."

"Let's hope!" all the people in the *bottega* said together. "Let's hope!"

Once everyone had taken their sip, the mayor spoke up. "Tizzoni," he began, but he was interrupted by an incredible explosion of thunder. "As I was about to say," said the mayor, "I think we ought to send you on your way. You have a long road to travel to Rome, and I don't think the weather will make it any easier for you."

"He's right," Milena said to Renato. "It's time for you to go."

"He's right," Tita said to Renato. "You really should go."

"The truck is parked just out front," said Cappelli, reaching into his trouser pocket and tossing Renato the keys. "You shouldn't wait. Go."

"I'm going," Renato said, nervous now to be going. "Fine. Time to go." He kissed Tita on her cheek. "*Ciao*. See you in a couple of days. Think about the grape-picking. Think about what I said."

He waved to Duncan and Meg Barker, who were happy in their conversation up at the far end of the table.

"*Ciao*," he started saying to Milena, but she stopped him.

She said, "I'll walk you to the truck."

"I'll walk you to the truck, too," said Petula.

They walked toward the door, and everyone started to follow. "Nice for everyone to say good-bye," Maria Severina called out. "But don't forget to come back in afterwards. There's the bill to be paid. Renato, we'll settle yours later."

"*Grazie,*" Renato said to her. "*Ciao.*"

He raised his chin in a nod to Tonino. Tonino smiled and raised his chin in response. "*Ciao.*"

Renato smiled at Daniele and said, "Thanks for the toast." He tried not to be touched by the open-eyed nod that Daniele gave him in return.

Renato and his family left the *bottega*. People watched from the door. Somehow the priest had managed to exit before Renato. When Renato stepped over to the truck, he saw that the priest was waiting for him. "Didn't think you'd get away without your blessing, did you?" Don Luigi said.

The priest reached into a pocket of his black cassock and pulled out the same water-shaker that he had used to bless the bones of Renato's parents in their new small caskets. He muttered a blessing that only God could hear, and walked around the waterworks truck, sprinkling water on each of its four corners. When he was very close to Renato, Don Luigi muttered, "I've been thinking about your state of mind. You know, we are taught that after confession the soul is made new again, fresh as it was the day you were born. Perhaps you want to confess?"

"Thank you for the thought," Renato whispered back. "I'll think about it some."

A wind blew and the sky flashed bright. A second later, everyone felt the thunder shake their bodies.

"The storm's close," the priest said. "*Buon viaggio,* Tizzoni. Come back safely."

Renato realized everyone was watching him from the other side of the *bottega*'s big front window and from the doorway. Maybe he was expected to say something momentous, but he could think of nothing momentous to say. "Thanks for the dinner. See you in a couple of days. Let's hope things go all right. *Ciao*."

People echoed, "*Ciao*."

He sat down inside the truck, leaving the door open so that he could kiss Milena good-bye.

"*Ti voglio bene*," she said. "I love you." She kissed him. "Maybe when you come back, maybe you'll be a happier person."

"I hope so," he said.

"*Sì*. I hope so, too."

She stepped back, and Petula leaned in to say good-bye.

"*Ciao*, Petula." He kissed her cheek and patted the other cheek with the palm of his hand. "My little girl. My pregnant little girl."

"*Ciao, babbo*," she said. "And don't worry. I won't forget to take care of the sheep."

"You're a good girl," he said.

"Who ever told you otherwise?" said Petula.

Renato shut the door to the truck, turned the key in the ignition, switched on the headlights, put the truck gratingly into gear—for this clutch wasn't so perfect, either. He released the parking brake, put his foot on the accelerator, and eased away.

From the lit-up entrance to the *bottega*, people waved.

Just before he drove off up the *corso*, Renato turned, to catch Milena's and Petula's eye.

Driving away, he looked in the truck's rearview mirror. He saw a radiant oasis of warmth down the road behind him, a glow of men and women, the front of the *bottega* full of light. He drove on and the bright forms in the mirror became smaller. He turned the corner in the piazza and took the road that led out of town. Another corner, and the rearview mirror showed blackness.

He had gone less than half a mile when the rain came down fast. Renato drove the old white waterworks truck into the darkness that was broken only by cold flashes of lightning. He was doing exactly what his dream had told him to do, he reminded himself, yet somehow he felt dreadfully alone.

THIRTY-SEVEN

Night

It was close to one o'clock in the morning when Renato reached the outskirts of Rome.

The rain had stopped. He didn't need his windshield wipers at all now. The streets were slick with water, as smooth as oil.

He was following the signs pointing toward "Roma." When he got even closer, he'd look for signs to "Centro," and then to "Stazione F.S." What could be more central than the railway station in any town? And wherever there was a station, there was sure to be a hotel.

It was all very strange to Renato. His trips to hotels had not been many, a couple of overnight outings to the sea when Petula was a child. Had he ever slept in a hotel bed without his wife by his side?

He looked around the nocturnal world that lay just outside Rome: an apparently endless row of street lamps, mile after mile of apartment blocks, a honeycomb of sleeping people tucked into bed. "*Quanta vita c'è*," he said aloud. "How much life there is!"

In the center, he let himself get lost, excited to be in Rome. There were buildings and squares he had seen on postcards and on television and in films. He crossed the River Tiber and rode up along the embankment. He recognized the Ponte Sant'Angelo and the Castel Sant'Angelo glowing in the beams thrown out by floodlights. Could that be the same Sant'Angelo, Renato asked himself, who gave his name to our town?

An impulse grabbed him when he saw a sign for "Citta del Vaticano." He followed the sign to the Vatican, telling himself he'd only take a look tonight before heading toward the station to find a hotel. A moment later the waterworks truck was driving up the Via della Conciliazione with the Vatican rising ahead, like a palace worthy of a king.

An anticipatory shiver shook him, as if he had an official meeting with the pope all booked. As if destiny had already made the arrangements. As if the pope were resting up in preparation for their encounter.

Cretino! he reprimanded himself. I'm thinking about the pope, but the pope certainly isn't thinking about me.

He drove away, losing himself again in the labyrinth of streets.

He was tired when he at last found the station. He had done enough nocturnal tourism. He wanted a bed.

After much looking, he spotted a small parking space for the truck. He squeezed the truck in, nudging the car in back of him only four times, the car in front only three. He took his overnight bag and locked the truck up tight, not that it contained anything worth stealing. A couple of screwdrivers on the floor of the passenger seat. A pair of pliers. A wrench.

Near the train station he saw two policemen busy talking to a man who was lying on the pavement. The man was telling the policemen to fuck each other up the ass.

Renato felt far away from Sant'Angelo D'Asso.

A neon sign said HOTEL DUE GATTI but the sign was turned off. He rang the "Night Manager" bell beside the door.

Silence.

He rang the bell again.

More than a minute later, he heard the crackle of the intercom under the bell. The intercom said, "*Sì?*"

"*Buonasera,*" Renato said. "I was looking for a room."

"I'm coming," the intercom said, then clicked dead.

Several minutes later the front door opened. A bald man in pajamas stood in the doorway, tying his bathrobe around his waist. "Forty-nine thousand for the night." In getting out of bed, the man had apparently not bothered to put in his teeth.

"Forty-nine?" Renato said. A little more than he had hoped for, but what could he expect in the center of a big town like Rome? "Fine. Do I pay now?"

"No." The man stepped back, letting Renato in. "Give me a document. Your identity card. I'll keep it until the morning. You can register tomorrow." The man took a key off a hook behind the front desk. "Room twenty-three. Second floor. Down the corridor on the left. Bathroom is across the hall."

"*Grazie.*" Renato took the key. "And excuse me for waking you."

"It's my job."

"Still, you must have been sleeping deeply at this hour."

"It's my job."

"Thank you, in any case."

"For nothing."

"Well. Good night." And Renato went upstairs while the man watched.

Renato found the door to room 23. He had been born on February 23, and the number 23, which represented luck, had much to do with his interpretation of his first dream. The number 23, now that he thought about it, was half his reason for being here. So he took the room assignment as a kind of positive sign.

He turned the key and saw a single bed beside the sink in the corner of the tiny room.

It's only a place to sleep, he told himself as he lay on the sagging bed of room 23 in the Hotel Due Gatti. Tomorrow I've got important things to do.

The color of the curtains hanging in the window was an indeterminate pale gray, or perhaps it was white grayed by city soot coming in through the window. The edges had turned brown.

Renato switched off the light. It had started to rain again outside. Renato listened to the rain. The foam-filled pillow was hard. There was no Milena in this bed. This was not home.

THIRTY-EIGHT

Roma

Renato stepped out of the hotel. The morning sky had been washed to a clean blue by the rain the night before. Puddles on the road and sidewalks were the only proof that it had rained at all. Renato had hardly slept. Still he was in Rome. *Roma!*

He was happy to walk to the Vatican. He didn't want to move the waterworks truck only to have to weave through Roman traffic and look for a space in the center of town. Besides, the morning was cloudless, perfect. Walking suited him fine.

Emptiness in his stomach, he entered a bar on a corner and ordered a coffee. "And to eat," he said, "I'll take that." He pointed to a fancy-looking pastry in a glass case. Different from home, he thought. Bread and some pecorino cheese from his own sheep was breakfast at home. Maybe anchovies marinated in pesto sauce sometimes, when he wanted a change. Or some prosciutto with bread. Strange, having breakfast today without milking his sheep first and taking them to graze up on their hill.

Renato ate the fancy-looking pastry. He listened to people talking around him in the crowded bar. This is what life is like outside my town, he thought. This is what life will become for us when we have to leave. The people around him seemed friendly enough, but they were unknown to him. This was not like the *bottega* back in

Sant'Angelo D'Asso. Probably right now back home in the *bottega* Milena and the customers were talking about him, wondering how he was getting on. They knew him. They cared.

Here in this Roman bar he was a stranger and no one even saw him. Life will mean this from now on, once the town becomes a lake. Life will mean being alone in the world.

Never really alone, though. He thought: Milena will be with me, no matter where we have to go.

Then he thought about all the people he knew who had to face every day alone. He thought about Don Luigi and Cappelli and Il Piccino and Sculati and now Signora Vezzosi, too. Loneliness, he thought. Mother of all other fears. He found himself thinking about Daniele, about the aloneness that Daniele must be living, now that his parents were dead. He thought how relieved Daniele must be to have Petula in his life, as happy as Renato had been when, after being orphaned at seventeen, he came to notice the magical presence of Milena that first time he had seen her juggling snowballs. What a luxury it was for him now, to sip loneliness and know that it wouldn't last.

He drank the last of his coffee, paid for it, said good-bye to the bartender, and went back out to walk some more. Coffee lingered on his tongue.

The arms of St. Peter's Square were open to embrace him. He walked up Via della Conciliazione and the Vatican rose before him, as welcoming as a mother.

He walked past the stands that sold snacks and cold drinks. He entered the great piazza, his eyes rising along the obelisk, as throngs of people converged from every direction toward the front door of the basilica high atop the steps, for Mass was about to begin. His heart pounded in his ears. He could hear himself breathe.

Renato followed the gravitational pull, anxious to be sucked inside the basilica. He saw other people drawn the same way. There was a yearning readiness on every face he saw, a desire to receive.

A group of Japanese walked beside him to his left, a group of Germans to his right. Other voices spoke English.

Flocks of nuns, in black and white, were everywhere, and priests in black walked in groups or alone. There were nuns and priests with Oriental faces, others with African black skin, others with Nordic fair complexions, others with the features of India, others still with Mediterranean olive skin. All the world seemed to be in St. Peter's Square.

He walked up the steps. Crossing himself and giving his head a small reflexive bow, he entered the basilica which looked larger than the entire town where Renato had lived his life.

The bell rang. The Mass was about to begin.

St. Peter's Basilica was a cosmos inside, a firmament of marble, gold leaf, painted saints, sculpted angels, dark recesses, bright lights. The marble Madonna held her dead son. Stepping in, Renato heard the silence fall over the many people whose backs were turned to him, faces turned forward.

They hushed because way up front, a procession of priests was entering. Renato found the side aisle. Walking as swiftly as he could, he kept his eyes on the processional. He wasn't sure at first, but then in the center of the group of priests and bishops and archbishops and cardinals and other such men in bright robes, men who were of unquestionable importance in the hierarchy of the church, all of them walking up toward the altar, there was the pope himself, looking as he appeared in the many photographs Renato had seen. A little older, perhaps, a little more stooped, but definitely the same man.

A peculiar silence filled the basilica, a special reverence for the pope. The reverence smelled of incense.

The prayers began, the responsive readings between the congregation and the several priests who were officiating. Hymns were sung. Renato recognized the liturgy from a lifetime of listening to the very same words. He did not, however, follow this morning's Mass in the way that one holds a missal in hand and reads and stands and sits and kneels in all the right moments. Renato stayed on his feet, and he avoided the rows of seats altogether. He kept moving along the side aisle, coming ever closer to the front of the hall, closer even to the fantastic spiral columns that marked the corners of the altar.

He had a mission. It was not to let himself get caught up in the Mass. Were he to do that, then he'd find the Mass finished and the pope escaped before he had a chance to so much as say hello. No. If shaking hands with the pope was what he had come to do, then he'd better position himself now in the right place. But where was the right place?

There, he decided, his eyes finding one wing of the altar. That's where the pope and all the other priests and bishops and archbishops and cardinals in the processional had entered. It seemed logical that the aisle between the altar and the door far off to the side of the basilica should also be the route they would take for their eventual retreat.

The organ blasted out a chord, making the building quake, and everyone started to sing. Renato didn't sing; he steered a steady course to get as close as possible to the door through which, he was sure, the pope would make his exit after Mass.

Drawing near the side door along the wall, he realized that he was not alone in his reasoning. A crowd of people was already there, forming a human corridor between the altar and the door. Renato stood at the back of the group, which was three or four people deep. Would he manage to get up front?

I'll get as close as I can to the door, Renato decided. That way I can shake his hand just before he leaves.

He went to the wall and started to squeeze his way in between the side doorway and the last woman in line to speak with the pope. Other people pressed against him from behind, making him in turn shove the woman in front of him.

"*Aa-eey!* Don't push!" The woman turned.

"*Scusi, signora.*" His voice was a whisper, because he was feeling the incense-scented reverence in the air.

"Where do you think you are?" she said. Her voice was not a

whisper. "Do you think you're in the marketplace? Don't push, I tell you!"

"*Signora*," he said, trying to maintain his whisper, "you think I want to push you? These people behind me are pushing me and, you know, it's like a chain reaction that happens. What can I do?"

The people in back pushed again, and Renato leaned against the woman despite himself, and she was thrust forward, too.

"*Ay-ah!*" a child's voice shrieked. "You're stepping on me!"

Looking over the woman's shoulder, Renato saw what he hadn't noticed before. A dark-haired boy stood in front of the woman. Young, he must have been, for the top of his head came up to the woman's breasts. She was a chunky woman. Her hair wanted to be taken for blonde, but a good two inches of dark roots betrayed its genuine color. The boy complained, then jabbed his elbow into his mother's gut.

"Huh!" the woman said upon impact, her diaphragm contracting. She slapped his cheek, which was a difficult operation because his face was turned away from her. The heel of her hand must have caught his ear, because he immediately held the side of his head and started to whine. "Be quiet and behave! That's what you get if you ever think about elbowing your mother again! Little brat!"

The people behind Renato's shoulders gave another shove. This time he planted his feet and resisted with all his strength, not letting himself touch the woman or her son. "Oh!" he said, turning his head as best he could to address the people behind him. "Come on, guys. The Mass has hardly started and it will be a long time until it ends. A little space in the meantime, please!"

"See that, Marco?" the mother bent over to talk to her son, who was still rubbing his ear. "You should get yourself some manners like this man here if you want people to listen to you." And she turned to talk to Renato. "He's not really bad, though, my little Marco. The teachers at school say he's bad. But I tell him, 'Marco,' I tell him, 'it's not you who is the bad one at that school. It's them who's bad.' That's what I tell him because it's the truth. He gets upset sometimes, that's all. And when he gets upset he can't help himself. He expresses himself, and people think he's bad for that! But those will be problems of the past now, because the Holy Father himself is going to sort it all out."

"Sort it all out?" Renato said.

"Of course, that's what he's here for, isn't it? That's the pope's job, no? That's what my sister told me. And she's been here before to get herself blessed. She said, 'You take Marco to the pope and the pope will sort him out. If he can't, no one can.' That's what my sister said."

"I see," Renato said. "And that's why you're here?"

"That's why everyone's here. Everybody's asking for something."

"I'm asking for help to get over my liver trouble," said the man standing next to the woman.

"I'm asking for my nephew to take the vocation and become a priest," said a woman on the other side of Marco's mother.

"You see?" Marco's mother said, proud at being proved right. "Everyone wants something. And the pope will take care of things. Works better than just praying for things to happen. Better to get help from a live pope than from a dead saint, don't you think? So tell me, Toscanaccio," she said, having recognized the Tuscan sound of Renato's accent, "what have you come here to ask?"

Renato rubbed his beard with his hand. "It's a long story," he said. "I wouldn't know how to explain."

"Well, get your thoughts clear by the time the pope walks by, otherwise it's like how it works with a shooting star on the Eve of San Lorenzo, you know? You have to get your wish ready ahead of time. Or else the star shoots past in the sky and you haven't found the words yet to say your wish, and in a minute the star is gone and you haven't asked for anything. He's old, the pope, but when he walks by, all those bishops and cardinals and people just keep pushing him along fast. That's what my sister told me. So you have to be even faster to tell him what it is you want him to sort out."

❧

"Exchange a sign of peace," a priest's amplified voice intoned.

"Peace be with you," Renato said, shaking hands with the people around him within easy reach. "Peace," he said, shaking hands with Marco's mother when she turned to him. "*Pace,*" he said, deciding to give Marco's hair an affectionate tousle.

Marco pulled away, making a face.

"The Mass is finished." said the amplified voice of the priest. "Go in peace."

The pope waved and smiled at the great assembly of people, then started to make his way in Renato's direction, escorted by the group of bishops and cardinals and important-looking priests.

Renato's heart jumped. He watched the pope bless the first people in line on the way to the side door. Blessing one person, then another, the pope smiled at some, shook a hand or two, let his sleeve be touched, let his hand be held, let his ring be kissed, put his hand on a head bent in supplication, moved along, moved along, a shepherd among a flock of many sheep. Hands reached out, hoping to be touched in return by the papal hand.

Maybe Marco's mother is right, Renato thought. Everybody wants something. Help for a son who makes trouble at school. Help for a failing liver. Help for an end to loneliness. Help for a shortage of cash. How many lives—he asked himself—how many lives could be described in terms of what's missing, of what they haven't got but would love to have?

Marco's mother squealed. "You see, Marco? The pope's almost here."

"Oh God," Renato muttered. He tried to swallow but his mouth was too dry. Before he realized what he was doing, he slipped his left hand into his pocket, on top of the list. He was ready.

The pope, a few people away, bent over. A beautiful woman sitting in the wheelchair whispered something in his ear. Standing up again, the pope smiled, then placed his hands on her head in benediction. He moved on to an elderly man who stood beside the wheelchair. The man was crying.

"Marco, get your wish ready in your head." Said the boy's mother. "Remember, you wish for him to make you good, you understand me?"

The pope moved from one person to the next.

Renato heard the words of Marco's mother and, feeling absurdly like a child himself, he thought: Here comes the moment that was promised to me in my dream. And what have I come here to ask for?

He had the list clenched in the palm of his left hand inside his back pocket. He tried to remember as many people as he could from the list, and all the things they each hoped for in their lives. I hope Milena's life with me changes so that she can be happy, too, Renato said to himself. Yes, and Petula, I hope I can learn to accept what she's doing with her life, even if maybe she's about to ruin everything because she got knocked up by Daniele, but I hope Daniele's life turns out okay also, and maybe I can accept him. Maybe I can be strong by being flexible, like Petula says. I hope Signora Margherita Vezzosi can start to live again, even though my poor Signor Vezzosi is dead and the signora's life doesn't feel like anything more than a forgotten dream right now. I hope her seasons change and she can see that life renews itself. I hope for Duncan that he finds love at least as beautiful as the love he had with Angie. And, while I'm on the subject, I hope Meg Barker finds whatever it is she wants, but not with me. And I hope that Il Piccino finds that maybe some of the rips in his life can be mended. And I hope Don Luigi the priest can maybe be less lonely, even if he is a priest, and I guess I hope the same for Sculati the gravedigger, and why not? Same for Cappelli, too, because even though he blasphemes more than any other person I've ever met, he's a good person inside and maybe he would have a secret talent for loving someone. And I hope for—

His hopes weren't coming to him anymore, not because he had run out of people to hope for, but because there were too many people to hope for, and the pope was only two people away now, busy talking to the middle-aged couple with money problems on the other side of

Marco's mother, and Renato knew he'd never have time to get all his hoping done by the time the pope got to him. And he was almost starting to feel mean, only hoping for the people in his own town, because there were millions and millions of more people around and they all were probably pretty much in the same boat, so why not hope for them, too? But the pope was about to talk to Marco's mother now and Renato's excitement at the nearness of the pope was a powerful distraction from his own hoping.

And I can't pretend to forget myself, he thought quickly, because that was what I came here to sort out in the first place. So I hope for myself to find life's taste all new again. *Voglio rinascere.* I want to be reborn. It's been too long now that I've walked around feeling dead.

"Papa! Papa!" Marco's mother pleaded to the pope's face, panicked that he might dematerialize in front of her before she had gotten her business done. "Papa, I want you to do something—" She interrupted herself, eyeing the pope's hand as if she had neglected some vital step in protocol to make her wish come true. She grabbed the pope's hand and planted a kiss on his ring.

Renato watched where her lips landed. He was quite sure he recognized the masculine hand. He had seen it in his dream. But the ring wasn't the same. In the dream there was a red stone. The pope's ring was golden and beautiful, yet it had no stone. But that didn't make a difference. The hand was more important. And the hand that had visited his sleep again and again, reappearing holding a feather pen and the list over water, the dream hand had guided him at last to this real living hand with blood in the veins beneath its skin.

"There," Marco's mother said, pulling her mouth from the hand of the pope. "I kiss your ring," she said, reciting a ceremony she seemed to be inventing as she went along. "And now I ask you to do something for this child here, this little Marco of mine; he and I have come here now to ask you to do something for him. Make him good, Papa! He is good, of course, I mean. He is not a brat, like they say. But his teachers at that school are very bad, so they tell me he's the bad one. Please, Papa! Make my little Marco so good that his teachers will feel ashamed if they ever want to call him bad again!"

"What does Marco say?" asked the pope. He put a hand on Marco's head. "Hmm? What do you say, Marco?"

Marco lowered his eyes. He mumbled, "I don't know."

The pope chuckled. "I'll tell you something. I think you're a very good little boy. And I bless you in the name of the Father and the Son and the Holy Spirit." He made the sign of the cross over Marco's head. "Try to love other people, Marco, because God loves you."

He pulled his hand away.

"*Grazie,* Papa, *grazie!*" Marco's mother was wild with emotion.

Some priests in the procession had already passed through the door. Those who remained recognized that the pope was ready to move on, ready to turn his attention to Renato, the last person before the door.

THIRTY-NINE

Renato and the Pope

Renato watched everything with incredible concentration. He had watched the benediction of the child, had seen the pope remove his hand from the head, had noticed the pope begin to shift his own weight from one foot to the other, the body's natural preparation for the single step that would bring him to Renato. And now Renato—his senses attuned by nervousness—saw what no one else saw. He saw Marco's foot move a little, up under the hem of the pope's long robe. Was the boy doing it on purpose? Or was he merely trying to leave? Whatever the motivation propelling the foot, Renato saw the danger, knew that the foot could upset the balance of the scene, but somehow, terribly, as in a nightmare, Renato found himself tongue-tied, heavy-bodied, unable to speak or to move, his reflexes wretchedly slow.

The pope turned to Renato and fell, tripped by Marco's foot.

It wasn't much of a fall, more of a misstep, more of a lean. But before the weight of the pope had time to come up against Renato's body, two motions occurred with simultaneous speed. "Don't trip the pope!" Marco's mother screamed out, her supersonic hand giving her son's face a hard slap.

The other motion was of Renato's hands—both of them, for the left hand, too, flew from his pocket—as they grasped the pope's shoulders, completely cushioning the fall.

"*Ay-ah,*" Marco moaned, holding his cheek.

And Renato was eye to eye, nose to nose, with the pope.

Senses alert, he saw the man before him. He saw a man. He saw a man as old as Vezzosi, who was now dead. Renato was close enough to smell the man's breath, to see the softness of his skin the way old men's skin turns soft. The man looked vulnerable in Renato's eyes, as all people can be vulnerable sooner or later. Most people in their vulnerability, though, have someone to look after them. Renato had Milena. Who has this man got in the world? he wondered. Who's he got, except the group of cardinals and bishops who follow him around and wonder about their own careers? Everybody's always asking of him, but who gives to him?

Renato and the pope beheld each other for an instant. Renato's hands were on the pope's shoulders. The pope's hands, in the expectation that the fall might have proved worse than it had, had raised themselves automatically and had grabbed the lapels of Renato's jacket.

"Thank you," said the pope.

"You're welcome," Renato said. "Are you all right? Did you hurt yourself?"

"No. It was only a little trip." He turned to look at Marco. Marco was holding his cheek, still in pain because his mother had connected with force. The pope put his hand over Marco's, the pope's big hand engulfing almost half the face.

Marco looked up. Something must have happened to him then, looking up into the eyes of the pope, because he said, "Sorry."

The pope laughed. "That's a good start, don't you think?"

"I'll show you to be sorry," Marco's mother sang in.

"I'm sure he's sorry enough," the pope said. "He didn't mean to trip me, did he? It was by accident. Wasn't it, Marco?"

Marco's face somehow hurt less. "By accident," he said. "I didn't want to." And Marco's mouth became a smile.

The pope kissed him on top of his head.

Old man or not, Renato thought, he's got a power that makes people change.

The pope straightened up, turned to Renato, and said, "And for you? What did you come here to ask?"

"I came here—" But it was no use. What was he supposed to do now? Shove his left hand into the pocket with the list, thrust out his right hand, and insist on giving the pope's hand a good shake? No, the moment for shaking hands had already passed. "I came here to give you this." Unexpectedly, Renato felt he had to give something, not take. He pulled the toy boat from his jacket pocket and gave it to the pope. "It's nothing," he said. "And I'm sure you have lots of nicer things. But I found it, anyway, and I wanted to give it to you."

The pope said, "A lovely object. Thank you."

No sooner had he given the little boat to the pope than Renato felt like an idiot. Of course the pope gets given things. Every time he makes a trip somewhere in some part of the world, people are always presenting him with gifts. They show it on the TV news all the time. Ceremonial offerings of silver chalices and crystal statues and fancy headdresses and all kinds of expensive, precious things. He must think I'm an imbecile to be giving him a child's toy.

"A lovely thurible," said the pope.

"A what?"

"A thurible. A censer. For burning incense." The pope's eyes smiled at Renato's.

"And I thought it was just a little boat!"

"They often used to make them in the shape of boats in the old days. The *navicula,* they called it in Latin. Or *navicella* in Italian. Little boat, yes. But for carrying incense during prayers."

"Who'd have thought?" Renato was relieved that at least his offering wasn't out of place.

A priest accompanying the pope placed a hand on the papal elbow, a polite signal that it was time to move on. "God be with you," the pope said to Renato.

Renato said, "And with your spirit."

The pope left. He walked through the door.

The corridor on the other side was well-lit. Peeking in, Renato saw paintings in elaborate gold frames along the walls.

"Good-bye, then, Toscanaccio," Marco's mother said. "I have to get this one home. I have to cook some lunch for us. When I tell Marco's father he tried to trip the pope! I wouldn't dare to think how angry he'll get! Or maybe it was an accident, if the pope said it was. Maybe Marco wasn't trying to be bad. We'll wait a bit and see. Come on, Marco. Time to get you home." She walked away, pulling Marco along by his wrist.

"*Arrivederci,*" Renato said. "*Ciao,* Marco."

Marco, without turning, said, "*Ciao.*"

The other people had left, too. That's that, Renato thought.

He took one last look into the doorway the pope had just gone through. A Swiss guard on the far side was just about to close the door. Cardinals were walking away. Renato saw the pope stop in the middle of the corridor. The pope turned around, his face bent down in careful scrutiny of the little boat he held in his hand. "A minute, please," the pope called out to the Swiss guard.

He came back through the door, back into the basilica, and looked happy to have found Renato still there.

"This little bronze boat," he said. "It's a very beautiful *navicella* indeed. Looks very old."

"Yes, I'm sorry. I tried to polish it up after I found it, but I couldn't get rid of those corroded spots. Maybe your people in here will have something special for old metal. They can probably make it look as good as new."

"Where did you find it? You said you found it, no?"

"*Sì,* I found it next to the roots of a fig tree, down along the river-bank near the bridge in my town. And thinking about it, the fig tree was there in that little cave, and down in that hole it's probably worse than just a little damp."

"Do you recognize this symbol?" The pope held up the little boat. "This insignia here?"

Renato looked.

"Ah, yes," Renato said. "I noticed that, too, when I was polishing it. It's part of the design, no?"

"No. That's the interesting thing. That symbol isn't usually found on *navicelle* like this one." The pope studied it some more. "The use of the *navicella* for burning incense, you see, goes back to the earliest centuries of Christianity. These little cups attached to the sides are where the incense was placed. See? And the little boat represented the newly emergent church offering safe passage to mankind along the River of Life all the way to the Sea of God at the end of the river. See the two men in the boat? The one up front is St. Peter, and the man in back is St. Paul, with their faces looking outward toward the world. Probably had a chain attached to it once, through these holes here, to hang it on the wall. Incense was often used in the meeting places of holy men, or in hermits' caves."

"I had no idea," Renato said.

"Lovely, no?" said the pope. "They made *navicelle* like this for hundreds of years. This bronze *navicelle* could be one of the earlier ones, those used by the first Christians. But this symbol here, etched on the side, is unusual for an artifact like this. Very ancient symbol. It's the sign of the fish. And the symbol, this same symbol, was used by the earliest Christians as a kind of secret code. They put it on buildings to mark out meeting places and safe-houses in the first centuries after Christ when the Romans were trying their hardest to suppress the cult. You and I are standing in St. Peter's right now. This symbol would have been known to St. Peter himself. And you found it, you say?"

"*Sì*, I found it," Renato said. "I was there with my wife, walking by the river, and when I went to get her some figs from the tree, I found this little boat."

"Your accent isn't from Rome," the pope said. "Tuscan, no? Where's the river you're talking about?"

"In my town, where I live. Sant'Angelo D'Asso. Not too far from Siena. Just a ways to the south."

"Sant'Angelo D'Asso?"

"*Sì*. Sant'Angelo. Very beautiful place. And if you ever want to see it, then you better come fast. Soon it won't be there anymore. Who

knows when? But soon. They're going to start building that dam farther up the valley and the town will disappear underwater. *Sì, sì.* If
you ever want to do us the honor of a visit, you better come quickly."

Renato saw color rise in the cheeks of the pope. "Sant'Angelo
D'Asso!" He shook his head, smiling, as if meeting a memory he hadn't
encountered for years. "Incredible. I studied the patron saint of your
town when I was a student in seminary. Everyone, each of the students,
had to do the life of a saint, and your Sant'Angelo was my saint.
Remarkable example of courage, he was."

"*Davvero?* Really? Don't know anything about him myself. We
were never really taught. You know how it is. But I was wondering
since I got here in Rome, I mean, I saw the Ponte Sant'Angelo and
the Castel Sant'Angelo nearby, and I started to think—"

"No, no. That's a different Angelo. Your saint lived in the earliest
days, when the cult had only just come to this peninsula from the Holy
Land. He was a young man from a well-off family in Arezzo. A man of
culture, like most of the first Christians in Europe. When he received
the gift of faith, he turned away from all the comforts of his old life and
went to live like a hermit instead. A mystic. Left his rich, soft bed and
chose to sleep on the stone floor of a cave in the valley of the River Asso,
there, where your town is. His cave became the meeting place for a
small group of followers. They called him Angelus: the messenger."

"I didn't know," Renato said. All priests, he realized, love to give
lessons. Even the pope.

"His only possessions were those necessary to survive and to pray.
On everything he owned, they say, he etched the symbol dearest to his
heart." With his finger, the pope pointed to the fish etched on the side
of the little boat. "Alphabets had grown from this sign. The aleph in
Hebrew. The alpha in Greek. Our own letter *a*. Jesus had identified
himself as alpha. The Greek word for fish? *Ictus.* The early
Christians of learning read meaning into the word that became an
acrostic, *I.C.T.U.S. Iesus Christus Theu Uios Soter.*"

Renato was only halfway keeping up. He was nervous speaking
with the pope. And the pope was finding a scholar's delight in ancient
history and classical languages, subjects Renato had always been

happy to leave for other people to study. He was glad, at any rate, that the pope liked his present.

"And Sant'Angelo," the pope went on, "saw in the fish a sign of primordial life. 'God first,' the fish symbolized to Sant'Angelo. A brave man, because the Roman authorities of the period saw his teaching as a threat to the paganism they practiced. Angelo set himself against paganism. The Romans went to his cave, accused him of treason against Rome, arrested him, and wasted no time in killing him. His followers became cleverer at keeping themselves to themselves. They remembered him always, though, as a martyr. Pius II, the Renaissance pope in the fifteenth century, had Angelo canonized as a saint. Pius was from that area himself."

"Of course," Renato said. "The town of Pienza. Interesting, this story about Sant'Angelo. Thank you for telling me. Martyred right there. To think!"

"His body was never found, after the Romans got through with it. No one knows where his remains are. Neither is it known where the cave was in which he lived." The pope looked at the little boat. "And you found this by a cave?"

Renato laughed. "Who knows? Could be the same."

"Could be. And now you say the town is about to disappear?"

"Unfortunately, yes. Already been decided by the region and by the national government and by everyone who has the power to decide."

"I'm sorry," said the pope. "It must be difficult for people in your town."

"Difficult? Yes. Everyone, I suppose, has been in a peculiar frame of mind since we got the news, very peculiar indeed."

"You know, I've seen people without homes all over the world."

"Of course," said Renato. "And things aren't that tragic for us, I know. The government will compensate everyone. We'll have new homes somewhere else in not too long. We're lucky in that way. It's just that the town, you understand, it will—" With his hand Renato described something disappearing into air.

"I'm sorry for your town," said the pope. "As you will understand, decisions of this sort are political. About a political matter such as this, I can do nothing. Nothing but pray. Be assured that I will pray."

"*Grazie*. That's already something."

The pope thought for a moment. "And before they put everything under water, perhaps I could send in some people—archeologists—to investigate the site where you found this *navicella*. See what they might find."

"Archeologists? Why not? But they better come quickly. If they wait too long, there won't be anything left to research."

"And if you perhaps could show them where you found the little boat?"

"But of course. Send the people along. Whoever you want. When they get to Sant'Angelo D'Asso, all they have to do is ask for Renato Tizzoni. Or if they don't remember my name, they can ask for the waterworks man. They'll find me. We're a very small town."

"The waterworks man. Fine, then." The pope inclined his head, a gesture that meant good-bye. "Thank you again for the *navicella*."

Renato, too, gave his head a little bow.

He waited. He hesitated. Now was his moment. He still had time. He could still put his hand in his ass pocket and touch the list and offer his other hand for the pope to shake. Maybe it would even seem natural, though of course he had already spoken to the pope, for a good long time, too, but they had talked about other things, about the little boat, about the saint, and now he'd missed his chance.

While Renato equivocated, the pope had turned to go. It would be too difficult now. Now Renato would have to call for the pope's attention and make him turn around if he wanted to shake his hand.

Too late. The pope was gone. The guard shut the door.

Stepping out into the bright midday heat of St. Peter's Square, Renato asked himself how he intended to face the people back home upon his return. They had sent him off like a hero, with a big dinner and everything. Now he'd come back a fool. He hadn't even managed to shake the pope's hand.

FORTY

The Puddle

Renato walked down the steps, the façade of St. Peter's Basilica behind his back. He squinted, disoriented by the white sunlight of the square. People brushed past him going in and out of the doors. Renato was miserably confused. What had he done? He hadn't managed something as easy as a handshake.

Renato walked toward the center of the square, the many people swirling past him. An old man in tattered clothes stood as still as a statue with outstretched hands, pigeons perched fearlessly on the man's shoulders and arms. Boldly they pecked his pockets and poked their beaks into his hands for crunchy kernels of seed. The man let them eat.

Near the old man was a young girl in a short white dress. And there was the girl's boyfriend, a would-be photographer, capturing images of his beloved to preserve on film.

The young couple in love did their turns amid the multitude of people like dancers moving through a crowded ballroom. Renato, too, was dancing in a way, though his steps felt awkward and unguided. He walked gracelessly, drunk with confusion. Only by chance did he notice he was about to walk into a large puddle full of last night's rain, now reflecting the fresh blue sky.

He stopped in his steps to steady himself, staring at the puddle before his feet. He thought about what had just happened inside the basilica. The list, he said to himself. What will I tell them all now? They're expecting so much.

He took the list from his pocket and looked it over. His eyes passed over the names of the people who were important to him. More than names. He noticed the things the people had said, thoughts those people had put into his head, each thought expressing the truth of that person's life. And each thought was true not only for that other person but for Renato, too, pertaining so much to him that the names could almost disappear.

Renato read and reread the lines. He thought about the people who had spoken with him, the people who surrounded him in his daily life. I've been trying to give something to them, he thought, the way I give water to their houses. But look at these lines. Look at what these people have given to *me*.

"In an instant, a lifetime disappears like a dream," he read again. "But life renews itself."

That was what he had wanted in the first place. He had wanted to be reborn. Instead he found himself living with death. Every time he had looked in the mirror lately, he saw death in his face. Not his own death, but the death that had encircled him. His parents' death, resurrected by the death of Aristodemo Vezzosi, his second father. He hadn't wanted to look at that death squarely, but death had left its shadow over him anyway. Life tasted of nothing; nothingness was death.

But it wasn't time for Renato to die. It was time for him to be reborn. He had lost. He feared losing everything. Yet to live is to lose. How could it be any other way? And then, after loss, rebirth comes.

He looked at the list and the sentences written in his own hand-writing seemed to fight against each other. "That things may change!" was his wife's hope, and his own, too, but change was terrifying because it made beloved things impermanent. "The ephemeral is beautiful" was true for him although he couldn't accept that thought, yet before his parents' open graves Sculati had said "The past is always present, it's just hidden most of the time," and there was Petula's voice, which could have been his own voice telling himself "You can only accept." The choice to accept, or to do anything else, was his, because "Choosing is good." And he wasn't the only one torn apart by the clash of true thoughts, because Duncan was torn apart, too, as were most people, because we're all in the same *navicella* together, and people go through what most other people go through, as the voice of Cappelli reminded him: "You are another I."

All the lines on the piece of paper in his hand were part of him, given back to him by other people, yet the lines seemed impossible to reconcile.

Maybe it's the *ambiguity* itself, he thought, maybe it's the ambiguity of everything that gives life its taste.

What he was missing was the faith to let himself choose to savor once again the rich ambiguity that surrounded him. Yes, what he lacked was faith.

He looked at the list, and the lines were beautiful in his eyes. What if the list had nothing to do with the pope? he asked himself. What if this list was meant for me? What if the dream sent me here to Rome only as a way for *me* to find this list? Could this be the treasure shown to me in the dream?

Standing before a puddle in the middle of St. Peter's Square, his head bent over the piece of paper he had been treasuring, Renato started to laugh. I am absurd, he thought, and he laughed some more. Laughing, he started to feel light. No cynical snickering, this was a deep laughter to make him free. When was the last time he had let himself openly laugh?

These people will think I'm a lunatic! Who laughs alone? Crazy people, that's who.

Then the thought of his laughing alone seemed funnier than what he was already laughing at, so he laughed louder, laughing at himself, and the list fell from his fingers.

A few feet in front of the tips of his shoes, the list floated on the water, ink side down. A breeze made a current in the shallow water and sent the list sailing even farther away.

Feeling frantic, not caring about whether or not his shoes got wet, Renato stepped into the puddle to reach the list.

When Renato snatched the list from the water, he saw that the ink of people's names and their thoughts had become nothing more than a watercolor smudge. The paper itself was too soggy to be of any use.

Renato sighed. Water seeped through the seams of his shoes. He balled up the ruined list. Looking down he saw his reflection in the puddle: a bearded man in baggy trousers, standing in a puddle, head down.

Catching sight of his own hand holding the list, Renato felt an electric chill spread from the small of his back. I've seen this before, he thought. He saw a masculine hand with the paper of his list in its palm. And below the hand was the water of the puddle, like the water in his well back home, and the hand was like the hand he had seen hovering over the well, the hand that had led him here.

"*Dio boia,*" Renato said aloud. The hand over the water in his dream had never been the hand of the pope. It was his own.

And the ring I saw on the finger in the dream? he asked himself. What about the ring with the red stone? Then he laughed. A dream is a dream. How much can you expect from a dream? A dream can't foresee everything.

A long elusive sensation of peace began to spread inside him. He had completed what the dream had instructed him to do. His list had vanished from the paper it had been written on, but that was fine with Renato, because the words that had been on it were written in him.

He put his free hand in his ass pocket and stretched his back. A sensation pulsed. New blood. Electricity crackled inside him molecularly. He opened his lungs and the air that rushed into his mouth was as astonishing as the first breath ever. His eyes saw the sun, white-sparkling through clear air. His skin was warm. His feet stood in water on the hardness of stone. He heard the splash of water in the fountain not far away. Pigeons dipped their beaks in the puddle for a drink. The photography couple waltzed by, and Renato smelled the cigarette of the young woman in the short white dress. She twirled close to him. His nose sniffed her perfume and her sweat. Renato felt the momentariness of the moment, the ephemeralness of all the beauty right there in the piazza, including each person present, present only for this instant, miraculously present all the same.

The photography couple ran off, the boyfriend stopping to take a photograph as she ran across the square.

Renato had wet shoes on his feet and a soggy piece of paper in his hand.

"Here," the old man with the birdseed in his pockets said. "Take this." He plucked a pigeon feather out of his pocket and offered it to Renato.

"Thank you," Renato said. "But no."

"Take it!" the man insisted.

"Why?" Renato asked.

"It's a feather to fly on," the man said. "Have to keep flying, no?"

Renato didn't want the dirty feather, but how can a person be rude to a man who takes care of birds? Then he remembered his conversation with Don Luigi on the steps of the church back home. Faith, Don Luigi had said, was like a feather. It kept the creature aloft.

Renato laughed. "In that case, all right." He accepted the feather from the man, and slipped it into his own pocket. "I suppose I might need it."

"Never know," said the man, turning his attention back to the birds.

"*Grazie,*" Renato said. "*Ciao.*"

"*Ciao,*" said the man.

When he reached the edge of the piazza, Renato threw the water-logged list into a public trash can.

The feather he kept.

Renato was nearly outside the piazza when a taste started inside his mouth. It was the taste of his first love for Milena. The thought of it made his mouth water now. Pecorino cheese, honey, and black pepper. That had been the dessert after dinner when, as a young man of eighteen, he had told Artistodemo and Tita Vezzosi of his love. It was a wonderful taste. The cheese had been salty and sharp, the honey bittersweet with a tang, and the pepper had tickled his nose from inside. To Renato's mind, the taste contained every taste in the world. Salty, spicy, sweet. Every taste in the world all in one.

Now that I think about it, Renato said to himself, when I get home I'll take some of that pecorino cheese of ours and I'll make myself a nice little treat.

Behind him, people were assembling in front of the Vatican. He saw them and realized they were waiting for the pope to appear at the upper balcony to give his weekly address. Maybe he should stay to hear the pope speak.

No, he told himself. What more could I hope to receive? His tastebuds were hungry again for taste. Renato was *rinato,* reborn.

He walked away, hearing the crowd at his shoulders explode in applause, for the pope had appeared and was waving, ready to begin his speech.

Half a minute later Renato was out of St. Peter's Square, walking toward a telephone booth on the corner. He dialed the number of the *bottega* back home. "Ah, Milena!" he said, glad that she, and not her mother, had answered the phone. "I knew you'd be there getting things ready for Sunday lunch."

"Renato!" What happiness there was in her voice! As if Renato were telephoning from a million miles away, as if he had been gone for a year and not a day. "It's Renato!" she called out.

He heard a chorus reply on the other side of the phone. "Oh, Renato! *Ciao!*" many voices said.

"Who's there with you?"

"Who isn't? Half the town is here in the *bottega,* waiting to hear word from you. Renato, it's you! I miss you. You've never been away before."

"I miss you, too. I'm coming home."

"And how did it go? Did you do what you wanted to do in Rome? Did you see the pope?"

"Went well. No, what am I saying? A disaster! But a beautiful disaster. So yes, it went very, very well, you could say. Not in the way I expected. You understand? I'll tell you all about it later when we can talk eye to eye."

"Come to the *bottega* when you get home and you can have some dinner here. Then we can go home together. And I can have you back in our bed."

"*Bella idea,*" Renato said. "Oh. And if you see Petula before I get back, tell her I've decided. She can have the key to the house."

"You can tell her that yourself when you see her. She'll be happy for the talk. You've been such a wall lately. She'll be happy now. And I have a message for you from Tita Vezzosi. She telephoned yesterday. A surprise it was, because she's not a person who likes to use the phone. But she telephoned yesterday because she's got herself all worried that you're never coming back, or that you're coming back too late to help her pick her grapes."

"So she's decided to make wine this year after all?"

"*Sì.* Says she thinks it's crazy, but says you convinced her somehow. Says that even if none of us is still here to drink the wine next year, she didn't spend fifty years working with her husband in the vineyards just to let the grapes go bad on the vine, unpicked. And she said another thing. She said Petula was right."

"Right about what?"

"About accepting," Milena said. "About how you can only accept. Petula was right, Signora Vezzosi said. And she said she has to try to accept. That's why she wants to pick the grapes."

Renato was quiet for a moment. Then he said, "If you see *la Vezzosi,* tell her I'll help. Tell her I'll pick the grapes with her."

Milena, too, went quiet. "Then we'll see each other later on."

"See each other in a little time." Renato was about to hang up.

After a pause Milena said, "I did what you asked me to do."

"What did I ask you to do?"

"You don't remember? You asked me to notice. I noticed."

"Noticed what, Milena? I don't follow what you're saying."

"You asked me to notice some little physical thing that I liked. Well, I noticed."

Renato thought. Then he remembered. "*Brava!*" he said. "And what is the thing you noticed you like?"

"Your beard. Last night it was hard to sleep without the beard that rubs my cheek when you hold me close to you, rubs my neck when you hug me from behind."

Renato was silent for quite some time before he realized he was standing in the telephone booth, grinning into the receiver without saying a word. "And I like your cheek when I rub my beard against it," he said. "I like your neck."

"I'm glad you like my neck." Milena's voice took on an intriguing energy. "There are other things I notice that I like, too."

"Really? Like what?"

"I like your chest. I like your thighs. I don't think I've ever told you, but I like the small of your back."

"If you want to talk about the small of the back," Renato said, "yours is a work of art. To say nothing of your hands."

"You like my hands? I wanted to tell you that I liked yours."

"I like your hands very much," Renato said. "And how I like your feet!"

"My feet, too?"

"The most beautiful feet I've ever seen," Renato said. Saying it, he realized he was telling the truth. "But we can talk more about this when I get home. I'll tell you about all the lovely parts of you, and about everything else. The coin is finishing in the phone. *Un bacio*. A kiss."

"*Un bacio.*"

"*Un bacio. Ciao. Ciao.*"

He started to walk up Via della Conciliazione, then turned back on his own steps. He went to one of the roadside food stands that sold sandwiches and cold drinks. "This fresh fruit you've got on the counter, is it for the pretty display or is it also for sale?"

"If you've got money," said the vendor, "then it's for sale."

"Give me three tangerines," Renato said, reaching for his wallet.

I wonder, he thought as he walked away with the tangerines in a brown paper bag. I wonder if Milena still remembers how to juggle. Well, we'll see in a little bit. We'll see. She can always try again.

FORTY-ONE

For Now

Dawn. A clear Sunday morning in spring.

Renato's beard was a few years grayer. The sheep were a few years slower in their steps. Seconda wasn't there anymore. She had died giving birth the year before. The lamb had died as well. Three sheep had seemed like an unbalanced number to Renato; he was used to having four. So he had kept one of the lambs born to one of the other sheep, a little female to whom Quarta had given birth. Quarta, immersed now in the responsibilities of motherhood, seemed a bit more solid, a bit less fearful of life. Her lamb, though, was the exact image of the way Quarta herself had been. Even a faraway rumble of thunder made the lamb tremble. Renato told her frequently not to worry so much about everything, but she never listened. When the lamb was frightened, she ran to find her mother. Only when she was flank to flank with Quarta's warm wool did she let herself calm down.

Renato sat on the ground, as he did every morning. Beside him sat the little boy who had just turned four years old. They looked out over the valley together. "Tell me, Beniamino," Renato said. "Sitting here like this, what do you feel under the seat of your pants?"

After thinking for a moment, Beniamino said, "I feel the grass. And pebbles. I feel the hill."

"Exactly," Renato said. "*Bravo*. You feel the grass and the pebbles and the whole hill. You feel *la terra*. The earth. Ours. That's why I like to sit here like this every day."

They sat some more. Then Renato said, "Oh look! Your little lamb wants to talk to you."

The lamb came over and nudged its head into the boy's arm. Beniamino started standing up. He wasn't much taller than the lamb. Before the boy had found his balance, the lamb nudged him again with the surprising strength that lambs have. Caught off guard, Beniamino fell over.

"Hoopah!" Renato laughed, making him laugh, too. Renato mussed his grandson's hair.

Weekends like this, when Beniamino came over to spend the night in Petula's old bedroom, Renato was beside himself with joy. Who would have imagined that a little human presence could bring such big happiness, as big as the sea? It was good to be a grandfather.

Renato and Milena were constantly repeating the offer to Petula and Daniele. "Give yourselves a break for the weekend. You both work hard enough with the bar. We'll look after Beniamino. No trouble. Really." Every now and then the offer was accepted, and Renato and Milena had the pleasure of living weekends like this one.

Renato stretched his back, scratched his belly, and looked down over the valley, for the sun had risen now past the top of the hills. He heard bells ringing in the church tower. The tower was still there. So was the bridge. So was the entire town.

No one could say for certain why the dam had not been built. Very possibly the delay had something to do with the team of archeologists who had been sent by the Vatican. They had arrived in town not long after Renato's visit to Rome. They asked around for the waterworks man who had spoken with the pope. When they tracked Renato down, he was amazed that they had actually come. He took them to see the grotto by the river in front of which he had found the little bronze boat. The archeologists did some digging for several weeks, finding other artifacts. A little cross carved from animal bone. A metal bowl for food. The sign of the fish had been etched on every object they found. Tests showed that the objects dated back to the Late Roman, Early Christian period. Certainty does not exist in archeology, of course, but the archeologists let it be known that, to their minds, the *navicella* and the other artifacts discovered in the grotto appeared to confirm the notion that the cave had, in fact, been the place where Sant'Angelo had lived as a hermit.

"*Che colpo di culo!*" everyone said. "What a stroke of luck!"

A group of townspeople—including Mayor Morelli, Sculati the gravedigger, Tita Vezzosi, Pellegrini the cobbler, Domenico the barber, Il Piccino even though he was Jewish, Cappelli, Milena's father, Tonino, the *comandante* of the police, Petula and Daniele, Milena, Duncan— along with Meg Barker of course—all got together, led by Renato himself, to build a small stone tabernacle, the kind often seen along country roads. They built the tabernacle next to the grotto where the fig tree had its roots. Inside the shell-shaped nook they placed a small statue of the saint. The tabernacle had nothing grand about it. The intention had been no more than to commemorate the martyred hermit who had given the town its name. Don Luigi came along, said a few prayers over the tabernacle, sprinkled it with water from his silver water shaker, and consecrated it, in the name of the Church, as an official shrine.

The question then arose as to who might be the owner of the now consecrated tabernacle. The regional administration said that, like the entire riverbank, the little plot of land on which the shrine stood was public. Don Luigi, however, pointed out that the tabernacle itself had been blessed by the Church and should therefore be considered Church property. His stance was backed up by a letter from the archbishop. People said the cardinal, too, was willing to lend his solidarity. That's what people said. People even said that the Vatican would be prepared to give support, if necessary, at the very highest levels. The pope, people liked to say, had become a friend to the town.

If people pressed Renato for details about what had occurred between him and the pope, he would shrug and say, "It's a mystery to me. I only gave him a little bronze boat. I didn't even manage to shake his hand."

Construction of the dam farther up the river never quite seemed to start. Everyone in town became an expert at debating the finer points of property law. There were many disagreements, but the consensus maintained that, according to Italian law, certainly the government had the right to expropriate private property to be used in projects for the public good, yet the government could not touch holdings belonging to the Church. "That's what the law says," people talking in the bars and in the barbershop and at the newsstand and in front of the butcher's counter said to each other. "If you don't believe it, look it up yourself."

"*Che colpo di culo!*" everyone said. "What luck!"

Many people predicted a nasty legal battle. Then the bureaucratic technicality came along, the technicality being that the building permission authorizing the construction of the dam had expired. As simple as that. Work hadn't begun within the predetermined period, and time had run out.

This wouldn't be a permanent obstacle for the region, or for any other party absolutely hell-bent on getting the dam built, but it would mean starting again from scratch. When a building permit expired, the parties wishing to build were then bound by law to go back to the first steps, even as far back as putting in a new proposal to all the legislative bodies concerned.

"*Che colpo di culo!*" everyone said.

There was nothing to stop the regional authorities from trying to launch the dam proposal again. Maybe they still would. Someday.

Most people figured that Sant'Angelo's tabernacle was what stopped the building of the dam, because the Church seemed in no way disposed to let the tabernacle sit on the bottom of a lake. But maybe people who thought this way were just exaggerating. Maybe they overestimated the power of the Church. Didn't people always say that the Church never interfered in local politics? So it couldn't have been the Church that stopped the dam. Maybe.

Or maybe the truth lay on the part of those other people in town who shrugged their shoulders and said, "Huh. How much does the government ever really manage to do? Governments come. Goverments go. They accomplish very little. Life goes on." Maybe they were right in asserting that the plan to build the dam, like so many other projects in Italy or anywhere else, merely ran out of steam.

Did it matter which explanation was right? Wasn't it enough for destiny to reveal itself in its own good time, without people always having to understand why?

"Oh, Beniamino!" Renato called out. "If you tug on the lamb's ears like that, they'll come off in your hands! Come on." He picked the boy up and gave him a ride on his shoulders. A good sensation to give a child a shoulder ride, Renato thought. A better sensation when the child is your child, he remembered from when he used to give shoulder rides to Petula. And possibly even better still, he thought, when it's your grandchild.

The little legs holding tightly to Renato's neck made him feel he was participating in life's own endless process of giving new birth to itself.

"Let's take the sheep back down to their stalls, and we'll see if we have any olive branches left over in the feed room for you to give to your lamb. Then we can think about feeding ourselves. We'll have breakfast with your grandmother, no? And what would you say about a little treat for breakfast? How about some honey and pepper and pecorino cheese?"

Renato and Beniamino, the lamb, and the three aging sheep walked down the hill. The bell clanked around the first sheep's neck.

Sant'Angelo D'Asso is still where it always was. For now.

Photograph © 2000 by Valeria Indice

JEFF SHAPIRO is an American who moved to Italy in 1991. He writes for travel magazines and works as an English instructor in the Tuscany region. *Renato's Luck* is his first book.